One
Perfect Flower

by

Roberta C. M. DeCaprio

This is a work of fiction. Names, characters, places, and incidents either are the product of the author's imagination or are used fictitiously, and any resemblance to actual persons living or dead, business establishments, events, or locales, is entirely coincidental.

One Perfect Flower: Between the Rifle and the Spears, Book Two

Contact Information: info@thewildrosepress.com

Cover Art by *Nicola Martinez*

The Wild Rose Press
PO Box 708
Adams Basin, NY 14410-0706
Visit us at www.thewildrosepress.com

Publishing History
First Cactus Rose Edition, 2010
Print ISBN 1-60154-741-2

Published in the United States of America

His emerald gaze caught and held hers. "What's your name, lass?"

"Raven… Raven Amelia Eagle," she blurted out.

He chuckled. "Ah now, 'tis a unique name for a unique lass."

"Not so unique really," she said. "My father is Chief Proud Eagle of the Western Apache tribe."

He smiled. "Then you are an Indian princess?"

She never thought of herself in such a way, but by tradition she was a princess. She nodded.

He regarded her quizzically. "But your eyes are blue, and the manner in which you speak—"

"My mother is white," she broke in. "It is her family I am going to visit in England."

He searched her face as though he wished to memorize it. "Aye, that explains it, then."

She realized it was growing very late. If Sunny woke to find her gone, she'd be very worried. "I must go." Gathering her skirt, she ran up the stairs.

"Wait," he called after her. With a few strides of his long legs he was soon standing at the foot of the steps looking up at her. "I meant no offense."

"None was taken," she assured him over her shoulder, making her way to the landing. Then she stopped and looked down at him. "Thank you again, sir, for your help. And…for your kindness."

He bowed from the waist. "The pleasure was all mine, Miss Eagle."

A smile trembled over her lips at his gentleman ways. "May we live to meet again, my friend."

He gave her a slight nod before she disappeared around the landing.

Praise for *ONE PERFECT FLOWER*

"*ONE PERFECT FLOWER* takes you from the dusty Midwest to the lush greens of the Emerald Isle, bringing two cultures together and binding them by love and respect. My pick on this book is a mixed berry pie. You get a little bit of everything in it...absolutely delicious reading!"

~Jaclyn Tracey, author of ***EDEN'S BLACK ROSE*** *(The Wild Rose Press)*

"*ONE PERFECT FLOWER*, the second story in the Between The Rifle and the Spear series, proves Roberta C. M. DeCaprio has an incredible imagination. With flair and flavor she continues the unusual love-swept journey with her last heroine's grown daughter seeking a new heritage a continent away."

~Deb Tompkins, author of ***MIKE, THE MOLLY AND ME*** *(The Wild Rose Press)*

Dedication

To my father, Anthony T. DeCaprio,
who passed away June 28th, 2009.
I thank him for his constant support
and faith in my writing career.
Also many thanks to
Great-Aunt Lucy Formichelli Doyle,
who drove me to elementary school every day and
instilled in me the importance of a good education.
To my Godparents,
Uncle Carmine DeNofio and
to the memory of Great-Aunt Annette Formichelli,
who also encouraged brain power.
And to Aunt Peg DeNofio Wos, who showed me
that above all, having fun at what you do is
important for a happy and healthy life.
As well as to Great-Aunt Jane Formichelli
Bohunicky, whose zest for living has inspired me to
embrace life to the fullest.
To my fellow writer-friends and critique partners,
Elaine Stock, Deb Tompkins and Jackie
Kearney/AKA Jaclyn Tracey,
to the memory of the late Kathleen E. Woodiwiss.
(her "*Shanna*" inspired the writing of this book),
and to my editor Patricia Tanner
for again giving this second book of my saga
a chance for others to enjoy.

"'Tis the seed planted with love, from which one perfect flower grows.
And love always finds a way:"

Chapter One

Western Apache Reservation, Phoenix, Arizona
Spring, 1892

Raven Amelia Eagle lay still, the night breeze cooling the moist, sticky film coating her thighs. The desecration of her body took only a few moments, yet she would remember it for the rest of her life. With trembling hands she pulled her skirt over her knees and stood. Her legs shook, and she found it necessary to steady herself against the trunk of a nearby tree. With laborious steps she made her way to the river, her mood veering sharply to anger. She seethed as she washed the abuse from her flesh; vigorously scrubbing away the reminder.

Will I ever feel clean again? Violently her body quivered, the cold river water trickling down her legs.

She dared not breathe a word of the violation to her family. Her father and brother would want to avenge her honor and could wind up dead. She would not be the one to bring more trouble, more hardship to her people. This nightmare she must keep to herself, so no one else would get hurt. Besides, it was her fault.

She was well aware of the danger an unaccompanied woman could encounter by the hands of the white agents controlling the reservation. They knew no mercy, turning the men of the tribe into scouts and mistreating the women with physical abuse. They also destroyed the corn and melon fields to keep her people dependent.

Clothing, blankets and other items intended for the Indians were sold instead to traders in the town of Globe. There was not even enough hide left to make moccasins, they too had to be purchased from the agents, if needed.

Many nights her stomach rumbled with hunger from the inadequate rations doled out each week. Twenty people were expected to live on one small shoulder of beef and twenty cups of flour. Scarce food and poor conditions left her people's spirits low. Hopelessness filled the reservation, and sadness consumed the faces of those she loved.

Usually she complied with her parents' rule, but tonight she had no choice. An hour before sunset she had been sitting by the river with Water Lily, her cousin Rising Star's wife, when she went into labor. By the time she had helped Water Lily to her *gowa*, fetched the midwife, and found Rising Star, night had fallen.

She squared her shoulders now, brushed the dirt from her clothes, and took a deep breath. With a heavy heart she lifted her face to the night sky. A slight breeze played with the tendrils of hair that framed her face. The treetops stirred. She shivered, wrapping her arms around herself and casting her gaze ahead. The passageway to her *gowa* stretched eerily before her. She braved the distance, glancing back with caution, stomach clenching. With each step fear her attacker would return mounted.

Sweet Lord of the heavens let me make it home safely, she silently prayed and picked up her pace.

When she entered the wickiup, her mother and siblings sat around the fire pit.

Her brother, Gabriel Golden Eagle looked up from his meal, his brows furrowed beneath the strip of pale hair that splashed across one side of his crown. The same splash of pale hair graced their great-grandfather's crown and to the Apache it looked like he'd been kissed by lightning. "I was just ready to come looking for you." His sharp, impatient tone made her jerk to a stop.

She forced a smile and took a seat beside her sister, Sunny Eagle. The younger sibling's hair was golden, like their mother's. "I had to fetch the midwife, then search for Rising Star." Graciously, she accepted the dish of corncakes and juniper nuts her mother handed her. "Water Lily is about to give birth."

Her mother, Golden Lady, smiled. "Ah, a baby is being born."

"I am not so sure bringing a new life into this hell is wise," Gabriel mumbled.

She understood why her brother felt as he did. A baby's birth meant anything but good news to him, since his young wife had died in childbirth three years ago. *Nahdaste,* Fire Star's death left him overwhelmed with loneliness. Once he confided in her losing his wife and infant son left him old and worn. He vowed never again to love another woman, and at only twenty-seven, he went through the motions of life without really living. Raven knew his sorrows also included concern for the family—most of all his sisters.

Both she and Sunny turned the heads of the white agents. A maiden who had not yet chosen a warrior to marry became more of a target for the lusty appetites of those who intruded upon her people's land. She neared twenty, and Sunny, her golden curls framing an angelic face, just entered her eighteenth year. Gabriel was very protective of his younger sisters, although they were women in years. Being nine years older than Sunny, he shielded her like a parent. He feared daily for their welfare, taking it upon himself to watch out for them whenever he could.

"Stay close to our wickiup," he warned, over and

over again. "And never walk the reservation alone after dark."

He had suffered more than grief for his wife and son's passing in the last few years. Gabriel was one of the scouts for the white agents. They had molded him for the job perfectly. Other than the deep brown of his skin and shoulder length black hair, he could pass for any other trader roaming the countryside; wearing a white shirt, buttoned down vest, and leather boots—castoffs with cracked soles that seeped water when it rained. For all his hard work and efforts, the reward and pay were small. Many times the *indah,* as her father called the white men, left Gabriel no bedroll at the end of a journey, forcing him to endure the cold Arizona nights without a blanket. Upon his return to the reservation, he was exhausted and sore, his body full of insect bites, and his spirits low.

Her mother sighed. "My heart is saddened by what our homeland has become. Gone are the days when I could run alone from the wickiup on a hot night, down to the river for a swim. Now, the joy of living free has disappeared. Our village has been turned into a reservation." Her large blue eyes looked around the fire pit, resting momentarily on each of her children's faces. "And we're the prisoners." With a downhearted expression upon her delicate face, she stood and made her way to the bed she shared so many years with Raven's father, Chief Proud Eagle. "I wanted so much more for all of you."

Raven set her meal aside and went to her mother, placing an arm around her shoulders and pulled her close. "Do not be sad, my mother." Her own grief surfaced, stomach churning as she rehashed what had just happened to her. She forced the grief down deep inside of her for fear she would blurt out the abuse she endured in the woods. That would only cause them all more pain. She took an audible breath. "We must only think of the good times."

Her mother's eyes twinkled through her sorrow. "And there were so many years of happiness, especially when all you children were small." There was a trace of laughter in her voice. "Your father and I had our hands full teaching the three of you everything you needed to learn." Golden Lady stroked her cheek. "You enjoyed your grandmother, White Dove, and her wisdom. All of you listened with wide-eyed excitement as she told her stories of the old times." Casting a glance at the fire, Golden Lady watched the flames dance. "I have fond memories of the first Thanksgiving celebration I brought to the tribe," she said. "Your grandfather, Cunning Eagle had been eager to learn of my traditions. I even danced for the old chief. This left your father boiling with jealousy while my dear friend, Reverend Joshua Holmes, looked on." She sighed. "Oh, how I miss the beat of the drums vibrating in my soul, the songs and sense of humor that our people were noted for."

"With the agents taking over the village, we do not celebrate much of anything anymore. Most of our concerns now are how we are to keep from starving," Gabriel mumbled.

Golden Lady sighed again, ignoring her son's words. "How I miss Josh."

"He was the holy man who had been like family to you after the death of your parents, right my mother?" Sunny asked.

Golden Lady nodded. "It's been twenty-seven years since I last set eyes on him. When he realized my heart was only for your father, Josh set sail to his homeland in England. I've heard bits and pieces from him through Ben Newcomb."

Raven knew Reverend Newcomb was the preacher who replaced Josh. He and his wife Sylvie brought food and blankets to the reservation and school supplies so her mother could continue to educate the Apache children.

Sunny stood and sat on the opposite side of her mother. "You look so troubled, my mother."

Golden Lady searched her youngest child's soft features. Out of the three, Sunny looked the most like her, though all of them had the rich blue of her eyes.

"I was just thinking how much I wish the good people of the past were still with us."

Sunny moved closer, curling her legs beneath her. "Tell us again about the first time you met grandfather."

"Ah, yes, Cunning Eagle." Golden Lady stretched her arms out to embrace both her daughters. "Now, there was a wise and honorable man. The day Proud Eagle first brought me to the village to be accepted by his people was quite a day." She looked into each of her girls' faces, and then cast a glance at her son, still sitting beside the fire. "It was a time when Indian and white man feuded openly and violently, so the union between your father and I was not something either side wanted. When I first caught sight of your grandfather, his stern face shook me to the very core. But later I found him to be a very loving and gentle man." She smiled. "How proud he'd have been of all of you."

Raven could not help secretly wondering if her grandfather would be proud of her now that she was tainted and spoiled by a white man's lust. She sighed, returning to sit by the fire, and silently watched the flames dance within the pit.

****

Amanda lay awake; dreams of her and Proud Eagle riding bareback through the hills would not appease her thoughts tonight. They were too filled with concern for her children, especially Raven.

Within the last few days her middle child was preoccupied, jumpy, and withdrawn. Though she tried several times to pry from her the problem, the girl's lips remained sealed. She had seen this behavior before, amongst the other women violated by the agents. She kept their secret, knowing full well the tribesmen would be forced to fight for their women's honor if they were told. None of the women wanted their men dead, so they hid the issue.

Raven was unmarried and the daughter of the chief. Proud Eagle would be compelled to act. She was sure this was why her eldest daughter kept silent, harboring the trauma alone. The sorrow Raven endured broke her heart. Should Raven become with child was something she couldn't bear to imagine.

She traced the straight line of her husband's nose with the tip of a finger. "Are you asleep, my *shikaa*?" Using the affectionate Apache word for *husband* always turned his heart tender... not that Proud Eagle ever was anything but tender toward her.

His eyelids fluttered open, a smile curved his lips, and he turned his gaze her way. "We both know by now it would not matter if I was. When you are troubled, no one sleeps until you are troubled no more."

She snuggled against him, laying her head upon his warm muscular chest. "The conditions here are getting worse, aren't they?"

"Yes."

"What are we to do, Proud Eagle?" She raised her head, searching his large black eyes. "I fear for our children."

He pulled her close. "I love you, Golden Lady... and our children. I would never allow any harm to come to any of you."

She placed her head again upon his shoulder.

He may not allow them any harm, but he could not prevent it from happening. There was a better than good chance Raven had already been compromised.

Proud Eagle tightened his arm around her. “Trust me, as you have always done.”

“I pray for our children to live happy and free,” she whispered.

He placed a finger beneath her chin and raised her face to his. “You have my word our children will live happy and free.”

His mouth gently covered hers, the shape of his lips memorized by way of a thousand searing kisses, consuming for the moment all her thoughts and fears.

She responded, desire carrying her away to a world of sensuous feelings and unbridled pleasure. For the time they explored each other’s bodies and climbed to the peak of their burning passion, all else was forgotten.

Lying fulfilled in his arms she smiled. “Twenty-eight years with one man and he still makes me feel newly wed.”

Proud Eagle playfully pinched her backside. “That is because the woman still acts like a bride.”

****

Proud Eagle rode up beside his son, dressed in his full Apache attire. “I wish to ride into town with you, my *ciye*.”

Gabriel flinched at the sound of the Apache word for *son* and eyed his father’s way of dress, resentment and shame flashed across his face.

Proud Eagle’s lips thinned. “Come,” he said, turning his eyes to the road and riding on ahead. Though he sat tall upon his horse, chin held high, a pang of disappointment swept through him. Lately his son shied away from his Indian customs. Wearing traditional clothing caused problems amongst his white employers, and Gabriel needed to keep his job. Even meager pay was better than no pay at all.

Gabriel caught up. "If not for you teaching me how to hunt and track, I would be of no use to anyone." Guilt edged his voice. He took a deep breath. "But you need to understand my side in all of this. Traditional dress is not welcomed, my father. Times are changing, and to survive, we must change, too. An Apache is accepted better dressed in the white man's clothes."

"You must honor your heart, Golden Eagle, and I must honor mine," he said. "But remember this, my son, a man who follows the ways of others can never be true to himself."

In silence, both men rode the rest of the way to town.

****

Proud Eagle thought with the passing years the town of Willow Creek grew in size and noise. As he passed the mercantile, now double its previous size, he remembered the time he was held prisoner in the back room by the white lawman, Lieutenant Ryan Duffy.

There was a bank now in town, a sheriff's office, and a jail as well as a post office. Even the standard way of travel changed. No longer just by horse, but by something called the *iron horse.* His son explained to him all about the boxed carts running on a track, pulling other compartments behind it.

"Its faster and a safer way to travel," Golden Eagle said. "And I take up where the train leaves off, guiding the wagons."

When they rode past the hotel and saloon, a drunken man stepped from the double doors shouting curses at him. An uneasy expression formed on Golden Eagle's face. "Do not let him trouble you, my son. His head swims with the *indah's* fire water."

"What did you need to come into town for anyway?"

He took a deep breath. "I need to send word to the holy man who lives across the big waters."

Golden Eagle frowned. "Always you and mother speak of this man, how he helped to save your life years ago. But he is too far away now to help, my father."

"If this friend chooses to help, the distance between us will not matter." He turned his horse toward the parsonage.

He mounted the back steps, remembering the day he came for the holy man, Josh, to invite him to the Thanksgiving celebration. His housekeeper, Grace Thomas, a good hearted old biddy, had opened the door. When she took a look at him standing on the porch stoop, she fainted dead away.

Grace's niece, Sylvie opened the back door today. She was married to the holy man, Benjamin Newcomb, who had taken over for Reverend Josh after he left for England.

Sylvie smiled, making a gesture of welcome with her hand. "Good day to you, Chief."

He inclined his head in a polite manner, grateful for this woman and her husband's friendship. If not for their kindness, village conditions would be much worse than they already were.

Golden Eagle removed his hat and gave a courteous nod, standing beside his father. Sylvie returned the gesture with a polite bob of her head and ushered the two men into the kitchen. Motioning for them to take a seat at the table, she moved to the cupboard, reached for two glasses, and filled them with lemonade.

He sat by the window, the white cotton curtains stirring in the warm afternoon wind. Glancing out onto the garden, he remembered the time he came into town to fetch Golden Lady after she received word her aunt from England was arriving. He was arrested by Lieutenant Ryan Duffy, a cavalry officer staying in town, whipped, and sentenced to hang. If not for the dual efforts of his wife and the Reverend Joshua Holmes, he would not be sitting in this kitchen today.

"What brings you to town," Sylvie probed, interrupting his thoughts and handing him a glass.

"I thank you, Miss Sylvie," Golden Eagle said, when she handed him a glass. He downed the cold yellow liquid within a few gulps.

Inwardly, Proud Eagle cringed. Never could he master the flavor of the sour drink and could swallow it only if he took tiny mouthfuls at a time. He placed his own glass down on the table. "I wish to send word to Josh in the place called England."

Sylvie nodded. "Benjamin is in the den."

He and Golden Eagle followed the reverend's wife through the foyer and to the room where Reverend Newcomb sat behind a large desk.

Benjamin looked up from his reading, stood, and made his way to his guests, shaking their hands with a large smile upon his long thin face. "Vhat a pleasant surprise." Frowning, he added,"All is vell vith the family, yaw? Everyone is in good health?"

He stifled a grin. Ben's homeland was a place called Sweden. Even after all these years his words still sounded strange. "All of us are in good health, thank you." He took a seat where Ben indicated beside the desk. "But I do need your help."

"Vhat can I do for you today, Chief?"

"I ask your help in sending a letter to England."

"To the Reverend Holmes," Sylvie added, reaching for her husband's stationery ledger on a nearby shelf.

Ben pulled a fountain pen from the drawer and held it up in admiration. "This marvelous vriting tool vas made by an American insurance agent in

1884; his name vas Levis Vaterman."

"Lewis Waterman," Sylvie translated.

"Yaw, yaw, that's vhat I said... Levis Vaterman." He handed the pen to Proud Eagle. "I enjoy very much penning letters vith it, only drawback is a change in temperature altars the ink's appearance. And should I carry the pen in my pocket it varms the ink and then..."

"It leaks out of the pen and ruins a perfectly good shirt," Sylvie finished the sentence, placing a sheet of paper in front of Proud Eagle.

When he first brought Golden Lady to his village, he instructed her in the ways of the warrior's fight and how to hunt with a bow and arrow. In return, she taught him how to read and write the white man's words. He placed the pen's tip to the paper and began to draw a letter, but he pressed too hard and out oozed the ink, forming a large black splotch on the white stationery and staining the tips of his fingers.

"Till you are used to it, the pen can be messy," Benjamin stated, motioning for Sylvie to give him another piece of paper.

He looked down at the fresh sheet and hesitated. Drawing letters in the sand with a stick, which was the way he first learned to write, or using the chalk and slate boards the Reverend Josh brought to the village was much easier to master. If a mistake was made it could easily be wiped away.

"Perhaps a pencil would be better," Sylvie offered.

Benjamin nodded and pulled a pencil from the same drawer where he kept the pen, handing it to him.

Many times he watched his daughter Sunny draw pictures on sketch paper with the pencil. The lines and swirls she created copied things she saw around her. He set the pencil to paper and began to write, but again pressing too hard broke the black tip.

"Hmm, this may take some time," Benjamin commented.

He nodded in agreement and turned toward his son. "It might be faster if you wrote what I speak."

Golden Eagle combed his fingers through his hair. "I need to get to work." He looked over at Ben. "Would you mind, Reverend, helping my father with this letter?"

Ben smiled and picked up the pen. "I don't mind a bit. You go on to your job, Gabriel. Sylvie vill see you to the door, and I vill help your father." He turned to Proud Eagle, his smile deepening. "Then ve vill have lunch together in the garden and a good talk before you ride home, yaw?"

He chuckled and mimicked Ben. "Yaw."

****

Two months passed before a letter from England arrived. On the day Ben brought Josh's response to the reservation, Proud Eagle took a walk to a secluded place in the village and ripped open the top of the envelope. Reading his friend's beautifully scripted words brought tears to his eyes. Josh complied fully with his request and made all the arrangements. Benjamin Newcomb was instructed to help carry out the plan. He sighed with relief. Now all there was left to do was explain the plans to his wife and children.

****

Gabriel's bones were beyond aching when he rode into the village. Just as he stretched out on the cot in his wickiup, his younger sister burst through the door's flap with the news he was needed at his parents' *gowa* for a family talk.

"They can talk without me," he groaned, pulling a blanket over his head. "And the next time you come uninvited into my home, I will paddle your backside till you cannot sit down."

Sunny ripped the blanket off her brother, not the least bit intimidated by his threat, and stood with hands on hips. "Mother said you *must* come now. She has exciting news."

Gabriel gave her a menacing look. "You do not hear well, little sister." He pulled the blanket back over his head. "I said they can talk without me."

"Get on your feet now, Golden Eagle," Proud Eagle demanded.

Gabriel peeled away the blanket to find his father standing at the foot of his bed, in the same fashion as his sister, with hands on hips.

He sat up, his annoyance mounting. "Am I not entitled to my privacy?" He frowned over at his sister. "First she comes pushing her way in here, not knowing if I am dressed or not, and now you—"

"You are never to walk into this wickiup without asking first to be invited." Proud Eagle interrupted with a scolding to Sunny.

She relaxed her stand, casting her gaze to the ground. "I am sorry, my father." She turned to glare at Gabriel. "But what right does he have to threaten to paddle my backside."

Proud Eagle arched a brow. "He has no right at all." Their father shook his head in disgust. "You two act like you are still small." He pointed to the door opening. "Go to your mother now, *dayden*."

Sunny folded her arms across her chest. "I am not a *little girl*."

"Then stop acting like one," Gabriel grumbled.

Proud Eagle narrowed his eyes at his daughter. "Leave us, now, Sunny."

With a huff she marched out of the wickiup.

Proud Eagle then turned his attention on his son. "I am giving you the chance to walk to my *gowa* on your own two feet, but the offer will not last long."

Gabriel threw the blanket aside and stood. "When do I start receiving some respect from this family?"

"Respect is given to one who shows it, my *ciye*," Proud Eagle retorted, striding out the door.

Gabriel's mother held out her hand to him and smiled when he entered his parents' wickiup. "Come, sit around the fire with us and listen to the good news."

Reluctant, tired, and only wanting the good news of a night's rest, he obeyed.

"Your father," his mother began, looking around the circle at each of her children, "has sent a letter to England, asking our friend, Reverend Joshua Holmes, to help us."

"And has he agreed?" Raven asked.

"Yes, he has," she said, squeezing Raven's arm with affection. "His reply came today."

Gabriel's heart sank. He had an idea he would not like the outcome of this family meeting. "How can he help us?"

His mother turned to look at him, her eyes bright with a satisfied glow, one Gabriel had not seen in them for a long time. "He has sent money for the three of you to travel to England."

His voice, cold and exact, was almost an affront to his mother's joy. "It is Sunny and Raven who must leave. It is dangerous for them here."

Proud Eagle stirred the fire with a stick. "It is dangerous for them to travel alone as well."

He stood with an angry glare. "Have you forgotten I have a job to do here?"

"Ah, the white man's bidding," Proud Eagle snapped.

"That may be so, but the extra rations I receive as pay has helped this family many times," he argued.

Proud Eagle raised a defiant chin. "I have taken

care of this family all these years, my son, and I will continue."

His voice grated. "Am I not in line to be chief, my father? How can I do this if I am in England?"

His father locked eyes with him, his voice calm yet stern. "Golden Eagle, sit."

He remained standing, his eyes challenging his father. "You have not answered my question."

Proud Eagle's large black orbs stayed fixed on his face, his tone mounting with anger. "Must I make you sit in front of the women?"

He did not want to think how his father would carry out the threat, but there was no doubt in his mind he could. Though he was strong, Proud Eagle was stronger and a head taller. Trying to hold his own against his father would be difficult and humiliating, especially in front of his sisters. Again, with much reluctance, he obeyed, folding his arms across his chest and staring into the flames.

"Please, Gabriel," his mother pleaded. "I need your help or this plan will not work. Your sisters need to get away from what's happening here. They need to go to England, where it is safe, and my Aunt Kaylena can care for them." She reached over and caressed his hand with the tip of her finger. "They will have a better chance of a future there."

"Does it not matter I have a place here?" he grumbled. His mother cupped his chin, turning his face toward her. The soft blue of her eyes always tendered his heart. "Please, my mother, do not ask me to do this."

"I wouldn't, Gabriel, if it wasn't so necessary," she said with a broken whisper. "And I ask this not only for them, but for you as well. You will be a man of great means."

The words stuck in his throat. "H-how so?"

"You know the story of my mother coming from England to teach the children of Willow Creek?"

He nodded.

"As the eldest she was in line to inherit Bentwood Manor, the Bentley estate. But she died of a fever when I was only a small girl, therefore bequeathing her rights to me. Upon my grandfather's death my mother's sister, Kaylena traveled to America, hoping to return to England with me as the next heir, but I was already married to your father and refused to leave, signing all the Bentley fortune back to her. Now, Kaylena is getting on in years and wants to pass the family's estate to the next of kin, which is you, Gabriel, because you are the eldest of my children."

He sighed. "I know nothing about being the head of a manor."

"Then you will learn." Proud Eagle's gruff voice made him stiffen. "The holy man will help you."

"What if I do not want to learn?"

"You're always saying you want to help our people, set them free," his mother said, placing a hand upon his shoulder. "With the money you'll inherit, you'll have the chance."

He frowned. "How can I help the tribe if I am in England?"

"After you claim your inheritance you will be a rich and powerful man, able to do whatever you want and travel wherever you choose. Then, Gabriel, you can return and do great things for our people," she said. "But this cannot happen if you don't go to England now, with your sisters, and claim what's rightfully yours."

For the first time in years, hope rose from the center of his being and filtered to the tips of his toes. If he could do this for his people, release them from the white man's oppression, it was his duty to leave. "For this reason…to help my people and keep safe my sisters, I will go."

Proud Eagle stifled a grin. This night reminded

him of so many that passed. What would take harsh words from him to make his son obey, only took a bit of soft logic from his wife to achieve.

"When do we leave, my mother?" Sunny asked.

"In fourteen days. You will leave Willow Creek by stagecoach and travel to Silver City, and then travel by train to Texas. From there you will board a ship going to England."

He watched his wife swallow the emotion that now welled in her eyes. He reached over to take her hand.

She gave him a timid smile and cleared her throat. "Enough money has been sent to purchase traveling clothes and several other outfits for you to wear. Miss Sylvie and Reverend Ben will bring them the morning you are to leave, and then they will take you to the stagecoach."

"Then that...that will be the last time we will see you, my mother?" Sunny said, moving closer and placing her head upon her mother's shoulder.

She gave her daughter's face a gentle pat. "Yes, my sweet *dayden*, for a while I'm afraid..." her words trailed off as she glanced over at him.

"I want you always to remember you are born of proud blood," he added. "Never feel shame for who you are or where you come from. Do not allow anyone to take your pride." He sighed. "Most of all, forever know that your mother and I love you. This is why we must let you go."

****

On the morning her children left the reservation, Amanda's eyes grew moist watching them board Benjamin Newcomb's wagon for the trip into town.

Raven looked stunning in an apricot traveling suit; the deep peach brought out the rich golden brown of her skin and the shine of her black hair. Sunny wore a deep blue outfit that matched the intensity of her sapphire eyes. The long golden curls, pinned high and elegant atop her head, framed her angelic features like a halo. Gabriel took his stand as a gentleman, assisting his sisters into the wagon before mounting his horse. He looked dashing and handsome in a white shirt, gray vest, jacket, and breeches to match. Black boots and a fine hat topped off his sophisticated look.

She bit her bottom lip to keep from crying. It was a very real possibility she'd never see her children again. This paralyzing thought circled her heart while packing Raven's belongings, so she placed her mother's wedding dress in the satchel as a precaution. She wanted her eldest daughter to have the dress Amelia Bentley Gregory wore the day she married Ethan Gregory. The same dress she wore in a second marriage ceremony to wed Proud Eagle.

She waved her good-byes, swallowing hard the tears stinging the back of her throat. Proud Eagle stood straight and silent beside her, his brave exterior shielding the heart she knew was breaking within.

Together they watched the wagon pull away.

Chapter Two

Raven shifted on the hard stagecoach seat, wanting to be free from the tortures of her clothes. White women wore entirely too much beneath their dresses. The cumbersome petticoat and tight bodice all overheated and suffocated the woman's natural form. And the narrow-toed shoes squeezed the life from feet and toes. She tugged at her collar and wished she could slip her feet from the confines of the shoes, but with all the laces to untie, accomplishing such a task would be awkward and most inappropriate in public. The thought of running barefoot to the river occupied her mind throughout the long, tedious journey to Silver City.

The first stop was in the small town of Black Rock. Gabriel secured two rooms at the hotel for them, trudging off with weary steps to his own quarters. She and Sunny took turns helping each other remove the layers of clothes they wore, stretching out upon the bed to relieve their aching bones.

Sunny propped her chin upon a hand. "Do you find this trip as exciting as I do, my sister?"

She hesitated with an answer, her flesh still stinging from the hard stays of the bodice. "I am in some ways, and in other ways I am not."

Sunny inched closer, laying her head upon her shoulder. "In what ways are you pleased?"

"I am relieved to be away from the white agents, to be going to a place where I will be looked upon with respect instead of scorn. The idea of not being hungry or cold, or the dread filling my heart while walking our village, is all pleasing."

"And what displeases you?"

"The fact we do not know if we will see mother and father again and wearing those horrible clothes," she concluded.

Sunny raised her head, her large blue eyes wide. "What are you saying? The clothes are beautiful." She giggled. "And I like the way the bodice makes my breasts look beneath the dress."

She narrowed her eyes. "Sunny Elizabeth Eagle you are a wicked girl."

Sunny frowned. "Raven Amelia Eagle," she countered. "I am not wicked at all, just happy to finally look like the grown woman that I have become. No one ever noticed on the reservation."

"Be happy they did not, for with everything comes some sort of price. Like the price for looking beautiful in the new clothes and being squished and stifled."

Sunny's frown deepened. "They do squish and stifle and getting dressed *does* take so long. But in time I am sure I will get used to it."

"Humph, I will never get used to such torture," she snapped, turning onto her side.

Sunny slipped a hand beneath the quilt and pinched her backside.

"Ouch!" She thrust a hand over the hurt and turned to face her sister. "Why did you pinch me?"

Sunny flashed a quirky smile. "Now you will think of the bruise on your behind instead of the uncomfortable clothes."

"Well, I will not be the only one," she said, ripping the blanket off her sister and wrestling her onto her belly. "Since mother is not around to keep you in line, the duty will now have to fall on me."

Sunny was weak with hysterical laughter while she playfully spanked her bottom. "No more... please," she hiccupped. "Or I will tell Gabriel."

"He will not come to your rescue; he has wanted to thrash your bottom for years," she said, sitting back on her knees and looking down at her little sister. Tears blinded her eyes, and she blinked them away.

Sunny, still giggling, rolled onto her back. "Oh, now I am not going to be able to sit for a..." Her words caught in her throat when she spotted the tears. "What is it, my sister?"

"We will never be apart, will we Sunny?" she choked out.

Sunny sat up and gathered her into her arms. "No, never. We will always have each other." She stroked her hair. "And I know we will see mother again... father as well."

Lonely already for her parents, she sighed. "I hope you are right, Sunny, truly I do."

****

All too soon the light of dawn approached the sky and after a quick breakfast of buttered rolls and tea, Raven found herself confined to sit out the boring hours of another day's ride. It was very late when Silver City came into view. Gabriel helped her and Sunny down from the coach and made his way to the hotel. Lively music blared from a building across the street, and she found herself drawn to its beat. She stopped to listen and saw a man stumble his way out from the double doors.

Gabriel reached out and took her arm. "Come, it is time to rest."

She pointed to the dwelling of interest. "What is there, Gabriel?"

He arched a brow. "Danger, my sister, and no place for a lady." He pulled her by the hand like a curious child and secured two rooms, parting from them till morning.

No sooner did Sunny place her head upon the pillow; she fell into a sound sleep. Raven guessed the novelty of looking all grown up took its toll on her little sister. The few times she cast a glance Sunny's way, she also appeared to be miserable in the fancy clothes. She stared up at the ceiling, listening to Sunny's even breathing. Exhausted as she was, sleep would not come.

Not to wake her sister, she crept out of the bed and to the window, looking down at the street below. From her position she could see people coming in and out of the swinging doors, the faint sound of music and laughter rising to her ears. She donned the dress she laid out for the next day's travel, omitting what went underneath in her haste, and slipped on the shoes. Tying back her hair with a piece of ribbon, she tip-toed from the room and down the stairs to the street below.

Raven took a deep breath and squared her shoulders before making her way to the curious building. Peering over the double doors, she swept a look around the smoke-filled room. Women dressed in bright colored skirts sat on men's laps, laughing and throwing their hair over their shoulders; their cheeks and lips painted red. In a corner, a man played a tune on the piano and people danced. She smiled, happy to tap her toe in rhythm to the music, until someone grabbed her by the waist and pulled her through the doors, into the smoky confusion of the room. She gasped and looked up into the watery blue eyes of a gray haired man.

He smiled down at her. "Come on, sweetie." He twirled her around with the music. "Get them purdy legs a movin'." She pushed him away to free herself from his grasp, but he tightened his hold. "Are ya thirsty, sugar?"

His toothless grin and foul breath reminded her of agent Hall. In her mind's eye she was again back at the reservation, enduring the violation of her body. Again she pushed him away, panic rising.

"Please, let me go."

"Sit," he said, shoving her down into a nearby chair and taking a seat beside her. He handed her a glass. "Drink." The man raised his own glass and clicked it against hers, sloshing the honey colored liquid over the rim. "Here's to ya and me, sweetie, and a little fun." He brought the glass to his slobbering lips and poured the brew down his throat.

She set her glass down on the table and stood.

The bearded man caught her by the arm, pulling her toward him. His cold, blue eyes impaled her with their gaze. "Where ya headed, honey? The night's young."

She struggled to free herself. "I just want to go. Please, let me go."

"Not just yet, I won't," he bellowed, pulling her down onto his lap.

A crushing fear rose to smother her. "Take your hands off me."

"Now, now, I ain't gonna hurt ya none, sweetie." He caressed her back. "If ya play ya cards right we can both enjoy the night."

Every bone in her body stiffened. She was ready to scream, scratch, kick, do whatever else it took to get away from the man.

A deep voice snapped from behind. "Let the lady go, Baxter."

She turned to look straight into the eyes of a tall dark-haired man; his broad shoulders and muscular arms filled the brown jacket he wore. There was an inherent strength in his face, clean shaven, except for a thin mustache sitting beneath an aquiline nose and above a generous upper lip.

"How do ya know she's a lady, Shannon?" Baxter retorted with a sneer, still holding her on his lap. "And whatcha still doin' here, thought you were headed back to Houston?"

"When I leave Silver City is none of your

concern." The tall man moved closer to Baxter, his emerald green eyes glaring. He ground out the words through gritted teeth. "I said, let the lass go."

Baxter cursed beneath his breath and pushed her off his lap.

She fell with a thump to the worn, wooden floor. Baxter and the other men at the table laughed at her ungraceful plunge. Her face burned as she stood, but her foot caught on the hem of the skirt, and she hit the floor again. The whole place roared.

The man called Shannon leaned forward and extended his hand. His deep voice, now softer then before, urged her to take assistance. "Please, allow me to help you, lass."

She accepted, wanting nothing more then to get back to her hotel room. His warm firm hold pulled her to her feet. He smiled, the dimpled cleft in his chin deepening.

"'Twould be my pleasure to see you safely home."

Her throat went dry. She searched his handsome face, gazing deep into the green of his eyes.

"I have no home—not here. I am, I am," she stammered, mesmerized by the dazzling display of his straight, white teeth. "I am staying at the hotel across the street."

He offered her is arm. "Then let's be getting you back to where you belong."

She placed a hand on his forearm, inhaling the clean scent of his cologne. "Thank you, most kindly, sir."

"Are you traveling alone, lass?"

She lowered her eyes. "No, sir. I am with my brother and sister. We are on our way to England and will be leaving on the morning train bound for Houston."

He frowned. "And let me guess—your brother has no idea you're running about, asking for trouble."

She raised a defiant chin. "I was not running about asking for trouble."

He arched a brow. "Aye, lass, you were, the moment you stepped into the saloon. And most likely you would have found it, if I hadn't come along. 'Twas a good thing I decided to have a bit of ale before I moved on."

Her lips thinned. "Well, I am sorry if I have ruined your plans."

"Not to worry, lass. I have hired a private coach and the driver doesn't mind traveling throughout the night. So when I leave is of no concern, but I'm a wee bit worried about you."

"You need not worry further."

His eyes roamed the length of her. "Didn't you realize the stir you'd cause half dressed?"

She flushed under his scrutiny. "I am afraid I do not understand, sir?"

"Where's the rest of your clothes, lass. The things that go beneath?"

She cleared her throat. "I am not quite used to…to wearing all the things…that…that…and I was in a hurry to see what made the music." She swallowed hard, mortified. "I do not usually dress like this."

The genuine concern in his eyes, the gentle tone of his deep voice, left her pulses racing.

"Every man's eyes were upon you, lass. None of which, I might add, had honorable notions in mind."

She knew all too well about dishonorable notions. Her cheeks burned with the memory of agent Hall and the dreadful abuse forever marking her soiled. How would she ever be fit to love in a proper way? She cast her eyes to her feet. "You are right, sir."

He raised her chin with a finger. "I assure you, lass, I speak the truth about the danger you put yourself in."

His mere touch made her breath catch in her throat.

His emerald gaze caught and held hers. "What's your name, lass?"

"Raven...Raven Amelia Eagle," she blurted out.

He chuckled. "Ah now, 'tis a unique name for a unique lass."

"Not so unique really," she said. "My father is Chief Proud Eagle of the Western Apache tribe."

He smiled. "Then you are an Indian princess?"

She never thought of herself in such a way, but by tradition she was a princess. She nodded.

He regarded her quizzically. "But your eyes are blue, and the manner in which you speak—"

"My mother is white," she broke in. "It is her family I am going to visit in England."

He searched her face as though he wished to memorize it. "Aye, that explains it, then."

She realized it was growing very late. If Sunny woke to find her gone, she'd be very worried. "I must go." Gathering her skirt, she ran up the stairs.

"Wait," he called after her. With a few strides of his long legs he was soon standing at the foot of the steps looking up at her. "I meant no offense."

"None was taken," she assured him over her shoulder, making her way to the landing. Then she stopped and looked down at him. "Thank you again, sir, for your help. And...for your kindness."

He bowed from the waist. "The pleasure was all mine, Miss Eagle."

A smile trembled over her lips at his gentleman ways. "May we live to meet again, my friend."

He gave her a slight nod before she disappeared around the landing.

****

The *iron horse* sputtered steam from its stack, the large wheels creaking and groaning with each turn. The engine chugged, moving the train ahead, slowly at first, then faster and faster.

Raven watched her brother sit back in his seat.

"I am thankful the train compartment is larger than the stagecoach. Now I have more room." Gabriel sprawled out his long legs, sitting more comfortable and relaxed near the window. The droning of the train seemed to soothe him, and soon his eyelids grew heavy. Before long he was deep in sleep.

Sunny was occupied watching the countryside fly by. "This is all so wonderful and exciting. We are almost flying as fast as the birds."

"Birds are free," Raven grumbled, pulling at the frilled collar of her blouse. "Oh, I do not think I will ever like these clothes."

Sunny cast a frown her way. "It is the way we must dress now, can you not try harder to get used to it?"

She sighed. "I am trying hard, but wearing all this material is—is—"

"I think you are ungrateful," Sunny snapped. "Why can you not be as appreciative as I am and enjoy the beautiful garments? After all, the holy man, Josh, went to great trouble to outfit us in style and to make it possible to leave our village." She glanced back out the window. "As much as I love our heritage and traditions, I am tired of the sorrows, the hunger, and the fear of living on the reservation."

"I am sorry if I sounded ungrateful," she apologized.

Sunny turned again toward her, and they shared a smile. "All will be fine, my sister. Just you wait and see."

She nodded and thought of the green-eyed man. He came to mind many times throughout the four days she endured on the train. The man, Baxter, in

Silver City called him *Shannon*. Would that be his first or last name? So obsessed was she with his green eyes and deep voice, that when she closed her eyes she conjured up his handsome face. She wished she could share the experience with Sunny, but knew she would have Gabriel's wrath upon her if she divulged anything about her little excursion to the saloon. It was a shame, too, because the girl gossip would have entertained her. After four days of eating and sleeping in a seat, she was restless and bored.

Gabriel was content to sleep away the hours, and Sunny sat with her sketch book and pencil, engrossed in capturing the faces of the other people aboard the train. But she, who enjoyed helping her mother teach the children, was not so cheery sitting idol. Wearing hot wrinkled clothes over a stiff and aching body was anything but pleasure. Only when the city of Houston loomed ahead did her spirits rise.

Again, Gabriel secured two rooms for the night, and before turning in, they enjoyed a meal together in the hotel's fancy red and gold dining room. The chicken and dumplings melted in her mouth, and the fresh bread, slathered in creamy butter, sopped up the homemade gravy swimming in herbs at the bottom of her plate. After eating all the delicious food, she could hardly keep her eyes open. With heavy steps, she climbed the stairs to her room.

"How much farther do we have before we get to the ship?" Sunny mumbled while waiting for Raven to unlock the door.

"Gabriel said from here we have another day's ride by stagecoach to the coast. There we will board the ship going to England, and travel several weeks across the deep waters of the North Atlantic Ocean."

Sunny yawned. "Are you any closer to getting used to the new clothes?"

"Somewhat." She closed the door behind them,

securing the lock as Gabriel warned. "But it is still going to take a heap of trying."

****

Raven could not believe her eyes. The ship was immense, floating like a monster on a sea that ate hungrily at the land. Beside it were docked two other large vessels, each one headed for a different destination. Beneath her feet the floor rocked. Steadying herself using the ship's wall, she followed the cabin boy through the crowded corridors to the compartment she would share with Sunny. It was bigger than the one on the train; the bunks positioned one above another. The first line of business was deciding who would sleep on the top bed.

"We will call numbers for it," Sunny suggested.

She narrowed her eyes. "You always cheat."

Sunny's tone was indignant. "I do not."

"Yes, you do," Gabriel interjected, coming into the room. "But I can settle this right now." He pointed to Sunny. "Since you are a bit daft when you first wake and would probably forget you are sleeping in a second story compartment, you take the lower bunk."

"I am not daft," Sunny protested. "I am just a little groggy."

Gabriel arched a brow. "Whatever the case, I do not need you plunging to your death."

The cabin boy placed the luggage on the floor beside the washbasin, giving each of them a smile. His coal black eyes and unruly dark curls framed a child's face. Raven thought he could be no more than fourteen years of age. He took the time to explain where certain comforts could be found and when the meals would be served.

Gabriel's room adjoined theirs, no doubt to keep a look out for them. There were lots of men roaming about the ship; each one craning their necks to eye her and Sunny as they came aboard. She knew Gabriel saw the looks as well because he reached for each of their arms, tightening his grip while he escorted them to their quarters.

"Neither of you are to walk about this ship alone, do you hear?" he cautioned.

It was the same warning she received at home. She knew the danger firsthand and did not quarrel. Staying in her room, away from the leers and stares, was just fine with her. Even the thought of a man touching her made her flesh crawl, and she welcomed the security of the tiny cabin. But keeping Sunny confined would be hard. Naturally curious and completely oblivious to certain dangers, her younger sister would be a target for the first sailor looking for a woman's charms.

She shivered and edged closer to her brother. "You need not worry, we will stay together."

"Good," he said, making his way to his room. "I have to go below and see to my luggage now, and I want you both to stay put. Lock the door when I leave."

"When do we sail?" Sunny asked.

Gabriel glanced at the pocket watch he pulled from his vest. "In two hours."

"Why not just wait for the cabin boy to bring the bags to your room?" Raven suggested.

"I just want to make sure all is in order." Gabriel pointed to the portal's handle. "Remember, lock the door and stay in the room."

****

Raven sat on the lower bunk, looking through Sunny's sketch book, when the cabin boy called through the door they would sail in twenty minutes. Each drawing was exactly as it looked in real life. The one of her dressed as a traditional Apache woman, standing with a foot upon a rock, one hand on her hip and the other on a spear, did her proud.

She could not help thinking how much she did look the part of an Indian princess and wished the green-eyed man she met in Silver City could see the drawing.

"Do you think Gabriel has come back from his luggage search?" Sunny asked, looking up from her task of placing toiletries beside the washbasin.

"There is only one way to find out." Laying the sketch book aside she walked over to the door adjoining their cabin and rapped on it with a knuckle.

No response.

"Gabriel," she called out. There was no answer. She frowned. "Should I try the knob?"

Sunny's eyes widened. "I would not if I were you. He could be undressed. And the last time I barged in on his privacy he threatened me with a thrashing." She folded her arms across her chest. "Father was there to stop him, but he is not here now."

"Well, Gabriel dares not touch me." She turned the knob and peered into the room.

It was empty.

Sunny stood beside her, wringing her hands. "Oh, poor Gabriel. I bet his belongings are lost."

She pointed to the bunk. "I do not think so, look there, Sunny."

"His bags are already here…then why…where is—"

"I think I know where he might be." She narrowed her eyes. "I have no doubt our dear brother is at the place where the men drink the fire water. We passed one on our way to the ship." She made her way to the corridor portal. "I am going for him."

Sunny followed, reaching out a restraining hand. "Gabriel said to stay in the room, besides he knows when we are to sail."

"If he is drunk, Sunny, he might not be able to

make it back in time."

Sunny folded her arms across her bosom. "This is very unwise."

"I will tell you what is unwise—to leave our dear brother passed out somewhere. You know the stupor he is in after he drinks."

Sunny bit her bottom lip. "But Gabriel said to stay here with the door locked."

"What if a thief finds him passed out and robs him of the funds he carries, how will we pay for things on this journey?"

Sunny placed hands on hips. "Though you have a very good point, you are still being unwise."

She threw her hands up exasperated. "Oh, stop acting like mother. I am going to find Gabriel, and that is that."

"Please, wait here," Sunny pleaded.

"You wait here and make sure you lock the door behind me. I am going below to find him, and when I do..." her voice trailed as she shook an angry fist in the air.

****

The cantina reeked of stale smoke and sweat, much like the saloon in Silver City. She scanned the room for her brother and shuddered when she spotted a man reaching out to fondle one of the scantly clad girls. Another man fell off a chair in a drunken faint, and she worried further what condition she would find Gabriel in. If he tasted too much of the drink, it would be difficult for her to manage getting him back to the ship by herself.

"Hey, you! Mestiza!" a man shouted from his seat at a table. He grabbed a handful of lace that trimmed the bottom of her skirt and tore it free. She was twirled into his lap. "You have too much on." His sour breath wafted from his meaty lips.

She shoved him away and wiggled free, but he caught her by the hand and with a tug, ripped off her sleeve. She was horrified. Her blouse hung in shreds, exposing a shoulder. Scenes of agent Hall and Baxter swam in her mind. Her heart pounded, panic mounting.

"You will not touch me," she shrieked, doubling her fist and slamming a crushing blow to the man's nose.

Blood poured from his nostrils.

"Little whore," he cursed, bringing both his hands up to his injured face.

She fled with a mixture of fear and rage, running blindly to the ship and stepping onto the plank. Breathless, she gripped the rail on deck and looked down at the crowd below. She was not going to leave this ship until it docked in England, with or without her brother.

She lingered on deck, calming her thoughts and cooling her rage while she watched the seamen pull up anchor. The large vessel lurched ahead, making its way out into the vast stretch of water looming at the forefront. Looking out to where the sea met the sky made her queasy.

Raven turned away from the rail and searched down the corridor for the causeway to her cabin. Back and forth she wandered, growing confused. Everything aboard looked strange to her. She could not find the living quarters or the cabin boy. And where were all the people? The ship's horn bellowed, nearly deafening her. The floor swayed beneath her feet, and she lost her balance. Making her way back to the deck area, she fought to keep her nauseous stomach calm and her wobbly legs straight. There she spotted a tall man with a bushy beard. He was leaning on the rail, smoking a pipe; his fiery red hair blowing in the breeze.

"Please, sir," she said, struggling to keep her feet beneath her. "Where would the passenger's cabins be?"

He turned, his large blue eyes widening at her torn clothes. “Are you alright, lass?”

Her cheeks warmed. “I will be, once I can find my cabin.”

“There are none on this ship, lass. ’Tis a private owned vessel carryin’ cargo bound for Limerick.”

“Is Limerick in England, sir?”

“Nay, lass,” the man said. “Limerick is in Ireland.”

Chapter Three

"Wonunicun," Raven whispered.

The man frowned. "Beggin' your pardon, lass?"

"A mistake has been made," she translated, biting her lower lip to keep from crying.

The man chuckled. "Well, if there has, lass, 'tis you who've made it."

Her knees were as weak as a newborn colt's. She held onto the rail, tears slipping down her cheeks. "I fear you are right, sir. Somehow I have gotten aboard the wrong ship."

The red-haired man embraced her waist with a steady hand. "'Twill take a wee bit for you to get your sea legs."

She shivered, the wind growing stronger and whipping strands of hair from her chignon.

He smiled down at her, his eyes softening. "I'm Terrance Murphy, the ship's physician." He took her arm. "Let's go below to the galley, and while a hot bowl of soup warms your bones you can be explainin' to me how 'tis you've come to be on the wrong ship."

She did not trust herself to speak, fearing she would either cry or be sick all over the deck. Giving the doctor a slow nod, she allowed him to help her away from the rail and down the stairway. At the bottom, stood a long narrow room where a stocky built woman of middle age worked at a table cutting meat with a cleaver.

The woman raised her gaze to meet Raven's. With a frown she put down the cleaver, wiped her hands on the apron tied about her chubby waist, and made her way to the foot of the stairs.

"Saints preserve us, Terry, what have you brought me here?"

"This misfortunate lass mistook this ship for one bound for England, Molly."

"Mother of God," she whispered. "And you've family aboard the other ship?"

She nodded, pushing aside the hair from her eyes. "A brother and a sister." A burning lump lodged in her throat at the thought of how worried they must both be by now. Just a day ago she and Sunny pledged they would never be apart, and now she had no idea when she would see her sister again.

"Fill a bowl o' potage for the lass, Molly, me dear. The poor child's chilled to the bone," Terrance said, offering her a chair.

Molly placed the soup on the table and with a kind smile, took a seat beside her. "You poor dear, you must be frightened out o' your wits."

She did not believe she could eat a thing in the state she was in, even though she had not eaten since the morning meal, but accepted the woman's kindness as not to hurt her feelings. She spooned the soup into her mouth, the warmth of the broth slipped down her throat. It tasted good, filling her hungry belly.

Molly broke a piece of wheaten bread from a loaf sitting on the table and handed it to her. "How have you come to be on this ship instead o' your own, lass?"

She took a deep breath and explained to Molly and Terrance the reason she left the England bound ship and the rude man at the pier's cantina.

Molly threw a hand up in disgust. "Those rogues have no respect for women."

Terrance took a seat opposite her. "Well, there's not much we can be doin' about the situation now, since we're already afloat." He flashed an encouraging smile and reached out to give her hand a pat. "But not to fear, lass. When we dock in Ireland, we'll contact your family in England and send you safely home."

Home is not England, but a tiny village in Arizona I fear I will never see again.

Molly frowned. "And what will we be tellin' y'r lordship? She hasn't the proper passage. He gets testy about such things, always makin' sure all papers are in order."

"I can cook and clean for my keep," she offered.

"'Tis settled then," Terrance said, glancing at Molly with a humorous twinkle in his eyes. "You're always complainin', Molly, me dear, the workload gets a wee bit much for you. Now you have an eager helper." He stood and made his way to the stairs, turning to add. "When need be, I'll settle all this with m'lord."

Molly nodded in agreement and turned to her. "If you've finished your broth, child, I'll be takin' you to find some other clothes for you to be wearin'." She reached out with a chubby hand and fingered the torn blouse. "You certainly can't be expected to be runnin' around like this throughout the voyage."

She followed Molly to another room behind the galley.

Handing her a dress, the elder woman giggled. "Saints preserve us, I've fed you and now I'm clothin' you, and I don't even know your name."

It was true; in all the excitement neither of them had asked her name. "Raven Amelia Eagle," she supplied. "I am the daughter of Chief Proud Eagle of the Western Apache tribe." She squared her shoulders and added with pride. "I am an Indian princess."

****

Molly, skilled with a needle as well as with a cooking pot, made over a few of her own dresses for Raven to wear. They were cut to fit and quite comfortable. With her long black hair braided and hanging down her back, Raven went about her duties, learning the routine in just a week's time and fitting in with the rest of the crew. They were all a kind bunch of people, doing their best to make her feel at home.

When the work day was done, she joined everyone around the long galley table where they sat laughing, eating, and sharing stories about their homeland. Hans, one of the cabin boys, had come from Sweden and sounded just like Reverend Ben when he spoke. The deck hands, Victor, Hugo, and Boris were brothers. They came from a place called Russia. But her stories gathered the most interest. The crew listened intently as she told them about her Indian chief father, white mother, and of the reservation's sad state of affairs.

The only person yet for her to meet was the man who owned the ship. The one they all called the Lord of Limerick. She believed the man to be sick and aging, always needing to travel with a personal physician on board and his meals brought three times a day to his cabin. Her people taught the young to respect and revere the elderly. But what if the Lord of Limerick was a mean, stubborn, old goat who would have her thrown off the ship? In any case, she was perfectly content to have Terrance speak on her behalf and relieved the ship's owner never ventured below deck. She hoped it remained that way till the end of the journey.

****

Raven lie now on her cot, cramps and their slicing pain having her down for the day. She could hear Molly and Terrance discussing the situation in the next room.

"She's a blessin' in disguise," Molly confided. "A hard worker often doin' more than her share o' the chores."

"I'm pleased to hear this, Molly." Terrance answered.

"And what have you told y'r lordship?" Molly probed.

"Only that we acquired an accidental stowaway, and you put her to work for her passage."

"And he wasn't concerned as to what will be happenin' to the lass once we dock in Ireland?"

Terrance's tone softened. "Not to fret none, Molly, me dear. I assured m'lord I'd take full responsibility regardin' the matter when we reached Limerick. And he was satisfied with that, so I saw no reason to concern him further."

"Well, I'm a wee bit concerned for the lass's health, Terry."

"You're concerned over everyone's health, Molly. 'Tis your nature." Terrance chuckled. "Maybe you should have been appointed the ship's physician."

"Now, quit teasin' me here and listen to *why* I'm concerned."

Terrance sighed. "Speak your fears, woman."

"The lass hardly eats, has such a wee appetite, and what she does eat, doesn't stay down long."

"Sounds like a classic case of seasickness to me," Terrance concluded. "Give her another week, and she'll bear up." Terrance laughed again. "I've seen heartier souls then her turn green around the gills."

"Nay, 'tis somethin' more," Molly went on. "She's tired all the time, has severe stomach cramps durin' the night." She lowered her voice. "I hear her groanin' and fussin' from me own bed, and I'm tellin' you, Terry, the child's ailin'."

"Where's the lass now?"

"I've sent her to her cot, gave her a cup o' tea and a warm compress for her stomach," Molly said.

"And so what would you be needin' me for, Molly, me dear? 'Tis all I would have recommended."

"I know, I'm probably fearin' the worse for

nothin'. But all the same, I'd feel better if you'd take a look at her." Her voice sweetened. "'Twould take a load off me mind."

"Now, don't be gettin' yourself all agitated, love. 'Tis probably somethin' she ate." Terrance sighed again. "Take me to the lass now. I'll have a look at her and give her a powder to help her sleep."

Raven heard them make their way to her cot, but she kept her eyes clenched tight, breathing in quick, shallow gasps as the pain cut through her middle like a sharp blade. Ice spread through her stomach, and she shivered, pulling the blanket up to her chin.

At the touch of a gentle hand upon her forehead, her eyes flew open, looking up into the face of Terrance Murphy. His eyes, almost opaque, searched her face, the tiny lines around his mouth creasing with concern.

"You're burnin' with fever, lass," he said, pulling the blanket down to her waist. "Show me where it hurts."

She moved a trembling hand over her lower abdomen.

Terrance pulled the blanket down to her knees and lifted the nightgown.

"No," she protested, curling her knees to her waist. "I am…I am not wearing anything beneath."

"'Tis alright, lass," Molly consoled. "Terrance is a doctor and is here to help. There is no need for you to be ashamed."

She relaxed her legs and rolled onto her back so Terrance could examine her. She shuddered; turning her face aside as he probed with delicate fingers at the base of her stomach and between her thighs. Glad for the semidarkness hiding the flush in her cheeks.

Terrance recovered her and knelt down beside the cot. "Raven, lass, look at me."

She turned, her face burning with fever... humiliation...the pain that wracked every part of her body. “What is wrong with me?”

The doctor’s voice was soft but alarming. “You’re miscarrin’ a babe, lass.”

A baby? I am having a baby? No, I am losing a baby! “I do not understand...it cannot be,” she sobbed.

Terrance turned to Molly. “I need clean cloths and a basin of warm water.”

She glanced at Molly’s frightened face.

“Why didn’t you tell me you were with child, lass?”

Her heart sickened with the remembrance of agent Hall touching her body, taking her virtue. “I did not know. I was taken against my will one night on the reservation by an agent that brought food to the village.”

Molly leaned over and squeezed her hand. “’Tis his sin, not yours, lass. And may he be damned for his actions.”

It seemed like an eternity before the pain subsided, the bleeding controlled. Deep within her heart she wrestled with a mixture of relief and sorrow. To want her rapist’s child was something she knew she could not bear, but still...what she had carried beneath her heart was a baby...innocent of its father’s actions and also a part of her. In some strange way she grieved the loss of the small life, her tears of mourning adding to her physical pain. If not for Terrance Murphy’s gentle, experienced hands continuing to care for her body, his calm, caring voice soothing her spirit, and the sleeping powders he administered, she would have never been able to drift away from the loss and loneliness. The pang of being parted from her family quieted, and she was soon cast into the blissful state of nothingness.

****

Terrance sat in the large stuffed chair of Braiton's cabin and looked at him with weary eyes. Slowly, the physician took a sip of whiskey from the glass. "How many times have I examined you, m'lord, in the years since you were a lad?"

Braiton pulled his shirt over his shoulders. "I can scarcely count them, Terry, but each time I held my breath for a positive result."

Terrance sighed. "Aye, 'tis good when the news is positive."

He searched the other man's face. "What is it, Terry? Have you bad news for me this time around?" He moved closer. "I have a right to know if I'm falling apart."

Terrance placed his glass on a nearby table. "You're far from fallin' apart, m'lord. In fact you're the perfect picture o' health. I'm quite sure you'll surpass us all," he added.

"Then why the grim face?" He took a seat beside Terrance and buttoned his shirt. "Saints preserve us, man, you look as though you've been up all night."

Terrance rubbed his fingers over red-rimmed eyes. "That's because I have been up all night, m'lord and right now me eyes burn with exhaustion."

His voice softened. "Why, Terry?"

Terrance sighed again, heavier this time. "Do you remember me tellin' you about our wee stowaway?"

"Aye, the young lass who mistook our ship for one she was supposed to board for England."

Terrance nodded. "Well, she's not as wee a lass as I led you to believe."

Braiton frowned. "How old is she?"

"Oh, in my opinion, near to her twenties."

He stood, reached for the whiskey bottle and refilled Terrance's glass. "Suppose you tell me the whole story."

Terrance thanked him with a slight nod of his

head and took a sip. "I'll start with her name, a beautiful name actually." He cocked his head sideways. "Raven she's called. Raven Amelia Eagle and she's an Apache lass. Her virtue was compromised by an agent who brought food to her village. Unbeknown to her, she became with child." Terrance's eyes saddened. "She miscarried last night."

His mouth dropped open as Terrance's words hit a recollection he held vivid in his mind, and for a long moment he just stared ahead speechless. When he could finally speak, the words were a mere whisper. "And how is she now?"

The doctor arched a brow. "Not good, m'lord, 'tis why I've been up all night."

"What's still ailing her, Terry? Is she hemorrhaging?"

"Nay, m'lord, the bleedin', thank the Lord, is under control. 'Tis a fever troublin' her body now. I'm afraid the damp servant's quarters aren't helpin' her condition," Terrance explained. "She's been accustomed to a dryer climate. Even though Arizona nights can get cold, they aren't as damp as what she's experiencin' here. The poor lass can't stop shiverin', the dampness penetratin' through to her very bones."

"Have her brought up to this cabin, Terry," he said, going over to the bed and straightening the quilt. "She should be warm enough here."

"Nay, m'lord, surely not your bed?" Terrance protested. "I'll have the cabin boy bring her cot up for her."

"I said she takes the bed," he said firmly. "I will use the cot." He gestured to the portal. "Now, off with you, man. Let's get the lass well again."

****

Raven ran through the brush with Sunny, laughing and enjoying the warmth of the noon sun, high and blazing in the sky. Then, in an instant the sun disappeared, surrounding her with a cold, lonely darkness. Frantic, she searched for her sister, but Sunny was nowhere to be found. In the distance she heard her name being called, the voice soft, deep. Where had she heard this voice before?

Opening her eyes, she focused on the face of the man bending over her. The kind, strange green eyes twinkled, a slow smile spread beneath the mustache.

"Welcome aboard my ship, lass," he said, covering her hand with the warmth of his own.

She looked around the room, confused. "This is your ship?"

"Aye, you're aboard *The Sweet Maureen*."

She took an audible breath. "Then you...you are the Lord of Limerick?"

"Aye, Lord Braiton Shannon." He inclined his head. "At your service."

Again she looked around the spacious room. "Where am I?"

"You're in my cabin."

She pulled her hand from beneath his and brought the quilt up to her chin. "And this...this is your bed?"

"Aye, lass, 'tis much warmer for you here than below."

She cleared her throat. "And where have you slept?"

He chuckled, the cleft in his chin dimpling. "Have not a fear, only the quilt kept you warm." He pointed to a cot set up in the sitting area of the cabin. "There is where I took my slumber."

She sat up, leaning on her elbows, to get a better view of the splendid quarters. "How long have I kept you from your bed?"

He fluffed the pillow behind her head. "Three days."

"I am so sorry I have troubled you," she said,

lying back down.

"'Tis no trouble, lass." His eyes saddened. "The good doctor Murphy explained your circumstances. I am truly sorry for all you've been through and wish now for you to be well."

Humiliation coursed through her body. She turned away from him, rolling onto her side, burying her face into the pillow. Tears stung her eyes, wetting the clean white linen.

His weight jiggled the bed, and a gentle hand touched her shoulder. Slowly, he turned her to look at him.

"'Tis no reason to be ashamed, lass." He pushed aside a long strand of hair clinging to a moist cheek. "The shame belongs on the head of the man who so ruthlessly took what wasn't his." For a moment his eyes grew hard, the muscles at his jaw throbbed. "He's fortunate I know nothing of his whereabouts, for I'd make him pay for what he's done."

She believed he would, remembering the way, with one command; he saved her from Baxter's clutches in Silver City.

"But I'm sure your father already has," he added.

She sighed. "He would have, if he knew."

"And why doesn't he know, lass?" He softened his tone. "If you were my daughter 'twould be my right to know, to avenge your honor."

"And that is exactly why I did not tell him."

He frowned. "I'm afraid I don't understand, lass."

She gazed deep into his emerald eyes. "No, I suppose you do not, then again, how could you? I am sure all your life you have been able to live and speak and do exactly as you please." He opened his mouth to respond to her words, but she held up a hand to silence him. "I mean you no disrespect. But you do not understand the circumstances my people live with."

"Then tell me."

"My village was taken over by the white agents. Nothing belonging to my people is theirs anymore. We are robbed of our goods and our dignity. And if any of us fight for our rights, we are beaten or hanged."

Braiton again laid a hand on hers, the warmth of his touch sending heat waves through her body. "And so you feared for your father's safety?"

"For his life," she said, glancing down at his hand. His fingers were long; the nails clean and clipped evenly. "As chief he is a very proud leader. He would take a stand against the white agents. I could not allow them to take his life."

"And what of your mother, lass?"

She raised her eyes to meet his. "I believe deep down she figured out what happened, and that is why she sent her children to England."

He smiled. "She sounds very protective of her family."

"She is, and I know she kept quiet for the same reason I did."

Tenderness filled his eyes. "Do you remember your last words to me, lass?"

She frowned confused. "My last words?"

"Aye, in Silver City, before you disappeared around the landing. You said you hoped we'd live to meet again."

She smiled. "Yes, I remember."

"And we have." He arched a brow. "It seems you have a knack for being where you shouldn't, and me for rescuing you."

"I owe you much, for then and now. I am grateful for all you have done, and do not wish to be any further trouble."

"I'm not worried, lass."

"I gave my word I would work to pay for my

passage, so in the morning I will return to the galley and help Molly."

He frowned. "You're not in any condition to move from this bed or to labor at chores."

"But I gave my word, and I always keep—"

This time he silenced her words by placing a fingertip on her lips. "Since we're old acquaintances from our Silver City days, I must insist you be my guest for the remainder of the voyage."

"You are very kind, sir, and I thank you, but I will keep my agreement and work for my food and passage. All I ask is your help in sending word to England when we dock."

Braiton took in the deep golden brown of her flesh and the sheen of her dark hair laying in disarray against the white linens. He admired her determination, her honesty, spirit, and the strong sense of pride flickering through her intense, blue eyes.

Women he knew were frail and dependent. *Featherheads*, he called them, only concerned with the latest fashion. They sat in their gowns like stiff stone statues, not a curl out of place. They'd never dream of getting their hands dirty. But this fresh young beautiful lass lying in his bed was warm and genuine, full of life and wanting to live every moment of it. She denied the luxury he offered to stay duty bound by an agreement. She honored her word, and he would honor her in return.

"That is all I ask," she said, interrupting his thoughts. "That you send word to my family."

He nodded. "I'm acquainted with Captain Rafe Cavendish of the vessel *The Entrenous*." He raised a brow. "Which was the ship you should have boarded. 'Twill be no trouble to contact him when we reach Ireland."

She gave him a satisfied nod.

"But now, lass, might I ask something of you?"

"And what might that be, sir," she muttered a bit uneasily.

"I can tell you assume the request is that of a blackguard." He rose from the bunk.

"I did not mean..."

He stood looking down at her. "If I had cared to, lass, I could have taken my pleasure from your womanly charms while you raged in fever. You would've been none the wiser."

Her eyes widened, and she pulled the quilt up to her chin.

"And you hide nothing from me beneath that coverlet, for 'twas I who tended you these past three days." He moved to the foot of the bunk. "Did you know you have a tiny crescent shaped birthmark right on–"

"You have made your point clear, sir," she interjected. "If you wanted to shame me, you have done so."

"Nay, lass, 'twas not my intent," he corrected. "And I beg your pardon if I have. I only wished to prove to you I am not a man who would abuse a woman."

"Then you are like my father and brother," she countered.

He smiled. "If they are gentlemen, then aye, I'm just like them."

"They have always prided themselves as honorable men, respectful to women," she said. "And I have never seen them be otherwise."

"I was merely going to ask for your friendship in return, to learn more about your family over a shared meal, perhaps, nothing more."

Her tone softened. "I should very much like to befriend you, sir."

He made his way to the portal. "Enough said, 'tis best now that you eat, regain your strength. I'll send Molly up with a tray of food."

"I thank you most kindly, sir," she said, sending him a warm smile.

He closed the cabin door behind him, leaving the Indian princess lying in his bed to collect her thoughts. Or was it he who needed to gather his? For some reason the lass's smile totally disarmed him.

He combed his fingers through his hair. All his life he steeled himself against womanly wiles, the curse he suffered a constant reminder to keep buried all such desire. Normally, 'twas not an issue, thoughts of the sadness he'd bring upon a mate was enough to keep intimate notions at bay. But when Raven gazed upon him with her sapphire eyes, an unexpected wash of pleasure coursed through his entire being. The jolt of gratification so pure, so strong, it gave him a genuine thrill and almost knocked him to his knees.

He knew, after he found Molly and ordered Raven a tray of food, 'twould be necessary to seek out a private place; someplace quiet, where he could just sit and think.

Chapter Four

For three days, Raven recuperated in Braiton's bed. Her dreams took her back to her village, sitting around the fire pit and listening to her father's stories. If there was one thing the Apache people liked to do the most, it was telling fables and tales, many having a moral to live by.

After her fever broke there was no need for the Lord of Limerick to keep constant vigil beside her bed. The cot he slept upon was moved to the good doctor's cabin, the two men sharing diminutive quarters to give her privacy.

She was now back in the room she shared with Molly and working in the galley.

"You're indeed foolish, lass," Molly chided as she prepared a lunch tray. "I hear Lord Shannon offered for you to ride the rest o' the voyage as his guest, yet you've chosen to work up a sweat down here with me."

She kept at her task, chopping potatoes for the dinner stew. "It would have been terribly inconsiderate of me, Molly, to continue sleeping in the man's cabin throughout the entire voyage, leaving him and Terrance cramped for room."

"Obviously it mattered not to him, or he wouldn't have offered," Molly retorted.

"And did anyone care to ask Terrance's opinion on the matter?" she countered.

"He would have agreed."

"Speaking of agreements...ours was I work for my passage. I will stand by my word." She dropped the vegetable pieces into a large pot filled with water. "I am learning quickly no one gives something away without wanting something in return."

Molly responded somewhat annoyed. "As I hear it, all m'lordship wanted was your friendship."

She brought the pot to the stove and set it to boiling. "And do you truly believe it is all he would take?"

"Aye, lass, I do." Molly came to stand beside her, folding her chubby arms across an ample bosom. "Lord Shannon is a man who also stands by his word and says what he means. If he asked for your friendship, then 'tis all he'd be takin'."

She wiped her hands on the apron tied around her waist. "And why would he want my friendship?"

Molly sighed. "Perhaps he believed you held somethin' new for him to hear, would make him laugh a wee bit, or be a listenin' ear yourself."

"Does he not have Terrance to talk to?"

Molly reached out and pushed a tendril of hair from Raven's forehead. "Now why would he be wantin' to gaze upon Terry's face when he could be lookin' at this one?"

An unwelcome blush crept to her cheeks, and she busied herself by stirring the potatoes with a wooden spoon.

"Besides," Molly concluded, "we're all busy doin' our jobs, lass. M'lordship doesn't pay us to sit around and chat. Who would be runnin' things for him if we did?"

Raven grabbed an onion from a bowl and began to slice it.

Molly stood beside her. "He gets lonely on these voyages."

The onion's fragrance made Raven's eyes water. She dabbed each one with the end of her apron. "I am sure, the handsome man that he is, many women want his attention. When he arrives home he will be lonely no longer." For a reason she could not explain, the thought of the young lord having anything to do with another woman bothered her.

Molly shook her head, wiping her own eyes with her sleeve. "You're wrong, lass. He has no one."

She gathered the sliced onions into her hands. "Now, how would you know, Molly?"

"Me sister, Anna O'Leary works at Shannonbrook. She's been tendin' the place since Lord Shannon was a wee lad. Her husband, Patrick, drives the lord's carriage, and he can attest to the fact he visits no women, nor do they call on him."

Again, she could not understand why Molly's words brought her a sense of relief. What was it to her whether Lord Shannon entertained other women or not? "He is just good at keeping his business a secret."

Molly came to her employer's defense. "Nay, lass, 'tisn't the case at all. M'lord is a gentleman in the true sense o' the word."

She shrugged and dropped the onions into the boiling pot before she covered it. "If he is or if he is not, it has nothing to do with me. The deal was I work for my passage, and it is what I intend to do."

"Fine, if that's the way 'tis to be." Molly made her way over to the tray she prepared for Lord Shannon and handed it to her. "Here you go, me stubborn lass, take him his lunch tray."

Molly calling her stubborn annoyed her. A deal was a deal, and she was keeping her end of it. She needed nothing from the Lord of Limerick but a way to get to England. She took a deep breath to compose herself, then knocked on the portal with one hand, while balancing the tray with the other.

"Aye, enter," his deep voice called from within the cabin.

She opened the door, raising her eyes to spot his whereabouts. He sat working at a large desk, his head bent in concentration over a pile of papers.

"Just lay the tray on the table in the corner," he instructed without looking up.

She made her way to a table at the far end of the cabin and set the tray down, then turned to face him. "Is there anything more I can do for you, sir?"

At the sound of her voice, he met her gaze. The slow smile that curved his lips deepened the cleft in his chin. Rising from his chair, he moved to stand beside her.

He was a tall man, and she had to crane her neck in order to meet his eyes. She licked her dry lips and forced a smile in return. "Would you like for me to pour you a cup of tea?"

He pulled a chair from the table and sat down. "Aye, thank you, lass."

The scent of his cologne filled her senses, his very presence unnerving. With trembling hands, she picked up the pot and poured the tea, then handed him the cup.

Lightly his fingers brushed hers as he accepted the hot brew. The mere touch of their flesh connecting made her insides quake.

His eyes engulfed her with concern. "I hope you aren't doing too much too soon, lass."

She pulled her hand away, folding them behind her back. "I am fine, sir. Thank you for asking."

He sat back in his chair and searched her face. "Do I frighten you, Raven?"

It was the first time she had heard him say her first name. The way the *R* sounded rolling off his tongue thrilled her. "I do not frighten easily, sir."

A mischievous twinkle gleamed in his eyes. "That's good to know."

Her voice was shakier than she liked. "Will that be all then?"

"Aye, thank you."

She could feel his eyes watching her leave. Her

steps were awkward as she walked to the door. Once the portal closed behind her, she leaned against it and let out the breath she had been holding.

What in heaven's name has come over me?

The pounding of her heart could wake the dead, and the palms of her hands were soaked with sweat. She wiped them on the apron, whispering to herself. "Get a grip less you appear the fool." She looked around, in the hopes no one heard her talking to herself, before she made her way down the causeway to the galley—feeling confused and elated all at once.

****

Braiton trusted Captain Rourke Kirby, a skilled sailor in his day who weathered many storms. His hair and beard were white with age, but his mind was as clear as a crystal goblet. He was sharp at a game of cards, quick with a snappy remark, and more than capable at the helm of *The Sweet Maureen*.

Standing before him now, Kirby's hazel green eyes shone with concern from beneath bushy brows. "I've spotted the buggers a few miles behind us, m'lord."

Braiton poured them each a whiskey and handed a glass to Kirby. "And you're sure they're Sea Patrol?"

"Aye, m'lord." Kirby took the whiskey and threw the honey colored liquid down his throat. His ruddy cheeks, permanently chapped by the wind, swished, and he savored the taste of the expensive liquor before swallowing it. "Most likely they want to check the cargo against receipts."

Braiton twirled the amber drink around in the glass before downing it as fast as Kirby. "All is in order. I have nothing to fear from these men."

Kirby's heavy white brows knit together. "There's a problem other than the cargo, m'lord."

He sat back in his seat, laying his glass aside and reached for his clay pipe. “What might that be, Captain?”

“The young American lass, m’lord. She doesn’t have the proper passage to show she legally belongs aboard.” Kirby removed his cap and combed his fingers through his unruly hair. “The authorities could conclude she’s bein’ smuggled for the sellin’ o’ carnal pleasures. Many ships have hustled women aboard for such purposes.”

He lit the pipe, taking a few quick puffs. “And what happens to the women?”

Kirby replaced his cap upon his head and folded his large hands in front of him. “They’re removed and taken off to prison, m’lord.”

It disturbed him to think of Raven in one of those lock downs. His stomach churned, and he rose from his seat, coming around to lean a hip against the desk. “Perhaps if I explained the situation, offered them a few coins, they might overlook her.”

“Save your breath to cool your porridge, m’lord. These knaves are a crafty lot.” Kirby chuckled sardonically. “One look at the lass, and they’ll not only be takin’ her, but havin’ their fill with her as well.”

Inwardly he recoiled. Raven at the mercy of these men…of any man. With jaws clenched he paced the cabin floor. “Then what can be done to save her from these scoundrels?”

“If the lass were your wife, m’lord, the Sea Patrol would have no right to do a thing.”

Kirby’s words slammed him in the gut, stopped him in his tracks. “I have vowed never to marry, Captain. Surely there has to be another way?”

Kirby’s brows furrowed. “Sorry to say, m’lord, I cannot think of another as bindin’. As ’tis, I’ll have to date the marriage papers to when we first left America.”

He ran a hand through his hair, blood pulsed in his head, and resumed pacing. "If that be the only way, then make the arrangements."

Kirby gave a taut nod and walked to the portal, stopping short before opening it. He turned to face Braiton. "What if the lass refuses?"

"Explain to her the consequences she'll face if she doesn't go along with the plan."

Kirby shook his head. "The lesser of two evils."

"Aye, something like that, Captain."

****

At first Raven was too startled to object, but as Molly braided her hair, she continued to ponder the situation. The whole idea became absurd.

"*Aco'tndn'nil'gon'ye*...what is the trouble? Why can he not just hide me?"

"The trouble is if the authorities found you, lass, we'd all be in a fix." Molly reached for the yellow ribbon on the table and entwined it within the braid. "You should be feelin' grateful m'lord decided to marry you instead o' handin' you over to those men."

She could barely swallow the lump growing in her throat. "I always hoped when the time came for me to marry, it would be for love."

"We never know what's ahead o' us in this life, lass. Could be in time the two of you—"

Annoyed, Raven interjected, "We are scarcely friends, so scarce he could not even come to tell me all this himself." She turned around to look Molly in the eyes. "He sent the captain to demand...not ask...I wed him."

Molly smiled. "I'm sure 'tis because he's so much on his mind, he must be ready for these men." She narrowed her eyes. "Don't you think every girl who's had a marriage arranged hasn't gone through the same...felt the way you do?"

"I do not care about other girls," she protested.

"Hush, now child, and let me finish here," Molly

said, placing a hand on her shoulder and turning her back around. "There is no other choice before you, and the Sea Patrol is on our tail. There must be enough time for the ink to dry on the weddin' papers so that everythin' appears in order, or else we'll all be seein' the inside walls of a prison."

"None of this is happening the way it should be, Molly. I am supposed to be sent to England, to be with my family, after we land in Ireland. How can that happen if I am Lord Shannon's wife?"

Molly pinned the braid atop Raven's head. "Now, don't you go worrin' so, lass. M'lordship 'tisn't daft, and I assure you he hasn't forgotten his duty to you. But first and foremost he knows these men must leave our ship and be on their merry way." She gave her an affectionate pat on the arm. "'Twill all turn out for the best, you'll see, and what a vision you'll be when I'm through here." She giggled. "'Tis all so romantic."

Becoming the wife of a man she hardly knew was anything but romantic. She always thought when it was her time to wed she would wear the dress her grandmother and mother wore to take their own vows. Tears welled in her eyes. Her sister, Sunny, would wear the traditional gown now. Hopefully, it will be under better circumstances.

Molly reached for the dress she'd cut down to fit Raven and draped it over her shoulder. "Look how the yellow brings out the rich darkness o' your hair."

She gave a taut nod. "You have done a fine job, Molly."

Molly smiled, eyes twinkling with satisfaction. "Now stand and let me help you on with it, lass."

She obeyed, allowing Molly to fasten a row of tiny pearl buttons up the back.

When finished, Molly stood back to admire her work. "You're a vision, lass." Molly brushed a tear from her own eye. "If only me sister, Anna, could be here." She took her by the hand and led her to the stairs. "The next time I set me eyes on you, you'll be the Lady of Limerick."

She clutched Molly's hand. "Oh Molly, I am so scared. This is not the way it should be." Tears burned the back of her throat. "I do not want to be the Lady of Limerick. All I want is to be Raven Eagle and join my family in England."

Molly's tone sharpened. "For now 'tis how it must be, lass. We're not all given what we want, and so we must make the best o' what we have." Then she gave her an encouraging smile. "You must trust m'lordship. He is a good and honorable man. He'll make everythin' right in the end, you'll see." She softened her tone. "Now go, lass. Lord Shannon awaits you."

She made her way up the stairs, careful to hold her full skirt above her ankles to keep from tripping. By the time she reached Lord Shannon's cabin she was numb with fear and uncertainty. *How could this be happening to me?*

"Trust him," Molly had said.

She hesitated before knocking on the portal and calmed herself by taking a few deep breaths. *What choice do I have?*

It was Captain Kirby who opened the door, bowing as she entered.

She managed a polite smile in return and looked over at her husband-to-be. An expression the mixture of admiration and awe crossed his face, and it set her already weak knees to knocking.

Making his way to her, his emerald eyes took in the entire length of her with a long, slow sweep. Then they rested ever so slightly on the scooped décolletage of her gown.

Her face grew hot beneath his scrutiny. Molly had made the neckline way too low. With trembling fingers she adjusted the lace collar.

Lord Shannon commented with quiet emphasis. "I'd say you're like a rare gem, lass. When polished, you shine magnificently."

She inclined her head in a small gesture of appreciation. "*Ashoge,* thank you. I am most grateful to you for what you are doing."

He took her hand, closing his fingers over hers. "Shall we begin, then?"

She nodded in agreement, a warm glow flowing through her with his touch.

He led her to stand in front of the large desk and gave a quick nod to Captain Kirby. "We're ready."

No drums beat, no women danced, her parents were not smiling as she spoke the vows. The whole ceremony—a few words read from a book held by Captain Kirby—was over in a matter of minutes. Her voice shook repeating her part, the promise to *honor and obey till death do them part* was a lie and sounded hollow to her ears.

When he finished agreeing to his part, he placed upon her finger a gold band. In the center of the ring sat a large blue stone, flanked on each side by diamonds. The brilliance almost blinded her.

"I cannot accept this ring, sir."

"You not only can, my lady, but you must. 'Twas my mother's wedding ring and 'tis tradition it be my wife's." The warmth of his smile echoed in his voice. "The sapphire is the same blue of your eyes."

"But under the circumstances I understand if –"

"'Tis yours now, Raven," he interrupted softly.

She wiggled her finger, admiring each gem. "I will guard it with my life, sir."

He poured red wine into three glasses, handing one to her and the second to Kirby. "Here's to my wife, Lady Raven Shannon," he toasted, raising the third glass high.

"Here, here," Kirby chimed in.

She smiled and raised her own glass. "And to

you as well, Lord Shannon."

"You need not be so formal, Raven. 'Twould please me to hear you call me Braiton."

Though she felt anything but comfortable being so familiar, she nodded in agreement. He was now her *shikaa,* husband. How would it sound to others, especially the Sea Patrol, if she stood on formality?

After the marriage certificate was signed, a heavy knock sounded at the door. Braiton blew on the papers to dry the ink while Captain Kirby answered the call.

A slim built man with beady eyes stood in the doorway. "Beggin' your pardon, Cap'n, the Sea Patrol approaches."

Kirby nodded. "Thank you, Riley." He faced Braiton. "Are you ready, m'lord?"

Braiton's jaw thrust forward. "Aye, Captain."

Her husband studied her. The same air of authority that stopped Baxter's torments upon her in Silver City was present again. There was an inherent strength in his face, an appearance of one who demanded respect and instant obedience. With him by her side, she knew there was little to fear.

He extended an elbow to her. "Are you ready to greet our guests, my lady?"

She squared her shoulders and looped her arm through his. "I am now, sir"—she hesitated and then added—"I mean, my *shikaa*."

He arched a brow. "And what is it now you've just called me?"

"Husband, *shikaa* means husband in Apache."

They shared a smile and together walked out on the open deck.

Chapter Five

In silence, hoping only she could hear the rapid beating of her heart, Raven watched the three men come aboard. They were dressed in double breasted jackets of red wool and black breeches. The heels of their shiny black boots clicked on the wooden deck floor with their quick steps, their eyes cold and faces stern.

Secretly thanking Braiton for rescuing her, she shuddered at the fate she could have endured at the hands of these heartless looking men. The Sea Patrol reminded her of the white agents who infiltrated her village, ready to take what was not theirs. The comparison was accurate. *Netdahe, death to all intruders.*

Braiton lowered his head to hers and whispered in her ear. "Are you all right, Raven."

"They make my blood grow cold," she whispered in return.

"Aye, they are a pirate looking bunch at that, but you have nothing to fear from them now. You're Lady Shannon; no one would dare to harm you. Besides," he added in a tone ringing with command, "they'd have to get through me first."

Startled by his response, she glanced up. "You would protect me with force?"

Braiton's large green eyes caught and held hers. "Aye, I would…to the death."

The last thing she wanted was for him to fight on her behalf or to die in the process. The chance of him being injured, or worse, paralyzed her with even a greater fear then the Sea Patrol posed. Now she sympathized with her mother...why she kept silent...never telling her father about the white agents' crude remarks and lecherous stares.

"No, my *shikaa*. Never should you fight for me."

His answer carried a unique force. "'Tis not for you to say, Raven."

She knew there would be no use to try and persuade him differently, even if there were time ...which there wasn't because the tallest man of the three coming aboard now stood before them, introducing himself and the others.

He bowed to her and nodded to Braiton. "I am Captain Marshall Langley." He gestured to the thin man standing to his left. "This is Lieutenant Addison Gray." Then he indicated the stockier-built man to his right. "And this is Lieutenant Martin Breck."

Braiton acknowledged each man with a taut nod. "'Tis my pleasure, gentlemen. Welcome to *The Sweet Maureen.* I am Braiton Shannon, Lord of Limerick." He gestured to her. "And this is my wife, Raven."

Captain Langley cocked his blond head to one side. His large gray-blue eyes sharp and accessing, swept the length of her. "Raven, is it?" His mouth spread into a thin-lipped smile. "That's a most unusual name."

Braiton kept his features composed, the tiny muscle at his jaw throbbing. "My wife is part, Apache, Captain."

Langley's eyes darkened. "Have you two been married long, my lord?"

She stiffened.

Braiton moved closer, placing an arm around her waist and pulling her to him. "Fact of the matter, Captain, I met my wife on this last voyage to America in Silver City. We were married aboard ship. My captain, Rourke Kirby, presided over the ceremony."

She found it impossible to steady her erratic pulse, though everything Braiton said was the truth, even if the events did not happen quite as he led Captain Langley to believe.

Langley's continued leer reminded her more and more of the white agents or that of an animal ready to attack its prey. He turned his cold gaze on Braiton. "I trust you have the necessary documents to prove what you say is true, my lord?"

Braiton returned Langley's look with a sharp one of his own. "Aye, Captain, I do." He removed his arm from around her waist and extended an elbow to her. "If you'll follow us to my cabin, I'll be glad to show you the marriage certificate, cargo receipts, and anything else you wish to examine."

She had to force her legs to move, her steps rigid walking beside her new husband to the cabin, the men's boot heels clicked with authority behind her.

Braiton opened the portal and motioned the men to precede him. "Everything you seek is laid out upon my desk." He escorted her to a chair before shutting the door. "I'm sure you'll find it all in order."

Again, Langley's eyes brushed over her, his words loaded with ridicule. "You must miss your family, my lady, or are you a poor orphan, hoping to better your station?"

This yudastcin, bastard, is making me out to look like a bija'n'ata, whore. Anger singed the corners of her control, rippling along her spine. "I have left many loved ones in America, sir."

Braiton's tone, though quiet, had an ominous quality. "My wife is an Indian princess, Captain Langley. And her mother comes from a prominent English family."

Langley was courteous, but patronizing. "I know many prominent families in England, which might yours be, my lady?" he challenged.

She forced her voice to remain calm, steadying her gaze. "Bentley...Kaylena Bentley of Bentwood Manor in Brighton, England." She raised a defiant chin and counter challenged. "Do you know of her, sir?"

Langley's face suddenly went grim. "Aye, my lady, I do."

Braiton cleared his throat and made his way to the desk. "I know you are a busy man, Captain, shall we carry on with our business?"

"You are a most fortunate man, Lord Shannon, to have such a beautiful, well-bred wife," Langley managed to reply through stiff lips.

"Thank you, Captain, I quite agree." Braiton handed the papers over and turned to her with a smile. "My lady, would you please pour each of these men a glass of whiskey?"

I would not mind dumping it over their heads. She forced a polite smile. "I would be happy to." Desperate to keep her hands from trembling, she went about the task, filling each man a glass as well as one for her husband. She served their guests first, Langley letting his fingers slip over hers as she handed him the glass. She met his bold stare with an indignant glare.

"May this warm you for the journey home."

She served Braiton last, smiling up into his eyes.

He returned the smile, reaching out to take her hand and giving it an affectionate squeeze, sending her pulses racing.

Langley sipped his whiskey while scanning the papers. Finally he admitted, "I see nothing that concerns me." Dragging his eyes from the documents he glared over at Braiton. "I'd like to check the cargo now, my lord."

"Certainly," Braiton agreed, placing his glass

upon the desk. "Everything is below deck."

Langley and the other two men set their glasses down on the table.

She was about to ask Braiton if he wanted her to join them when he answered the question for her. "You remain here, my lady. 'Tis much warmer." Turning to Langley Braiton explained, "My wife is not yet accustomed to the dampness of the sea."

"I understand." Langley bowed to her. "It has been a pleasure, my lady, one I assure you I shan't forget."

She inclined her head. "I am sure of that as well, Captain. And would you be so kind, should by chance you meet my Aunt Kaylena, to please give her my love?"

Langley gave her a taut nod. "Most definitely."

Braiton stifled a smile and gestured to the portal. "After you, gentlemen."

As soon as the door closed behind them, she sighed with relief and made her way to one of the stuffed chairs. She eased her body down into the soft cushion, and then leaned forward to free her aching feet from the tightly bound shoes. She unlaced the torturous leather binds and kicked them aside. Reaching beneath her skirt, she unhooked each stocking from its stay and slipped them down her legs, off her feet, and wiggled her bare toes. Next, she unpinned her hair from atop her head, letting the braid fall to her shoulders. Then she rested her head against the high-back of the chair and closed her eyes.

****

"Will you be wanting dinner, my lady?"

She opened her eyes to find Braiton looking down at her. She stifled a yawn. "Have those horrible men gone?"

He arched a brow. "Aye, well over an hour ago. And they won't be back, you are safe now."

And who will keep me safe from you? She rubbed her eyes with the backs of her hands. "Why did you not wake me sooner?"

Braiton took a seat opposite her. "You looked like you needed the rest." He reached for the clay pipe on a nearby table and lit the end, puffing on the mouthpiece. The smoke swirled in circles above his head. "Besides, I enjoyed the ramblings of your dreams."

The blush crept into her cheeks. "And what did I say so amusing?"

He cast a glance at her bare toes. "You were raving on about your shoes."

She pulled her feet back, hiding them beneath the hemline of her dress.

Braiton chuckled. "When we get home I'll buy you a pair that fit."

Home...not my home. With the memory of her village flooding her thoughts, she blurted, "Nothing could be as comfortable as wearing a pair of moccasins. They are light and easy to kick off before running into the river. You cannot imagine how wonderful it feels to have the mud squeeze between your toes, the cool water rush against your legs."

He stopped puffing on his pipe and leaned forward in his chair. "Tell me more about your people."

"Well, they dress in tunics, skirts, or dresses made of soft buckskin." She looked down at her full skirt and wrinkled her nose. "It is much easier to work dressed in clothes coming only to your knees, then like this."

He placed the pipe aside. "I take it you're not pleased with your new apparel?"

She shrugged, folding her hands in her lap. "It is pretty at times, but for the most part it is bothersome... way too much goes on underneath."

His interest awakened. "And what goes on

beneath the buckskin?"

Her cheeks warmed. "Nothing," she murmured, casting her eyes down to the hands she held clasped in her lap.

Braiton's hearty laughter brought her eyes up to meet his. "Then I beg you, lass, to make an honest effort to conform to our ways." He gestured to the neckline of her dress. "Should you have decided this evening not to garb yourself appropriately beneath that garment, all that you're about would have surely been in full view." Touches of humor remained around his eyes and mouth. "Langley and I would have definitely come to using our fists." He arched a brow. "He was quite enthralled with your beauty, talked of nothing else while we were below."

She frowned. "That man reminded me of a sly *baya,* coyote."

"Aye, I agree. And if it was discovered you lacked for proper passage, that sly coyote would have you aboard his ship, stripped and bedded by now."

For a moment she studied him intently. *Is that not what you wish to do?* She stood and made her way to the desk, keeping her back to him.

He came to stand beside her. "What is it, lass?"

She cleared her throat. "What happens now? What do you expect to happen between us?"

His voice was velvet-edged and strong. "I married you only to save you from those miscreants. You have nothing to fear from me, nor has our agreement changed. Is that clear?"

She turned to face him, the heat emanating from his body. "Yes, it is very clear."

The muscles quivered at his jaw. "This marriage is one of convenience only and shall always remain as such." His lips thinned with displeasure. "Throughout your illness I cared for you, and not once did I compromise your virtue." A probing query came into his eyes. “How could you believe I would start now?”

She moistened her lips. “I have come to learn that no one gives something without wanting something in return. And you would have every right, now that we are married, to—to...” she stammered.

His expression was one of pained tolerance. “Aye, you’re correct, lass, ’tis my right to take you to my bed,” he interjected. “But ’tis one I won’t be acting on, now or anytime in the future. ’Twas necessary to keep you aboard this ship, and that’s the only reason I married you.” His burning eyes held her still. “Make no mistake about it, my lady.”

“Then our agreement stands?” she managed to reply through stiff lips. “When we reach Ireland, you will keep your word...send me to join my family in England?”

Braiton leaned forward, lowering his voice. “Aye lass, I will. Like you, I always keep my word.”

“Then we have nothing further to discuss,” she said, stepping aside to find her shoes and stockings. Once she had her belongings, she made her way to the portal.

Braiton sighed in exasperation. “Where are you going now, lass?”

She turned to face him. Tired lines appeared around his eyes. “To my bed.”

“Nay, you’ll sleep here,” he said, blocking her way. “I will share Terry’s quarters.”

She frowned. “His cabin is way too crowded for the two of you.”

“There will be no more discussion on the matter, my lady.” He turned the knob and opened the door. “Molly will bring you up your dinner momentarily.” He motioned to the built-in wardrobe in the corner. “You’ll find a nightshirt in the drawer. Sleep well, Lady Shannon,” he said, shutting the door behind him.

****

Raven tossed all night in the soft, roomy bed, more than *The Sweet Maureen* did upon the sea. The sharp pain of remorse consumed her as she mentally rehashed her conversation with Braiton. The man was a life saver on three occasions, always presenting himself the gentleman. His kindness and generosity surpassed any she'd ever known. What possessed her to doubt his intentions?

She sat up in the bed annoyed with herself. Braiton was not like agent Hall, Baxter in Silver City, or Captain Langley. He was different, and she needed to start seeing him in a better light, believe him, trust him to keep his word, as Molly said.

He did assure me the marriage was in name only, and he would never touch me.

Appeased, she snuggled beneath the quilt in a last attempt to get some sleep. While doing her best to relax another realization struck her. Sitting up again, a gasp escaped her. *I have nothing to fear because I am soiled goods.* This bitter reflection slapped her hard, crushed her esteem, and tears welled in her eyes. Braiton would never touch her because she was tainted—damaged merchandise. What man would want a used woman? Especially a man as rich and handsome as the Lord of Limerick who could have any woman he chose?

She swallowed hard, fighting the humiliation that burned her flesh, remembering his words. *"What happened to you was not your fault and is not your shame."*

Were they said just to comfort her? She groaned. *An easy statement to profess because you never imagined you would marry me.* A mixture of humiliation and rage swept through her veins. Covering her face with her hands, she wept. She hated being on this ship and wished she was with

Gabriel and Sunny. How she missed them. How she missed her mother and father. Seeing them in her mind; sitting together by the fire-pit, laughing and singing in spite of their sorrows, made her long for them even more than ever. Then she heard her father's words, so clear were they that she expected to look up and find him in the cabin with her.

"Never allow anyone to make you feel badly about yourself. Remember, you are born of proud blood."

New found courage and pride flowed through her veins. She dried her eyes with the backs of her hands and squared her shoulders. "I will remember, my father," she whispered. "I will remember."

****

Braiton found it impossible to sleep, especially with the scene playing over in his mind of Raven running to the river scantly dressed in buckskin, ebony tresses flowing freely behind her, and long bronzed limbs shimmering with moisture.

He swung his legs over the side of the bunk he'd taken from Terry and sat upon the edge, combing his fingers through his hair. The thought of her tormented him. Easily, he could get lost in her deep sapphire eyes. Every time his gaze met hers, his heart turned over in response. When she entwined her delicate fingers with his, heat surged through his entire being. Full, lush lips tantalized him, begging to be kissed.

He clenched his jaw, fighting desire. The curse he was destined to live with denied him such pleasure, and Raven's presence made it all the harder to bear. He grabbed for the robe tossed over the bottom of the bunk and lit the lantern beside the bed. She had no right to occupy his thoughts in such a way. *Nay, 'twas not her fault, I am wrong to let her.* He paced the tiny quarters.

"Does somethin' ail you, m'lord?"

Not something, someone to be exact. He turned to find the tolerant Dr. Murphy, who slept on a cot in the corner, watching him. Braiton chuckled sardonically. "Bad enough I keep you from your bed, now I interrupt your dreams."

Terrance rose up on his elbows. "They weren't much to speak of anyway." He arched a brow. "What o' yours, m'lord, could they possibly be about a certain young lass I know?"

"They dare not be," he grumbled.

"All the mates on this ship vision her in their sleep and you, the only man aboard who can do more than dream, spend the night with me," Terrance teased.

He frowned, uncomfortable to learn his men were mentally ravaging Raven. The fact only added to his aggravation. "You know very well why I am not in her bed. My bed," he corrected.

Terrance swung aside the blanket and stood, reaching for his own robe. Taking a seat on a nearby chair, he folded his arms in front of him. "Oh, aye, I remember, she is your wife in name only."

He gave the doctor a narrowed, glinting glance. "Besides you, Raven, and myself, only Molly and Captain Kirby are privileged to that information and 'tis the way I want it to stay."

Terrance sighed, leaning back in his seat and crossing one leg over the other. "I think 'tis best no one else knows as well, so have no fear, me lips are sealed. But..."

Braiton's frown deepened. "I don't like the sound of that *but*."

"Well, I was just thinkin', m'lord, if 'tis your hope this marriage appears genuine, would it not be better for you to be in your own cabin?"

The teasing glint in Terrance's eyes changed his troubled mood to one of irritation. "Now, how do you think I can manage that?" Frustration rose to choke him. "The last thing either of us wants is to share a bed."

Terrance's smile was smug. "You're in me cabin, and we're not sharin' a bed."

He tightened the robe's sash around his waist. "If you can't see the difference, I feel sorry for you man!"

"I'm perfectly aware of the difference, but I think 'tis important to keep tongues from waggin'."

"What's the difference if they wag now or later, when she leaves for England?" he countered.

"Time has a way of smoothin' a situation over, m'lord." He leaned forward in his seat. "You've helped the lass above and beyond your duty, now 'tis time you ask somethin' in return for your graciousness."

"Nay, I won't. 'Tis what she expects, she said it to me herself. No one gives something without getting something in return." He shook his head. "I won't have her thinking I'm just another rogue."

Terrance's voice was heavy with sarcasm. "I'm not sayin' you should ravage the lass. Just that she allow you to share your cabin. Sleepin' arrangements as 'tis here."

"Not much on privacy," he snapped, "hers or my own."

"M'lord," Terrance began impatiently, "you are a figurehead in Limerick, a prominent business man. Every move you make is scrutinized. Grant you, 'tis hard to live like a fish in a glass bowl, but that's how 'tis for a man with a title."

"Terrance Murphy, what you're suggesting is—"

Terrance held up a hand. "Let me finish, m'lord."

Braiton gave a taut nod.

"Explain your status and position to the lass." He smiled. "She's good-hearted, a bit spirited, but always eager to please. I saw how accommodatin' she was when she helped Molly in the galley. I know she'll work with you on this matter as well."

He sat down on the edge of the bunk to ponder the idea.

"Tell her you will send her to England within a year's time," Terrance advised further. "By then all eyes won't be gapin' so much at the two o' you. And should anyone question her departure, by then you'll be safe in sayin' she's simply gone to visit her family in England for a few months."

Braiton frowned. "And what do I say when she never returns?"

Terrance shrugged. "Circumstances happen in a marriage, 'tis not uncommon for a husband and wife to drift apart, to live separately."

He nodded in agreement. "Aye, sadly enough I know many who do. One in a townhouse in the city, the other at the summer home. 'Twouldn't be how I'd want to be married, if I truly could be, that is, but it seems to be fine for others." He sighed. "Then the lass can go on with her life and so can I." For some reason the thought of never seeing her again bothered him.

"As far as all are concerned," Terrance added, "you're a married man who has a wife spending time with her family. Raven will never have to know the truth about what physically ails you, and you will never have to worry about bein' available."

His good friend and physician had a valid point. With everyone believing he was already wed, he'd never again have to endure the matrons of society trying to introduce him to their daughters, sisters, or nieces in the hopes he'd take one for a wife. "It all seems to work out perfectly for all of us, doesn't it Terry," Braiton admitted.

"It can if..."

He arched a brow. "If what?"

A mischievous twinkle gleamed in the doctor's

eyes. "If you're able to guard against your manly desires, m'lord. The lass *is* quite tempting."

Aye, that she is. But I would never inflict my hell on her or curse a child of my own, as I have been cursed. "I haven't a choice, Terry, but to keep my feelings at bay."

"I'm sorry, m'lord."

He turned his gaze toward his friend. "So am I, Terry, so am I."

Chapter Six

Molly stared at Raven when she entered the cabin bright and early the next morning carrying a wash basin filled with warm water, toiletries, and fresh clothes.

Her gray-green eyes shone with motherly concern. "And so what is this?" Molly pushed aside a strand of hair from Raven's forehead. "M'lady's eyes are all red and swollen, and on the morn after her weddin' night, too?" She clicked her tongue in reprimand. "'Tis bad luck, lass."

Raven cast her gaze to the hands she held clasped in her lap. "It is what it is, Molly."

Molly arched a brow. "And who says it has to stay that way?"

She was too tired to argue differently.

"Lord Shannon wishes for you to join him in the doctor's cabin for breakfast, m'lady," Molly said, laying out the clothes she brought at the foot of the bed.

She watched the elderly woman's short, stubby fingers place the grooming items on a nearby table. Molly did everything with such love. "Do you have family, Molly?"

"Aye, a son named Michael. Father Michael Darby he's called now." She smiled with pride. "He leads a congregation in Dublin."

"And what about your husband?" she probed.

Molly's eyes softened. "Ah, me sweet lovin' Chauncey went home to be with the Lord about five years passed now."

"I am so sorry, Molly."

"Ah, me, too, lass. They'll be no other like him, that's for sure." She smiled. "He was the captain of Braiton's father's ship, and me, his first mate. Together we sailed to many lands for Lord Broderick, and we saw some beautiful sunsets." She giggled. "I think Michael learned to take his first step aboard a ship out to sea before he did on dry land."

"Is that why you continue to come on Lord Shannon's voyages?"

"Aye, I love the mist, the smell of salt in the air." She gazed down at the toiletries she'd set out. "'Tis enough about me now, m'lady or else your breakfast will grow cold. And since you barely touched your dinner last night, you should be quite hungry."

Strange enough, she had no appetite.

"Come, lass," Molly coaxed, pulling down the quilt.

She stood as Molly soaked a cloth in the water and lathered it with scented soap.

"Off with those bedclothes, now, so that I can wash you," Molly said over her shoulder.

Her eyes widened. "Wash me?"

Molly squeezed the wash cloth over the basin. "Aye, m'lady."

She wrapped her arms about herself. "I do not need you to wash me."

"Ah, 'tis a modest one you are, but 'tis customary for a woman with a title, such as yourself now, to have a personal attendant."

She wrinkled her nose. "Let me guess, Lord Shannon has instructed you to assist me."

Molly's plump cheeks rounded with her broad smile. "Aye, 'tis the way o' it. And so here I be, at your service."

She frowned. "You have too many other things to do on this ship than to add bathing me to the list, especially when I am perfectly able to do it myself."

Molly arched a brow. "And then am I to catch the devil from me employer when I relay to him I've left you to your own devices?"

It was certain she did not want Molly to get in trouble because of her. She pulled the nightshirt over her head, her face scalding with humiliation, and covered her breasts with her hands.

"'Tis nothing to be shy about, lass. We've all got the same parts, you know. Yours are just a wee bit newer than me own."

Raven giggled at Molly's assessment and turned around so Molly could rub the warm, wet cloth down her back. The gentle strokes relaxed her shoulders and spine. She moaned with pleasure as the stiffness seemed to wipe away.

"See," Molly beamed. "'Tis not so bad."

"Do you wash Lord Shannon's back, too, Molly?"

Molly giggled like an embarrassed school girl. "Mercy, nay child, Lord Shannon's attendant is Brian O'Malley."

She raised her arms so Molly could wash under them, ticklish and flinching with each stroke. "I have not met Brian."

"Brian doesn't travel with m'lordship on voyages. The poor man turns greener than a shamrock just lookin' at a ship. When Lord Shannon is aboard he tends himself." Molly dried Raven's back and thighs with gentle pats. "You will meet Brian when we get home. He's got a heart o' gold, he does, and goes out o' his way for m'lord at every turn."

"Home," she repeated. Her home was a tiny wickiup by a river. "It is not my home."

"'Twill be, m'lady." Molly turned her around and gave an encouraging smile. "Shannonbrook is in bad need of a woman's touch, hasn't had one since Lord Shannon's mother, Lady Maureen. May she rest in peace."

"He has named the ship after her, then?"

"Aye, he loved his mother very much, still mourns her death." Molly slipped a chemise over her head. "Perhaps you will bring him happiness."

She smoothed the undergarment down her hips. "Lord Shannon married me to save me from the Sea Patrol and for no other reason."

"I don't believe it has to stay that way, m'lady," Molly reflected as she helped her on with the dress.

"I do."

"We never know what lies ahead of us, m'lady." Molly motioned for her to sit in a nearby chair. "Now, let me have a go at that hair."

She allowed Molly to braid her long tresses, pondering the elder woman's words. *The only thing lying ahead for me is to be with my family, people who love me and are not ashamed of me.*

Molly stood back to admire her work. "Ah, a beauty you are at that, m'lady." She handed Raven the stockings and shoes. "Be quick now, child. Your food grows cold."

She slipped on the sheer leg wear and laced up the ties of each shoe.

Molly opened the portal and summoned her through. "I ask nothin' more o' you then to let each day take its course." She smiled. "And can't the two of you have fun in the mean time?"

She shrugged. "I suppose it would not hurt."

Molly's smile broadened. "Nay, m'lady, 'twouldn't hurt at all."

****

Terrance Murphy's cabin was not luxurious or as spacious as Braiton's, but what it lacked in lavishness, it made up for in comfort. A warm feeling filled Raven as she entered the cozy quarters, as well as the aroma of bacon, boiled eggs, and toast with marmalade. A table spread with fine china displayed the delicious fare, along with a steaming pot of tea.

Braiton, in his emerald green, high-necked sweater, looked dashing. His eyes twinkled with tiny gold flecks as he bowed from the waist. "Good morn to you, my lady," he said, pulling out a chair for her, and then taking a seat opposite.

She smiled and reached for the pot of tea. "Would you like me to pour you a cup?"

He inclined his head in agreement and pierced a piece of bacon with a fork. "I trust you slept well?"

"No, I did not."

He set his fork down beside his plate, giving her his full attention. "What disturbed you, lass?"

"I was very rude to you last night, and I suppose it was my actions keeping me awake." *That and the realization you are completely ashamed of me.* "You have been very kind to me," she added, wetting her dry lips, "and I had no right to accuse you of any wrong motives. I hope you can forgive me."

Braiton's eyes softened and searched her face. "There is nothing to forgive, my lady."

The slow way he explored her features made her heart pound. She cast a glance down to the empty plate set before her. "I do not know how I can repay you for all you have done for me."

He spoke in a half-whisper. "I know of one way."

She raised her eyes to meet his.

He chuckled. "You needn't fear, 'tis nothing compromising. As I said before, this marriage can only be one of convenience."

She listened to the terms of the agreement he proposed between them. To appear happily wed when others were around, for a year's time, so as not to jeopardize either of their reputations. He would take care of her needs and while she was in Limerick, she would want for nothing. With the marriage never consummated, an annulment would be easily granted, she would be given a handsome stipend upon departure for her time, and then both of them could go their separate ways.

His terms filled her with humiliation, crushing her confidence, and she blinked back the tears that stung her eyes. *I will be given a handsome stipend upon my departure to cover my time. Services provided like a business deal. And that is all I am to you...all I will ever be. You pity my plight, but could never see me as someone you could love.* She wanted nothing more than to be reunited with her siblings, but for some unexplained reason she was saddened by his feelings toward her and the idea she would never see him again.

Braiton broke through her thoughts. “Do you accept these terms, Raven?”

If agent Hall had not taken my virtue, would you see me in a different way? “Yes, I accept and will be glad to do whatever you ask.”

He smiled. “Then what we need to do now, lass, is get to know each other better, so we will appear convincing.”

She spread marmalade on a piece of toast and took a bite, not really tasting it. “I suppose you are right, my *shikaa*.”

He sunk his teeth into his own toast, a small bit of bread clinging to his mustache.

Without thinking twice, she picked up the cloth napkin beside her plate and wiped his face.

He blinked, astonished.

The blush heated her cheeks. “You had a piece of bread trapped in the hairs of your *nneezi*,” she explained.

“*Nneezi*,” he repeated. “Is that how you say *mustache* in Apache?”

She nodded, soaking the egg in the plate with the rest of her toast.

“Teach me more of your language, Raven.”

“What would you like to know?”

He reached into his pocket and pulled out a

small purse. Opening it he held up a small, round piece of currency. "How do you say *coin*?"

"*Beso*," she answered.

He repeated the word.

"*Nzhoo*, very good," she praised.

His eyes twinkled. "How do you say *water, salt, medicine*," he questioned rapidly.

"*Guesa* means water, *inchi* means salt, and we say *izee* for medicine," she tutored.

Once again he repeated each word the way she pronounced it.

"You catch on fast, my *shikaa*," she admitted.

"And how do you say, *my wife*?"

"*Shi'aad*," she translated.

His hearty laugh was cut short by a knock at the door.

Braiton stood. "We will continue this lesson when I return."

She smiled at his exuberance. "I will be waiting."

When the portal was opened, Riley entered. He bowed toward her and lowered his voice when he spoke to Braiton. She strained her ears to hear his words, but Riley's thick Irish brogue made it hard for her to understand, especially at such a low volume.

When her husband returned to the table his brows were creased with a worried frown. "Some trouble brews, lass." He grabbed his jacket draped over the back of his chair. "We're sailing into a storm." He took her by the arm and escorted her to the door. "Get yourself to my cabin, 'tis much safer there."

She looked up into his eyes, now clouded with concern. "Please, be careful."

His gaze went to her lips. "How do you say *all right* in your tongue?"

"*Haua*," she replied, his gaze sending ripples of

excitement down her spine.

He flashed a lopsided grin. “I will be *haua,* my lady. Now, go. Take shelter in my cabin.”

On her way to Braiton’s cabin she glanced up at the gray sky. The darkness seemed to envelope *The Sweet Maureen,* as the vessel sailed through the choppy waters and into the eye of the storm. Rain pelted down upon her head, and she ran for shelter. Terrified, she took refuge on the large bunk. The ship pitched from side to side, groaning and creaking as it rocked, and her stomach churned. Swallowing hard the nausea rising to choke her, she curled herself into a ball, covered herself with the quilt and held onto the bed’s post.

The large desk and table were bolted down, but the chairs slid from one end of the cabin to the other. Each time an item from Braiton’s desk smashed to the floor, she winced. Fearing the ship would flip onto its side and sink to the bottom of the sea, she prayed the good Lord would pardon her sins. Then she prayed for Braiton and his men. How were they coping on deck? In her mind’s eye, she pictured them all plunging to their deaths, swept overboard into the vast, dark waters.

“Spare us, Jesus,” she whispered, pulling the quilt over her head.

****

The angry waves splashed over the rail, swallowing the bow. Braiton stood with legs apart and feet braced, struggling to keep balanced, straining to hear Kirby’s words.

“’Twould be best, m’lord, if the ship were taken off course, pulled away from the storm.”

“I’d rather muster through, Captain. I can’t take the chance this storm will rage for days.” He wiped aside the wet strands of hair that clung to his face. “I’ve got a deadline to meet with this cargo.” He looked around at the others on deck, working hard at baling water. "We'll take her through," he decided. "She'll hold; she's a strong ship. And I'd like to get through the worst of it while we still have daylight."

"Aye, aye, sir; as you say," Kirby agreed, leaving Braiton to man the helm while he bellowed a few commands to the other mates.

Fighting to keep his footing on the wet, slippery deck, he ventured the ship ahead.

"Everythin' has been secured, sir," Kirby announced upon his return. "She's a bad one, m'lord." He helped Braiton hold the tiller to the starboard side. "We've got a good hour o' this before we're through."

"She'll hold, Captain," he said again, confident *The Sweet Maureen* would get them through and set his focus on the angry waters at the forefront.

Chapter Seven

She watched the water seep through the cracks around the portholes each time waves crashed against the outer walls of the ship. Her hands, stiff from clutching the bunk's post, ached.

Is this how it will end for me, my lifeless body floating in the cabin of this ship at the bottom of the cold, black sea? Her thoughts were broken by men's voices and heavy footsteps in the passageway. The loud banging on the portal made her jump out of her skin.

"M'lady," Terrance called. "Please, open the portal."

The urgency in his voice made her scurry off the bed. "I am coming, Terrance," she called back.

The ship pitched beneath her feet, and she fell to her knees in the disarray. Creeping to the portal, she reached up and slid the bolt free, then stood braced against the wall to pull it open. The thick oak door flew out of her hand, wind and rain gushing in her face. Thrown off her feet, she landed hard on her backside. Stunned momentarily, she stayed on the floor, watching Terrance and Riley carry Braiton's limp body to the bunk. She crawled to the bed, pulling herself to her feet using the same post she held onto for hours, and looked down upon Braiton's form. A large gash burned across one side of his forehead, the blood streaking down his face and soaking the collar of his sweater.

"What happened?" she gasped, stumbling to the side of the bed.

"A beam broke and caught him in the head,"

Terrance explained, while his quick, experienced hands administered to Braiton's wound.

The strange surge of concern and affection she felt for Braiton frightened her. "Will he be all right?"

Terrance's low and unruffled tone helped to compose her emotions. "Aye, m'lady, the wound's not as deep as it appears. It looks as though the beam grazed him, but he'll be out for a wee bit."

"If you'll not be needin' me further, Doc, I'll be takin' meself back to the cap'n," Riley said, pushing aside with his foot the debris littering the floor beside the bed.

"Lady Shannon can help me now, lad," Terrance assured Riley. "Go where you're needed more."

Riley nodded and made his way to the portal, struggling against the wind and rain to close the door behind him.

She moved closer. "Tell me what to do, Terrance."

Terrance began to remove Braiton's boots. "We've got to get rid o' these wet clothes, lass. He's soaked to the bone and will catch his death." He moved to unfasten the trousers. "I'll hold up his bottom while you slide down the breeches," he instructed.

It is not right for me to be here, see him undressed. Stepping back, she tightened her hold on the bed's post. "Terrance, I-I cannot..." she stammered.

"Hurry, lass," he snapped, ignoring her protest.

She braced a knee against the bunk's frame, and then placed the other knee on the bed. Gripping the waistband of Braiton's pants, she managed to pull them down to his ankles. Terrance lifted each of Braiton's legs, while she tugged the saturated garment off his feet. The breeches came free, and she lost her balance, falling backward and hitting the floor with a loud *thump*.

"Saints preserve us, are you all right, my lady," Terrance inquired concerned.

She gathered up her skirt and rolled onto her knees, her behind throbbing from the impact. "I am fine," she lied, again using the bed post to stand.

Terrance removed Braiton's jacket and sweater. She was caught off guard seeing him naked. Helpless to halt the heat rising to her cheeks, she glanced away, but curiosity had her at a disadvantage. This time she surveyed him fully, her slow gaze easing from his muscular arms and chest to a taut belly. Her eyes swept over his hips and to the patch of dark hair at the juncture of his thighs. On further assessment she took in the strapping long legs that allowed him to tower over her.

Terrance's voice snapped her thoughts back to the task at hand. "Can you manage to get to the wardrobe, lass, to fetch dry towels?"

She pulled her gaze free from Braiton and looked over at Terrance. He kept a close eye on her, a small smile curving one side of his mouth. "I hope your wifely admiration for your husband never leaves you, m'lady, but if you don't fetch the dry towels, you might find yourself a widow."

She blinked, embarrassment turning to annoyance, and glanced away. She pushed aside the chairs and other wreckage littering the cabin, making her way to the wardrobe and back.

When she handed the towels to Terrance, he stepped out-of-the-way. "I'll leave the rest to you, m'lady." Another slow grin spread across his face. "Dry him well and keep him warm." A mischievous twinkle danced in his pale blue eyes. "Body heat is much better than a quilt."

And with that he was gone, leaving her standing by the bed with the towels in her hands.

I guess I have no choice in the matter. She knelt beside the bunk and with a shaky hand dried his powerful set of shoulders. Unexplained warmth flooded her body when she moved to dry his chest. The desire to run her fingers over his flesh overwhelmed her. Placing the towel aside, she caressed an arm with timid strokes, admiring its magnificent hardness, awed by the strength coiled within. The thought of being engulfed by his embrace made her tremble with excitement. She knew, in spite of his strength, he would be gentle—tender and considerate.

She gazed upon his face; a generous mouth, aquiline nose and a straight forehead. With a light touch, she fingered the bandage shielding his wound. *What would I have done if your injury had been fatal?* She shuddered to think and covered him with the quilt. The ship settled to a lulling rock, the storm's rage now quiet. The waters calm.

Her own eyelids grew heavy. She climbed over her husband to the other side of the bunk and slipped beneath the quilt, listening to him breath evenly beside her. *Thank you, Lord, for getting us through the storm,* she silently prayed before she fell asleep.

****

Braiton woke to find Raven's warm, soft body cradled in his arms. Delicate, slender fingers rested on his chest, a golden brown cheek familiarly nuzzled against his shoulder. He turned to look into her sleeping face, taking in the fine sculptured details of her full mouth, nose, and cheekbones. Even in sleep the slant of her eyes was prominent. Wisps of shiny black hair curled around her face, cascaded down her shoulder and across his chest. He reached for a lock of hair. Twirling a curl around a finger, he brought it to his face, inhaling her scent. Sweet and clean. Everything about her was feminine, yet firm. *Aye, firm.* Like her breasts. He smiled remembering their fullness erupting from the neckline of the dress she wore the night they were wed. *How is it you feel so right in my arms, lass, warm against my naked flesh?*

He froze.

What am I doing here, lying naked beside her? He removed her hand from his chest and slipped out of bed. The room spun. Reaching for the bedpost, he took a moment to steady himself before stepping over the debris. He found his breeches amongst the wreckage littering the floor and dressed in a corner.

"How are you feeling, my *shikaa*?"

He turned to find her watching him, her eyes dewy in the morning light. "I've a wee bit of a headache."

She arched a brow. "Just a wee one," she coined his phrase.

He frowned and made his way back to the bed, sitting at the edge. "What happened last night?"

She sat up against the pillow. "You do not remember?"

"Nay, lass, 'tis all a blur."

Raven motioned to his forehead. "You were knocked unconscious from a falling beam."

He brought a hand up to his forehead and touched the bandage.

"Terrance and Riley carried you to the cabin." She cleared her throat. "Your clothes were soaked, so they had to be removed."

His frown deepened, not quite sure he really wanted to hear the answer to his next question. "Who removed them?"

Raven's cheeks turned a deep crimson. "Terrance. And I helped." She cast a glance away.

The blood drained from his face, a sickening horror vised his heart. "Did I do...did anything happen?"

Her eyes met his. "You need not worry; all is still in order with our agreement." She tugged at the sleeve of her dress. "As you can see, I am still fully clothed."

He reached for her hand. "You don't understand, lass—"

She pulled free from his grasp. "I understand only too well," she interjected, raising a defiant chin. "I know my place; make sure you do the same."

"As I've said before, I always keep my word." He stood to fetch his boots. Pulling them on was a chore in his condition. He reached for his jacket, anxious to leave the cabin, and remove himself from her surveying gaze. With awkward steps he made his way to the portal. "I'd better check on the damage done from the storm." With a quick sweep of his eyes, he made an inventory of the room. "I'll send Molly up to tidy the cabin; bring you up clean clothes and a bit of breakfast."

With that said he shut the portal behind him and made his way to Terrance's cabin. Entering the room without knocking, Braiton found the good doctor sitting at the table, sipping a cup of tea.

At the sudden intrusion, Terrance arched a brow. "And a good morn to you, too, m'lord."

He studied Terrance intensely. "What the hell are you up to, Terry?"

Terrance's wide eyes feigned innocence. "I can't imagin' what you mean, m'lord."

"Oh, can't you now?" He moved closer to the table, wrestling the anger rising to get the best of him. "Was it just not yesterday you cautioned me to keep my manly desires at bay?"

"Aye," Terrance agreed, stifling a grin. "I remember somethin' was said to that nature."

He failed to see the humor of the situation, the rage he harbored nearing eruption. "And yet you left me, unclothed, in her presence. You're not helping me here, Terry," he admonished.

The doctor leaned back in his chair. "I brought

you to your cabin, m'lord. Where you belonged." He frowned. "Was I to kick your wife out?"

He ground out the words. "Aye, Terry, 'tis exactly what you should have done. Long enough to remove my wet clothes and put on dry ones."

Terrance replied with staid calmness, "You wanted the marriage to look genuine." He shrugged. "I thought this would be a good way to do that, and what did it hurt for her to look a wee bit? It seemed only fair, since you got a good look at what she's about."

His cheeks burned with the remembrance of how he cooled Raven's feverish, naked flesh. The memory stirred his very core, left him aching for her from deep within.

"With you unconscious, m'lord, I didn't think 'twould go much farther."

"And there lies the crux of it. You didn't *think*." He chuckled sardonically. "Or didn't you count on me ever waking up?"

Terrance arched a brow. "Well, of course, I knew you'd awaken, the beam merely grazed you."

His frustration mounted. "And what then, Terry my friend...if at this point I can still call you a friend...was there not one thought in your head as to what might happen when I did open my eyes?" His irritation became a scalding fury. "I am only human, by God! Didn't you realize lying naked beside her in bed would be disturbing?"

"I-I..." Terrance stammered.

He cast Terrance a wary glance. "Aha, I thought I'd never see the day when the good Dr. Murphy was at a loss for words." He narrowed his eyes "Listen to me, and listen well, so we never again have to have this conversation. My reasons for deciding never to marry have not been by choice...Lord knows I've had my share of lonely nights...but out of necessity. You of all people, my personal physician, understand better than anyone the penalty at hand. This prank you pulled could have led to dire consequences. For the lass especially." He combed a hand through his hair. "If you haven't a care for my feelings, Terry, at least think of hers. She doesn't deserve to be caught up in my hell."

Terrance's expression stilled and became serious, his tone apologetic. "I beg your pardon, m'lord, truly, I do."

He gave a tight nod. "I thank you for that."

Terrance motioned to the seat opposite him. "Now, that all is well between us, won't you join me for a wee bit o' breakfast?"

"Nay, I need to find Captain Kirby, and see what other havoc that beam caused."

To his relief *The Sweet Maureen* suffered only minor damage. For the remainder of the voyage he lent a hand with the repairs, a good excuse to keep his mind on something other than Raven and the morning after the storm. He felt awkward in her presence; the large ship became very small.

How good 'twill be to finally be home.

****

Three days after the storm, Braiton stood at the rail using the scope to verify Captain Kirby's sighting of land. He sent for Raven, wanting her to experience the moment with him, but didn't blame her if she decided not to show. He purposely avoided her, harboring himself in the Captain's quarters with the excuse of paper work.

The light tap of her heels on the deck's floor surprised him. Turning to face her, he smiled and handed her the scope. "Peer through the glass, my lady, and behold the glorious sight of home."

Raven raised the viewing instrument to her right eye. She held her chin high, shoulders straight, slender fingers adjusting the position of the scope.

His admiration grew as he studied her further;

full, firm breasts erupted teasingly from the lace neckline of the violet dress she wore, slim waist, and well-rounded hips.

Aye, a tempting lass she is.

When she turned to hand him the scope, his face warmed with embarrassment at being caught.

"You must be pleased to finally be home."

He smiled again. "Aye, that I am."

She dragged her lips into a reluctant smile, quick to fade. "Then I am happy for you." She looked deep into his eyes. "Since we did not have the opportunity to get to know each other as we said we would, this might be a good time to tell me about your village."

Well, I had that one coming, since I intentionally made myself scarce. He searched her face. She looked exhausted. He felt a mixture of pride and pity for the lass. Being at sea was hard enough on a veteran sailor, what was it like for her?

Did I take enough into consideration the fact this woman never stepped foot on a ship before this? Not to mention helping Molly in the galley, being forced into marriage to escape the Sea Patrol and weathering a storm, all while missing her family.

"It is quite all right if you would rather not tell me," she said, breaking through his thoughts.

"Nay, lass, I want to share Limerick with you." He cleared his throat and began to recite. "*The Sweet Maureen* will dock in Shannon Harbour, the port built in 1830 for the use as a transshipping center. Over two hundred and fifty thousand people use the canal, many of them to emigrate from Limerick and Cobh, to America, Canada, and Australia."

Raven's giggle was soft and light, infectious enough to lift a person's spirits.

"Your words sound like a page from a history book Reverend Newcomb brought to the reservation when I was younger."

“Aye, ’tis where it came from,” he admitted. “When I was a lad my father thought a good prerequisite to sailing was to learn facts about the harbour.”

“Well, why not tell me about your village in your own words,” she suggested.

“There are many shops in Limerick, a few taverns, some nice…some not so nice. Christopher O’Donnel runs the smithy and livery, families live in the cottages and there’s a Grand Hotel. The warehouses are bonded, along with a customs and excise post and the Royal Irish Constable barracks are filled with holding cells.”

Raven’s bemused expression caught him off guard. “All that?” She arched a brow. “Then your village is quite large.”

He nodded.

“I will look forward to seeing all of it during my stay,” she concluded.

“And I’ll look forward to showing you around.” He reached out and took her hand. “Welcome to Ireland, Lady Shannon.”

She entwined her fingers with his. “*Ashoge*, thank you, my *shikaa*.”

Together they turned to watch the approaching shore.

Chapter Eight

Raven stumbled when she got off the ship, her legs the consistency of the molasses her mother made and her father loved to eat.

Braiton caught her before she hit the ground, helping her reclaim balance. “You haven’t yet gotten your land legs, lass.”

Sea legs, land legs…it does not matter… either way they are taking me where I do not belong. Where then did she belong? She was alienated in her own village by the white agents, was sent to an aunt she never met, and ended up marrying a stranger.

“This is Limerick, my lady,” her new husband exclaimed with pride, interrupting her thoughts. “Welcome to the bustling village of Shannon Harbour.”

She remained silent, taking in the grandeur of the beautiful stone buildings populating the waterfront. Inhaling deeply, she filled her lungs with the crisp air.

She cast him a glance and discovered he was smiling down at her, green eyes sparkling with excitement.

“This place is such a part of my heritage, my lady.”

“You own all this?”

“Well, not exactly, but Limerick has been governed by the Shannons for centuries.” He pointed to a horse drawn carriage. “Our bian awaits, my lady.” After helping her into the carriage, he climbed in beside her, and then rapping on the roof he called to the driver. “Home, Patrick.”

The carriage drove over brick and cobblestone paved roads, bringing her closer to her new life. There was nothing more she could do but get comfortable, sit back against the fine velvet seat, and take in the sights they passed. A bunch of noisy baby birds trying to take flight from a stone wall caught her attention.

"Those fledglings come from Bullock Island," he explained. "Here they're called callows."

"They seem to have much to say."

He chuckled. "Aye, they do at that."

She craned her neck to look at the tiny shops lining each side of the street, their windows displaying all sorts of wonderful items.

"All those shops will be at your disposal."

Astonished, she turned to look at him, finding he kept a close watch on her. "I can buy things?"

Braiton nodded. "I will take you there myself, after you've nestled in a wee bit at Shannonbrook." He settled back in his seat. "The new Lady of Limerick must have the best there is to have. Anything you desire is yours for the asking."

She gasped. "But why, my *shikaa*?"

He shrugged. "Why not, my lady?"

"Do not worry, I do not need much to keep me happy," she offered.

"'Tis not so much what you need as 'tis what's expected of you."

She frowned. "What do you mean?"

"In my position 'twould not be appropriate for my wife to be arrayed in anything but the best."

Her mouth tightened. "Then I am to dress for the sake of others?"

He sighed. "I don't like to think of it in that way, but aye. There are too many troublemakers and gossip seekers waiting for a chance to ruin or bring disgrace down upon my good name."

"It must be hard living for all others to see," she

reflected.

His voice was shadowed. "Doesn't your father, as the chief, have to set an example for his people?"

"Well, yes..." she hesitated, thinking of the times her father wore the full-feathered headdress for ceremonial events. "But mostly his duty is to provide for the tribe, make sure all the families have food."

He gestured toward the window. "Look out there, lass."

She cast a glance in the direction he indicated.

"All the area you see is known as the *Townland of Cluain Uaine Beag,* Gaelic meaning *the small enclosed meadow area of the one intended for deputy,*" he translated. "My ancestors had great adversaries in those times, acquiring their land and holdings after many conflicts. They stood courageously against those who tried to take their wealth. Many lost their lives in the process."

Her shoulders tensed. "My people lost the land they inherited from their ancestors and many died trying to take it back."

His face grew solemn. "My forbearers faced many sorrows, as well, my lady. Fortunately, they pulled through, becoming respected and even prosperous in spite of it all. Truth be told, lass, they never let their tenants starve and worked along with them to make the land thrive. As leaders though, they were constantly in the public eye, and their position made them vulnerable to scandals and lies." He stretched his long legs out in front of him. "Not much has changed, that's why I go along on my business voyages. Sometimes I need to get away to a place where no one knows who I am or cares what I do; a place where I don't have to maintain the stand of a leader. If I want to fling off my boots and high step in the river, I can."

She giggled.

His face broke into a puzzled frown. "What amuses you, lass?"

"The thought of you flinging off your boots and dancing in the water. It is something I would do, but not—"

"Someone like me," he finished her sentence.

"I only meant- that you are—are so—" she stammered.

He laughed. "I know what you meant, my lady." His eyes danced mischievously. "I have to take on the appearance of what is expected of the Lord of Limerick. But by no means is it what Braiton Shannon, the man, is really all about."

The gleam in his eyes stirred her heart. "Then I will enjoy getting to know the real man behind the title."

He returned her smile, his mustache rising at one corner of his mouth. "You sound confident you'll accomplish your mission."

"We're home, m'lord," the driver called from his seat atop the carriage.

Braiton leaned forward. "There she be, lass. Shannonbrook."

Her jaw dropped open as she scanned the beautifully landscaped bushes and trees that surrounded a great mansion. She could not even begin to count the number of large windows gracing the front of the building, looking like many watchful eyes.

The front double doors, made to accommodate a giant, stood the entire length of the front veranda and reached almost to the second floor.

"And she's all yours to run," he added.

"Me?"

"Aye, she needs a woman's touch. Perhaps you could wake her up a wee bit."

She turned to look at him. "You would trust me with the task?"

He shrugged. "Who else should I trust?"

She licked her dry lips. "But, my *shikaa*, I do not know the first thing about—"

"You know colors," he broke in. "And what makes you feel warm and comfortable, don't you?"

"Yes, but I—but..." Why was she finding it so hard to make her tongue work today?

"That's all that's needed. I trust you fully with the endeavor."

"I know nothing of cost or quality." The whole idea frustrated her down to her hair roots.

"Cost is not a problem, and as far as quality, well, Molly or Anna can advise you there."

She cast a glance to the hands she held clasped in her lap. "It might be best for them to do it all."

"Nonsense, lass. 'Tis your touch the manor needs. You're the Lady of Limerick." She raised her gaze to meet his encouraging smile, the cleft in is chin deepening. "I have every confidence the woman, who dares to discover the real Braiton Shannon, will also be able to redecorate Shannonbrook." He arched a brow. "But if you're truly undecided or become confused about anything, you need only to ask me. I will always be close by for you to seek advice."

"I would be honored if you sought my advice as well. I am a good listener, and I can keep a secret."

Braiton hushed her with a finger upon her lips. "My dear Raven, I do believe you could drag a confession from the devil himself." He inclined his head. "And I will remember your kind offer."

"You will not forget?"

"Somehow I have the strangest feeling you'll not allow me."

She cleared her throat. "That is exactly what my father says to my mother."

He smiled. "Then I'd say we're off to a good start."

The carriage came to a halt in front of the

mansion, and a tall balding man rushed from the double doors, followed by a woman wearing a wide smile across her plump face.

The man opened the carriage door. "Welcome home, m'lord. I trust your trip was pleasant?"

"'Twas a successful one, thank you, Brian," Braiton responded, his long legs unfolding out the carriage exit.

Other servants emerged from the mansion, taking the baggage the carriage driver handed them and bringing them inside. They worked fast and were efficient. She hoped she could be as well-organized in her role as Lady of Limerick.

"'Tis good to have you home, m'lord," the woman chimed in cheerfully. "And I've a meal waiting, in case you're hungry."

"'Tis good to be home, Anna," he said and turned to offer Raven a helpful hand. "And you'd best set the table for two." He smiled down at her, the cleft in his chin deepening. "I'm sure my wife is hungry as well."

The woman's eyes widened.

Braiton chuckled. "Aye, a wee bit of a shock to me, as well. But I trust all of you will make Raven feel welcome and comfortable in her new home." He gestured to the balding man. "This, my lady, is my personal attendant, Brian O'Malley. And this charming lass," he said, looking over at the woman, "is Anna O'Leary, Molly's sister and Patrick's wife."

Raven gave the man a gracious nod. "I am pleased to finally meet you, Mr. O'Malley."

Brian's blush rose from his neck to encompass his round, balding head, ears and all. "No need to stand on formality, m'lady. Just callin' me Brian will do."

"Very well then." She turned to acknowledged Anna with a smile. "And then may I call you Anna?"

Anna nodded.

"I have heard so much about you from your sister, Molly." She bit her bottom lip. "I just hope I will not get in your way."

Anna's return smile consumed her face. "Nay, m'lady, 'tis I who hopes to please you."

Braiton took her by the arm. "It has been a long journey, and I'd like you to rest a wee bit before we're served a meal."

She nodded in agreement and allowed him to escort her through the large set of double doors. Once inside the mansion, she could not believe its size. Her bedchamber alone was bigger than three wickiups put together. The carpet, thick and plush, cushioned her footsteps as she made her way to the large canopied bed. It was covered with a lacey spread and adorned at the head with oddly shaped pillows in a deep pink and cream combination, touches of gold splashed here and there.

She wandered to the dressing table in a far corner. It was draped in lace that matched the bedcovering. The tiers hung in flowing beauty to the floor. Upon the dressing table sat a three sided mirror. She gazed for a moment at her reflection and fingered the gold-handled brush, comb, and hand-mirror placed to one side.

At the glass doors, she stroked the soft velvet drapery and gazed out at what appeared to be a private garden, the view breathtaking. The trees rocked with the wind, and she shivered. Even standing in the sun, she felt cold in this new land.

She stood before the large stone fireplace, letting the warmth from the flames penetrate her flesh. Slowly, the chill left her bones. She realized she had not felt this warm since leaving Arizona and turned to warm her backside, surveying the room a second time. She wondered why Braiton thought her touch was needed. The bedchamber lacked for nothing and was lovely just as was. Certainly she could do no better.

When he had escorted her to the room, he explained it once belonged to his mother. "'Tis only right it now be yours," he said, throwing open the doors to a walk-in wardrobe. "'Tis empty now, lass, but be assured 'twill soon be filled with gowns specially tailored to fit."

She self-consciously looked down at her makeshift dress and then back at him. "I suppose that would be nice."

"Not that you don't look fine in what Molly has supplied," he added, "but to have your own style is always better."

Then he showed her the private cubicle behind a curtain, revealing a table with a wash basin and towels upon it. And in a far corner there was a strange looking chair with a hole in its seat and a pot beneath. Braiton had laughed at her perplexed expression and explained what the strange chair was for.

She blushed, and he chuckled again at her modesty. "'Tis a perfectly normal function."

Now, as her backside warmed, her needs rose, and she decided to use the convenience. She made her way to the strange chair and for a moment stood before it, looking down into the hole at the bottom of the empty pot. She sighed, remembering his words; *it's a perfectly normal function.*

"And one I need to do," she whispered, turning around and lifting her skirt. She managed to secure the material beneath her chin while pulling down the undergarment. The white bloomers slipped down her legs and wrapped around her ankles. She made sure her skirt was out of the way before she sat her bared bottom down upon the chair.

The day's accumulation filled the pot, hitting the basin with a loud trickle. She cringed. Relieving yourself in the woods was much quieter, the dirt absorbed it all. Then a thought struck her. Where was she to get rid of what was in the pot?

Molly entered the room and seemingly read her thoughts. “When you’re finished there, m’lady, I’ll empty the pot for you.”

Her face heated. “There is no reason for you to have to do that, Molly, just tell me where I should bring it.”

Molly rolled down the quilt and fluffed up the pillows. “’Tis not a bother, lass, so trouble yourself no longer about it.”

She did not want to argue, but the thought of Molly having to empty a pot filled with...with... made her uncomfortable.

“I know you’ll be wantin’ to wash away the salt o’ the sea from your flesh, so Anna and I will be bringin’ up a tub to fill with water for a bath.”

Embarrassed over the whole situation, she gathered, rather awkwardly, the full skirt of her dress and reached down for the underwear, now tangled around her feet. Just as her bare behind rose from the chair, Braiton entered the room.

She gasped and sat back down with a *thud*.

Upon spotting her whereabouts, his full lips twisted into a lop-sided grin. “I beg your pardon, my lady.”

She frowned. “You could have knocked.”

He turned his gaze away. “Pardon on that account as well, but I was going to ask you to join me for a cup of Irish coffee. I see, however” he cleared his throat, “you are otherwise engaged.”

Her humiliation at the intrusion turned to annoyance. “I have more privacy behind a tree.”

His eyes met hers.

Her heart hammered in her ears as he made his way across the room.

He smiled down at her and reached for the curtain. “That’s what this is for, my lady.” He closed the drape around her.

She sat quiet a long time to compose herself, staying behind the curtain long after his booted footsteps left the room.

****

Braiton savored the hearty meal of roasted potatoes, ham with onion soup, and soda bread Anna prepared. After the lavish spread, a delicious rice pudding was served for dessert. Brown bread and oysters later accompanied them as they sat in the drawing room. He lit his clay pipe and sat back in his chair, enjoying a potent stout of Guinness, while Raven sipped Irish coffee from a delicate china cup.

He watched her from the corner of his eye. She thoroughly enjoyed the warm brew, relaxed and looking refreshed after a bath and a good meal. The yellow dress Molly made over for her dramatically swept off each bronzed shoulder. And her thick, dark hair piled atop her head, complemented the graceful length of her neck, little wisps of hair framing an angelic face.

"I thought you'd be happy to hear word has been sent to your family in England."

She looked over at him from where she sat; blue eyes hooded by dark lashes. "*Ashoge*, thank you."

"And tomorrow I will take you to the village, where I will introduce you to Metilda O'Flannaghan. She owns a woman's shop and will help you choose a wardrobe."

"I do not need much. At home, a few simple buckskin dresses, a skirt, tunic, and a pair of moccasins serve me fine."

"I'm afraid much more is called for here, lass. But if you're fond of leather, perhaps Matilda can fashion for you a riding habit." He took a sip of the Guinness, picturing the luscious curves of her body draped in leather. "Do you like to you ride?"

"Bareback or with a saddle?"

Her response startled him. "You can ride either way?"

She nodded.

He sat forward in his seat. "Well, my lady, I'm quite impressed. What other talents are you keeping secret?"

She brought the cup to her full lips and took a sip of the coffee before answering. "I can hunt, trap, and fish; shoot with a bow, spear, or rifle, and I can sew, cook, read, write, and cipher."

Her list of accomplishments astonished him. "I dare to say, lass, you far surpass any lady you will meet in Limerick."

She arched a beautifully formed brow. "Did you think all I could do was a war dance beneath the moon?"

"I make no assumption of you or your people, Raven," he said, watching the play of emotion upon her face. "I was merely making the comparison of your skills, to that of the women here."

"And what are the Limerick women like?"

He sat back in his chair and reached for his pipe, taking a few puffs while pondering his answer. "Commoners, peasant born women, have no opportunity for an education. First they help their parents tend the land, and then do the same for their husbands after they're married. Genteel women, the ladies of society, settle into different wifely duties. They spend their time hosting gatherings, planning what silver and china to use, embroidering samplers or purchasing the latest fashions. I call them featherheads."

Her eyes widened. "Certainly you do not expect me to be like them?"

"I don't believe for one moment, lass, anyone could make you be anything other than what you are." *Which is intriguing.*

She frowned. "Then you do not like the

featherheads?"

"Truthfully, my lady, they disgust me. Turn my stomach. For I find they lack ambition."

She giggled. Her lilting mirth lifted his spirits. She rose to put another log on the fire.

"That's not your job, my lady. Ring for Brian."

She turned from her task to face him, hands placed upon perfectly curved hips. "What, and be a featherhead?" She shook her head and reclaimed her chair. Before taking another sip of the coffee, she muttered into the cup, "I think not, my *shikaa*."

More satisfied then he believed he could be, he smiled to himself and puffed again on his clay pipe.

****

The next morning her new husband and the carriage waited for Raven in front of the mansion. She ran down the long staircase, taking the steps two at a time, and climbed into the carriage beside Braiton. "So sorry for keeping you waiting." Out of breath, she gave her curls a careful pat. "I have never seen such a fuss over the way one wears their hair."

He positioned his long legs in front of him. "And how is a lady's hair worn in your village, lass?"

"A maiden wears her hair in a nah-leen, which is an odd-shaped widget that holds the hair back. But married women wear their hair down, flowing freely about their shoulders."

"Aye, I can see how that would please a husband," he mused aloud.

"If you would like, I could wear my hair in such a way." She quickly added, "When there is only the two of us at Shannonbrook."

A warm smile spread his lips. "I believe I'd like that, lass."

The tiny shops along the main street of the harbour village were bustling with people. She found it hard to contain the excitement rising within.

Braiton helped her from the carriage and escorted her down the street to Metilda O'Flannaghan's shop. "When I was a wee lad," he explained, "I'd sit in a large chair in the corner of the shop while my mother tried on every gown that caught her eye." He smiled fondly with the memory. "Then, I thought the day would never end." He sighed. "Now, to have her back..." his voice trailed off, and she saw the sadness etched upon his face.

She was quick to change the subject. "Tell me a bit about Metilda O'Flannaghan."

"A smart lass, that one," he began. "She was married at a young age to a rich, old bugger. He left her a small fortune when he died and the freedom to travel wherever she pleased."

"And where did she travel," she asked.

"France, Italy, the Orient, bringing back silks and other fine fabrics. When she returned to Limerick, she employed a dressmaker from Paris to fashion all of her gowns." Braiton paused before the shop's door. "Soon Metilda, or Tilly as she likes to be called, was the most fashionably dressed woman in many surrounding areas of Ireland. Being the talk of the town gave way to the birth of her shop." He gestured to the door. "Shall we meet her now?"

She nodded and preceded Braiton into the shop. A tiny bell ringing above the door announced their arrival.

The muted shades of pink and aqua gave the tiny boutique a soft, feminine appeal. The sitting room's high-backed chairs, covered in cream-colored upholstery, accentuated the décor and looked comfortable. No doubt, this was where Braiton, as a boy, waited while his mother tried on dresses.

Hanging on racks were gowns of every color and size, and for every occasion. Hats of all shapes and styles, some with feathers, some with bows, hung on hooks or were displayed on shelves beside elegant matching scarves and gloves.

Tilly sauntered into the salon from the backroom. She was of slender build with fiery red hair piled high atop her head. The wide-set chocolate eyes widened as she spotted her new customers. Thin, red lips broke into a grin that consumed most of her delicate face.

Tilly took Braiton's hand in both of hers. "Ah, Lord Shannon, 'tis a pleasure." She glanced at Raven, and then turned her attention back to Braiton, gazing deep into his eyes and fluttering her transparent lids. "What brings you to me shop on this day?"

Braiton, removing his hand from Tilly's grasp, reached for Raven's arm and drew her close. "May I present my wife, Raven Amelia Eagle Shannon."

Tilly's hand went to her throat. "Then the rumor 'tis true, you have wed." Again she turned to Raven, this time taking her hand. "'Tis me pleasure, m'lady." She inclined her head with respect. "I'm at your service." She smiled and gestured around the shop. "What can I interest you in today?"

Braiton answered for her. "Everything. I wish for my wife to purchase an entire wardrobe, Tilly. I trust your people will help her in whatever she may need to be the most fashionably dressed woman in Limerick."

Tilly's dark eyes widened. "Aye, m'lord. In fact, I will assist her meself." She looped an arm through hers. "Come, m'lady. We will first have refreshments, and then we will begin with the essentials."

Raven looked back at her husband and cast him a reluctant glance.

He smiled and gave her an encouraging nod. "I have business at my warehouse, lass. Enjoy shopping. I will return for you in a few hours, that is, if Tilly can handle such a tall order within such a time."

Tilly waved a hand in the air. "Go about your work, m'lord, and leave it all to me." She smiled at Raven. "Your beautiful wife will lack for nothin' when I am finished. And will be the talk o'the town," she added.

Braiton gave her a taut nod. "I thank you."

"What colors do you favor, m'lady?" she asked, pulling Raven to the back room. Before she could answer, Tilly rattled on. "Wait till you see the new arrivals from Paris. They are simply divine."

She cast one last look over her shoulder at Braiton.

He winked at her and made his way to the door.

"Right this way, m'lady, so that I can measure your form," Tilly said, whisking her through a heavily draped archway.

She heard the tiny bell ring as Braiton opened and shut the door behind him. Alone with Tilly now, she took the seat offered her and accepted a cup of tea.

"After you've had your tea, m'lady, I will start from scratch." Tilly took a sip from her own cup, leaving a red lip print on the white china. "Like a beautiful paintin', I will begin on a blank canvas and build from there." Tilly reached for a tiny bell on the table and gave it a shake.

A young woman appeared from another room. She had large gray eyes and a mass of blonde curls, which were pulled back at the nape and fastened with a gold clasp. "Oui, madam?"

"Bridget, this is Lady Shannon," Tilly said, placing the bell aside.

Bridget smiled and curtsied. "Welcome, madam."

She gave Bridget a polite nod, setting her tea cup down upon the matching saucer.

"She is in need o' everythin'," Tilly continued.

"Take her to the dressin' room and help her to remove all her clothes."

"Oui, madam." Bridget took her by the hand.

She stood and looked over at Tilly. "Must I remove everything?"

Tilly again waved a hand in the air. "I will start from scratch, m'lady. Everythin' must go."

She was sure it was going to be a very long afternoon.

Chapter Nine

Raven did not believe she'd ever stood so long without a stitch of clothing on. While Tilly and Bridget measured every inch of her body; breasts, abdomen, hips, thighs, legs, and even her backside, she stood with her arms out, head up, and back straight.

"Now, I have your exact dimensions for the special gowns and riding habit I will create," Tilly boasted. "But you'll need somethin' ready-made to take with you for everyday use."

She tried on an endless array of day-gowns, nightwear, fancy undergarments, gloves and hats to match. She slipped her feet into soft leather slippers, pumps, and boots. Each outfit was accessorized with a variety of purses, pouches, and hair clips, not to mention the different scents of cologne and bath oils added to the lot. Tilly left nothing out, putting together a wardrobe fit for a queen.

The dress she wore to the shop was discarded, Tilly curling her nose up at Molly's handiwork. "I suppose the poor woman did the best she could."

The last day outfit she donned, a light blue, full-skirted, day frock trimmed in dark blue lace, she kept on to wear back to Shannonbrook.

"You're simply divine," Tilly said, dramatic emphasis placed on the word *divine*. "'Tis your color, matches your eyes and against the dark hair and complexion, simply divine," she repeated.

Bridget stacked the items purchased, folding them with care, placing them in various sized boxes and garment bags.

Raven's eyes grew wide at what was accumulated. "There is not enough room in the carriage to fit all these packages."

Tilly's head flew back with laughter, red curls flopping to one side. "M'lady, such worries are not your concern." She took Raven's hand in both of hers. "Pierre will deliver all of your packages." Again she rang the bell for Bridget.

Bridget looked as exhausted as she felt. "Oui, madam."

"Bring Lady Shannon's things to the outlet room for your father to deliver to Shannonbrook," Tilly instructed.

Bridget nodded.

"*Ashoge*, thank you, Bridget," she offered, wondering if the young woman ever had time to make a pretty outfit for herself.

"You are most welcome, madam," Bridget said and hurried off to complete Tilly's orders.

Tilly's red lips curved into a satisfied smile. "We have done well, today, Lady Shannon and by the time you arrive home, everythin' will be waitin' for you."

She sighed, relieved to be done with it all herself. "I thank you as well, Tilly. You have been so helpful and kind."

"'Twas me pleasure, m'lady, now sit and be comfortable, have another cup of tea while you wait for Lord Shannon."

She had three cups of tea, and still Braiton had not come to fetch her. Looking out the shop window, she scanned the cobblestone street for a trace of him.

"Men, when they get with their business dealin's, they lose all track o' time."

She turned to find Tilly standing behind her. "Can you show me then, the way to Lord Shannon's warehouse?"

"Aye, m'lady." Tilly opened the shop's door and

pointed with a slim finger to the left. "Do you see the large platform where a crowd has gathered?"

She nodded.

"That is the town's square, and when you arrive there you must cross over to the other side of the street," Tilly explained further. "To your right you will see another street. You cannot miss the large brick buildin' at the end. That is Shannon Warehouse and Holdin's."

She thanked Tilly again and stepped onto the sidewalk, the bell ringing behind her when Tilly shut the door. Walking through town, Raven lingered at each shop's window, admiring the displays. There were so many beautiful things to buy. Her father would love to have the pipe in the tobacco shop's window, and her mother the patchwork throw in the quilting shop. Her sister, Sunny, would beam with excitement to have the pens and pads from the art shop. How she would love drawing with all the colored pastel chalks.

When she came upon the town's square, the people pushing and shoving made it impossible for her to cross over to the other side. She found herself being swept up in the confusion and forced to the front of the platform.

"What goes on here?" she asked the man standing beside her.

"Brady is holdin' one of his weekly contests, lass. Today is an archery exhibition." The man pointed to the right of the platform. "And there sits the prize."

She stood on tip-toe, her eyes following the man's finger. There, sitting gaunt and panting, was a large red-haired dog. Her heart went out to the animal. "What kind of dog is he?"

"An Irish Setter and a darn shabby one at that," the man answered.

"He looks starved," she said, annoyed anyone could be so cruel.

"Aye, he probably is, but someone will get one more hunt from him before there's a need to put him down."

"Put him down where?"

The man turned to look at her. "To death, lass."

She gasped. "Why would there be a need to kill him?"

"Look at him, lass. There's not much fight left in the old beast," the man said.

"He just needs to be fed, that's all," she protested. "Given the chance, he will be a faithful pet for many more years to come."

"Folks gathered here today aren't lookin' for a faithful pet, lass."

"What must be done to win him?"

"Gettin' the arrow closest to the circled center o' the target board, will make him yours," the man explained.

Three men mounted the platform, each taking a turn at winning. Their aim did not even come close to the circled center.

"Any more among you," Brady shouted. "Come now, have we no more who would like to try?"

"I would like to try," she called out from where she stood.

Eyes turned her way, and the crowd broke out in hearty laughter. Brady craned his neck to get a better look at her. "You're just a wee lass." He frowned. "These bows are the real thing. They'll rip the muscle from your arms."

She raised a defiant chin. "I thank you for your concern, sir, but I will be fine."

"Let the lass try, Brady," the man behind her shouted. "'Twill be more entertainin' to watch then your other exhibitions."

The rest of the crowd agreed and cleared a path for her.

Stepping onto the platform, she made her way

over to the dog. "I would like to take a look at him first."

The crowd laughed again.

Brady placed hands on hips. "I haven't all day, lass, so make it fast."

She nodded and knelt before the dog, running a hand over his matted fur. Not much flesh covered his bones. She could feel his ribs. "You poor thing," she whispered. The dog, sensing her kindness, licked her hand. "All you need is some food, definitely a bath, and lots of love to make you strong again."

"Time is wastin', lass," Brady scowled. "If you wish to make a fool o' yourself, then let's be done with it." He threw a bow and arrow at her feet. "Let's see you hit the center o' that target board."

****

Braiton walked past the platform to Tilly's shop. "Another of Calvin Brady's exhibitions, I see."

"Aye, m'lord," Patrick said, a twinkle in his eyes. "Shall we see what the bugger's up to today?"

He glanced at his pocket watch. Already he was past the time he said to fetch his wife, but remembering how his mother lingered at Tilly's shop, led him to believe he was afforded a few moments more. "Perhaps there's still a wee bit of time left after all."

They pushed their way through the other onlookers, Patrick craning his neck to see what was taking place on the platform.

"Who is old man Brady making a fool of today?" he asked the man standing next to him.

"A pretty little dark-haired lass." The man chuckled. "And she's a spirited one at that. She's got the old bugger all fired up."

Patrick pushed ahead farther, his mouth dropping wide at what he saw.

"What is it Patrick? Do you know the woman?" Braiton asked, moving beside him.

"Aye, m'lord, I do." Patrick swallowed hard and cleared his throat. "She's your wife."

"What?" He strained against the crowd to make his way to the platform.

"Should I get her down, m'lord," Patrick said, following close behind.

Craning his neck to see past the heads in front of him, he saw his wife place the arrow into the bow. She got down on one knee and pulled her arm back into position. Her form, straight back, head held high, brought a wave of pride washing through him.

"Should I get her down, m'lord," Patrick repeated.

"Nay, let her try." He watched her take a deep breath, aim the arrow, and pull back on the string. He was awed by the way she made it appear so easy. She released the arrow. It flew through the air, hitting the target dead set in the middle.

"By God, 'tis a bull's eye," the man in front of him shouted.

The crowd cheered, and his heart swelled with pride. This amazing woman was his. They were legally wed, and by law, all her sensational attributes belonged only to him. He shook his head to clear it, bringing himself back to the situation at hand.

Raven stood and threw the bow at Brady's feet, like he had done to her. "I believe the dog is now mine, sir."

"How about we shoot for her, Brady," a man yelled from the crowd.

Brady's fat face broke into a devilish grin. "Who will be first?"

Again, the crowd cheered, and two men stepped up onto the platform, leering at her with hungry eyes. She witnessed the same look in the agent Hall's eyes. With a racing heart she stepped nearer to the dog. "I wish only to take my prize and go."

"Let's see what we're gettin', Brady." One of the men sneered, lifting the hem of her skirt.

"Leave me alone," she shrieked, doubling her fist and catching the man on the chin with her blow.

The man stumbled back, and again, the crowd cheered. But in an instant, he was near her, grabbing her by the arm and twisting it behind her. He slammed her against the pole where the dog was tied. The animal jumped to his feet, growling at the man. She knew, if the dog was not secured by such a short leash, he would have set his teeth into the man's leg without hesitation.

"Let the lady alone," a deep, familiar voice boomed from the front of the platform.

She twisted her head around to see her husband, standing with feet placed far apart, hands on hips.

The man threw her to the floor and spun around on his heels, ready to aim his doubled fist into Braiton's jaw. But her husband was quick, landing his own powerful punch into the man's stomach. Bent in half by the potent blow, the man fell off the platform. Seeing Braiton in action, she understood now why the man Baxter in Silver City cowered upon only a word. Obviously, her husband's formidable reputation preceded him.

By now the second man made his move.

"Behind you, my *shikaa*," she warned.

Braiton swung around and took the other man in a strong hold around the neck, then flung him into the archery board. The round target came loose from its stand and slammed down on the second man's head, knocking him unconscious.

Brady stepped forward. "M'lord, surely you have better things to do, then to bother comin' to the aid o' this little wench. For a shillin' she'd probably go with any o' these men."

Braiton grabbed Brady by the collar of his coat.

"Never call her a wench again," he said through grit teeth. "If I ever hear you speak disrespectfully about the lass in any way, I'll rip your tongue from its root." Releasing Brady, he reached for her hand and helped her down off the platform. "Patrick, fetch her dog," he called over his shoulder.

Brady's voice grated harshly. "What's the lass to him?"

"His wife," Patrick said, leaving the platform with the dog following close behind.

****

Raven held her shaking hands in her lap and licked her dry lips as Braiton stared out the carriage window, his jaw muscles clenched. His even features appeared set in stone. Obviously, he was rehashing the whole incident in his mind.

"I am truly sorry," she managed to choke out. "I never meant to bring shame upon you." She swallowed hard the lump of fear lodged in her throat. "You have every right to be mad at me."

He glared at her, gold flecks of anger flashing in his eyes. "Is that why you think I'm mad, Raven? Because you feel you've disgraced me?"

She nodded, not trusting herself to speak without sobbing.

"Well, you are wrong." He sat forward in his seat. "If I was delayed by just a few moments, or had gone straight to Tilly's shop, do you realize what you'd now be suffering at the hands of those rogues?"

"Only too well." Tears sprang to her eyes. "I know I should have waited for your return. But when I saw this poor dog, *sno'ta'hae*, just lying there all dirty and half-starved..." She reached over and patted the dog's head.

"If you wished to have a dog, Raven, why didn't you simply ask for one," he snapped.

"I did not wish to have a dog until I saw this one. I knew I had to win him, to save his life.

Sometimes, to right something wrong, the thought of your own safety is the last thing on your mind. Do you understand, my *shikaa*?"

He sighed. "Aye, lass, strange enough, I do." He looked down at the pitiful animal, lying on the seat between them. "And now that you have him, what will you call him?"

"I thought *Nalyudi* might suit him."

"And what is the meaning?" he inquired.

"It means, He Runs About. Once he is given lots of food, he will be running about again."

He frowned. "Perhaps Brawn might be easier for all of us to remember, lass. With the proper care he will soon be a brawny one."

She smiled and tried out the name. "Brawn. Yes, I think it fits him well."

"Well, Brawn," he said to the dog. "Let's hope with lots of soap and water you'll smell better, too."

"Then I can keep him?"

"Aye, but first we wash him."

She giggled. "*We* will wash him? You plan on helping me with the task?"

He smiled. "Aye, I do at that. Who knows, maybe this old bugger does have a few more hunting days ahead of him." He scratched the dog behind the ears. "I'm really quite proud of you, Raven."

She frowned. "How?"

"There is no one in Limerick, including myself, who could have beaten you in that contest today."

"*Ashoge* for that, but now I fear I have opened the way for troublemakers and gossip mongers to turn the whole thing into something horrible."

"There is no doubt, my lady. You definitely made an impression." He smiled. "But you were also a marksman and such a skill deserves respect and praise."

Patrick brought the carriage around to the back of the manor, and Brawn was taken into the kitchen area. Braiton removed his waistcoat and rolled up his shirt sleeves, reaching for the huge basin that hung from a hook upon the wall. His arm muscles tightened as he set it down on the floor, reminding her of the night aboard the ship, during the storm, when Terrance brought him injured to the cabin.

The splendor of his naked body excited her to the very pit of her stomach. She yearned now for his muscular arms to embrace her and fought the urge to run to him—caress again his hard chest and slim belly beneath her finger tips.

He picked up two buckets and made his way to the door. "I'll fetch the water from the pump," he said, breaking through her thoughts.

"Braiton," she called. The breathless way it came out made him stop in his tracks. It was the first time she had called him by his name, and he quickly turned to look at her. Their eyes met, and she could tell she stirred something within him. Her pulse quickened, and she licked her lips. His eyes went to her mouth, and he swallowed hard. "My father would say you have the roar of a lion but the heart of a lamb."

His gaze met hers, a slow smile playing at the corners of his mouth, the mustache spreading across a full upper lip. "Let it be our secret then, lass. People hark far better to the lion than they do the lamb."

Once the basin was filled, she went about coaxing Brawn to get in, but the big red dog was having none of it. He straddled his large paws and braced himself in a stubborn stand, making it impossible to budge him even an inch.

"Come on, now, laddie," Braiton pleaded. "Have some respect for the lady who saved your mangy hide." He made his way to the straggly animal and picked him up, placing him into the basin. "I'll hold him, my lady, while you wash."

She set about soaping the matted fur. The dog squirmed and jerked. With all the squirming, coupled by his slippery body, Braiton was having a hard time keeping a grip.

Brawn shook, spraying soap suds everywhere, soaking the front of her new dress. "Oh, Brawn, you are making such a mess," she scolded. "You need to hold him tighter, my *shikaa*."

"I can't, lass, he's too slippery." Braiton braced his feet against the wall. "Take the other bucket of water and rinse him a bit."

Brawn broke free from Braiton's hold and lunged out of the tub, knocking her off balance, and dumping the bucket of water over Braiton's head.

He gasped, looking up at her with the most shocked expression. Sitting in a puddle of water, hair flattened over his ears, and his shirt drenched made for a comical scene.

She stifled a giggle. "I am so sorry."

He pushed the wet strands of hair from his eyes and began to stand, but the floor had become just as slippery. He lost his footing and with a *thump*, hit the floor.

This time she could not suppress her laughter.

He scowled at her mirth. "This amuses you, my lady?" Once more he made an attempt to stand.

"Forgive me," she said through her hysterics. "But if you could only see how funny you look."

He glanced down at himself and then back at her and began to laugh as well, a mischievous twinkle glowing in his eyes. "My lady, you are still soapy." He maintained his balance this time and came around the tub toward her.

She backed away from him. "Now, Braiton, what are you going to do?" she squealed.

He reached for the bucket and filled it with the basin water.

She screamed and started to run.

He followed close behind.

"Do not dare to do this," she scolded over her shoulder.

They ran around the chopping block, laughing like a couple of children.

She made her way to the other side of the spacious kitchen, Braiton on her heels. Brawn barked and raced around the table, slipping and sliding on the soapy floor. She fell to her knees, doubled over with laughter at the clumsy dog.

Not expecting her to stop short, Braiton slid into her, falling backward and spilling the water over them both.

Soaked to the bone, her dress clung to the curve of her breasts. In that moment, she was aware of nothing else in the room, but him. His emerald eyes stared at the beads of water trickling down her cleavage. So captivated was he, she almost believed he would reach over and trace their path.

"Saints preserve us," an angry voice snapped from the archway. They both turned to find Anna standing, hands on hips, her plump face screwed into a scorn. "What in heaven's name has happened in here," she demanded, looking around the room.

Braiton stood, pushed the wet hair from his eyes, and extended a hand to Raven. How quickly he composed himself, where as, her heart still raced.

He cleared his throat. "Good afternoon, Anna," he responded in a calm manor. He made his way past her, his boots squeaking with each slushy step. "Please see what can be done about this room, 'tis a mess."

Anna's mouth hung open as she watched him leave the kitchen.

"I am so sorry, Anna." Raven bent down to retrieve the bucket. "I will clean this, you need not trouble yourself."

"Nay, m'lady." Anna took the tin pail from her

hands. "'Twill be the death o' you if you don't get out o' those wet clothes."

"But Anna," she protested.

"Not another word about it, m'lady." She pointed to the archway. "Now, off with you."

She nodded.

"Saints preserve us," Anna screeched. "What is that?"

She turned to find Anna's attention on Brawn, sitting wet and matted in the corner.

"That is Brawn, Anna, my dog. I won him today in the village square."

Anna pointed a finger toward the archway. "You, too, out!" Brawn rose and walked with a dejected gate toward the door, but before leaving he stopped directly in front of Anna and shook the wet fur that hung from his bony body, splattering her crisp, white apron with water.

"Out!" Anna shouted again.

Both Raven and Brawn hurried from kitchen and ran up the stairs.

Chapter Ten

Tilly had kept her word. All the items Raven purchased that morning were waiting for her in her bedchamber. Molly had removed each garment from the boxes and neatly hung them in the wardrobe. The bottles of cologne adorned the dressing table and the bath oils were arranged with care, ready for use.

Molly gasped when Raven came into the room, soaked to the bone. “M’lady, what in heaven’s name happened to you?”

She pointed to Brawn.

Molly set her sights on the wet dog, which looked somewhat like a large drowned rat and gasped again. “And what is that?”

“That, or rather, this, is Brawn, my new dog. I won him in an archery shoot this afternoon in the town square,” she boasted. “He was in need of a bath.”

“It looks to me like you’re the one who had the bath.”

She giggled. “If you think I look *dit’ood*, wet, you should see Braiton.”

“Lord Shannon helped you?”

She nodded. “He is far more soaked than I am.”

They both laughed. Brawn casually made his way to the warmth of the fireplace and plopped himself down on the floor.

She shivered. “He has the right idea.”

“Get out o’ those wet clothes, m’lady, before you catch your death,” Molly insisted, helping to remove the saturated material and enveloping her cold flesh in a red velveteen robe. At the dressing table, Molly removed the pins from her sagging curls. "'Twill never dry enough before the evening meal to rearrange properly."

"Then I will wear my hair down, like the married women of my tribe."

"But m'lady—"

"It will be fine, Molly," she reassured her with a smile.

"Very well then," Molly finally agreed. "What will you wear this evening?"

"The light blue dress embroidered with white flowers on the collar."

Molly went to the wardrobe and retrieved the dress Raven requested, laying it on the bed along with the necessary undergarments. Shrugging off the robe, she slipped the dress over her head.

"You've forgotten what goes on underneath, m'lady."

"I have not forgotten."

Molly frowned. "But, m'lady—"

"I have decided, when I am here with just my husband, I will dress without the undergarments, like the women of my village."

"What will Lord Shannon think?"

"He said he wanted me to feel at home." She turned so Molly could fasten the buttons up the back. "And this is how I will feel at home."

"I think you might have misunderstood him, lass."

"It will be fine, Molly," she said, turning to face the elder woman and giving her arm an affectionate pat. "Could you ask Brian to set the meal table in front of the drawing room fire? I would like for us to have our dinner served in there this evening."

Molly sighed. "Aye, m'lady, as you wish."

Braiton waited for her at the bottom of the staircase, watching her descend the stairs in bared feet, the lace-trimmed hem of her dress swishing around her delicate ankles. The garment hugged her tiny waist, the neckline showed a teasing glimpse of cleavage. Her shiny black tresses hung free around her shoulders, and the entire sight of her rendered his mouth dry. Upon her reaching the bottom step, he extended a polite hand to her, and she accepted it with a smile.

"You don't like your new shoes?"

She shrugged. "They take some getting used to."

She leaned into him, and his elbow brushed against the side of her breast. She wore nothing beneath. He cleared his throat. "Were the undergarments not to your liking?"

"They will do."

He raised a brow. "Then I don't understand why you're not—"

"You wanted me to feel at home, did you not?" she broke in.

"Aye, my lady, but—"

"With my hair free, feet bared, and no fuss beneath my clothes," she interrupted again, "I feel very much like I am at home." She searched his face. "It does not trouble you, does it?"

Trouble me...nay. Disturb me...aye. He swallowed hard. "That's not the point, lass."

"What is the point, then?"

He cleared his throat again. "Well, 'tis just not appropriate for you to be so scantly clad."

"Oh, I would only dress this way, of course, when there is just the two of us having dinner," she added.

His gaze roamed the length of her. *How will I manage to swallow one morsel?* "You are full of surprises, lass, never ceasing to amaze me."

She giggled. "I have another for you tonight."

He rolled his eyes heavenward. "I'm almost afraid to ask what that might be."

"Come," she said, leading him by the hand to the drawing room. Slender fingers entwined with his, her mere touch brightened the cave of loneliness that surrounded his heart.

Before the fire, the dinner table sat, covered with a lace tablecloth and fine china. Candles were lit and the wine glasses filled.

"I thought we would eat by the fire, as my people do."

He escorted her to the table, and over wine, she told him more about her village. Anna brought the first course of the meal and shook her head confused.

After Anna left the room, Raven broke out in laughter. "Poor Anna, first she finds her kitchen a mess, both of us drenched to the bone, Brawn sitting all ragged and wet in the corner, and now she is serving dinner in the drawing room. She will believe for sure we have both lost our senses."

I have lost all sense of reason, lass, wondering what to expect from you... finding each new day something to look forward to.

She popped a boiled potato in her mouth, savoring it as she chewed. "Eating good food is such happiness."

He leaned forward in his chair. "It pleases me to hear you say that, because your happiness is of the utmost importance to me."

She smiled. "*Ashoge*, my *shikaa*."

Brian removed the table after dinner and brought in a tray of Irish coffee and pastries. Braiton moved to sit in the armchair by the fire, puffing on his clay pipe.

Raven recited to him from a book of sonnets. Her soft voice dipped and rose with each stanza. She sat at his feet, her legs crossed and the skirt of her dress pulled up to her knees, revealing shapely, bronzed legs. Looking down at her from where he sat, he had a clear view of her erupting neckline.

I would love to know how those rounded breasts feel, naked and free, in the palms of my hands. His loins grew thick beneath his breeches with the thought, and he shifted in his seat, casting his gaze to the fire, concentrating instead on the poem she read.

"Is anything wrong?"

He took a puff of his pipe, keeping his focus on the flames. "'Twas a full day, my lady and it grows late. Perhaps you could save the rest to read another night?"

He heard her stand and place the book upon a nearby table. She moved closer, standing over him, the luscious scent of her cologne filling his senses. He made no attempt to look her way, not chancing the temptation to reach out to her, pull her down upon his lap, and kiss her full lips. Tormented, he closed his eyes. *If you only knew the turmoil you create within me.*

"*Ashoge* for all of my beautiful clothes and for allowing me to keep Brawn." She leaned over, kissed him on the forehead, and whispered in his ear, "Sleep well, my *shikaa*."

So close you are to me, lass. Can you hear my pounding heart?

"You as well, my lady," he managed to choke out. He didn't open his eyes until she was long gone from the room. He hated what he had been destined to live with, the isolation, the fear of getting too close to her. All of it was torture and his spirits plunged. *Ah, my beautiful wife, shi'aad as your people would say, if you only knew what you did to me.*

****

Raven sat up in bed, gazing into the fire and sipping the last of the hot milk Molly brought up to her. Brawn slept at her feet. The mansion was still, and she wondered now if Braiton was asleep. She bid him goodnight with a gentle kiss upon his forehead.

How she wished he'd embraced her, kissed her in return. She groaned.

"I cannot sleep thinking these thoughts." She pulled back the quilt and swung her legs off the bed, reaching for her robe and slipping it on. Brawn lifted his head. "I am only going for more milk," she said, taking the mug from the bedside table. "Go back to sleep, this does not concern you." He obeyed, and she made her way down the stairs and to the kitchen.

Molly, Anna, and Brian were still awake, and discussing her and Braiton. She was not usually a part of eavesdropping, but these three people knew Braiton well. If she could learn more about her husband, it would make their time together so much better. Stepping off to the side of the archway, she listened.

"M'lord has such a preoccupied look upon his face," Brian said. "I brought him his mug o' hot milk, and he didn't even glance me way. I set the drink upon the table beside his chair, and he merely thanked me without takin' his eyes off the fire. 'Tis so unlike him. Always he tries at some sort o' small talk while instructin' me on what outfit to lie out for the next day. But tonight 'twas different." He sighed. "I asked him, 'what will you be wantin' to wear on the morrow, m'lord'," Brian rehashed. "And he told me not to fuss about it, that he needed a wee bit o' time alone."

"Somethin' must have happened," Molly said. "M'lady was in the same sullen mood, sittin' up in bed, watchin' the fire with longin' in her eyes."

"I've seen him lookin' lonely, Molly, but 'twas not the look he had tonight," Brian said. "Nay, tonight there was somethin' else botherin' him. Somethin' more."

"He's confused, and a wee bit frightened," Anna chimed in. "Lady Shannon's got a way of wedgin' herself into his heart, and he's fightin' it every inch o' the way.

"Aye," Molly agreed. "I sensed the same when we were aboard the ship." She giggled. "Poor souls. When do you suppose they'll realize they've fallin' in love with each other?"

"Ah, it might be sometime, dear sister," Anna said. "It took lots o' lilac water and mutton stew to bring me Patrick around, and sometimes he still needs remindin'". She sighed. "But m'lady's got a strong spirit about her. If she keeps at him, he'll break. And there's nothin' sayin' we can't help them along a wee bit."

"How are we goin' to do that, Anna?" Molly asked.

"We can keep her encouraged by praisin' his qualities, let her see the good man that he is, so she'll not be givin' up," Anna suggested. "And you, Brian, could drop pleasantries about her, keep her always on his mind."

Brian chuckled. "I think she's already on his mind."

"Good, then 'twill be an easy task," Anna said.

Brian sighed. "I'll not be conspirin' against him."

"You're not conspirin' against *him*, but for *them*, Brian," Anna added.

"Not to worry, Brian," Molly said. "Anna and I will do most o' the work." Then she giggled like a school girl with a secret. "I'd better get to sleep, mornin' comes early." Her chair scraped against the floor as she stood. "Good evenin' to you folks, sleep well."

Not wanting to be caught listening, Raven flew up the stairs and into her room, securing the door behind her. Brawn lifted his head to look at her and focused his gaze on the empty milk mug she still held in her hand.

She arched a brow. "So, I did not happen to get more milk." Frowning, she said again. "Go back to sleep, this does not concern you."

****

Braiton's news would bring his wife great joy. Barely able to contain his excitement, he burst through the foyer's double doors, almost knocking Brian off of the step-stool he stood upon.

"Brian, my man, where might my lady be?"

Brian moved to clean a lower shelf of the large bookcase he dusted. "Ah, in her chamber, m'lord, but she's—"

He didn't wait to hear the rest of Brian's answer, taking the stairs two at a time to her room. Without knocking, he entered her chamber and stopped in shock at what he saw.

Raven emerged from her bath, her back to him, drying her hair with a towel. Golden brown skin glistened with water droplets, her long shapely legs spread slightly apart. And there, sitting on the fleshy part of her thigh, was the crescent shaped birth mark he'd glimpsed while tending her fever aboard the ship.

"I am glad you are here, Molly. I would love to soak all day, but enough is enough. My fingers and toes are all wrinkled." She wrapped the towel around her head and turned around.

Upon meeting each other's glance, they both froze.

His voice, caught somewhere down near his toes, failed him. His gaze was riveted on her naked splendor. The heat coursing through his veins as he scanned the length of her; from the erect, pink peaks capping full breasts to the slim belly, down to the roundness of her hips and finally resting on the triangular patch of dark hair between her thighs.

"Braiton," she gasped, bringing him back to his senses.

He lowered his gaze and spun around. "I'm so sorry, Raven. Truly, I had no idea you were..."

She scampered to the bed. "You could have knocked."

"Aye, aye, you're right, my lady." He raked a hand through his hair. "I must remember to do that." He cleared his throat. "And I apologize for my rudeness. There is no excuse for my behavior, other than the fact I was excited over a surprise I have for you."

"A surprise for me?"

"Aye, may I turn around?"

"Yes."

He turned to find her tightening the cord of the robe around her tiny waist. A waist he could picture naked again. Forever that image of her would be etched in his mind.

"What is the surprise?"

He cleared his throat, pulling his wits together. "I have invited a business client for dinner this evening, by the name of Lord Morgan Wade. Actually, 'tis he who has the surprise for you."

She frowned. "But I do not know this Morgan Wade."

He chuckled. "Well, he knows you."

She neared, affording him a whiff of the jasmine oil. "How does he know me?"

"If I told you that, lass, 'twould ruin the surprise." He made his way to the door. "I will leave you now to your day. Lord Wade will arrive at seven. Please join us in the drawing room. Oh, and my lady, you must address him as *my lord*," he added, stifling a smile, "and be sure to wear everything that goes beneath the dress this evening."

****

Raven thought Molly worked her magic with her hair, the sides brought to the top of her head in a cascade of ringlets, the back left down, curls flowing freely to her waist. The gold satin gown trimmed with white lace was a stunning contrast against her skin. The empire bodice and scooped neckline revealed a tempting amount of cleavage.

When she entered the drawing room, Braiton stood by the fireplace, smoking his pipe. Morgan Wade sat in a nearby armchair sipping brandy from a cut glass goblet. Both men turned her way.

Her husband's eyes twinkled with admiration, scanning the length of her before shifting to look at Lord Wade. "Morgan, may I present to you my wife, Lady Raven Shannon."

She extended a hand, the way Molly taught her earlier and addressed him as Braiton advised. "It is so nice to meet you, my lord."

Lord Wade placed a kiss upon her knuckles. "The pleasure is all mine, my lady." He smiled. "I have heard so much about you."

She cast a glance at Braiton. "I apologize if my husband has bored you."

His smile deepened. "Talk about you could never be boring, my lady. However, what I learned about you I didn't hear from your husband."

She frowned. "Who, then, have you been talking to?"

"That is the surprise, lass," Braiton said, extending an elbow for her to take. "And you'll find out after dinner."

She did not think she would be able to eat a bite, as anxious as she was, but made every effort to hold her excitement in check, accepting her husband's escort into dinner.

Morgan Wade, a handsome man of middle age, sat to her left. Tall, slender, and well-built, his wavy brown hair was colored gray at the temples. A clean shaven face and even features rounded out his arresting looks. Well-educated, he spoke like a gentleman and had a sense of humor. She could not help but think her father would enjoy the man's company. Lord Wade found a way to include her in the dinner conversation, even the business topics, and she enjoyed the visit, glad Braiton invited him to dinner.

After dessert and coffee was served, Morgan sat back in his seat and set his full attention upon her. "You have been so patient, my lady. I'd say the time has arrived to present the surprise promised you, but first I must tell a story."

With hands clasped in her lap, she smiled. "My people are great storytellers."

"Then I am sure you will enjoy this one, which begins with my sister, Lady Eugenia Abbott and her husband, Lord Stanley."

She could not imagine what Lord and Lady Abbott had to do with her surprise, but she listened patiently.

"They were returning to their home after a visit with their daughter, Annabella, who lives with her missionary husband in Texas" He stopped talking long enough to take a sip of his coffee. "Aboard the ship they met a young American woman and her brother, quite beside themselves with worry. The pair had been separated from another sister."

Her heart raced, and she wet her lips.

"The young woman was so overwrought, my sister, being the motherly type, took it upon herself to become her companion throughout the voyage." He added a teaspoon more of sugar to his coffee and stirred. "Of course, by the time the ship docked Lady Abbott befriended the girl and invited her and her brother to meet the rest of the family, being myself and my daughter, Fiona."

She swallowed hard. "Did the ship dock in England?"

"Aye, my lady, it did. How could you have possibly known," Lord Wade teased.

Tears welled in her eyes.

Morgan Wade reached into his jacket pocket and

pulled out an envelope, placing it upon the table in front of her. "Your sister asked me to give you this letter."

She stared at the envelope through her tears. Glancing over at her husband, she whispered, "Braiton, it is from Sunny."

He smiled, his own eyes appearing misty. "Take it, lass."

She took an audible breath. "Thank you, Lord Wade. I cannot tell you how happy you have made me." She wiped her eyes with the backs of her hands and picked up the envelope. "Would you excuse me?"

He nodded. "Aye, my lady. Go read your letter."

She ran up the stairs, securing her chamber door behind her. The gas lamp Molly readied for her added a soft glow to the room. She sat by the fire, holding Sunny's letter to her heart. "Thank you, God," she whispered before opening the envelope.

****

It was late when Morgan Wade left Shannonbrook, Patrick driving him back to the Grand Hotel in the harbour village. Braiton passed Raven's room on his way to his own and seeing a light from beneath the door, decided to say goodnight. This time he remembered to knock.

"Yes, come in," she called out.

"I saw your light still on, and I wanted to make sure all was well," he said, closing the door behind him.

She smiled from where she sat at the writing table. "At least you remembered to knock this time," she teased.

He smiled. "Aye, that I did."

She motioned to the chair beside the fire. "Come, sit, and let me read to you Sunny's letter."

She sat at his feet, as she'd done the night before, and read to him Sunny's fear when they discovered she boarded the wrong ship. She suffered, praying Raven wouldn't be taken by the Sea Patrol, and was grateful later to learn she was safe and wedded to Braiton. She went on about Aunt Kaylena, Bentwood Manor, of Captain Rafe Cavendish, and Fiona Wade.

When Raven finished reading, she looked up at him. "Sunny has gotten on quite nicely with her new life."

He locked his gaze on her beautiful eyes, the deepness of their color drowning him with desire. "It certainly sounds that way." He sighed. "Have you, my lady?"

"I am trying," she whispered, standing and making her way to the writing table. "It would please Sunny and Gabriel to have a letter from me as well." She handed a sealed envelope to him. "Would you give this to Lord Wade before he leaves?"

He nodded. "I will see him in the morn." Their fingers brushed together when he took the letter from her and heat surged through his body. He was tempted to bring her slender digits to his lips and kiss each one.

"Thank you, Braiton, for everything."

He stood. "*O idche mhath,* good night, my lady. Sleep well."

She walked to the veranda doors. "You, too, my *shikaa.*"

If only I could with you etched so deep within my thoughts. He made ready to leave the room, but took one more look at her. She was so striking in a light pink negligee with a flowing robe to match. It gave her the appearance of an angel. His angel, sweet to the touch, sweeter even to the eyes. Did he ever want to stare at anything other than her gorgeous face?

She pulled aside the drapery, glancing up at the sky. From where he stood, the full moon hung like a beacon in the night.

"Do you think Sunny is looking at the same beautiful moon?" she wondered aloud.

"'Tis possible she could be," he answered.

"Yes, it is possible," she whispered, pressing her sister's letter to her heart.

Chapter Eleven

Braiton put in a full day and was exhausted. His business with Morgan Wade took longer then expected, running into dinner and drinks at the local pub. After bidding Lord Wade a safe journey and giving him Raven's letter for her sister, he returned to the warehouse to complete the paper work from the day's dealings.

Now, all he wanted to do was crawl into bed, but when Patrick pulled up in front of Shannonbrook, there was quite a commotion brewing.

Anna, eyes wide with fear, ran to the carriage.

"What is it, Anna, me dear?" Patrick asked, climbing down from the driver's seat of the bian.

"'Tis lady Raven, Patty," she said out of breath. "We've looked everywhere for her, but she's nowhere to be found."

Braiton exited the carriage in a leap, the pounding of his heart echoing in his ears. "What do you mean, she's nowhere to be found?"

"Just that, m'lord." Anna wrung her chubby hands in front of her.

Besides being tired, he was now confused and annoyed. "How could this be, Anna?" he demanded.

"She went out for a walk with her dog before the noon meal and hasn't returned."

"Did you check the stable?" he snapped, thoughts of Raven injured or worse coursed though his mind.

Tears welled in her eyes. "Aye. Dooley hasn't seen her either."

Fear sunk his heart, and he hurried into the

mansion.

Anna ran to keep up with his long strides. “Molly and Brian have combed the grounds, callin’ her name over and over, and she’s nowhere to be found.”

“Damn it all, Anna,” he bellowed. “How could this have happened?”

Anna cringed. “She likes to be outside, m’lord.” She sniffed and wiped her eyes with the hem of the apron tied around her plump waist. “She’s not a prisoner here and has the right to wander where she wishes.”

“But she hasn’t the knowledge of the area as of yet, Anna. Someone should have gone with her.”

“’Tis true, what you say, m’lord,” Anna choked out. “But she’s a spirited lass, ’tisn’t happy bein’ followed around. She likes time to herself.”

“She can have time to herself, woman.” He sighed and added with a harsher tone. “But just not when she’s going far from the mansion.”

His stern words caused Anna to wail with regret. “I’m so sorry…so very sorry, m’lord. You’re right. I should have paid her more attention, gotten Dooley or Brodie to take her about.”

He forced himself to speak in a calm voice. “Stop your blubbering, Anna.” He sighed again. “I’m sorry for being so sharp with you,” he apologized. “I fully realize none of this is your fault.”

“We all love the lass, m’lord,” she sobbed. “None o’ us want her hurt in any way.”

He pinched the bridge of his nose with a thumb and forefinger. “I know, I know, Anna.”

Patrick put his arms around his wife’s shoulders, and she turned into his embrace, sobbing harder against his throat. “Now, now, me love,” he whispered. He looked over at Braiton. “How can I help, m’lord?”

He threaded his fingers through his hair. “Have

Dooley saddle my horse while I change into my boots."

"Aye, m'lord," Patrick said and left to find Dooley.

Anna followed him up the stairs. "I'll ready a blanket for you to take, m'lord. It grows colder and m'lady hasn't anythin' but a thin waist coat about her shoulders."

****

Braiton sat rigid in the saddle, scanning the night for a sign of Raven. Every nerve in his body was raw with uncertainty and fear for the trouble she could encounter. About a mile into his search he spotted Brawn sniffing around a clump of thick brush. He climbed down from his horse and called the dog to him.

"Here, laddie," he coaxed, getting down on one knee. Brawn came to him and licked his face. "There's a good dog, now," he said, scratching behind Brawn's ears and running a hand over his back. "Can you tell me, boy, where my lady is?" The dog barked and backed away from him, twirling around in a circle. "Can you find her, laddie?" He glanced around the quiet surrounding him.

"She saved your mangy hide, will you return the favor?" The dog barked again and ran a few feet ahead. "That's it, Brawn, go find Raven." Mounting his horse, he followed Brawn deeper into the forest bordering his land. The dog stopped at the base of a large tree and howled. Reaching for the blanket, Braiton headed on foot to where the dog stood. There he found Raven huddled beneath the tree.

"My lady," he said, relief flooding his heart.

She glanced up dazed. "Braiton, is that you?"

"Aye, lass." He knelt beside her.

"How did you find me?"

"'Twas Brawn here, that led me to you."

"I went out walking with him this morning and

lost track of time," she explained. "When it began to grow dark I started back to the mansion, but tripped and twisted my ankle." She straightened her leg and winced.

With gentle fingers he probed the ankle bone. "It doesn't appear to be broken, lass, but I'm sure you've got a nasty sprain."

"I tried to stand, but it kept giving out on me." She grimaced. "And the pain..."

"Aye, you'll not be walking for a while." She shivered, and he placed the blanket around her shoulders. "Let's get you home, where 'tis warm."

She wrapped her arms around his neck. "I am so glad to see you, my *shikaa*."

He gathered her up and held her close, overjoyed himself to have her safe within his embrace. "And I you, lass."

At the mansion, he carried her to her bedchamber, Molly and Anna following close behind, crying and chattering.

"We were scared out o' our wits, m'lady," Molly said, placing pillows behind Raven's head.

He left her to be fussed over by the two elder women. Spotting Brawn standing in the hallway, he smiled and held the door open for him. "Set yourself down by the fire and warm yourself, too, laddie. You've earned it." The dog barked, and he chuckled. "I'd say, my lady was more on target then with just the arrows. Saving you was the right thing to do."

The dog sauntered past him, and he bent to ruffle his ears. "Thank you for your help in finding her."

Bone tired he made his way to his own bedchamber and sat down wearily on the bed. It had been quite a day, one he never wished to repeat. He was frightened for her safety clear down to the marrow of his bones. Just the thought of her injured or worse made his stomach clench. And though every fiber of his being cried out for sleep, he knew he couldn't rest until he made it clear to her, she should never wander so far from the mansion again.

He waited until Molly and Anna finished caring for her before he knocked upon the bedchamber door. Her own voice sounded tired when she called out for him to enter.

He made his way to the bed and sat at the edge. "I just wanted to make sure all was well with you before I took to my own bed."

"I am fine now, thank you."

She smelled of vanilla and lavender. The enticing scent filled him with a strange yearning to snuggle beneath the quilt and fall asleep with her in his arms. "Today brought back a few memories of my childhood." He stroked his mustache. "Shall I tell you why?"

She nodded and positioned herself comfortably against the pillows. He knew her people loved to tell stories, now she readied herself to hear his.

"I wandered into the same dense patch of the forest when I was a few months shy of my eighth birthday," he began. "My father warned me over and over again of the danger lurking about in that damp, overgrown part of the estate. But I didn't listen and repeatedly went on my little adventures in spite of anything he could come up with to deter me."

"Was your father troubled you did not listen?"

"Oh, troubled would hardly be the word to describe how he felt." He paused, that day coming to mind as clear as if it happened yesterday. "One day, after I spent an entire afternoon romping about the forbidden grounds, my father finally figured out a way to stop me."

She sat forward. "What did he do?"

He glanced over at the crackling fire, hesitating. Never did he speak of this to anyone. "My dear father, may God rest his soul, brought me into his study. Locking the door behind him, he said, 'Lad, this is going to hurt me a lot more than 'twill you', and placed me across his knees. Before I could protest, my breeches hung down around my ankles and my bared bum throttled. I don't know what stung more, my flesh or my pride." He turned to look at her. "I can still feel that thrashing to this very day, both the pain and humiliation."

He leaned closer to her. "Do you think such measures would work again for the same situation?" He pictured his hand on her firm, bared bottom...but not to punish her...that would almost be sacrilegious. *Nay, not under duress, but to caress.*

She gasped. "No, I do not."

"Then what would, Raven?"

She snuggled back against the pillows and brought the quilt to her chin. He stifled a smile. Did she believe he'd make good on his threat this very instant?

"My father feared for my mother's safety each day with the white lawman and the Mexicans scouting around the countryside," she said. "He asked her never to ride without him."

He arched a brow. "And did she listen to him?"

She nodded. "My mother knew how troubled my father would be if she did not do as he asked. He feared greatly she would be hurt or kidnapped. Out of honor toward him, as her husband, and respect for his concerns, she never rode without him by her side."

He searched her sapphire eyes. The deep blue pools sucked the breath from him. "Raven," he began in a softer tone. "Fearing for your safety blinded me with worry. My heart dropped to the very soles of my feet thinking of you in a *droch aite*...bad place. I can honestly admit I was numb with a panic I've never tasted before and hope to never taste again." He stood, looking down at her. "So, I ask you this...out of honor for me as your husband, and respect for my concern, please promise you'll never venture into the woods *alone* again."

"I am truly sorry for worrying you so, Braiton," she whispered, reaching for his hand and bringing it to her lips. His knees nearly buckled from the warmth of her kiss and heat raced through his body. If only he could throw caution to the wind…not care about the consequences for losing control. He'd have stripped her of the bedding covering her beautiful woman's form, and everything else she wore. On this night he would have his wife, over and over again.

He pulled his hand free from her grasp.

Stunned by his abrupt action, she cast her gaze to her lap. "You have my word. I will never go into the woods alone again."

He made his way to the door, but hesitated in his departure, least he leave her thinking he was a cold hearted bastard. "By all that's holy, lass, I want you to know I do everything…*everything*," he emphasized, "with only your best interest in mind." Before he shut the door behind him, he added. "I ask you please, to always remember that."

****

Within a few weeks, Raven was back on her feet. She did not see much of Braiton, since he was extremely busy this time of year at the warehouse. By the time she came down for breakfast, he was already gone for the day. And when he returned, she was already in bed. Without him around, she felt lonely eating by herself in the dining room. So one evening she decided to take her meals with Molly, Anna, Patrick, and Brian in the kitchen instead.

In time, she found herself growing close to them all, the four becoming almost as a family. And like family, when one member becomes ill, the rest pitch in to do what they can to help.

Anna awakened under the weather, and Raven

insisted the elder woman spend the day resting in bed. She won, in spite of Anna's protest. But there was much to be done before a guest, all the way from a place called Bunratty, would arrive for dinner. It was unfair to leave all the household chores for Molly to do, so Raven donned a simple dress and wrapped her hair up with a bandana. She baked bread, did the laundry, and was now scrubbing the foyer floor on hands and knees.

"Saints preserve us, lass, what are you doing?"

She turned to find Braiton standing behind her. She surveyed his feet. "If your boots are muddy, kindly wipe them on the mat by the door before you take another step farther. I have not the time to scrub this floor again."

He knelt down, his eyes level with hers. "And why, my lady, are you scrubbing it at all?"

"Because Anna is ill, and there is much to do before your Bunnyrat guest arrives for dinner."

He stifled a smile. "'Tis pronounced, Bunratty, and didn't you get the message I sent home with Brodie?"

She wiped her wet hands on the apron she wore. "No message came, my *shikaa*."

He frowned. "Damn that lad. Can't he ever pass an ale house without stopping in?"

"What did the message say?"

He stood and offered her his hand, helping her to her feet. "It said Rory O'Neill arrived earlier then planned and wanted to take us both out to lunch at the hotel restaurant. At noon, the two of us would be around to fetch you."

She gasped, looking down at her clothes. "And here I am dressed like this, hardly presentable to meet anyone."

"I beg to differ," a deep voice came from the doorway. "In spite of the flour that stains your cheeks and dressed as a scullery maid, you are positively bewitching."

Rory O'Neill's double breasted jacket hung snug on his tall frame, a crop of brown hair framing an interesting face. Topaz colored eyes, hooded by thick dark lashes, twinkled mischievously as he moved closer, bowing from the waist. "Let me introduce myself. I am the Bunnyrat guest, at your service."

Her cheeks heated. "I am so sorry, sir, for not being ready for your visit."

He smiled. "Nonsense, my lady. 'Twas not your fault, obviously."

She wiped her hand again on her apron and extended it to him. "Let me welcome you then to our home."

Rory studied her closely, and her face heated beneath his scrutiny. He brought her hand to his lips and pressed a quick kiss across her knuckles. "'Tis my pleasure, my lady."

Braiton cleared his throat. "Raven, I'll have Molly fix us lunch here, while you get yourself changed."

She nodded. "I will not be long." With that said, she hurried to her bedchamber.

She could not work Molly's magic with her hair, so instead she brushed it till it shone, tied it back with a green ribbon and let the curls fall freely to her waist. She chose an emerald green day dress, one with buttons down the front and much easier to get dressed in by herself. White lace trimmed the scooped neckline and cuffs, the soft color bringing out an aqua hue to her eyes.

She lingered by the drawing room door for a moment before entering. Rory O'Neill stood posed like a gallant sentry by the fireplace. She took in both men, her husband the handsomest by comparison. Braiton, by far was taller in stature and much more muscular.

"Braiton, *a dhiobhail*...you devil. How, on God's

green earth have you been blessed with such fortune, man?" Rory's bold gaze roamed the length of her as she made her way to stand beside Braiton.

"Down, lad," Braiton quipped. "The lady is quite spoken for."

"Only because you saw her first," Rory countered.

Braiton put a possessive arm around her waist. "You're an unscrupulous man, O'Neill, to eye a woman so boldly in the presence of her husband." His humorous tone held a note of annoyance.

"Then shall we go out onto the veranda, my lady?" Rory invited, gesturing to the double doors at the far end of the room.

She glanced up at Braiton. His jaw muscles pulsed. No longer was he finding their banter amusing. "I wish to stay here, by my husband," she said, nestling closer to him.

Braiton's expression relaxed with a smile, his arm tightening around her waist.

"Do I stand a private moment with you at all, my lady?" Rory teased.

"I think not, sir."

Rory threw his head back and laughed. "Ah, she's got spirit, Braiton. Do you think you can handle such beauty and spunk all at once, old man?"

Braiton arched a brow. "I believe I'm up for the challenge."

Rory studied her again. "I'd say you nabbed the pot o' gold at the end of the rainbow, for sure."

"And you, my greedy friend, better not let me catch you dipping your hands into my treasure," Braiton retorted.

Rory locked eyes with Braiton. "Oh, to be sure, my lord, you would not catch me."

"You, sir, are a scoundrel in every true sense of the word," Braiton snapped.

Rory laughed again, his gaze returning to her.

"How are we going to keep this possessive husband of yours at bay, when the other gents in Limerick get a look at you?"

"If they are true gentlemen, then there is little to worry over." She raised an eyebrow. "And if they are like you, then they will get what they deserve."

"Ouch, you wound me deep, my lady," Rory teased, grabbing his heart.

She giggled at his antics. "You are full of what Molly calls, *the blarney*."

Rory's eyes twinkled. "And she's quick-witted as well. Now, if she's got brains, you're in for some real trouble, Braiton."

Braiton chuckled. "I've already discovered that, my friend."

She was relieved when Brian announced lunch was ready and accepted the arm her husband extended to escort her into the dining room. Throughout the day and into the evening Braiton remained attentive to her, the two appearing the perfect married couple. Rory, unlike Lord Wade, only drew her into the conversation to flatter her in some way, or make a suggestive remark. By the end of the evening, she was very pleased to bid the man a goodnight. Rory climbed the stairs to the guest's quarters, and Braiton escorted her up the ones leading to their bedchambers.

She shut the door behind her with a sigh. How she wished Braiton's devotion was real. He acted tonight like the loving husband and many times he even appeared jealous at Rory's attention toward her. But she knew it was only an act, a formality in front of others, and it did not mean a thing. Their marriage was one of convenience only, an agreement that in a year's time would end.

She glanced at the ring she wore. It was just a formality, too. It meant nothing...she meant nothing to him. He treated her kindly, was most generous to her, but she would never win his heart. She sat upon the bed and fingered the lace that trimmed the sleeve of her gown. All the pretty clothes in the world would not make her desirable enough to him. She would always be the pitiful, young women who wandered onto his ship, and he was forced to rescue from the Sea Patrol. Her stupidity inconvenienced his life.

My life has been inconvenienced, too.

Her heart was discouraged, troubled, and even a little annoyed. She spotted the mug of hot milk Molly left for her on the bedside table, but tonight she'd need something more...the comfort of her Bible. Realizing she left it in the library, she crept down the stairs to retrieve it.

Once in the library, she found the book right where she placed it a few days prior, on an end table beside the leather wing back chair.

"You can't sleep either, my lady?"

Startled, she spun around to find Rory O'Neill standing by the window. "I just came for my Bible." She held the book for him to see and made her way to the door.

He blocked her exit. "Braiton tells me your father is an Apache chief and your mother is a white woman."

She nodded.

He moved closer. "Then you're an Indian princess."

She remained silent.

"No doubt, she's the reason for your blue eyes." He glanced at the Bible she held in front of her. "And how it is you can read."

She frowned. "My father's people can also read. They are smart and brave, not at all what others make them out to be. So you need not fear or lock your door. I will not creep into your room to take your scalp."

Rory chuckled. "I meant no offense, my lady. And I fear no such thing. But perhaps 'twould be wise for me to advise you to lock *your* door. You just might find me creeping about your bedchamber, and it won't be your scalp I'll be taking."

Rory O'Neill might be sophisticated, well-dressed, and rich, but he had the same look in his eyes as all the other scoundrels she'd encountered. In many ways, he was more dangerous, believing his irresistible charm was something every woman desired. Did he think he was now doing her a favor?

She raised a defiant chin. "Must I remind you, sir, I am married?"

A sardonic smile curved one side of his mouth. "To a husband who is obviously too inadequate to please you." He caressed the Bible's leather cover. "Otherwise why would you need to come for this?"

"We enjoy sharing scripture."

He laughed again. "Now, who's full of the blarney, my lady?"

Her cheeks heated. "You might try reading a passage or two, yourself." She gestured to the shelves covering the walls. "Or perhaps look for a book on manners." Pushing past him to the door, she added, "It might prove to be helpful."

In her hurry to return to her bedchamber, she ran into Braiton.

He stood by the library door, arms crossed over his chest, and a proud smile upon his face. "*O idhche mhath*, my lady."

"Good night to you, too, my *shikaa*," she whispered and hurried the rest of the way to the stairs.

Chapter Twelve

Dooley O'Connor was waiting for Braiton at the back door. The lad's love for horses and the ease in which he handled them was what secured his position as Shannonbrook's stable boy. Braiton trusted Dooley with the care and grooming of Grania, his dapple gray, and often found the lad admiring the beautiful animal. No doubt Dooley dreamed one day he would own such a magnificent mount himself.

"Has she come, then, Dooley?" Braiton said, donning his riding jacket.

"Aye, m'lord, and what a beauty she be," Dooley marveled.

Braiton followed him to the stables. "Then you think Lady Shannon will like her?"

"Oh, aye, m'lord, how can she not?" Dooley led him to the stall at the far end of the long building.

He stroked the nose of the chestnut colored mare he'd purchased a few days prior. "She's perfect." He smiled at Dooley. "Saddle her up, and mine as well, while I inform my lady we're going for a ride."

He found his wife in the garden, lounging in a chair on the veranda. It was her sanctuary, the place where she could always be located. She was reading from a book she'd discovered in the library.

He took a seat beside her. "And what is it you read today, my lady?"

"Richard Brinkley Sheridian," she said, saving her place with a marker and setting the book on a side table. "Do you realize, Braiton, books open new worlds to a person? Stories and poems contained within the bindings capture the imagination, stir the heart. Authors like Oliver Goldsmith, Congreve, and Swift fill the bookcases and are within a hand's reach."

Her exuberance intrigued him. "I'm glad you enjoy them."

"I do not only enjoy them," she went on. "They envelope my conscience, transport me to other lands and times. Happy novellas, tragic tales, even one of the unnatural fueled my interest."

"Aye, books are great friends." *They help to endure the long, lonely nights when sleep doesn't come.*

"I am sorry for rattling on," she said. "Was there something you wanted?"

"Aye, lass." He smiled. "For you to ride with me."

She looked down at the way she was dressed. "Now, like this?"

"Aye, right now." He took her by the hand and led her down the path to the stables.

She ran to keep up with his long strides. "Why are you in such a hurry?"

He stopped short, and she slammed into him, losing her balance. He caught her before she hit the ground, gathering her into his embrace. "I'm anxious for you to see the special gift I've purchased for you."

She wrapped her arms around his neck. "You have a gift for me?"

Her touch, the very nearness of her body so close to his, filled him with wanting. Her intense gaze fueled the longing within him. "Aye," he managed to choke out, leading her by the hand the rest of the way to the stable. Dooley guided the mare toward her.

She gasped. "This is my gift?"

He chuckled at her excitement. "Aye, she's all yours, lass."

She turned to him and wrapped her arms around his waist, burying her cheek against his neck. "*Ashoge*, Braiton."

Her fingers, splayed across the small of his back, sent a warm glow spreading through him. He fought to control the swirling emotions of her mere touch.

She gazed up into his eyes. "But why? There is a stable full of *chelees*, horses."

The urge to plant the most passionate and prolonged kiss upon her full lips overwhelmed his thoughts, and he struggled to calm his dizzied senses. "None of the others would suit you." He searched her face and mentally caressed her body. "You deserve only the finest mount in the country, a mount such as the mare that stands before you."

Her eyes welled with tears, their moisture glistening in the deep blue of her eyes. "I thank you from the bottom of my heart."

Oh, that I could postpone this ride and carry you to your bedchamber instead. Shut out any awareness of the world and become totally entranced by your compelling personage. To just forget all I loath, what I am destined to live with.

He shook his head to clear it and broke free from her embrace. "You are most welcome, my lady." He gestured toward the mare. "Now, shall we ride?"

Braiton got his first taste of what an excellent equestrian she was. Even inappropriately dressed, she handled the mare with grace and speed. She had no trouble keeping up with him, and he prided himself at being a seasoned horseman.

Raven's hair broke free from the pins holding it in the chignon at the base of her neck and tumbled down her back, the breeze cooling her face. Her cheeks grew raw from the crispness of the wind, but she did not care. Her body was alive, exhilarated, and singing with a mixture of pleasure and freedom.

She rode with fervor beside Braiton, and he

matched her intensity. She couldn't help but think how well he would fit in with her people. Gabriel and her father would enjoy riding beside him as well. Thinking of home brought a longing to her soul. She brought the mare to a slow walk, pulled off the path, and stopped.

Braiton came up beside her, a frown creasing his brow. "Is something wrong, my lady?"

"I wish to show you the real way to ride," she said, dismounting and pulling the saddle off the mare. She gathered the fullness of her skirt between her legs and straddled the horse, gripping a handful of the dark, thick mane. "I will race you back to the stable, my *shikaa*."

Dooley's eyes widened when she rode into the stable. "Saints preserve us, m'lady," he said, running over to her. "What happened?"

She climbed down from the horse before Dooley had a chance to help her. "All is fine, Dooley." She gave the mare a loving pat. "Will you tend her for me?"

"Aye, m'lady," he said, still looking bewildered.

When Braiton rode into the stable she beamed up at him. "I win."

He threw her saddle to the ground. "'Twas not an easy task to tote your saddle and still ride as swift."

"Ah-ha, then do you admit I am swifter than you?" she teased.

"I admit nothing," he quipped, climbing down from his horse. "Other than the match was unfair. I was riding with an extra load."

"Then strip your *chelee* of his saddle, and we will race again," she challenged.

"Nay, the horses are too tired now. Their performance would be poor."

She giggled. "You mean your performance would be poor. Without the saddle you would fall off."

He arched a brow. “You are a good rider, my lady, but your ability hardly surpasses mine.”

She placed hands on hips and threw the words at him like stones. “Why, because I am a woman?”

He frowned, his expression clouded with his anger. “Nay, that has nothing to do with it.”

“I think it has everything to do with it, Braiton Shannon.” She gathered her skirt, raising the hem high above her ankles, and stalked up the path to the mansion.

“Raven,” he called after her.

She ignored him and continued toward the mansion, seething with mounting rage.

“Raven,” he shouted now, catching up with her and grabbing her by the arm. “Can you halt for just a moment, lass?”

“Halt,” she snapped, flashing him a look of disdain. “Like a horse controlled by the reins?” She squirmed free from his grasp. “I think not!” She ran the rest of the way to the mansion.

Rory O’Neill stood on the garden veranda, puffing on his clay pipe when she came storming through the garden.

“My lady,” he said. “You look as though you’re being chased by a wild boar.”

She cast a hostile glare his way and pushed past him, slamming the door behind her.

Braiton followed close behind Raven. His anger singed the corners of his control and bristled down his spine.

Rory chuckled. “Aye, I was right. Here comes the wild boar.”

His sharp retort stabbed the air as he pushed past him. “Haven’t you some sort of business to attend to?”

“I’d much rather tend to yours,” Rory called after him. “’Tis far more entertaining.”

Braiton took the stairs two at a time, his heart

hammering. When he came to Raven's door, he threw it open and slammed it shut behind him. His words came sharp and ragged. "Would you listen to me, lass, for just one moment? For just one God given moment?"

She stood fuming by the fireplace, blue eyes flashing with rage. "No, you listen to me." Her angry gaze swung over him. "I had a life before I met you. I hunted in the woods, rode, swam, danced, cooked, and sewed." She neared him and with a finger, poked him in the shoulder, her tone cold and lashing. "I helped my mother teach the children in the village, I aided the midwife in birthing babies."

Her bosom rose and fell with quick intakes of breath, wisps of hair clinging in disarray around her face. "I even had friends who truly liked my company." Her sardonic laugh tempered his anger with amusement. "Perhaps that is hard for you to imagine, but it is the truth." She waved a hand around the room. "But here I am just the poor soul who needs rescuing and guidance."

A tear slipped down her cheek, and her lower lip quivered, yet she held her chin high. Pride and beauty emanated from her in volumes. She was intelligent, resourceful, caring, and enchanting. This he realized more times then he wanted to admit.

Truth was, he thought of her constantly. All he wanted to do was make her happy, take care of her, and love her. *Aye, God help me, love her!* He longed to hold her, feel her beneath him, kiss her…kiss her…kiss her!

He reached for her shoulders and pulled her against him, his mouth coming hard upon hers. He expected her to stiffen in his arms, step back and slap him hard across the face. But instead, her lips parted, and she fell into the embrace. Her breasts crushed against his heart racing within his chest.

With hunger he tasted her, his tongue teasing,

playing around inside her mouth. She slipped her arms around his neck, delicate fingers playing with the hair at his nape. The realness of her was a thousand times better than anything he could ever imagine. She felt right in his arms, her touch arousing in him emotions he never thought existed, that he never dared to hope for. Being this close to her he was alive, like he'd never been before.

The lass made his head spin, his knees weak. Her lips were soft and warm, and he never wanted this kiss to end. He inhaled her scent and caressed her back, his hands traveling up and down her spine. He wanted her...he wanted all of her.

But his torment stood between them, awakening him to the danger his actions would evoke. Bad enough he lived with the curse, he couldn't place such an injustice upon her. Aye, she beguiled his heart, but his selfishness couldn't start something that should never be allowed to bloom.

He broke away, and she fell back against the mantle. Her gaze was dazed, then hurt. "I'm sorry, Raven, for everything," he choked out and left the room.

Raven stood in a trance, her fingers caressing her lips. She could still feel his kiss there, warm and sweet. He made her body quake with desire. She could barely remain standing. He left the taste of his kiss upon her lips, the imprint of his touch down her spine. With a shattered resolve, she fell to her knees and wept.

She declined joining him for dinner, claiming a headache. He had Molly bring her up a bowl of stew. Before he retired for the night, he rapped on her door, bade her good night, and hoped she felt better in the morning. The man was infuriating, yet thoughtful and kind. He bought her a beautiful horse, and instead of appreciating such a wonderful gift, she showed off her riding skills.

Tears welled for the hundredth time in her eyes. What was it her father always said? *"As long as you know how to do a thing well, that is all that matters."* She pictured the outline of his proud profile and memories of home overwhelmed her.

The night was quiet around her, the moon casting a soft sliver of light through the half closed drapes of the veranda doors. She lay lost and consumed by the large bed. The grandness of the room was nothing but a large reminder of her loneliness. She knew sleep would elude her and crawled out of bed. Slipping on a robe, she tiptoed down the stairs. Brawn followed close behind as she made her way out to the garden. From there she stumbled barefoot on the rocky path, to the stables. She lit the lantern hanging at the entrance and went to her horse's stall. As she stroked the animal's nose, the mare nuzzled her hand.

"You are the greatest gift anyone could have. I believe I will call you, *Dayden*." A rustling came from the darkness behind her, and Brawn growled deep in his throat, baring his teeth. Raven spun around, fear gripping her heart.

Dooley emerged from the shadows. "What means *Dayden*, m'lady?"

She sighed, relieved it was only the stable boy, though she had no idea why he was still called a *boy*. He appeared to be just as old as she, perhaps even older by a few years. A male his age in the tribe would already have received his warrior's training.

"It is Apache for *little girl*," she translated.

He frowned. "'Tis not safe for you to be runnin' about in the night, m'lady."

"I just wanted to see my horse again, thought maybe I would take her for a ride."

He moved closer, his kind, green eyes coming into view by the lantern's light. "Nay, m'lady. To ride in such darkness is not wise."

"I have ridden by the light of the moon many times with my father."

He ran a hand through his thick curly hair. "But this is Ireland, m'lady. Nights are foggy here. A rider not familiar with the land could be in grave danger." He frowned, bushy dark brows knitting together in concern. "I cannot allow you to take such a chance. I would never forgive meself if somethin' happened to you, nor would Lord Shannon."

She nodded in agreement. "I understand, Dooley." The chill of the night penetrated her bones. She shivered and wrapped her robe tighter around herself. "Do you not ever go home?"

He gestured to the lantern. "I was about to, m'lady, when I saw the light. Thought Lord Shannon might be in need o' somethin' more."

"How long have you worked for my husband?"

Dooley leaned against a stall. "About two years now, m'lady.

"And are you happy here?"

"Aye, very. Lord Shannon has always treated me fairly."

She frowned. "How so?"

"About a year ago me mother took to her bed with an ailment. Bein' I'm the only family the poor woman has, 'twas up to me to care for her. Lord Shannon paid me a wage, even though I wasn't workin' and sent Molly over to our cottage each mornin' to help me mother bathe and pin up her hair."

She smiled. "Yes, he is a very kind and fair man."

"It does me heart good to see him so happy, m'lady. Since you've come to Shannonbrook, his eyes are shinin' as brilliant as the brightest star."

His words gave her comfort, lessening the despair. "Do you really think he is happy because of me, Dooley?"

"Aye, m'lady, I do for sure." She shivered again and Dooley frowned. "'Tis much too cold to be out and about in only your bedclothes." He glanced down at her bared feet. "You'll be catchin' your death for sure if you don't be takin' yourself by the fire."

"Yes, you are right, of course. I am sorry I have kept you from your own home fires."

"No one is there waitin' for me anyhow. Me mother died four months ago."

Her heart went out to the man. "I am so sorry, Dooley."

He shrugged. "'Tis the way o' life, m'lady." He forced a smile. "Come now, 'tis best I be takin' you to the mansion."

She nodded and together they walked back to Shannonbrook.

****

Braiton sat in the big arm chair by the fire, staring into the flames. All was quiet, except for the large clock beside the bed, ticking away each passing second. Brian raised an eyebrow when he traded his usual mug of warm milk for a tumbler of whiskey. "Don't be mothering me, now Brian," he snapped, when the man filled the cup only halfway. "I need a man's size snout full this evening, for sure," he grumbled.

Brian shook his head in disgust. "You drink and y'r lady runs barefoot in the night, with no more then her bedclothes on."

He frowned. "The devil, you say, man."

"'Tis true, m'lord, she's out and about as we speak."

He set the tumbler aside. "And how do you know this?"

"Molly saw her flutter by, like a little fairy, barefoot and scantly clothed." Brian clicked his tongue with his disapproval. "To be runnin' out on such a cold night dressed so...well, she'll be catchin' her death for sure."

He jumped from his chair. "Do you have a notion where she was going?"

"Molly said she was headin' for the stables."

A cold knot formed in his stomach. "Saints preserve us; she wouldn't try…where are my boots?"

Brian hunted around the room for the discarded footwear. Once found, Braiton hurried to slip them on, then took to the staircase like a storm to the sea; thundering down with heavy, booted steps. When he rounded the corner to the kitchen, Raven's shriek of surprise startled him.

"Braiton," she gasped, her hand going to her throat.

He glanced at her dirt-stained feet and frowned. "Have you been riding, lass?"

"No. I just wanted to see my horse." She sighed. "I am sorry if I troubled you again." She walked to the far end of the kitchen and filled a tiny basin with water from a jug. Then she sat in a chair, placing each foot into the tub, and washed her soiled feet.

"Raven," he said in a softer tone.

She raised her gaze to his, hands splashing the water over her feet.

He made his way to her. "I'm sorry if I upset you. You're an excellent bareback rider. And you're right. I'd just fall off."

"I am the one who should be apologizing. I should have been thankful for your gift. It matters not who rides better, only that we ride together."

He reached for a towel and got down on one knee before her, spreading it open. She placed her wet feet between his toweled hands. Gently he dried them for her.

"I will clean up here," he offered, reaching for the basin. "You go on up to bed."

She stifled a yawn. "I am sorry I troubled you, again."

"Nay, lass, you didn't." He opened the back door to dump out the water.

"But you were angry when you thought I had gone riding."

He placed the basin on the hook. "I wasn't angry."

"Then why were you rushing out the door?"

"To find you, lass, and stop you, before you broke your neck."

She frowned. "Because you care about me?"

"Aye, Raven," he admitted. "You are all I do care about." He raised an authoritative brow. "Now go to bed."

She cast him a triumphant smile and ran up the stairs.

Chapter Thirteen

What caused a person to fall in love with another? When was the exact moment in time all the elements fit together to create the first *spark*, igniting all the emotions that followed? And when was it you knew for sure it was love? Raven did not have the answers to any of the questions plaguing her, but something inside kept giving her signs.

She was anxious to see his face upon the dawn of each new day. A heated flush of excitement spread up her spine with just his mere glance her way. The deep, rich timbre of his voice trickled through her entire being when he said her name, like water through a sieve. She yearned, no, craved for him at night, wanting him to quiet her body with his own. She needed him to quench her burning desire with his passion, a caress of his long fingers, the thrill of a kiss.

She lay awake in the center of her large bed and imagined how it would feel to love him. Would her breasts tingle with the brush of his soft lips against them? Dreams of him left her moist and sticky. She woke tormented with desire, wicked and wanton, yielding to the fantasy.

By day, she loved the times they spent laughing, riding, eating together. She left her hair free, clad only in a simple gown. She enjoyed the way he marveled at the freedoms she took, becoming comfortable with her natural, unrestricted ways. He doted on her, took her to magnificent places, presented her with priceless gifts. He introduced her to the company of fascinating and intelligent people.

Her interests grew, her horizons broadened. She became cultured and refined, elegant in demeanor, matching wits and information with the best of them. And yet, through all his good intentions, not a morsel of love was ever professed. He pulled back from intimate moments, left her ardor hanging.

Unsatisfied, she spent sleepless nights counting the endless hours stretching before her. She memorized the shadows in the room, the embroidered flowers on the quilt, how many tassels adorned the valances.

Come the dawn, she would agonize at the first light filling her bedchamber. Finally, she would give in to her exhaustion, falling asleep with tears slipping from closed eyelids and staining the pillowcases. How much longer could she endure the loneliness, the detachment, the confusion this man put upon her?

****

Braiton spent another night smoking his clay pipe, sipping whiskey, watching the fire, and listening to the bothersome ticking of the bedside clock. He wondered now, if she slept? His mouth went dry when he overheard Molly telling Anna, Raven wore a nightgown to bed, but come morning it was found in a heap upon the floor. He pondered, from that point on, how she looked sleeping in her natural state. 'Twasn't hard to picture the deep brown of her skin in contrast to the white bed linens, dark hair tousled upon the pillow or falling in disarray around her naked shoulders. He envisioned one slender arm flung above her head, an angelic innocence settling on her serene face. He further imagined long ebony lashes fanning across each cheek, and her full peach-colored lips slightly parted. His breath quickened at the thought of the quilt hanging low upon her curved hips as she tossed in slumber, leaving her breasts uncovered. With every breath she took, they rose and fell, the musky-pink summits erect; a perfect shaped navel in the center of a slim taut belly. He swallowed hard, his loins growing hot and thick beneath his breeches.

Every night at dinner, the hardened peaks of her breasts pressed erect against her bodice. He struggled to keep himself from flying across the table and ripping every shred of clothing off her; taking her with passion between the boiled potatoes and the mutton stew.

After dinner, they'd retire to the drawing room, to sip coffee and share conversation. He'd take a seat in the arm chair. She sat cross-legged on the carpet, before the fire; skirt raised to her thighs, the bronze, naked splendor of her legs in full view. He learned to adopt an outward demeanor of complete control, but inside he erupted with the heat of an active volcano. He longed to ease her down upon her back, spread wide her crossed limbs, and taste her womanly charms in every way imaginable.

He shook his head to dispel the image from his thoughts. Each night his efforts became harder and harder to do. He'd wake from erotic dreams that left him swelled and wet, aching for her. He squeezed his eyes shut, but the vision of her remained to torment him. The bronzed-skinned goddess lying naked only a few feet away from him was his for the taking.

She was his wife and by law he had every right to look, touch, and enjoy the pleasures of her body. Thoughts of her pressing naked against him, her flesh warm and soft, made his swollen member throb. He took an audible breath. *Why do I continue on this way when I can go to her this very moment, climb into the bed and take feverishly what is mine?*

Was he going mad? *Aye, I am. Mad to believe that's all that would be involved.*

He was reminded of his secret horror and how selfish 'twould be to make her a part of it. His blight kept him from her now and forever. The dull ache in his head from the whiskey was nothing compared to the one in his heart.

He moved to his bed and lay on his side, a tide of emotions rushing through his veins. He pressed his eyes shut and a sudden wave of exhaustion consumed every inch of his being. But he wouldn't fall asleep now. Nay, he'd first see the faithful dawn approach the sky…then he'd rest, but not before he whispered her name.

Come morning, he sat alone at the dining room table, waiting for her to join him. Rory O'Neill finally took his departure, business with Braiton completed. This meant Raven would come to breakfast with her hair falling about her shoulders and wearing nothing beneath her dress. He was anxious to hear her familiar light footsteps, but none descended the stairs.

"Anna," he said, sipping his tea. "Has my lady already eaten her breakfast?"

Anna busied herself arranging the silverware. "Nay, m'lord."

He set the cup aside. "She still sleeps, then?"

"Nay, m'lord. I believe she rang for Molly quite some time ago."

He nodded. "Then I expect she'll be coming down momentarily."

"Nay, m'lord. M'lady won't be down for breakfast this mornin'."

He frowned. "Is she ill?"

"Not exactly, m'lord."

"What do you mean by, *not exactly*," he snapped. "Either she's ill, or she's not."

"'Tis not me place to say, m'lord. Just accept she won't be down for breakfast this mornin'."

"Saints preserve us, woman, this beating-around-the-bush is enough to drive any man mad." He stood, his chair scraping loudly on the polished, wooden floor, and rushed upstairs to her bedchamber.

Braiton rapped upon his wife's door and after calling out her permission, he entered. Raven lounged upon the chaise by the fire, a cool damp cloth over her eyes. Puzzled and nervous, he made his way to where she sat.

"My lady, what ails you on this morn?"

She lifted the cloth from her eyes. "My stomach."

He looked down at her, concern for her well-being first and foremost. "Could it be from something you ate?"

"It is nothing like that, my *shi'aad*," she said, replacing the eye compress.

He couldn't bear for anything to be wrong with her. "Perhaps I should send for Dr. Murphy?"

She shook her head. "There is nothing Terrance can do for me, Braiton."

Confused and now somewhat frustrated, he sighed. "How do you know, lass, unless he has a look at you?"

She raised the cloth from her eyes again. "I already know there is nothing he can do. There is nothing anyone can do for what I have."

Her resignation unnerved him. "Mother of God, Raven, what do you think you have?"

She motioned to the bed. "Sit, Braiton. We need to talk."

His heart froze, and a wave of panic washed over him. "What is it, my lady? What's wrong?"

Raven sighed. "I imagine this is something a wife should not keep from her husband." Her own father always knew when her mother's courses came. But their relationship was a genuine love, where her marriage only one of convenience.

His mouth thinned. "You should keep nothing from me, lass, especially when it concerns your health."

"It is not all that bad," she reassured him. "More an inconvenience, really, than anything else, though I suppose complications could arise if I did not rest."

"What complications?" The muscles at his jaw pulsed.

She cast a glance at the compress she held in her hand. "My woman's time has come, and it is the first one since..." she paused, the blush rising to heat her cheeks. "Since my illness aboard the ship," she finally finished. It was a time she wished never to remember, but one she knew she would never forget. Agent Hall ruined her for all times, tainted her and left her a used woman. It was the reason Braiton would never consider their marriage anything more than a business deal.

He remained silent.

She raised her gaze to meet his, thinking she would see the disgust in his eyes, but instead he appeared distressed over her condition. "It did not come upon me like those I have had before, but Molly said it was to be expected," she added. "Staying off my feet for a while will help." She sighed. "Do you understand, Braiton?"

"Aye, my lady, I do now." Combing his fingers through his hair, he forced a smile. "I'm afraid I'm not use to such matters, so I ask you to forgive me for not knowing what to do, and then tell me what you will need."

"Just rest is all, my *shikaa*, and perhaps..." she glanced over at her meal tray sitting on a nearby table, "you could help me eat this breakfast. I do not know what Anna was thinking when she doled out such a large portion. This is way too much food for me to eat alone, especially this morning, when all I have a stomach for is dry toast and tea."

"'Twould be my pleasure, lass." He stood, pulled the dressing table chair beside her, and helped himself to her meal.

She munched half-heartedly on the dry toast as he talked about the fox hunt held each year at Glenview, the Lord of Bunratty's mansion. "I remember you mentioning you've hunted, so I thought you'd like to join me."

She smiled. "I would love to join you." She took a sip of her tea. "I have only hunted bear and mountain lion with my father, both being hard to bring down. But I suppose a *lupan*, gray fox could give a challenge as well."

He nearly choked on a piece of sausage he popped into his mouth. "Bears and mountain lions," he repeated.

She giggled. "Did you think I only hunted furry *gahs*, rabbits and bushy-tailed squirrels?" She batted her eyelashes. "Really, now Braiton, do I look that delicate," she teased.

"My dear woman, I'm hardly perceived as delicate, yet I'd consider carefully bringing down such animals as bears and mountain lions."

"Why so? One clean shot between the eyes does it every time."

He arched a brow. "What happens if you fail, lass? Surely you must have thought of that?"

She frowned. "Well, not too hard or for too long or else you will fail. It is you against the animal—one the hunter, the other the prey. I choose to be the hunter."

His eyes roamed the length of her. "I sincerely believe you'd not fit in any other role." He leaned forward in his seat. "And does the cat and mouse game you play with me also render me your prey?"

She smiled. "I suppose the answer to that questions centers on which you want to be, the *gidi*, cat or the mouse."

He poured them more tea. "Which is the winner?"

"That depends on how you play the game." She

took a sip of the tea, contemplating her next words. "If the mouse can get the cat boiling mad, then slips away, I would then say the mouse is the winner. But if the *gidi* frightens the mouse and then catches him, then the cat wins the day."

He threw his head back and laughed. "I'm at a quandary to choose, either way I could lose."

"Or win, it all revolves around the stand you wish to take."

"The law of the wild, my lady?"

"The law of life, my *shikaa*," she countered.

He searched her face. "You're a most clever woman, Raven."

"Not a featherhead?"

He laughed again. "Nay, definitely not a featherhead."

The cramps subsided while they talked, but now the pain returned, making its way to the lower part of her back. Stretching out in the bed would do wonders. "I think I need to rest now." She pulled aside the throw covering her and swung her legs off the chaise, but when she stood, the room spun.

He caught her before she hit the floor and carried her to the bed. Then wet the eye compress in a basin of cool water left on the bedside table. He swabbed her face and neck, pushing aside a strand of hair from her forehead.

"Just stay quiet and rest, my lady."

He was so close; the musky scent of his cologne filled her senses. Before she knew it, she stroked his clean shaven cheek with the back of her hand. "You look so tired, Braiton."

He forced a smile. "Then perhaps I should also take a nap."

"Nap here with me," she said, moving over to give him room.

He was silent for what seemed to her an eternity, then he sat at the edge of the bed, pulled off his boots, and climbed in beside her. He lay back against the pillow and stretched his arm out to her.

She rolled into his embrace, resting her cheek upon his shoulder, and placing a hand flat against his hard, muscular chest. It was heaven being in his arms. Peace engulfed her. She closed her eyes and slept the best she had in weeks.

****

Four days in bed healed her body but did nothing for her mind. Bored to tears of reading and embroidery, she decided to make her way downstairs to have her nightly mug of milk, before Molly brought it up to her. Brawn declined her offer to come along with a large yawn, returning to his slumber before the fire.

"You are becoming a lazy dog," she scolded, slipping on her robe and slippers. "I will leave the door open in case you change your mind." He yawned again.

Molly and Anna sat at the table, chatting over tea. Brian was preparing a night tray for Braiton when she entered the kitchen.

"I was just about to bring you your mug o' milk, m'lady," Molly said.

She took the seat beside Molly. "I thought I would have my milk with you ladies, tonight." She made a face. "I am growing tired of looking at the walls in my room."

Anna smiled. "Well, I'm glad to see you're feelin' better, lass."

"Me, too, Anna." She cast a glance at Brian. "What is it you are bringing up to Lord Shannon?"

"'Tis a snout of whiskey, m'lady."

She frowned. "I thought he drank warm milk before bed."

Brian sighed. "Nay, not anymore. He says the whiskey helps him sleep better."

"He has trouble sleeping, too?"

Brian nodded. "Sometimes he sits by the fire till the wee hours of the mornin'."

She stood and took the tray from Brian. "Lord Shannon does not need the power of spirits to make him sleep." She removed the tumbler of whiskey from the tray. "I remember my father saying, 'when you ease the heart, the mind will rest.' Besides, I know what will help much better."

"But he'll not let me bring him anythin' but the whiskey," Brian protested.

She gave his arm a reassuring pat. "Then I will bring the tray to him tonight."

"But, m'lady..."

"It will be fine," she interrupted. "Lord Shannon will enjoy the best sleep he has had in a long time." She turned her attention toward Anna. "Have we sleeping herbs, Anna?"

"Aye, m'lady." She rose from her seat and retrieved a tin canister from a nearby shelf. When she lifted the lid, it was filled with remedies. "I've some for fever, a few for consumption..."

"Any for relaxing," she broke in.

Anna nodded and pulled a tiny gauze bag filled with herbs from the tin. "That would be this one, m'lady."

She opened the bag and dropped its contents into two mugs. "Tonight we will both get the rest due us." Adding the tea already brewed, she placed the cups on the tray. "I would ask you all a favor now." She smiled, glancing at each one. "Please, do not come to us unless one of us rings for you."

They nodded in unison.

She mounted the stairs with more caution then usual, fearing she would spill the tea over the cup's rim; or worse yet, she would drop the fine china. A new found respect welled in her heart for Brian's talent of balancing the tray on just the palm of his hand. He made it look so easy.

She rapped on Braiton's bedchamber door, entering upon his request. She discovered him sitting with his back to her, in a chair by the fire, puffing on his clay pipe. The smell of spice and vanilla filled the room. She remained silent, placing the tray upon a large desk and bringing the cup over to the table beside his chair.

He glanced at the tea and frowned. "Where is the whiskey?" He looked up with a scowl, his mouth ajar when he saw her instead of Brian.

"Tea is much better for you." Before he could protest, she pulled a chair up beside his. "I thought I would join you tonight." She cast him a warm smile. "You do not mind, do you?"

"Nay, my lady, I don't mind," he grumbled.

She ignored his foul mood and retrieved her own cup from the tray, glancing around the room while sipping her tea. It was much bigger than her chamber, his done in deep blue and cream. The ornate carvings on the oak wardrobe and desk were done in detail and with quality craftsmanship. The huge bed, its elegant velvet drapery hanging down each post, was far grander than any she imagined.

She set her cup down and made her way to it, running her hands over the plush coverlet that matched the canopy and drapery.

Openly she admired the décor. "This room is magnificent."

He rose from his seat to stand beside her. "What pleases you about it?"

"It is so much like you, strong, handsome, and bold, yet warm and comforting." She turned around to look at him and was sure he blushed. She smiled and inhaled the tobacco's aroma filling the room. "I like the scent from your pipe as well." She moved to the veranda doors, caressing the soft velvet of the deep blue drapes. "What can you see from here?"

"I'll show you," he offered, pulling aside the long

curtains and unbolting the lock. He threw the double doors open and walked out onto the stone veranda.

She followed, the brisk night air stinging her cheeks. She shivered, pulling the collar of her robe up around her neck, and looked out over the dark, silent expanse of the property. The moon's reflection danced on the calm waters of the Shannon River in the distance. To one side of the estate, there loomed a building, half of it only a shell. It was outlined against the night sky. She pointed to the partial ruins. "What was once there?"

"The first Shannonbrook mansion." His voice was low and smooth. "The West wing was destroyed by fire when I was just a wee lad." He sighed. "I have little memory of the time I spent there."

A chill ran down her spine, and she shivered again. "It looks scary."

"Nay, lass, 'tis just sad, I'd say." He turned her way, concern edging his tone. "I think you're growing as cold as our tea." He gestured for her to precede him into his chamber.

She reached for two large pillows and a throw from the bed and laid them out by the fireplace. Then she picked up her tea cup and sat cross-legged before the fire.

"Come, join me."

He moved closer. "On the floor?"

She nodded. "My people enjoy a fire in this fashion all the time."

He smiled and retrieved his own cup before sitting beside her. "Tell me more about your people."

"Well, as I said, they enjoy sitting by the fire and telling stories."

The reflection of the fire flickered in the center of his green eyes. He sat back and relaxed against the pillow. "What kind of stories do they tell?"

She sensed his relaxation and was pleased with accomplishing her task. "Stories about the *lupan*, gray fox, and the *baya*, coyote, or the *mato*, bear, and the mountain lion," she explained. "All the tales are meant to teach a lesson and bring forth much wisdom."

He sat forward, placing his cup on the floor beside him and pulled off his boots. He wiggled his toes beneath his socks. "And did you learn from these fables?"

She smiled, fond memories of her childhood coming into her mind's eye. "I learned my share." She giggled. "My father would tell me I needed to listen harder than the others, because of my willful spirit."

Braiton laughed and lounged again against the pillow. "Your father is a wise man. His summarizing of you is perfect."

She placed her cup aside and lie back, too. "I hope I will be as good and wise a parent."

His eyes turned sad. "You wish to have children of your own?"

"Oh, yes, children are such a gift. How else could family traditions and legacies be carried on?"

He sighed and stretched his arms out to draw her close. "How, indeed; legacies both good and bad."

She snuggled into his embrace, the warmth of the fire and his body heat making her lids grow heavy. She yawned. "Can I stay here with you, Braiton?"

"Aye, lass," he whispered before they both fell asleep cradled in each other's arms.

****

He woke refreshed, 'twas the first good night's rest he had in months. The whiskey never accomplished such results. She still rested in the hollow of his arm, their positions proving neither stirred a muscle all night. The fire had died, yet he was warm. She was warm in his arms.

He glanced at her face; delicate lids shut in

peaceful slumber, thick dark lashes curling away from high cheekbones. Her full lips, slightly parted, invited him to taste their sweetness. He covered her mouth with his, awakening the sleeping beauty with a kiss.

Her hand moved to rest on the back of his neck, fingers playing with the hairs at the nape. His tongue wasted no time in claiming her, darting around in her mouth and exploring the soft corners. 'Twas as his dreams, though a thousand times better. She was warm, willing, and God he wanted her—all of her—to experience the pleasures of her body and cool the fires of passion burning within him.

He swelled beneath his breeches; desire a surging current of molten lava. His hands roamed to her thighs, his kisses to her throat. She threw her head back, giving him more of her soft, slim neck to suckle.

"Raven," he whispered, his body trembling with ardor. "This cannot be."

She placed each of her hands on his cheeks, bringing his gaze to meet hers. Sapphire eyes burned with fervor, their depths reaching to his very soul.

He grabbed her wrists and pinned her arms above her head. "This cannot be," he repeated, and in one fluid motion he was upon his feet, looking down at her. "Leave now lass, while you are still the hunter." He turned his back to her, moving to stand by the desk.

"Go, Raven. Now," he demanded.

He heard her scramble to her feet. "What is it, Braiton?"

He combed his fingers through his hair. "You need to return to your bedchamber, posthaste." He felt the chill of the room now. It seeped to his bones, surrounded his heart.

"Please, tell me what troubles you," she begged.

He shut his eyes, the hurt and confusion in her voice increasing the guilt consuming him. "There's nothing to tell, I just want you gone." He turned to face her. "Leave, now."

He watched her fight back the tears filling her eyes. "If that is what you wish."

"'Tis," he snapped.

She ran to the door, slamming it shut behind her.

"Damn," he hissed, picking up a ceramic horse from the desk and throwing it across the room. It shattered against the mantle, much like his resolve. Exactly like his heart.

He glanced over at the veranda doors. Morning's light seeped into the room between the half-closed drapes. He took an audible breath and folded his arms across his chest.

"It seems, once more," he whispered, "I am destined to meet the approaching dawn alone."

Chapter Fourteen

The Wee Lassie, Braiton's private passenger ship, carried them over the Shannon River to Bunratty. The cabins were on a much smaller scale than his cargo ship, *The Sweet Maureen*, but Raven's quarters served her needs well enough for the short voyage.

Raven watched from her bunk as Molly checked and rechecked the baggage, hoping nothing important was forgotten.

"All will be fine, Molly," she reassured the elder woman. "We have more packed for this trip then we need as it is."

"Nay, m'lady, 'tis not enough," was Molly's worried response. "You'll be havin' several formal dinners to attend, the opera, a ball or two, and the hunt. 'Twould not be proper for the Lady o' Limerick to be caught wearin' the same gown twice."

She sighed and rolled her eyes heavenward. "No, we must not let that happen. Wearing the yellow brocade twice would truly bring disgrace upon us all."

Molly frowned at her sarcastic tone and stopped fussing with the luggage, coming to sit beside her on the bunk and taking her hand.

"Was this trip not in your favor, m'lady?"

She sighed. "It was at first, but I am not so sure now."

"What has changed?"

"Not a thing, Molly," she lied, not wanting to explain what happened between her and Braiton in his chamber a few nights ago. She stood and made her way to the baggage, busying herself with arranging the compartments.

"Everything is just as Lord Shannon and I agreed upon. I was a fool to hope things could be different."

Molly rushed to her side. "Nay, m'lady, 'tis never foolish to hope."

She sighed. "I think Braiton is having second thoughts about saving a foolish girl who got herself lost."

"Nay, m'lady, what you think is far from the truth."

She tossed a bonnet she was holding on the bunk. "Then tell me what *is* the truth, Molly."

"Sometimes we need to get lost in order to be found, m'lady." She pushed aside a wisp of hair from Raven's forehead in a motherly fashion. "You're a beautiful and lovin' young woman, to be sure. All o' us marvel over your spirit and quick wit, and your husband is the first one among us to sing your praises."

She raised a questionable brow. "Blarney."

"Not a stitch o' the blarney, lass, 'tis all true what I say. There's not a day that passes your name doesn't come from his lips. The man lives for your presence, and I'm sure if you declined to come along on this trip, he would have canceled his plans as well."

She sighed. "If only I could be sure of what you say, Molly. I want so much for him to be proud of me."

Molly chuckled. "By all that's holy, lass, he is proud o' you. I've looked deep into his eyes and have listened closely to his words when he speaks o' you. He's your greatest admirer, and if you would just be a wee bit patient, wait this all out, you'll be happy one day you did."

She studied the concern in Molly's pale blue

eyes. "You are a wise woman, Molly. Are you sure you are not part Apache?"

Molly chuckled. "Nay, m'lady. 'Tis a pure Irish lass that I be." She gave her a little nudge. "Now go, join your husband on deck."

The Shannon River was calm and the sun hung low in the sky. She found Braiton rechecking their course with Captain Kirby. "'Tis an easy sail we have, Captain."

"Aye, m'lord. We should be dockin' upon Bunratty's shores sometime after the break of dawn," Kirby said. He tipped his hat to her. "Good eve, m'lady."

She smiled. "To you as well, Captain."

Braiton remained at the rail, gazing out over the water, searching the vast river far and wide while puffing on his pipe. She came to stand beside him, pulling her shawl tighter about her shoulders against the evening chill, and reaching out to grip the rail.

"I do not think I will ever be able to stand on deck without holding on to something."

He chuckled. "'Twill come to you in time, lass. I believe 'twas not until my fourth voyage I acquired my sea legs." He turned to look at her. "You're still way ahead of the game, though."

"How so?"

"It also took me as long to control my stomach."

She giggled, the tension between them fading. "My stomach has churned many times," she confessed. "But I have conquered the problem with the help of mind power."

He frowned. "That truly helps?"

She nodded. "My people conquer pain and weakness using the strength of their minds. The braves of the tribe must learn this skill before they can become *nagonlkadis*, warriors."

"Then how is it you've learned the skill?" His

eyes scanned the length of her. "'Tis obvious you're not a warrior."

"Ah, but you are wrong, my *shikaa.* A *nagonlkadi* is not only a brave off to war, but one who can survive life, carry on during hard times, and be the master of their mind and spirit."

His mouth curved into a lopsided grin. "You never cease to amaze me, lass." He shook his head. "I truly regret not having the chance to meet your family. You're young, lass; yet the wisdom of the elders fills your thoughts and grace your words. Your mentors must truly be the wisest of all."

She smiled. "My people also believe it takes wisdom to know wisdom." With that said, she made her way across the deck, to her cabin.

"Raven," he called after her, his voice mellow.

She turned to face him. His lips curled into a slow smile, the cleft in his chin growing deeper. She waited for him to speak, but he remained silent. His eyes said it all, surveying her with longing, then returning his gaze to lock with hers once again.

She raised a brow and moistened her lips with a smooth glide of her tongue. "Sleep well, Braiton." With a slight flick of her head, she tossed her dark mane from her shoulders and continued to her quarters.

Braiton was mesmerized by the easy sway of her hips. He wiped his sweaty palms on his breeches; only moments ago they were dry. Turning to look out over the water, he puffed on his pipe, his thoughts a vibrant mass of excited flurry. The way she looked, spoke, sauntered away, stirred him to the very core of his being. What was the power she possessed?

No other woman moved him like she did, drove him wild inside with desire. Passion mounted within just talking to her, his senses coming alive with her mere presence. The smell of her perfume, the rustle of her skirt, all of it left him with an overwhelming yearning to taste her charms, feel the warmth of her body beneath his. His loins distended with the slightest thought of her. His heart raced, his mouth went dry with the things he imagined her doing…to him…with him.

Even now he envisioned her opening her cabin portal and returning to him wearing only a sheer robe. Her long, slender legs would take easy strides toward him, shapely hips outlined beneath the translucent material. She would open the negligee, revealing all her womanly allure, and slip it off her shoulders. Down her back it would glide, spilling in a heap around her delicate ankles. The moon would cast a glow to her bronzed flesh, the wind playing with the dark curls, like the enchantress in the mythical legends he read as a lad. She'd be his goddess of the sea, standing naked on his deck. His throat tightened.

"All is well, m'lord," a deep voice boomed, dragging him from his fantasy.

He snapped from his thoughts, his flesh burning and spun around to find Captain Kirby standing behind him. He shook his head to clear it and straightened his collar.

"I'm sorry, Captain, come again."

"I said, all is well," Kirby repeated, then searched Braiton's face. "And is all well with you, m'lord?"

He nodded, pinching the bridge of his nose with a thumb and forefinger. "I'm just a wee bit tired." He straightened his shoulders and his waistcoat. "So, if all is as well as you say, then I will retire to my cabin."

Kirby tipped his hat. "Very good, m'lord. Sleep well."

He chuckled sardonically. "Aye, Captain, I will try."

****

The dawn faithfully lit the sky, leaving the morning dew to cling like a veil of moisture on the portholes of the tiny vessel. Braiton rapped upon his lady's portal.

"May I enter, my lady?"

"Yes," Raven called out.

He found her sitting on the bunk, a breakfast tray upon her lap, and eating a bowl of porridge. His eyes rested for a moment on the cleavage fully erupting from the neckline of her nightwear. Again strong emotions assailed his control. He pulled his eyes away and cleared his throat.

"We'll be docking in Bunratty within the hour, lass. And unless you take pleasure in watching me defend your honor, I suggest you clothe yourself a wee bit more modestly," he teased.

She smiled up at him. "I better not waste a moment then." She put aside the tray, swept off the quilt, and stood with her back to him. "Would you undo the buttons for me, please?"

He cleared his throat again. "Perhaps I should send for Molly."

She lifted her hair from her neck. "You will do."

His hands shook as he unfastened each button. With each slip of a tiny pearl through the hole, her smooth, naked spine came into view.

She spun around to face him, the nightgown slipping off her shoulders. "*Ashoge.*"

He turned and made his way to the portal. "Remember, within the hour."

"I will be ready. You have my word."

From the corner of his eye he saw the nightgown fly through the air and land on the bunk. He swallowed hard knowing she stood unclothed.

"Now, where are those bloomers," he heard her say before he rushed out the door and slammed it behind him.

****

Raven stood beside Braiton as *The Wee Lassie* approached the shores of Bunratty, wearing an elegant aqua dress trimmed with deep blue lace. Molly did her hair up, curls cascading down her neck.

Braiton looked at her and frowned. "The neckline of that frock doesn't hide much more than your nightwear."

"According to Tilly, it is the latest fashion from Paris."

He grunted. "And the cause, no doubt, for the men in France to challenge each other to constant duels."

"I could change."

He shook his head. "There's not the time, lass." He pointed to the carriage parked at the end of the dock they now neared. "There be Rory, himself, waiting for us."

She sighed. "I am sorry you are not pleased with the way I am dressed, my *shikaa*."

"I am very pleased, my lady, just not so happy you'll be pleasing Rory as well." He tugged at his collar and straightened his jacket. "That man leers at you like a hungry wolf."

"He is your friend, and I am sure he means no harm."

"And you are very generous to defend him after he cornered you in the library as he did, during his last visit to Shannonbrook."

She bit the inside of her lip. "About that night, how much of the conversation did you hear?"

He arched a brow. "How much I heard is irrelevant. That it never happens again is imperative."

Rory met them ashore and took her arm. She glanced at her husband, his clenched jaw a clear indicator he was displeased. Her father did something similar whenever another man paid too much attention to her mother. For a moment her heart soared at the thought he was jealous of another male's attention toward her. She freed herself from Rory's arm and moved beside Braiton. He smiled and put a possessive arm around her waist, pulling her closer.

Rory chuckled. "Good idea, old man. Keep a close watch on her, for every man will want to dance with her at the ball tonight." He cast a devilish grin her way. "I, myself, fully intend to keep you dancing until the wee hours of the morning."

"Don't you ever tire of throwing the blarney, Rory," Braiton quipped, assisting her into the carriage.

"Why you pierce me to the quick, old friend, implying I'd throw a line at your lady." Rory arched a brow. "Or is it you're too blind to see her beauty."

"I am neither old nor blind," Braiton said, climbing into the carriage beside her. "Just tired of your disrespect." Rory opened his mouth to protest, and Braiton raised a hand to silence him. "Save your breath to cool your porridge."

Rory nodded and took a seat opposite Braiton, but sent her a playful wink.

Raven gazed out the window, wanting to appear absorbed in the sights of the city. Rory, however, would not let it rest.

"My sister, Joleena is very interested to meet you, my lady."

She turned to look his way, wishing she could wipe the mischievous grin off his face.

Rory leaned back in his seat. "Though I must warn you, she had high hopes in snagging Braiton for herself."

Her heart sank to her toes. Meeting Joleena O'Neill now became the last thing she wished to do. With dampened spirits, she glanced again out the window and chewed on her bottom lip. No doubt

Joleena was sophisticated and beautiful, a true Irish lady, well suited to be a lord's wife. Her temples throbbed, and she closed her eyes with the pain.

"What is it, Raven," Braiton whispered, his hand coming to rest on hers. "Are you ill?"

She glanced at Rory first, to see if he heard Braiton's words. His head rested back against the carriage seat, and his eyes were closed. Relieved he slept, she answered her husband.

"My head hurts."

"Rest on my shoulder, then," Braiton offered, moving closer.

Their thighs touched and a bolt of heat coursed through her body. She felt the muscles through his breeches and inhaled the clean scent of his cologne, a mixture of musk and spice.

"What's bothering you, lass?" he whispered against her temple.

"I just want...just want..." she choked on the words.

"Want what, my lady? All I have is already at your disposal."

"I want you to be proud of me," she managed without breaking into tears.

He squeezed her shoulder. "I am, Raven."

She swallowed hard the lump growing in her throat. "You have been so kind to me, so caring. I would never want to bring shame upon you, especially in front of your friends," she said, neglecting to admit her concerns were mainly about Joleena O'Neill.

"You won't, Raven."

"You sound so sure."

"That's because I am." He planted a kiss upon her forehead. "You're a clever, resourceful, warrior, my lady, with much determination and spirit." He chuckled. "God knows you've set me back upon my heels more than once." He pushed a wayward curl from her forehead.

"I have every confidence in you, lass. Lord and Lady O'Neill will find you charming. And you needn't worry about matching wits with Joleena, because there's no problem there." He lowered his mouth to her ear. "She's one of the featherheads I spoke of."

She giggled. "Like her brother," she whispered.

Braiton chuckled. "Aye, it seems to run in the family. Though Lord and Lady O'Neill are warm, generous folks and cannot be responsible for the boorish ways of their children." He pulled back to look at her. "Feeling better now?"

She smiled. "Much, thank you, my *shikaa*."

They rode the rest of the way to Glenview in silence, her head quite comfortable resting on Braiton's shoulder. The ache at her temples left with his reassurance. It was all she needed to feel confident enough to meet the O'Neills...especially Joleena.

Chapter Fifteen

Raven was nudged awake by her husband's gentle hand upon her arm. "We've arrived at Glenview, lass."

She sat upright and straightened the full skirt, then smoothed the wisps of hair escaping her upsweep.

He gave her an encouraging smile. "You look radiant, my lady."

The carriage rounded a corner onto a cobblestone path and halted in front of an elegant mansion of white stone. The grounds were perfect, manicured, lush and green. Several different types of rosebushes adorned the long path to the front door.

Braiton, always the gallant man, extended a hand to help her descend from the carriage. Taking each step carefully, not to trip on the hem of her skirt and make a fool of herself in front of his friends, she kept her gaze on her feet.

When she glanced up, she locked eyes with Joleena O'Neill. The woman's gold-flecked orbs studied her, their strange color piercing and cold. Porcelain skin, high cheekbones, and a head full of copper ringlets completed Joleena's visage as the classic Irish lass. While introductions were being made, her heart raced. Featherhead or not, Joleena fit right into Braiton's life, would know how to decorate Shannonbrook and complement the title of Lady of Limerick.

Joleena forced a hospitable smile her way and neared Braiton, flashing him a warmer smile, eyes pools of seduction.

"You, my dear man, have been way too scarce." She placed a familiar hand upon his arm. "Have you forgotten all the fun we have together?" She leaned into him, moistening her thin red lips with a slow swipe of her tongue. "Let's go inside where we can talk more private. I have so much to catch you up on."

The other woman's bold stance caught her off guard. Though Molly swore no woman shared her husband's heart, Raven was not so sure. *Was Joleena in fact, a serious contender before Braiton was forced to wed?* At any rate, Joleena's behavior mirrored her brother's disrespect for the bonds of marriage. And since neither of them knew her and Braiton's was one of convenience, their actions were disgraceful.

Braiton was polite in the way he disengaged himself from Joleena's grasp and extended an elbow to her. "Raven and I would be very interested in what's been going on at Glenview."

She was sure Joleena did not want to catch up on things with her present, but she admired the way her husband put the other woman in her place. Proud of Braiton and thankful for his keen observation, her shoulders relaxed. She smiled up at him and accepted his arm.

Joleena's face flushed and to cover her humiliation at being rejected she cackled out a most nervous giggle while reaching for Rory's arm.

"Aye, we must all get acquainted, and reacquainted." She looked up at her brother. "'Tisn't that right, Rory?"

"Aye," Rory agreed, escorting Joleena toward the path to the mansion. In passing Raven heard him say, "Careful, little sister, your claws are showing."

****

After tea, Rory showed her and Braiton to the

bedchamber they would share while at Glenview. It was a spacious room done in burgundy and gold. The servants had already unpacked their bags, her accessories and toiletries arranged on the dressing table for her ease.

"I didn't think the chamber Braiton usually occupies on his visits here would be appropriate for a newly wedded couple," Rory explained, casting Braiton a devilish grin. "This room houses a much bigger bed."

"It is all so beautiful," she gasped, admiring the wood carvings along the bed post.

"Then I've chosen well," Rory said.

She fingered the delicate lace trimming the canopy. "Yes, thank you."

"I only wish to please you while you're our guest, my lady," Rory said. "I believe I've accomplished that much, at least."

"Yes, you have," she said, glancing up. "I will be very comfortable here." She turned to look at Braiton. "How about you, my *shikaa*?"

Rory turned to Braiton. "I'm sure your husband is comfortable wherever you are, my lady."

"Aye, 'tis the truth," Braiton said, drops of moisture clinging to his forehead.

She did not think he looked or sounded so convincing.

Rory slapped Braiton on the shoulder. "Not to worry, old man. This room is secluded from the rest of the house so you two will have complete privacy."

She felt the heat rise to her cheeks.

Rory turned his attention on her. "As you see Sinead already unpacked your belongings." He gestured to the tiny room branching off from the chamber. "A warm bath awaits you in there, my lady." Dipping his head, he backed his way to the door. "I will leave you two to freshen up a bit before dinner."

Securing the door behind Rory, Braiton sighed and sat down on the edge of the bed with a frown. “Well, it looks like we’ll be roommates while we’re here, lass.”

Her voice wavered. “Is that so disturbing to you?”

His square jaw tensed. “Aye, very disturbing.”

She made a dismissing gesture toward the door. “Then perhaps you should ask Rory for another room.”

“Nay, lass.” He stroked his chin, regarding her carefully. “That would be an unwise move.”

She managed to reply through stiff lips. “Then it looks like we are stuck with each other.” She gathered her toiletries together. “Now, if you will excuse me, I will take my bath.”

He had gone downstairs ahead of her, sending Molly up to help her dress. While Molly arranged her hair into a low chignon at the base of her neck, she thought back to the conversation she and Braiton had aboard the ship before docking. “I will wear the rose colored gown tonight, Molly. The one with the modest neckline.”

“Very good, m’lady,” Molly agreed, putting the finishing touches to her hair.

****

Braiton waited for Raven at the bottom of the staircase, eyes locking with hers as she descended each step. The unpretentious décolletage of her gown did little to conceal the fullness of her breasts. His wife was a beautiful and enchanting woman men admired and desired. Whatever she wore couldn’t diminish or hide the natural curves and splendor of her perfect body. Her shapely form held the promise and excitement of love and passion, in the way she walked, smiled, talked, and the demure way she cast her eyes.

Mother of God, I even love the way she laughs.

Braiton's eyes went to her lips, full and moist. He remembered their warm sweetness, the delight he felt in kissing them. Heaven. Ecstasy. Her cheeks flushed a deep pink like the rose of her gown, and the twinkle in her sapphire eyes ignited a flame deep within him.

He extended a hand to her. "You look lovely, lass."

She smiled. "And what of the neckline?"

He glanced at the front of her gown, throat going dry. "Much better, my lady."

Upon entering the dining hall, he escorted her to the head table and introduced her to their host, his dear friend, Shamus O'Neill. Her curtsy nearly brought her to the floor, and he stifled a smile. She must have practiced her bow.

"Rise, my lady," Shamus said. "I have no higher a title than your husband."

"But you are of many more years, my lord. I have been taught to respect the wisdom of the elders."

Shamus extended a hand. Braiton compared the contrast between the elder man's bony white fingers against her darker digits.

"I am honored to be invited to your home," she said.

Shamus gestured to the chair beside him. "Sit, my lady. I wish to speak with you while we dine." He reached for his wine goblet, raising it with a shaky hand to his lips. "Tell me about your family."

Braiton made his way to take the seat opposite her. She sipped her wine with an elegant manner, a beautiful addition to the meal.

"My father, Proud Eagle, is the chief of our tribe, and my mother is of English decent."

"Then you are what the Americans refer to as a half-breed," Joleena said, pronouncing *half-breed* like she'd tasted poison.

Braiton's hackles rose in defense for his wife, and he glared at Joleena from across the table.

Joleena's topaz colored eyes rounded, feigning innocence. "Well, 'tis true."

Raven sat rigid in her chair. "That reference is used by some."

"I don't care much for the word, myself," Shamus snapped at his daughter.

"I don't either," Braiton agreed, sending an encouraging smile to his wife. She forced one in return, and his heart went out to her. She was the bravest, most resourceful woman he'd ever known, and he wouldn't allow her dignity to be wounded.

"Tell me more about your people, my lady," Shamus urged.

A soft, loving curve touched her lips. "They are all good hunters and respect every part of their kill, using it to benefit the tribe."

Joleena grunted, her face a marble image of contempt. "I hear they have little respect for the lives of others."

He clenched a fist under the table, desperate to control his anger. "How have you heard this?" he challenged.

"I've read snippets here and there about the Indians and their unmerciful, savage tactics," Joleena sneered.

His wife stiffened as though she'd been struck, which is exactly what he wished to do to Joleena. Had Shamus reddened her bottom more as a child, perhaps she wouldn't have grown up to be such a wretched brat.

Raven answered with staid calmness he knew she didn't feel. He could tell she chose her words.

"Not all Indians are from the same tribe. Just as in any community, there are the good and the bad. My people are peaceful." Her tone was clear, strong. "If you are interested to know the truth, I will be glad to tell you over tea one afternoon while I am here."

"Perhaps," Joleena said smugly. "If I'm interested." She gestured around the room. "I can imagine how grand all this must appear to you, coming from where you have."

Raven took an audible breath. "It is not the size but substance of where you live that is everything." She nodded. "It is true, your home is lovely, but having riches is not where happiness lies. To serve each other and each new day with all your heart, matters most."

He caught her gaze, her eyes filled with raw hurt. She gave him a nod and smiled, in spite of the pain and embarrassment she had to be experiencing. He returned the gesture, proud she remained poised, intelligent, dignified, and controlled while putting Joleena in her place. She accomplished exposing the other woman for what she was. He couldn't have done better himself.

Throughout dinner he watched her laugh and talk with Shamus. The elder man was riveted, quite enthralled with the conversation. She was a quality woman, and she was his wife. Each day he became more and more aware of the tangible bond between them. Since she'd come into his life, all his senses leapt alive, he was drawn to her like a magnet. He wanted her. Even now he wished to take her to their bedchamber and make love to her. The intoxicating musk of her body was like a drug, lulling him to euphoria.

Ah, that I could be carried away by your sweet caress and searing kisses.

But as fast as the notion surfaced, he thrust it from his thoughts. His secret horror crept in to tarnish all that shined, squelched the hope of love burning within him. There was no other choice but to keep his distance from her as much as he could, remain indifferent. *Oh, if that were possible.*

He lowered his gaze to his plate and finished eating the rest of his dinner.

Raven listened to the conversations surrounding her, smiling when their idle chatter included her. The food she consumed was tasteless. She swallowed each mouthful with difficulty. When her husband looked her way, she forced a smile to please him. But inside she cried out to be rid of all those around her.

She wished to leave the dining hall and run to the solace of her room. Her head pounded, and she longed to be free from the bodice stays cutting into her ribs. But most of all she wanted to be away from the unnerving stares of Joleena O'Neill. The little witch impaled her with cold eyes. Hatred, potent and evil, sizzled from the woman all through dinner.

Shamus O'Neill escorted her into the ballroom, and she suffered to be polite and concentrate on what he said.

"You fascinate me, Lady Shannon." She sat beside him in a chair by the fire. "'Tis interesting hearing you converse about your culture, and I don't know when I've enjoyed talking with a woman as much as with you this evening."

"Are not Irish women interesting?"

"Most care little for the lay of the land or from whence their forefathers came. They leave such matters to their husbands and indulge instead with the frills of society." He grunted. "Afraid to get their hands dirty, the lot of them, and those that do, have little in their favor."

"Then would it not be wise to help the children learn to read and write, so they might better themselves as they grow to be adults?"

He cocked his head sideways. "You believe commoners should be educated?"

"Yes, both males and females. An education should be everyone's right."

He grunted. "'Twould be just a waste of time, lass."

She sat forward in her chair. "I think not. Those who have been taught have the means to find jobs, earn a better wage, not be cold, hungry, and in need of others to care for them. They can be a part of giving to their family, village, and helping it to prosper as well." The elder man was fully intent on her words, and this gave her the courage to speak her mind further.

"When I was just a girl, my mother told me of a man named Abraham Lincoln. As a boy, Lincoln was very poor and lived in a home made of logs. He walked miles in the cold to school, barefooted, because his family could not afford him shoes. He studied his lessons by the light of one small candle and grew to be a wise and important man. He became President of my country, freeing the black man from slavery and doing many more wonderful things for America. All Lincoln became and in turn accomplished, would not have happened if he did not learn from books. His education allowed him to go forward, and being all he could be, he helped others as well. This can be true for us all."

Shamus's eyes filled with admiration. "Your intelligence becomes your beauty, my lady. What a pity I am but a tired old man, for if I were once more in my youth, your husband would have much to fear."

"Well, I am still in my youth, and the music begins," Rory said, coming to stand beside her chair and extending a hand. "Shall we, my lady?"

"I should dance the first dance with my husband, but I thank you kindly, Rory."

"Your husband is rather otherwise engaged, my lady," he said, gesturing to where Braiton stood.

She glanced across the room to find Braiton. He and Lord Wade were having a heated discussion.

Braiton's brows knit together in a frown, his posture stiff and unyielding. Lord Wade appeared angry. His lips clamped tight, face strained. The evening she met Lord Wade at Shannonbrook, he did not act the temperamental sort, which was how he looked now. Something was very wrong between the two men and it concerned her.

Rory repeated. "May I have this dance, Raven?"

"Oh, go, have a whirl," Shamus encouraged. "My son won't bite."

Silently she begged to differ, but gave Rory a polite smile and accepted his outstretched hand. Two steps onto the dance floor she regretted her decision. Rory held her tight around the waist and very close. Not really a dancer, she found the nearness of him disturbing, not to mention having a hard time following the steps to the music.

He bent to whisper in her ear. "Every woman here is green-eyed with envy because their men haven't taken their eyes off you."

She pulled away. "I think that is unlikely."

He gazed deep into her eyes. "I fool you not, my lady, you're the most enchanting woman here, and your husband is a fool for leaving you unattended, delicious bait for all the hungry wolves."

She arched a brow. "You being the hungriest of all, sir?"

He chuckled. "Nay, my lady. I thought, as Braiton's dearest friend, 'tis up to me to step in and take over."

She wiggled free from his grasp. "I appreciate your gallantry, Rory, but I am quite capable of looking out for myself."

She left him on the dance floor and made her way through the crowd to the set of veranda doors. Warm and agitated, she believed a breath of fresh air would help, and pushed the doors wide to enter upon a stone terrace. Making her way to the rail, she gazed out into the darkness and inhaled.

Rory came from behind to join her. "All of this overlooks a most elegant garden," he said, gesturing to the landscape ahead.

"I should very much enjoy seeing it then, by day."

He moved closer, so close their shoulders touched. "'Tis my mother's project. Her creation and pride."

She stepped to the opposite end of the balcony, putting distance between them. "I look forward to meeting your mother in the morning. I am sorry she was not feeling well tonight."

He followed her. "Aye, well, mother always gets out of sorts around this time of year. You see, 'tis the anniversary of my brother, Corbin's death."

"I am so sorry, I had no idea you had a brother."

"Half, actually," he corrected, pushing aside a wayward curl from her forehead.

She stepped back, uneasy with his boldness. "I can only imagine the sorrow a parent feels after the death of a child. I truly pity her loss."

"What's a pity is that Braiton met you first." He searched her face. "You deserve a man who appreciates you, lass. Who smothers you with attention and loves you with a passion."

She raised a defiant chin. "My husband *is* that man, sir, and at this moment probably wonders where I am."

Rory pulled her close and bent his head to kiss her.

She pushed him away and with a pounding heart ran from the veranda to scope the room for Braiton. She found him still speaking to Lord Wade. *Did you even know I was gone from the room?*

She took a deep breath to calm herself before she approached the two men. By the time she reached her husband's side, his business with Lord

Wade concluded. Morgan spoke a few polite pleasantries to her before his departure. Braiton looked out of sorts, and her concern resurfaced for what transpired between them.

"What goes on, my *shikaa*?"

"'Tis a business problem, lass and nothing you need to concern yourself with."

"Are you treating me like a featherhead now?"

He frowned. "Nay, my lady."

"Then tell me what is wrong," she insisted.

He took her by the elbow and out to the terrace. She was relieved to see Rory was nowhere in sight.

"Lord Wade is a very prominent figure in England's import industry. His account with my warehouse is of an enormous sum, one that shouldn't be so high." He glanced ahead into the night. "Something is not correct, my lady."

"What do you think is not right, Braiton?"

"'Tis hard to put a finger on at this point, lass." He turned her way. "But I must look into the problem immediately." He searched her face. "Where did you run off to this evening?"

Her heart fluttered. *He did notice I was gone from the room.* "I just came out here for a breath of fresh air."

"Was all well with you, Raven?" he probed.

"All is fine," she lied, neglecting to mention Rory's bold advances. Her husband had enough on his mind at this time, she did not need to make matters worse.

He frowned. "Would you tell me if there *was* something bothering you, lass?"

She reached up and caressed the side of his face, changing the subject. "What bothers me right now is concern for your safety."

He caught her hand in his and bestowed a gentle kiss upon her knuckles. "I'll be fine, my lady, not to worry."

"When will you take care of this matter?"

"After the ball. I'm meeting Lord Wade in town for a late snout, and he said he'd explain his case further." He brought her hand to rest on his heart. "And I want you to lock your door while I'm gone, open it for no one but me."

She nodded in agreement. He did not have to ask her twice.

****

Raven lie in the center of the huge bed waiting for Braiton to return, eyes searching the shadows in the room, heart pounding in her ears. Her head still ached from the disastrous evening. First, dinner with Joleena, then the episode with Rory on the veranda, and now she worried for Braiton.

Why is he taking so long?

She squeezed her eyes closed, willing sleep to come. But all she managed to do was rehash the past few hours. As if in a trance, she danced around the ballroom floor with different partners, playing the part she agreed upon for Braiton's sake.

She was the perfect wife, the elegant Lady of Limerick. In spite of his pending problems with Lord Wade, Braiton put up the *devoted husband* front as well. He watched her dance with hawk-like eyes, never being far from her side, and then reclaiming her when the music stopped. She was desperate for each tune to end, for the evening to pass, so she could hide away in her chamber and Braiton could be through with the business at hand.

She opened her eyes and focused on the flames dancing in the fireplace. Memories of home filled her thoughts. She would sit in front of the fire-pit listening to her father tell stories about the coyote and the fox. The tales made her laugh and cry, held meaning and taught lessons. She wondered what her parents were doing now. Mother was probably bending over the fire, preparing a meal for her father. He would be cleaning his spear, glancing over at her with loving eyes.

They had the kind of love she admired and wished for herself. She remembered the nights she was sent to sleep at her grandmother's wickiup, so her parents could have time alone. Before she left she would hear her father ask her mother, "Will you dance for me tonight, my wife?" Her mother would flash him a demure smile and nod her head in agreement.

A wistful smile curved her lips with the fond memory, understanding now why they wanted to be alone. They were in love and yearned for the warmth and passion their bodies professed. She sighed, her smile broadening. How wonderful they are together.

Then as quick as her smile came, it faded. Her own loneliness crept up to surround her. Braiton gave her everything she could need or want, everything except love. Lost and empty inside she gulped, forcing back the hot tears of frustration scalding her eyes.

She shivered, snuggling beneath the quilt and praying despair would leave her heart and Braiton would return.

Chapter Sixteen

The tavern reeked of stale smoke and whiskey. Braiton followed Morgan Wade to a table in the corner of the dingy room. Sprawling his long legs to one side, Lord Wade sat back in his chair and lit his pipe.

"Aye, Lord Shannon," Morgan said between puffs. "I am purely distraught over the rising prices of your goods. French wines are costly, I agree. I also realize Ireland must import all her wine, but this isn't the case in England. We don't have to go through your channels, pay your high prices." Morgan sat forward. "I haven't wanted to deal directly with the French, my reasons being my reasons, but now you've grown too greedy, Lord Shannon."

He knew the damage Morgan could bring to his business if he were left unsatisfied. An import king, Lord Wade held great power amongst the other importers and exporters. Should he decide to pull his accounts, it stood to reason most others would follow.

The servant girl brought them each a whiskey and placed it on the table. He remained silent until she left, figuring a way to regain Morgan's trust. He took an audible breath.

"In all honesty, my lord, I know of no price increase. I've dealt fairly with you, as I do with all my clients. In truth, I have kept my fees the same."

"That is a lie, sir," Morgan accused, banging his fist upon the table. The glasses filled with whiskey jarred, the honey-colored liquid spilling over the rim.

"And I have with me the receipts to prove my case."

He squared his shoulders. "I should like to examine those receipts, my lord, since I'm being unjustly accused."

Morgan downed his drink then pulled a wad of crumpled papers from his vest pocket and threw them across the table. "I unjustly accuse no man, Lord Shannon."

He finished off his own drink then smoothed out the wrinkles and studied the receipts, anger swelling in his chest as he read each one. The handwriting scrawled across the paper wasn't that of his foreman and the price listed beside each item was an outrageous sum.

"I assure you, my lord, these prices are not correct."

"You're bloody hell right, they're not correct," Lord Wade snapped. "And unless something is done *to* correct them, I shall be forced to take my business elsewhere." He motioned for the waitress to bring them another round of whiskey.

"When I return to Limerick, I'll go over my books and the dealings pertaining to the goods you purchased."

Again the servant girl set down the drinks, her round, green eyes lingering on his. She cast him a demure smile. "Anythin' more I can be bringin' ye, me lord."

"Nay, lass," he mumbled, breaking eye contact.

Lord Wade dismissed the woman with a slight wave of his hand. "That'll be all for now." He chuckled. "It appears she's got an eye for you, my lord."

He frowned, picking up the second drink and taking a mouthful. "I am hardly interested, my own wife is quite enough woman for me to handle."

Morgan's laugh grew hardier. "Aye, that she is...quite enchanting. You're a lucky man, Shannon.

If I had that waiting for me at home, I'd find it hard to ever leave."

His personal business was his own, and he'd discuss it with no one. Combing a hand through his hair, he returned to the subject at hand. "I'll get to the bottom of this error, you have my word."

Morgan arched a brow. "All well and good to say, my lord, but what guarantee do I have you'll keep your word?"

He pulled a leather purse from his jacket pocket. "I will, at this very moment, square with you the overcharges from the readies of my personal funds. This should prove to you I conduct my business dealings in good faith." He searched Lord Wade's face. "Do you accept my offer, sir?"

"Aye, I do, Lord Shannon."

He sighed with relief and counted out payment in full.

Morgan called out to the waitress. "Bring us the entire bottle, lass." Smiling, he turned to Braiton. "Now we drink, my lord, and have us a hearty evening." Once the bottle was set upon the table, Morgan filled both of their glasses. "The night is young, and the whiskey flows plentiful to our table."

He returned the smile and obliged, not wishing to offend Lord Wade now that he regained his good graces. To refuse such hospitality would be a grave mistake. He drained each glass filled before him until his eyes blurred and the beat of his heart echoed in his ears. All resolve faded, and he laughed and enjoyed himself for the rest of the evening.

He didn't remember leaving the tavern or getting into the bian waiting to take him back to Glenview. Morgan Wade's assessment of Raven stuck in his thoughts. She waited for him now in bed. He laid his head back against the leather seat, and a deep longing for her coursed through his being. He envisioned her luscious mouth and pouting lips. They invited kisses and was his for the asking. 'Twas a perfect right he had to taste every part of her silky, bronzed flesh. His loins grew thick beneath the material of his breeches, wishing now to inhale her scent, feel the warmth of her flesh against his.

When the bian stopped in front of the O'Neill mansion, he stumbled up the walkway and to his room. Bracing himself against the wall, he knocked on the door.

"Raven, 'tis your husband. Open the door, lass, so I may behold you." He heard the patter of her bare feet on the hardwood floor, then the bolt released and the door opened. He smiled, his gaze roaming the length of her.

"Ah, there you are, *m'annachd,* my best beloved...especially so when you're naked and free beneath your dresses," he slurred.

Her face turned a deep shade of crimson. "Oh, hush, before you wake the entire household." She reached for his hand and pulled him into the room, bolting the door behind them.

He leaned against the wall, the room spun, and he cleared his throat.

She frowned. "You are full of spirits."

He smiled. He thought he did anyway. At this point he couldn't really feel his mouth. "Aye, lass, I am." He reached over and caressed her cheek with the back of his hand. "Your beauty leaves me breathless, *mo ghradh*, my dear."

"What you need is sleep, Braiton," she said, helping him over to the bed.

His body burned with desire. "Nay, my lady, what I need is you."

"Let me remove your jacket," she offered, slipping the coat off his shoulders and removing it from each arm. "And your boots," she said, kneeling at his feet to pull them off, one at a time, along with his stockings.

"Raven, look up at me," he whispered.

She raised her gaze to meet his. "It is time for you to sleep." She stood. "I have seen what drinking the fire water can do to a man."

He chuckled and reached for her hand. "Fire water, you say?"

She nodded. "It is what my people call the white man's drink."

He drew her close. "Aye, 'tis rightfully named, for a fire burns in me, *gu leoir*, plenty enough, for you."

"Braiton..."

"Nay, *monighean*, my lass, say not a word," he interrupted, placing a finger over her lips. "At this moment all I wish to do is taste your sweetness." He slipped the straps of her nightgown off her shoulders and pulled the garment down to her waist.

She gasped, the blush coloring her cheeks, and shielded her breasts with her hands.

He circled each of her wrists with his fingers, bringing her hands to her sides. "Nay, *mo ghradh*, don't hide now from me." He searched her face. "I'm a *duine*, a gentleman, and I'll not take from you, compromise you as the other did, but ask instead." Hungry desire spiraled through him. "Will you yield on this night to me, Raven?"

Raven's blood pounded in her brain, leapt from her heart, and made her knees tremble. With the tip of her tongue, she moistened her dry lips. "Yes," was her breathless response, and the only one he needed before he leaned in to suckle her breasts. His tongue teased and played with each hard peak. His lips left a trail of warmth in their path. She threw her head back, her entire being alive and aroused. Never did she known such pleasure existed. Everywhere he touched excited her flesh, set her deliciously on fire.

He pulled her down to meet him and captured

her mouth with a searing kiss. She tasted the sweetness of the whiskey on his tongue as it roamed the walls of her mouth. Her arms went up around his neck, and she leaned into him, his bulging loins pressed against her thigh.

"Raven, my Raven," he whispered into her mouth. "I want you." She pulled away, shocked at his declaration. But he drew her again into his strong embrace. "Nay, lass, don't be frightened, I'll not hurt you. I shall never hurt you," he whispered more tenderly while he slipped her nightgown off her hips and caressed her belly. His touch was a golden wave of passion tingling through her. Slowly, his hands moved downward, skimming either side of her hips and resting at her thighs. "Will you accept my burning body within yours?"

"Yes," again, all she could do was whisper, her flesh half ice, half flame.

She did not remember how their clothes ended up on the floor, or care how the two of them landed into bed. All she knew was how wonderful the tip of his finger circled her pulse of passion, teasing the tiny bud until it grew moist. Opening her thighs, his finger penetrated her, moving in and out. Passion piqued, she trembled, no longer able to disguise her body's reaction. Groaning with pleasure her arousal exploded, ripples of ecstasy spreading gusts of desire to every part of her being.

He rolled on top of her, spreading her legs wider with his knees. She arched her back and met his fullness, offering herself to him, completely.

"Aye, lass, that's the way now. 'Tis you who will let us soar together. 'Tis not like before. 'Tis not like before."

It was not like before, when she was taken against her will on the reservation. Braiton had asked, and she wanted to give…and give…and give.

He entered her and moaned with pleasure. "You

are so warm." Placing both hands beneath her hips, he pulled her up to meet him.

He was fully inside of her now, and she tightened around him, making him call out her name in a throaty whisper. She moved in unison to his thrusts, the two rocking faster and faster. Hurtled beyond the point of return, she dug her nails into his shoulders.

He shattered within her, hot juices bursting forth from his hardened shaft. As he filled her, he kissed each of her eyes, her nose, then captured her mouth.

"Did I hurt you, *mo nighean dubh,* my black-haired lass?"

"No," she whispered. His warm liquid trickled from her, leaving the inside of her thighs moist and sticky.

Spent, he rolled onto his back, his muscular chest rising and falling with each breath.

"Rest now," she said. He reached for her and drew her close. She sought comfort from the warmth of his body, reaching over to stroke the dark hair covering his chest. Indian men did not allow hair to cover their flesh. They found it offensive, and so a ceremony was performed at the first sign of manhood to pluck and destroy hair from growing. She liked the way hair looked on Braiton. The mustache above his lip, the hair upon his chest and thighs, added to his perfect sculpted body. He was as well proportioned as any warrior in her tribe.

"Raven," he groaned.

"I am here." She kissed his neck. "Now rest," she said again, closing her own eyes with contentment.

Together they drifted off to sleep.

****

A streak of sunlight found its way through the opening of the drapes adorning the veranda doors. She woke, dewy-eyed with the memory of the night before replaying in her mind. Her cheeks warmed with the thought of his fingers and lips teasing and caressing the most intimate parts of her body. He'd awakened and unleashed in her sensations she had no idea existed, taking her beyond her wildest dreams.

She listened to his heavy breathing, felt the beat of his heart beneath her palm, and wished she could start his day with a kiss. But he would not be as refreshed as she when he woke. The fire water had a way of making a body feel much worse than they did the night before. Perhaps it would be best not to disturb him.

She slid out of bed and tidied up the room, then performed her morning toilet at the wash basin. Donning a simple, deep purple dress with buttons at the front of the bodice, she brushed her hair till it shone and let it fall to her waist in a thick braid.

****

Slow, and with much pain, Braiton opened his eyes, vision blurred, his head pounded. There was no mistaking it; his head had been pummeled with a brick. He blinked his burning eyes into focus and groaned.

"Good morning, my *shikaa*. How does your head feel?"

He spotted her standing at the foot of the bed. She was dressed, looking radiant, and he was sure he would die. He groaned again and licked his dry lips. His mouth tasted like it was stuffed with cotton.

She moved to the side of the bed. "Ah, that bad?"

He nodded and squeezed his eyes shut. Even the sound of her voice made him flinch.

He heard her make her way to the wash basin to wet a cloth. She returned to swab his face and neck, then place the compress over his eyes.

"I thank you, lass." His own voice vibrated in his

ears, and he swallowed hard the bile rising to choke him. “I can’t remember the last time I’ve had that much whiskey to drink.” He frowned. “Truth be told, right now I can’t even recall how I got back to Glenview.”

She sat at the edge of the bed. “Do you remember anything at all about last night?”

“Nay, not a thing,” he whispered. He raised the cloth to look at her. “Care to enlighten me?” Her hesitation worried him. “Sweet Mother of God, Raven. We didn’t, I didn’t compromise—”

“No, you did not compromise me.” It was not an out and out lie, Raven told herself. She stood, making her way to the veranda doors and pulled aside a corner of the drapes, gazing out across the lawn. His outburst had her thoughts traveling back to the night of the storm aboard *The Sweet Maureen.*

He was upset then—as he was now—that something had transpired between them. He'd made it very clear, there must be nothing to prevent the marriage from being annulled within a year’s time, or that either of them breaks the agreement made.

He sighed in relief. “Thank God.”

Suddenly the spacious bedchamber became very small, the walls closing in on her. She could no longer bear to even look at him, the closeness of last night dissolving like the cubes of sugar she dropped into tea. She fought the tears stinging the back of her throat and went to the door.

“I will get you a mug of coffee. It will help to relieve the pain from the fire water.”

“Fire water,” he repeated. “You called the whiskey that last night, didn’t you?”

She turned to look at him, his dark hair in disarray, eyes red-rimmed and glassy.

“Yes, it is the name my people have for the white man’s drink.”

“Aye, I remember you explaining that to me.” He

frowned. "You helped to remove my jacket and my boots," he went on. His frown deepened. "Did you also remove my clothes?"

"You removed them yourself, Braiton," she supplied. "I did not think you were in any condition to sleep on the chaise," she motioned to the lounge by the fire. "So I shared the bed. But I was not compromised," she reassured him again. "So there is no need for you to be concerned further on that matter."

He groaned again. "Why the hell didn't I have the good sense to just pass out somewhere?"

It was all she could take; her pride shredded into tiny bits. She had to get out of the room. Away from him, away from the bed they shared before she choked on the sobs lodged in her throat.

"I am going for your coffee now."

In closing the door behind her, she overheard his angry voice.

"Damn, damn, damn."

Chapter Seventeen

Raven discovered tea time with Evangeline O'Neill quite pleasant. Lady O'Neill was not the drunken sort Rory led her to believe. But in her large hazel eyes there was a deep and profound sadness.

"Again, I must apologize for not meeting you upon your arrival," Evangeline said, taking a bite of a sugar cookie.

"Please, do not be concerned over it further."

Evangeline's thin gray brows knit together. "'Twas quite inhospitable of me, Lady Shannon. I am the hostess and you a guest. My dear husband Shamus is right, I am to be ashamed of my behavior."

She took a sip of the tea. "But I understand the reasons why this time might not be a happy one for you, my lady."

Evangeline sighed. "Aye, I see you've heard some talk."

She nodded. "Rory told me of his brother's death."

"Corbin was his half-brother." Evangeline corrected and sat back in her chair. "I suppose 'twould be only fair I explain it all to you."

"Only if you want to, my lady."

Evangeline gave her a timid smile. "Strange enough, I do, Lady Shannon. For a reason I cannot clarify, I believe you'd understand."

"I should very much like the chance to try, but I would also like you to call me, Raven."

Evangeline smiled. "Only if you'll call me Evie."

She returned the smile. “Agreed.”

Evangeline clasped her thin white hands together in her lap. “When I met Shamus he was a widower. Rory was only three and Joleena not quite two months old. The first Lady O’Neill, Ester was her name, died giving birth to Joleena. Shamus hired me to be the nanny.” She waved a hand above her head. “Needless to say, as time went on, things developed between us and within a year’s time we were married.” She paused to take a sip of her tea.

“I became with child soon after we wed. Corbin was the apple of my eye. Shamus, too, felt a special kinship with the lad, both being two peas in a pod. But as Corbin grew, Rory and Joleena became jealous of him, almost vindictive. At first Shamus and I just thought ’twas sibling rivalry, but I started to see things differently.” She sighed again. “Well, Shamus, of course, didn’t agree when I came to him with my worries. A father never wants to believe his children are capable of doing evil things.”

She frowned. “What evil things did they do, Evie?”

Evangeline shrugged. “Nothing one could really put a finger on, but there was something wicked in the way Rory and Joleena ganged up on Corbin. First Joleena broke or stole his toys, and then there were the humiliating beatings. And my son would never tattle, never complain, but when I discovered the marks on his body, he admitted Rory stripped him naked and beat him with a switch whenever he pleased.”

“Did you tell Shamus?”

“Aye, but again, he didn’t want to believe ’twas anything more than an older brother keeping his younger brother in line while the father was away.” She sighed. “And Shamus was often away.”

“Rory said this time of year was the anniversary of Corbin’s death.”

"Aye," Evangeline agreed. "'Twas six years ago, on the morning of the hunt the accident happened. Corbin and Rory had gone out together and within an hour's time, Rory returned with Corbin draped across his saddle, dead."

She gasped. "How?"

"According to Rory, he and Corbin split up, in order to corner the fox. For some reason Corbin dismounted from his horse and decided to continue on foot. Rory mistook him for the fox and shot Corbin."

Her eyes widened. "How terrible for Rory...for you...for all of you."

"Truth be told, Raven, Rory didn't seem all that troubled over the accident." Evangeline smirked. "If indeed 'twas an accident."

She sat forward in her seat. "What gives you a reason to think it was not?"

Evangeline shrugged again. "I haven't absolute proof of any one thing, I would say 'tis a mother's intuition. All I do know, is Rory wasted no time at all in consoling Corbin's fiancée, Rebecca Hennessey, the daughter of Shamus's good friend Angus. After Angus and his wife Anna died in a carriage accident, Rebecca came to live with us as my husband's ward, until she was of age to run her own affairs. The estate her parents left her in Dublin. But as time went on, Rebecca and Corbin fell in love and planned to marry. Rory envied Corbin and not long after his death, Rory persuaded a grieving Rebecca to marry him. They were wed the following year."

"Rory's married?"

"Was," Evangeline corrected. "Rebecca died two years ago."

"How?"

Evangeline took an audible breath. "Rebecca's parents left her a handsome amount of money and of course the estate in Dublin, as I've already mentioned. 'Twas there Rory and Rebecca moved after their nuptials. As her husband, Rory took over her finances and had a free hand in everything she owned.

"About six months after they wed, Rebecca summoned Shamus with the complaint Rory was running the till into the ground with his gambling. Well, Shamus and Rory had it out with each other, and my husband believed he'd mended the problem. He returned to Glenview and neither of us heard a word more on the trouble, but about a month later Rory sent word to Joleena, inviting her to come to Dublin for a visit. Joleena stayed for a week and one afternoon she persuaded Rebecca to go riding."

"Rebecca did not like to ride?"

Evangeline wrinkled her nose. "Nay, she was never an accomplished horsewoman, and Joleena knew that. Why she insisted on them going riding doesn't set well with me to this day. Nor why Rory allowed Rebecca to go." She stood and gazed out the large solarium window. "'Twas then Rebecca fell off her horse and broke her neck." She turned to face Raven. "And Rory, sole executer of Rebecca's estate, went through all she owned in a matter of months. He even had to sell the Dublin property in order to cover his gambling debts. He had no money and no where to go, so he came back to live at Glenview." Evangeline returned to her seat.

"Now, you know it all, Raven," she concluded. "Hopefully, you won't judge me for my actions." She cast a weak smile. "The only way I can get through the hunt each year is to become numb, disconnected. And the rum helps me to do that." The elder woman's lips thinned. "In fact, sometimes 'tis the only way I can live with my step-children."

****

Raven recalled the disturbing conversation with Evangeline O'Neill throughout most of the day and into the evening. Coupled with the bodice stays piercing her sides, and listening to the large woman on the Opera House stage bellow her song in a foreign tongue, she was quite miserable. The performer's bodice looked stiffer than hers, how the singer could get enough air into her lungs to sing the high notes, was something she wondered about. Braiton sat beside her and leaned over on occasion to explain the story's meaning, which was played out in song. The characters dressed in costumes and the instruments accompanying them were all quite fascinating. Actually, she enjoyed many of the scenes, when she was not self-conscious of her stupidity to understand the plot.

Joleena giggled every time Braiton translated the words, adding to her shame. The O'Neill woman's rude behavior caused Raven's stomach to churn, twist into knots. Had she not been a long time friend of her husband, she would have ended the humiliating cackling with a slap across Joleena's prudish face. After learning from Evangeline the spiteful ways of the O'Neill offspring, clouting Joleena would give her great satisfaction.

Joleena's dainty, porcelain hand touched Braiton's arm now and then, as she conversed about the play. This was done on purpose to aggravate Raven. She looked down at her own hands and grimaced. Though they were small, the nails clean and cut even; they were also tanned and weathered. Not the hands of a featherhead. They did more than hold a china cup at tea, a book, or an embroidery needle. She knew of Braiton's disgust for the featherheads, he boasted about his dislike many times, yet she was not what he wanted either.

How can I expect any man to want a tainted woman, such as I am? Used goods, is what I am now, and no man would want the shame of having me as their wife.

She realized Braiton's advances the night before were the cause of too much of the white man's drink, and she was repulsed at herself for giving into his drunken desires. Now, she hoped he would never remember what happened between them. It would only cause him anxiety and her embarrassment. She wanted nothing to change their agreement, or to keep her from leaving for England when the time came. Living in an unloving marriage, a union of convenience only, was something she did not want for her life.

The woman's performance ended and the people in the theater stood, clapping their hands and yelling, "Bravo." The singer bowed and threw kisses to the crowd. Then she was presented with a huge bouquet of roses. After the gas lamps were lit, Raven walked arm and arm with Braiton to the lobby and smiled like a good wife when he introduced her to others he knew. No one would ever guess the real status between her and her husband. To those looking on, they appeared a happy, newly wed couple.

At dinner, she ate without tasting the food, continuing to smile at whatever was said. She noticed Evangeline did not come down to dinner. The poor woman lived an unhappy life, and after all these years, too tired to smile when she did not feel like it, as Raven was doing. She frowned. When did she become such a fake? She supposed it was easy to do when practiced daily.

How time had a way of changing a person. She thought back to the first time Molly helped her bathe. She'd pulled away, embarrassed for another to wash her body. Now she stood with arms out, while Molly rubbed scented oils into her flesh. She did not even comb her own hair anymore. What would her father think of such behavior, about the things she'd grown accustomed to?

Morgan Wade broke through her thoughts. "Lady Shannon, as always, you look lovely."

She looked deep into his large dark eyes. They shone with genuine kindness and sincerity. Of all the people she had met, thus far, Lord Wade was the one she liked best, he was not artificial. "I thank you, my lord."

"I thought you'd like to know I sent the letter for your sister on ahead to England with one of my assistants. Miss Eagle should be receiving it any day now."

"I cannot thank you enough for all you have done." She sighed. "I miss my sister and brother so much, and up until now I worried how they were getting on."

Morgan gave her arm a paternal pat. "I know they've felt the same about you. Your letter will relieve their thoughts as well. And when I return to England, I will make it a point to tell them how well you've taken to your position as Lady of Limerick."

"May I speak free and in confidence to you, sir?"

Morgan nodded. "Always, my lady."

"I know of the troubles you and my husband are having, and I would want you to know, Braiton is a good and honest man. Whatever happened to make the problems, I have no doubt he will correct. I only ask you give him the chance to do so."

Morgan smiled. "Lord Shannon and I have come to mutual terms at this point, so no need for you to fret further on the matter." He searched her face and the heat rose to her cheeks beneath his scrutiny. "Your husband is a fortunate man to have you, my lady. If I were but a few years younger…" his words trailed off, and he shook his head. "Forgive me."

The same words Lord O'Neill spoke, though she wondered if they knew she was spoiled goods, would they still feel the same? "None is needed, my lord," she said, forcing a smile. "Thank you again."

She was relieved when the time came for her to retire to her chamber. She undressed and put another log on the fire. Too tired to care when Braiton would come up to the room, she slipped beneath the quilt and marveled in her quiet warm surroundings. All she wanted to do now was sleep.

****

Braiton was gone when Raven awoke, a blanket draped over the lounge by the fireplace the only indication he had been in the room. Molly bustled in with a cheery smile upon her plump face and hurried her out of the bed.

"Top o' the mornin' to you, m'lady." She pulled aside the quilt. "'Tis a fine day for a hunt."

She made a face and swung her legs off the side of the bed. "Oh, is that today?"

"Aye, m'lady," she said, busying herself around the room, setting out the riding habit and boots.

She stood, yawned, and stretched. "Where is Braiton?"

"Waitin' for you to join him downstairs," she said, helping her off with the nightgown. "Let's get you washed and dressed before his patience thins."

"It will do him good to wait," she mumbled.

Molly arched a brow. "'Tis not only him that waits, m'lady." She wet a cloth and washed her back. "Can't you hear the hounds all a howlin'?"

She nodded, hearing their cries. "Poor fox."

Molly dried her and slipped the camisole over her head. "Aye, but 'tis the way o' things."

"So, then I gather we will have fox for dinner?"

Molly frowned. "Oh, gracious nay, child. The fox is never eaten. The hunt is merely for sport."

She gasped. "Are you telling me the fox's life is to be ended, just for fun?"

Molly helped her on with the skirt. "Aye, m'lady."

"But why, Molly?"

Molly shrugged. "The hunters enjoy the challenge of bringin' the animal to bay, conquerin' its spirit, but have no taste for the meat."

She fumed. "But that is just wrong, so very, wrong."

Molly helped her on with the jacket. "Wrong or right, 'tis a sport they've been doin' for many years, m'lady."

She slipped her feet into the boots. "My people never kill an animal unless it was to be eaten, then every part of it is used to serve a need. We do not take a life just to waste it."

Molly pulled out the dressing table chair and reached for the brush. She sat down, and their eyes met in the mirror. "These folks are not your people, m'lady." Molly pulled the brush through her hair. "Their ways are different, and you must learn to respect the difference."

"But their ways are wrong," she protested.

Molly pinned up her hair. "Not wrong, just different."

Her mouth thinned. "I cannot do this today. I cannot do what I do not believe in." She folded her arms across her chest. "I will stay at Glenview and keep Lady O'Neill company."

Molly arched a brow. "You would disappoint and disgrace your husband, then?"

She bit her bottom lip. "No, I cannot do that either."

Molly smiled. "There are times, m'lady, when doin' somethin' for the ones we care about takes precedence over what we feel." She stood back to admire her work. "There you be, now, lookin' as lovely as ever."

She stood with a pout. "I will hate every minute of this day."

Molly ignored her grumbling, handing over the hat and gloves, then opening the chamber door. She cast an encouraging smile. "Your husband waits."

She found Braiton sitting with Shamus O'Neill in the dining hall. He stood when she made her way to him and pulled out the chair beside his own. "Are you ready to hunt, my lady."

She frowned. "As ready as I will ever be."

Shamus laughed from his seat at the opposite end of the table. "You don't look like it, lass."

She forced a smile. "I am just trying my best to adjust to another thing that is different."

Shamus gestured to the pastries on a tray in the center of the table. "Well, food is food wherever one lives, and since 'twill be a long time till the next meal, eat and enjoy."

She reached for a sweet roll and nibbled on it halfheartedly. Braiton poured her a cup of tea, and she drained the cup, the warmth of the liquid comforting as it slipped down her throat. After breakfast, they joined the others on the mansion's front lawn. She mounted her horse sidesaddle, which was not the way she would like to ride but did so for appearance sake.

Braiton checked the strength and circumference of the horse's legs below the knee. "In this way I can size up the weight a horse is expected to carry," he explained. Giving the horse's rump a gentle slap, he smiled up at her. "This one has good bones, my lady. You should have no trouble keeping the fox at bay."

Her horse broke into a gallop, and she sighed, still feeling sorry for the fox's fate. Because she despised killing an animal just for sport, she had a harder time mustering the excitement felt by the others.

Joleena pulled up beside her and brought her horse to a slow walk. Raven did the same so they could talk. The other woman's hat sprouted a silly looking feather atop the derby she wore and a ruffled blouse, the collar appearing tight. She eyed Raven's riding habit. "You look quite fashionable, my lady, even if you appear uncomfortable."

She straightened her spine, and forced a smile, thinking the same about Joleena's outfit. "I am fine, thank you."

Joleena allowed the men to pass. "Shall we take a wee bit of a rest?"

"Why, we've only just begun."

Joleena shrugged. "I thought perhaps we'd have a bit of time to get to know each other better. 'Twill be quite all right," she added. "We can catch up to the men in ample time, I know a shortcut."

She nodded and followed Joleena to a shaded patch of trees.

"They will jump over hedgerow and ditch," Joleena complained. "The scent of the fox will be caught by one of the hounds, and then lost again. And so goes it throughout the day." She halted her horse beside a tree and climbed down. "Finally after a long afternoon of such foolery, the fox will be at long last brought to bay."

She dismounted her horse as well. "You do not sound like you like this sport."

"'Tis because I don't," Joleena sulked, plopping down beneath the tree. "But 'tis better than sitting around an empty mansion, bored to tears."

Joleena reminded her of the china dolls she saw in the shop windows during her trips to town. They were pretty to look at, all dressed in their finery, but could only be admired from a shelf. A child could not really enjoy playing with such a doll, because it was too fragile. As a toy, it had no real purpose.

She summed up Joleena's life to be somewhat the same. The woman was always expected to appear a perfect and proper lady. Riding sidesaddle in tons of clothing was not really riding, and forced to listen to idle gossip while sipping tea, was not really fun. Talking about a gown recently purchased or arranging your curls in different ways for an evening guest was not really challenging.

She sat beside Joleena. "Does Ireland ever get warm enough to swim or bathe in the river?"

Joleena's eyes widened. "Saints preserve us, one does not *bathe* in the river, and a lady never swims."

She slipped off her gloves and set them aside. "Why not?"

Joleena gasped. "Because she'd be perceived as permissive."

She arched a brow. "Who would think this of a woman who only wanted to swim?"

"Why, everyone, or anyone that mattered," Joleena added. "Certainly no gentleman would seek her company."

"I think any man who judged a woman's virtue by such a thing, would not be worth the bother."

Joleena stood. "Things are different in Ireland than on the wild plains of your country, my lady."

She sighed. "So I have been told."

"Then 'tis best you begin to remember, learn to act accordingly so you don't bring shame upon your husband's good name." Joleena hurried to her horse. "Enjoy the rest of the hunt, my lady," she called over her shoulder and rode away.

Angry with herself for allowing Joleena to lead her away from the others, she stood with clenched fists and kicked her gloves aside. *How will I ever find the rest of the hunting party now?* She took a calming breath and scanned her surroundings. The early morning fog clouded most of her observation and she frowned.

"Which way should I go," she mumbled. Then, as if her father stood behind her, she heard his words..."*Just follow the holos.*"

What sun? This land does not have sun.

She gathered her full skirt between her legs and straddled the horse this time, glancing above the trees. Many times Braiton praised Ireland's attributes, talking about his country like it were a beautiful woman. He was fond of the rolling hills, admired the forest shrouded highlands, marveled over the glass lakes, mysterious bogs, semi-tropical bays, rocky cliffs and legendary seas. Right now, all she hoped to find was the sun.

She rode for quite a while, in circles, no doubt, the stays of her bodice stabbing her ribs. Disgusted and discouraged, she dismounted and stretched her arms high above her head. It was at that moment the fox darted across her path, startling her and the horse, which reared up on hind legs and ran away.

"Well, the day just keeps getting better," she grumbled, making her way to the clump of brush where the fox hid. Leaning closer to the shrub, she peered over the wild, green mass and caught sight of the little gray animal. Huge frightened eyes locked with hers, trembling with fear.

"Run while you can, *lupan*," she whispered.

The fox squirmed, but did not run. Closer she neared, spotting the hind leg caught in a mass of twisted vine. "Easy now, little *lupan*, I am not going to hurt you," she said, easing a hand down into the brush. But her cumbersome skirt made it impossible for her to bend low enough to reach the trapped leg. Stepping back, she removed the skirt and petticoat, kicking them aside, then approached the trapped animal again. Clad only in bloomers, she was able to squeeze between the scrub branches and pull apart the coiled vines, freeing the fox.

"Now run," she encouraged. "You are free." The frightened creature did not hesitate to depart its prison, or the death sentence the howling dogs issued.

"Lose something, my lady?" She spun around to find Braiton holding her skirt and petticoat in a gloved hand. "'Twould be wise to make haste in donning these, lass. Not far behind those barking hounds are the men of the hunting party."

He held out the petticoat for her to slip on and assisted her in securing the skirt. "How did you find me?" she said, smoothing the material over the petticoat.

"When Joleena rejoined the hunting party, *alone*, I did a wee bit of backtracking," he explained, fastening the buttons of her skirt. "I found your gloves, then followed your trail. Just now, when I came upon your horse, I knew you couldn't be far."

"And what excuse did she give for showing up without me?"

"She claimed you needed a wee bit more time to rest." He chuckled amused and turned her around to face him. "But knowing you to be the hearty outdoorswoman that you are, I believed not a word of it." His lips curved into a sardonic smile. "'Twasn't hard to figure she was up to her shenanigans and throwing me the blarney." He pushed a loose lock of hair aside and finished with a frown. "And you've let the fox go."

She nodded and cast her gaze to the ground. "He was so scared, Braiton, and there was really no reason for his life to end."

"Nay, there was no reason," Braiton agreed, lifting her chin with a finger, and looking deep into the blue orbs. His pulse raced with the thought of capturing her full, luscious lips with a kiss. The sound of barking dogs, growing louder, hurled him into action. He took her by the hand and led her to his horse.

"We'd better get ourselves clear from this area. If the others discover you're the reason they've lost that fox, things could get unpleasant." He swept her into his arms, sat her upon his horse, and climbed up behind her, straddling her with his legs. He reached around her for the reins and broke the horse into a gallop.

She leaned against him, resting her head upon his shoulder. He inhaled the scent of her, taking pleasure from the warmth of her in his arms.

"I love to ride," she commented, fidgeting with the collar of her bodice. "But not while wearing all of these clothes."

He smiled to himself, envisioning her riding uninhibited; hair floating behind her, a gentle breeze playing with the curls at her temples. *Aye, I can see clearly the bare splendor of her golden thighs spreading to straddle the unsaddled back of the mare, the bewitching light of the moon dancing in the deep blue of her eyes as she rides through the night.*

"Do you not see how wearing all these clothes while riding is foolish," she said, breaking through his thoughts.

"Aye, lass," he said, smiling to himself. "'Tis foolish indeed."

Chapter Eighteen

In spite of her husband's arms around her, Ireland's dampness penetrated every bone of Raven's body. She shivered all the way back to Glenview.

"Once we're home, lass, I'll have Tilly supply you with warmer undergarments," Braiton said. With fatherly concern he sent her up to the bedchamber and ordered a bath drawn.

She welcomed the way the warm water relaxed the stiff muscles along her shoulders and down her spine. Inhaling the lilac scent, she dipped a finger into the water, playing with the fragrant film the bath oil left. How nice it would be to just climb into bed after her bath, but that was not going to happen. There would be a concert after dinner. Musicians from France were commissioned to play for the O'Neill guests, and then another dance. She sighed and laid her head back against the tub's rim, closing her eyes. She was glad they would be leaving Glenview in the morning.

Joleena O'Neill once again made a fool out of her, and now she was worried she'd disgraced Braiton. Was he, at this very moment, being ridiculed and teased by the other hunters for having to ride off and find her? She groaned with a need to avenge herself, thinking of all the ways she could get even with Joleena. But what could she do to settle the score without bringing further shame upon her husband? She shuddered in disgust and sank lower into the water. Her stubborn Apache pride would be the ruin of her yet.

When Molly came into her chamber to help her

dress and do her hair for the evening concert, she overheard a loud conversation between Joleena and her servant woman taking place in the hallway outside her chamber door. Both Sinead and Tessie, Lady O'Neill's servants, were polite and had a sense of humor. Raven had come to like these women during her stay at Glenview. Perhaps it was because of her fondness for them that the incident disturbed her.

She was on her way to do something about it, when Molly halted her with a restraining hand upon her shoulder.

"Let well enough alone, m'lady. 'Tis none of your business what goes on between a servant and their employer in this household."

"I will just peer out from the door, Molly," she promised.

Joleena, admonishing her handmaiden, Sinead, screeched at the top of her lungs. "You little idiot, why is it you can't perform the simplest task?"

"Beggin' your pardon, Miss Joleena," Sinead said, tears brimming in her large green-gray eyes. "'Twas Lord O'Neill who ordered all hands to the kitchen."

Joleena raised her hand and slapped Sinead hard across the face. "How dare you blame your incompetence on my father's orders. Your duties to me should have been finished hours ago."

"Aye, Miss Joleena, I'm truly at fault. Forgive me," Sinead pleaded.

"See to it that it never happens again, or else 'twill be a switch to your bared backside I'll be giving you instead of a mere slap across the face," Joleena decreed and stalked away.

Sinead was visibly shaken and remained to compose herself.

It was then Raven went to her, placing an arm around her shoulders. "Are you all right, Sinead?"

Joleena's blow to her cheek already reddened.

"Aye, m'lady," she whispered, casting her gaze to the floor. "'Twas all me fault Miss Joleena is so upset. I'm such a scatterbrain at times."

"You are far from a scatterbrain, Sinead, and have been nothing but helpful and polite to me on my visit here." She wiped a tear from the girl's cheek with her thumb. "I am so happy to have the chance to know you and will miss you when I leave Glenview."

Sinead reached for her hand and held it tight. "Aye, m'lady, and I you."

"I want to thank you for all you have done for me this last week. You have made me feel at home."

Sinead's face brightened. "'Twas me pleasure, m'lady."

"And I would like you to keep in mind Shannonbrook's doors will always be open to you, should you wish to leave Glenview."

Sinead squeezed her hand. "I'll remember and be thankin' you, m'lady, for such generosity."

She stepped back, not wanting to get the girl in any further trouble. "I have taken enough of your time." She smiled. "Have a nice evening, Sinead."

"I bid you the same, m'lady." Sinead curtseyed and hurried down the stairs.

"You are a kind and gentle lass, my lady," a shaky voice came from the opposite end of the hallway.

She spun around to find Shamus O'Neill walking toward her, cane in tow, and taking careful steps. She went to him and offered her arm.

"Let me help you to where you are going, my lord."

"As a matter of fact I was coming to find you." He handed her a book. "I want you to have this, lass."

She scanned the binding. "But, my lord, this is

your favorite volume of sonnets. Why would you want to give it to me?"

He sighed. "Because you read them with the passion they were written. 'Tis my appreciation for the afternoons you were so gracious to read aloud. You have given me much pleasure." Lord O'Neill smiled. "I don't know when I've enjoyed myself more."

She returned the smile. "I have also enjoyed those afternoons, and every time I open this book I will be reminded of them." She held the book against her heart. "It will be my most treasured possession."

The elder man's watery eyes twinkled mischievously, reminding her for a moment of Rory's. "Aye, 'tis a good thing indeed I am an old man, or else your husband would have much to fear otherwise." He gestured toward the stairwell. "Shall I escort you to the ballroom, my lady?"

She nodded in agreement. "It would be my pleasure."

He chuckled. "Nay, the pleasure is mine."

The ballroom looked like the opera house, rows of chairs arranged to view the musicians sitting on a dais at the head of the room. Braiton caught her eye when she and Shamus O'Neill entered, making his way to her in a few quick strides.

He smiled at Shamus. "Good evening to you, my lord. I see you found my wife."

"Aye, lad, and now I suppose you want her back," Shamus teased.

"Aye, that I would."

Shamus nodded. "Very well, then." He unwound his arm from hers. "Thank you, my dear, for gracing my home with your lovely presence."

Her cheeks warmed. "I am honored to have been invited."

He gave her hand an affectionate squeeze and walked to his seat.

Braiton extended his arm and escorted her to a chair, taking a seat beside her. She studied his profile, a well defined nose and strong jaw. The dark mustache framed a full upper lip, and the cleft in his chin dimpled deeper when he smiled. She yearned now to reach over and place the tip of a finger inside the adorable facial hollow. Charming in every way, Braiton Shannon, The Lord of Limerick, caused her heart to race whenever he was around.

The musicians played an enchanting melody, and clutching the book of sonnets to her heart, she sat back in her chair to enjoy the evening's entertainment. Each instrument held a unique sound, when put together it was the most beautiful arrangement she had ever heard. The piano's rich tone was much different from the one she heard the night Braiton came to her rescue in Silver City.

The green of his eyes captured her then, and still did. She smiled to herself, comparing his bravery to a knight in shining armor. Just as the stories her mother read, Braiton defended her honor from an evil man's clutches; a hero, saving her from distress. As of late she had been distressed a number of times, Braiton always her salvation. He was good to her, and she owed him much. It broke her heart to realize she would never be able to win his love.

Jolted from her thoughts when the music stopped, she heard a musician introduce Joleena to play a waltz for the guests. Everyone in the room applauded. During Joleena's performance, her thoughts drifted again. This time she imagined Braiton dancing with her, holding her close, his eyes only for her. Lowering his head, she envisioned his mouth coming down upon hers, sweet, searing, consuming...

Again the music stopped and thunderous applause pulled her from the glorious daydream. Joleena curtsied and gazing straight into her eyes, announced, "I'd now like to give Lady Shannon the opportunity to entertain us."

She gasped and glanced over at Braiton. His lips were pressed together in a thin line, his jaw set.

"Would you do us the honor, my lady, on your last night at Glenview?" Joleena pressed with a mocking, sweet tone.

Again everyone applauded.

"Good God," Braiton managed to whisper through grit teeth. "She's gone to far this time. It all stops now," he fumed, rising from his chair.

She placed a restraining hand upon his arm. "It is fine, Braiton."

"'Tis not at all fine, Raven." He frowned. "You don't know how to—"

"Yes, I do," she interjected. "I *can* do this, my *shikaa*."

"I don't understand, my lady."

"The singing wood," she said.

His frown deepened. "The what?"

"The singing wood," she repeated, adding the translation. "The violin. I know how to play the violin."

She stood, placed the book of sonnets on her chair, squared her shoulders, and made her way to the dais. Joleena cast a smug smile and gestured to the piano. She returned the smile in the same fashion and walked past the large instrument, over to the musician with the violin.

"May I, sir?"

He nodded and handed her the violin.

Moving to center stage she faced the audience. "I will play a lullaby my mother taught me, handed down from her father, and his father before him."

Placing the violin beneath her chin, she closed her eyes and stroked the bow over the strings. Everyone was silent as the rich sweetness of her song filled the ballroom. Each note gripped her with the memories of home, transporting her to the little wickiup she shared with her family.

When the song was done, the room remained silent. The heat rose to sting her cheeks. She humiliated her husband again, along with herself this time.

But then the room exploded with applause. Guests stood and cheered, “Bravo, bravo,” as they had done for the opera singer. This meant they were pleased. She smiled, curtsied, and returned the violin to the musician, then hurried to reclaim her seat beside Braiton.

His face was exuberant with pride, smiling from ear to ear. “I had no idea you could play.” He sat and took her hand. “Why have you not allowed me to witness this musical talent of yours before?”

His touch sent currents of heat coursing through her body. “We do not have a violin.”

He chuckled. “Well, we shall get one, and you shall play for me again and again.”

“Then you are pleased?”

“Aye, lass,” he said, bringing her hand to his mouth and bestowing a light kiss upon her knuckles.

After the concert, well-wishers came to her and expressed how much they enjoyed her playing. When compliments had ceased, she brought the book of sonnets to her bedchamber, and took the time to freshen up a bit before she returned to the ballroom. The chairs were now placed along the walls, leaving the center of the room clear for dancing. Braiton was engrossed in a conversation with Lord O’Neill, so she made her way to the refreshment table to sample a delicious looking cookie covered in strawberry icing.

Rory joined her, his topaz hued eyes gleaming with mischief. “May I have this dance, my lady?”

Remembering the last time she danced with him, she stepped away and pretended to be interested in a crescent shaped chocolate concoction.

"I'd rather sit this one out, sir."

"So, the lovely Lady of Limerick has a sweet tooth," he teased. Before she could answer, he added, "Sweets for the sweet."

"Go away, Rory," she whispered.

He gestured in Braiton's direction. "Even I am not so bold as to make advances toward you, beneath the watchful eyes of your husband."

She glanced over to find Braiton observing every move Rory made.

"'Tis your last night here, my lady. 'Twould be only polite to abide by my wishes, since my family has been so hospitable."

"By rights then I should accept a dance with your father, and even your mother, since they were the O'Neills to show me welcome."

"I apologize for my sister's actions. She always was a spoiled brat."

She folded her arms across her chest. "It seems to run in the family."

He chuckled. "And I apologize for my behavior the other evening as well." He cast a playful pout. "Can you not forgive the past and honor me with just one dance?"

She sighed. "Very well, but we stay in the ballroom.

Braiton was so intent on watching Rory glide around the dance floor with Raven, he didn't notice Joleena beside him until she placed a hand on his arm.

"I'm truly glad you've come, my father is always happy to see you." Joleena smiled up at him, looking deep into his eyes. "He favors you so."

He nodded. "And I him. 'Tis been a grand few days."

She cast a glance at the grandfather clock and cleared her throat. "My, 'tis so stuffy in here." She placed the back of a hand to her forehead. "I feel as though I'm about to faint."

"It might help for you to sit, lass." He escorted her to the nearest chair. "I'll get you something to drink."

She reached for his hand. "Nay, Braiton, a breath of fresh air would be better." Her lips curved into a weak smile. "Would you be so kind as to walk with me to the veranda?"

He scanned the room for his wife and spotted her talking to Morgan Wade. Satisfied Raven was in good hands, he extended an elbow to Joleena.

She looped a hand through his arm and leaned into him as they made their way to the large double doors.

He helped her to a chair and went to the rail, looking out into the darkness. The night was brisk and still, except for the muffled sounds of music playing inside.

"Are you feeling better now?"

"Aye, a wee bit. The night air has helped to clear my head."

"Good," he said, turning around to face her. Only a lantern lit the terrace, casting their shadows upon the outer wall. "Perhaps now your head has been cleared, you might explain your behavior toward my wife."

"Why, Braiton," she gasped with wide-eyed innocence. "Whatever do you mean?"

"You know exactly what I mean, lass," he snapped. "You've done nothing but try to humiliate her since we've arrived at Glenview."

"Nay, 'tis not so, Braiton."

"Spare me the blarney, women. I'm not daft, nor am I your father, who believes everything you tell him." He frowned. "What in God's name has she ever done to you, Joleena?"

Joleena sprang from her chair and threw her arms around his neck. "She's married you, taken you from me," she sobbed.

He untangled her hands from around his neck and stepped back. "Have you gone mad, lass? There's never been anything between us other than friendship."

She reached for his hands. "Come now, Braiton, certainly you can't deny the fact I'd be more of a suitable wife for you."

He pulled free from her grasp. "I can and do."

"You should be thanking me for what I did today."

His eyes burned with his mounting rage. "And what was that, Joleena?"

She examined her fingernails in a snobbish fashion. "I was helping you see the ignorant twit for what she is."

He arched a brow. "Then I'm to thank you for your efforts?"

"Don't you see how bored you will grow with her simple ways?"

"Unlike your sophisticated ones, isn't that correct?" he grounded out with sarcasm.

She looked deep into his eyes, stroked the side of his face. "I know the proper way to be a lord's wife."

He grabbed her hand, holding it aside. "There is nothing proper about you, Joleena."

"Think about it Braiton," she hurried on, getting free from his grasp and snuggling closer to him. "I'd be such an asset to you in so many ways; running Shannonbrook, helping in your business. Far better a partner than that half-breed."

"Well, well, how cozy. I hope we're not interrupting anything," Rory remarked.

Braiton turned around to find Rory and Raven in the doorway. He set his jaw in anger.

"Nay, we're quite finished."

Rory turned to Raven. "I told you he slipped away with my sister." He folded his arms across his chest. "Here's the proof of his debauchery."

Braiton ground the words out through grit teeth. "The only debauchery is the sinister little game you two are playing." He glanced over at his wife, her face flushed. "'Tis quite clear, my lady, I've been set up to look as though I've deceived you."

Rory smirked. "Ah, a man concerned for his wife's feelings and anxious to make her understand. I'm touched beyond words."

Joleena's mouth curled with anger. "Nay, 'tis his humiliation for her stupidity you see, not his concern."

Raven licked her lips and cleared her throat. "These two have tried to shame us both on this visit."

Rory's tone hardened. "You believe him, my lady… just like that," he snapped his fingers.

Raven glared at Rory. "My husband has no reason to lie about being with another women." She turned her sapphire gaze to lock with Braiton's, the meaning of her words strangled his heart. "Do you, Braiton."

"Nay, lass," he whispered.

Rory chuckled sarcastically. "Is there not a first time for everything?"

Braiton said ominously, "I can bet 'twon't be the first time an irate husband thrashed the stuffing out of you."

Rory raised his hands in mock surrender. "I'm not the one caught in a compromising position."

"Braiton, please leave and take Rory with you," Raven said, making her way to Joleena. "This is between us women."

"Aye, my lady, 'tis a bit of man-to-man business I must deal with as well," he said, grabbing Rory by the collar and dragging him to the veranda doors.

"Nay, don't leave me alone with her," Joleena pleaded.

"Fear not, little sister," Rory quipped over his shoulder. "I've heard Indians never attack at night."

Raven watched the play of rage and fear cross over Joleena's features. She stood, raising her hand to strike.

Raven broke the slap with a quick chop to Joleena's arm. "I will not allow you to strike me, as you have Sinead."

The other woman shrieked and stepped back. "You deserve to be horse whipped."

She placed hands on hips, feet apart. "I dare you to try."

Joleena's eyes went wild. With hands raised and fingers set like claws, she went for her face. Raven stepped aside just in time, and Joleena fell into a veranda chair, landing hard on the stone terrace floor.

Layers of clothing hampered her from rising. "You little fool," she spat. "Did you really believe you could fit into Braiton's way of life?"

She raised a defiant chin. "Ah, but the truth is, I have fit in, Joleena."

The other woman moved closer.

Raven crouched like an animal ready to attack its prey. "I would think twice before you make your next move. You are no match for the things I know."

Joleena's jaw set, yellow eyes gleaming in the night.

She circled, watching, waiting for Joleena's next move.

Joleena shivered and hedged her way toward the double doors leading into the mansion. "This is by no means over," she choked out and hurried from the veranda.

Her heart raced. Gripping the rail, she inhaled the crisp night air. She knew now for certain Joleena wanted Braiton for herself. *She just might get her chance.*

After a year's time she would be leaving Ireland and her marriage to Braiton. That was the arrangement she agreed to aboard the ship. He reminded her often their marriage could be nothing more than one of convenience. She was sure it would be easy for Joleena to replace her, once she was gone. And although she trusted Braiton did not compromise his marriage vows tonight with Joleena, she did not believe it was out of loyalty to her. He was a man who had to uphold his reputation, being deemed a cheating husband was not a good way to do that.

Raven's back was to Braiton when he stepped onto the veranda. "Are you all right, my lady?"

She didn't turn around, but kept her eyes ahead. "I am fine, and you?"

He came to stand beside her. "Aye, as well as can be expected after having it out with a man you thought to be a friend."

"I think you should have a long talk with Evangeline. She has told me some things about the O'Neill siblings you need to hear." She turned to look at him. "She is not the drunken woman they make her out to be. And if there were some way Sinead could come to Shannonbrook, I would hope for that as well. It is a disgrace how Joleena degrades the poor girl." She sighed and raised her gaze to the night sky.

"I am sorry, Braiton."

He placed his hand over hers. "You have nothing to be sorry for. Joleena got what she deserved."

"My mother once had her troubles with an Indian maiden named Running Doe. She was a trickster, like Joleena. She believed if she shamed my mother in front of the tribe, she would then have a chance with my father."

He admired the side view of her face, the moon casting a glow to the black shiny curls atop her head.

"What did your mother do?"

"She fought Running Doe for her rightful place as my father's wife and won."

"You're truly your mother's daughter, then, for you've done the same."

"It is far from the same. In fact, there is a very big difference between us."

"And what would that difference be, lass?"

She turned to face him, tears glistening in her eyes, and swallowed hard. Her voice tinged with a sob. "My mother's husband loves her." She gathered her skirt and ran from the veranda.

Braiton stood alone, the stillness of the night surrounding him. "So does yours," he whispered, swallowing hard the lump in his own throat.

Chapter Nineteen

It was good to be back at Shannonbrook. Raven missed everyone there, especially Brawn. He greeted her with a wagging tail, wetting her face with his slobbering tongue.

"I missed you too, boy," she said, scratching him behind the ear. "It is good to be home."

Home. The word naturally slipped from her mouth. Perhaps it was because she finally considered Shannonbrook to be her home. She enjoyed each and every room, the garden, and stables, as well as all those who resided there with her.

Braiton, true to his word, bought her the most beautiful violin. Though she knew little about musical instruments, the violin he presented her with was of quality wood grain, and a most magnificent sound issued forth when played. The private concerts she gave him pleased them both, as well as the time they shared. They rode, dined, and laughed together. Many evenings she would read aloud to him, and time passed in a pleasant manner.

One night, about a month after her return from their visit to Glenview, she came downstairs to the library for a book. She spotted the light in Braiton's study and decided she would stop in to bid him goodnight. His head was bent over his ledgers, but upon hearing her enter the room, he looked up from his work. His face was troubled, strained. His eyes weary. Her heart went out to him.

He glanced at the mantle clock. "You're up rather late, aren't you lass?"

She stood before the desk, looking down at him. "I could say the same for you." Gazing at the pile of papers on his desk, she frowned. "You work too hard, and too long, my *shikaa*."

He ran his hand over his eyes. "Tell me something I don't already know."

"Very well, I will," she said, making herself comfortable on a chair beside the desk.

He arched a brow. "And what might that be?"

"I have an idea I need your help with."

He sat back in his chair. "Go on."

"While we were at Glenview, Shamus O'Neill and I conversed one night about the tenants and their lack of education."

He nodded. "'Tis the sad truth. They cannot afford private tutors and the nearest schoolhouse is in the next county. Not that the children would be able to attend if there were one closer," he added.

"Because they are needed to help with the chores?" she questioned.

"Aye, especially the boys during the planting and harvest time."

She nodded. "It is much the same situation children in my country face, but what if they could attend school when they were not planting and reaping?"

He frowned. "And who would teach them?"

"I would. I can read, write, cipher, teach scripture, and even the violin. In this way they will have better skills to obtain better jobs and a better life."

He smiled. "You have all this figured out quite well on your own, why do you need my help?"

She leaned forward in her seat. "I need a place to teach them." She gestured around the room. "I could teach them at Shannonbrook, in the great room, but I do not think Anna would appreciate it much."

He chuckled. “Nay, I don’t think she’d like the idea at all.”

“That is where I need your help, in finding a place to hold school.”

He stroked his chin. “I think I may have the perfect place.” His eyes twinkled with his smile. “The large stone building at the edge of the estate, which once served as a warehouse for the family business, has more then enough room for tables and chairs. There’s a wood burning stove in the center which will supply ample heat in the cold months, and ’tis in walking distance from every tenant’s cottage.”

She stood excited. “Oh, Braiton, it does sound perfect.” She ran around to his side of the desk and kissed his cheek. “I cannot wait to get started, but now I have so much to do.”

He laughed. “Do you plan on doing this all by yourself?”

She frowned. “I suppose I will need some help.”

“There is no doubt about it, lass. That old building hasn’t been used in decades. It will need to be emptied of what’s currently stored there, the chimney cleaned, and the roof mended. Not to mention furnishing it with all you’ll need to make it a proper school, like tables, chairs, a chalk board, and chalk. And those are just the major items.”

Her frown deepened. “Will you help me, Braiton?”

He stood, pushing aside a wisp of hair clinging to her cheek. “Aye, my lady, I will.”

She hugged him around the waist, resting her head against his muscular chest. “You are so good. The children will owe you so much.”

He stroked her hair. “Nay, Raven, they will owe you.”

She raised her gaze to meet his. “But I could not have done any of this without you.”

He searched her face. Her pulse raced. She anticipated his full warm lips consuming hers. But instead, he brushed a gentle kiss upon her forehead.

"Off to bed with you now, lass. A good night's rest is what you'll need, with such an undertaking ahead of you."

She glanced down at the pile of papers on the desk. "What of your own rest, my *shikaa*?"

He sighed. "I have yet more to finish here."

"Will you at least promise me you will not work too much longer," she said.

He nodded. "I promise."

Once in her bedchamber sleep eluded her and instead thoughts of the weeks ahead and all the work needing to be done raced around in her mind. She smiled to herself and snuggled beneath the quilt. How wonderful it will be for the children to have an education. She could not wait to begin.

Only a few days after their conversation in the library, Braiton called a meeting of all his tenants and explained her idea. They were all pleased and excited the children would be given such an opportunity. Many of the men offered their services in getting the stone building ready. The women sewed curtains for the windows and wove rugs for the floor.

One young woman in particular, by the name of Kathleen Grady, turned out to be a godsend. She was Raven's age, and the wife of Braiton's foreman, Kevin Grady. Because Kathleen's mother was a clergyman's daughter and well educated in her own right, Kathleen learned to read, write, cipher, play the piano, and speak French. Her grandfather's calling made Kathleen somewhat of an expert at translating scripture, and her eagerness to help was evident in leaps and bounds. The two also had much in common, each having an older brother and younger sister, a love for riding, hunting, and story telling. Upon structuring lessons and preparing the school for the children, the women grew to be good friends. Many days, after school was dismissed, they stayed on to laugh and talk, sharing childhood memories.

****

Braiton smiled when he thought of his young wife, which lately was many times within a day. She turned his household into utter chaos, but everyone loved and enjoyed having her around. Polite and respectful to the servants, she never demanded a thing, and could often be found working side by side with them to keep Shannonbrook clean and running efficiently. Teaching the tenant's children was not her only responsibility. Two days a week she took it upon herself to ride to each tenant's cottage, bringing them homemade bread and cakes she baked herself that morning. Staying to have tea with the women, she'd tell the children Apache folklore. She even helped to birth a baby or two.

He treasured the time they had alone, when she'd wear her hair down, curls falling to her waist, and void of undergarments. His favorite time of the day, and one he'd grown to appreciate the most, was sipping coffee after dinner in the drawing room. She'd sit on a mat in front of the fire, cross-legged, skirt raised high on her naked thighs and read aloud to him.

"Raven," he said, interrupting her one evening. She turned her sapphire eyes to meet his. "If I had a shilling for every time your skirt rose above your knees, I'd be very rich indeed."

She smiled. "And I as well, for every time you gazed."

He threw his head back and laughed, admiring her spirit. Her presence sparked a thrill through him. His eyes secretly seduced her, his heart yearned for her, his body desired hers, yet he dared not love her.

****

Raven dragged herself from the comforts of her bed. Each morning it took such an effort to start the day.

"Perhaps you need an elixir, m'lady, one to give you more pep and vigor?" Molly suggested, while fastening the stays of her bodice. "Doctor Murphy is expected in a few days to see Lord Shannon, maybe 'twould be wise for him to be lookin' in on you as well?"

She nodded. "I suppose it would not hurt."

"Nay, m'lady, 'twouldn't hurt at that. I'll tell Lord Shannon you'll be wishin' a time with the good doctor when he arrives."

"No, Molly, say nothing to my husband," she said.

Molly frowned. "But why, m'lady?"

"There is no need to give him cause for concern over my health, when I am sure I am just a little tired from all the work I have been doing." She sighed. "He has enough on his mind right now. I will not trouble him with more. When Doctor Murphy arrives, just send him to me first."

Molly nodded in agreement. "As you wish, m'lady."

The day Terrance Murphy came to call, Molly kept her word and brought him first to her bedchamber.

He neared the bed where she rested, concern filling his round face. "Molly said you've been a wee bit under the weather, m'lady."

"I am just tired, Terrance." She forced a smile and shifted into a sitting position. "There has been a lot going on here at Shannonbrook."

He returned her smile, placing his black bag at the foot of the bed. "Aye, I've heard you and Kathleen Grady are teaching the children, got a schoolhouse to boot."

She nodded. "And it has been quite an undertaking, yet so rewarding."

He opened the bag. "Let's be takin' a look at you then, shall we?" He grunted, frowned, and mumbled to himself throughout the examination, adding to her anxiety over what he might find. When finished he sat at the edge of the bed, stroking his chin.

"You're ailin' with somethin' there is not a cure for, m'lady."

Her eyes widened. "Good Lord, Terrance, is it bad?"

"Nay, m'lady, 'tis good."

She frowned. "I do not understand."

His face brightened. "You're with child, m'lady."

Her mouth dropped open. "Are you absolutely sure of this, Terrance?"

He laughed. "Aye, m'lady that I am."

Stunned, she laid back against the pillows. "I am having a baby?"

He laughed again. "Aye, that you are."

She swallowed hard. "Would you do me a favor and not breathe a word to my husband? I would like to surprise him with the news in my own time."

He nodded in agreement. "Of course you would, 'tis your right and half the fun. Although, I must admit I'd love to see the look on his face when you break the news to him."

"Yes, I am sure it will be a sight to behold."

"Imagine," he went on, "there'll finally be an heir to Shannonbrook. Braiton will be overjoyed."

She brought the quilt up to her chin, wishing she could disappear beneath it. "Oh, I do not think overjoyed would even come close, Terrance." She bit her bottom lip. "Not close at all."

Chapter Twenty

Braiton's body was as weary as a body could be. Sitting at his office desk, he rehashed the meeting with Kevin Grady. Remorse swept through him at the way he interrogated his foreman. Not much younger than himself, Kevin hadn't had an easy life. Abandoned by drunken parents at the age of ten, he grew up on the streets. The night Braiton met Kevin his nose was broken, shirt bloodied, and he was fighting with another lad in an alley over a shilling.

"If you need a shilling that bad, perhaps you might consider working for one," he'd shouted. The two men shrank back, staring in fear at his overwhelming form. He came forward, proposing to them a position in his company. The other lad ran away, but Kevin stayed to listen and was made a dock worker, moving up to foreman within a year's time. He was able to buy himself a tiny cottage in the village with the fair wage he was paid and made Kathleen O'Leary his wife. He trusted Kevin and never doubted his word. He didn't want to doubt it now.

He had handed Kevin the sales receipts. "They're signed in your name."

"But not by me hand, m'lord." Kevin sighed. "Have I not given you me loyal service for all these last five years?"

"Aye, that you have, Kevin."

"Then you must believe I would not cheat you?"

He rubbed his hands over his eyes. "If you didn't sign those receipts, then who did?"

Kevin shook his head. "I have no understandin'

o' the situation, m'lord."

"Have any strangers or unauthorized people been in this office, able to get the receipts from your desk," he had demanded, pacing the floor.

"Nay, m'lord, none," Kevin answered, clasping his cap in front of him.

"Have you left your post at any time, lad?" he snapped.

"Nay, m'lord, not once."

"You're absolutely sure of that, Mr. Grady?"

"Absolutely, m'lord."

Braiton returned to his desk, flopping down upon the chair. "This is quite a mess I'm in, Kevin." He shook his head. "How has this happened? Who could the culprit be?"

"I owe you me life, m'lord. You trusted me, gave me a chance to build a future. I will not turn me back on you, but stand by you throughout, and help you to expose the rogue who did this."

"I believe you speak the truth, Kevin, now go home to your wife."

'Twas time he went home to his own wife. Looking at the receipts again, he'd known from the start the handwriting wasn't Kevin Grady's hasty scrawl. But he had to ask. He rubbed his burning eyes and stood, making his way to the back door and bolting it.

"I'm ready to leave now, Patrick," he said, making his way to the main entrance.

"Aye, m'lord," Patrick said, rising from the crate he'd been sitting on.

Patrick had driven three generations of Shannon men to their destinations, and waited with utmost patience to bring them home. But never before this night, had he been summoned from his bed.

"Another wasted evening, Patrick."

"I'm sorry for that, m'lord."

"Nay, 'tis I who apologize for taking you from the comforts of your bed."

"Your apology isn't necessary, m'lord. I'm sorry your problem isn't solved."

He climbed into the bian. "So am I, Patrick, so am I."

****

Raven heard Braiton's heavy, slow footsteps climbing the stairs and met him at the top, looking down at him while he approached.

"I'm sorry if I woke you, lass." He was worn and pale, lines of worry etched upon his brow.

"You did not wake me. I have been too worried and frightened to sleep."

He sighed with his exhaustion. "There's nothing for you to fear, Raven. No one dares to harm you."

She threw her arms around his waist, placing an ear to his heart. "I do not fear for myself, Braiton, but for you. You are so troubled. I cannot bear to see you suffer so."

He drew her closer and groaned. "I don't know what to do, Raven. At this point I've lost all resolve. My heart is heavy with the weight of this situation."

He buried his face into her hair. "If this problem is not solved, and soon, all I've worked for, all my family worked for, will fall into ruination. Remaining clear headed is becoming harder and harder to do, yet I know I must stay in control or all will be lost."

She raised her gaze to his. "You need rest, Braiton." She took his hand and led him to his bedchamber. "Come, you cannot have clear thoughts when you have not slept." She left him standing by the door while she lit a gas lamp and pulled down the quilt on his bed.

"Come," she urged.

He made his way to her, as though he were in a trance, and lowered himself to sit at the edge of the bed.

She removed his boots, helped him off with his waist coat and shirt, then lifted his legs to rest on the bed.

Covering him with the quilt, she whispered, "Sleep now, and think no more of anything tonight."

She reached for his shirt and coat and hung them over the back of a chair. A wad of crumpled papers fell from the coat. She bent to retrieve them, bringing them over to the lamp. Unfolding the slips of paper, she scanned the list of goods purchased and the prices. Kevin Grady's signature scrawled across the bottom of the list. She studied the handwriting and frowned. There was something familiar about the strange way the letter "*I*" was dotted, with a fancy swirl, like a dancing snake.

Where have I seen this before?

She squeezed her eyes shut and searched her brain to recall the answer, but her memory failed her. Opening her eyes again, she continued to stare at the fancy script, hoping to jolt her mind, but her efforts were in vain.

Weary herself, she returned the papers to the jacket pocket, turned down the lamp, and made her way to her own chamber. Her heart ached for her husband's troubles, sharing his confusion and despair.

She sighed. *If I could only remember where I have seen that handwriting before?*

"It will come to me," she whispered to herself, climbing beneath the quilt and pulling it up to her chin.

****

The meeting Braiton set up between Morgan Wade, Kevin Grady, and Morgan's assistant, Steven Bates would be the final one. Steven Bates arrived in Limerick that morning, and he hoped the man could help them figure out who signed Kevin's name on the receipts.

"This is not the chap I dealt with, my lord," Steven confirmed, dark eyes darting from Morgan, to Braiton, and then back to Kevin. "He was of slight build and clean shaven."

"And 'twas me name he gave, Mr. Bates?" Kevin inquired.

"Aye, sir, it was. He signed the receipts as such," Bates claimed.

Kevin glanced over at him. "I signed nothin' for this man, Lord Shannon. Up until this very moment, I never set me eyes on him."

"Aye, I can vouch for that as well," Bates agreed, crossing his arms over his chest. "This was not the chap I did business with."

Braiton raked a hand through his hair. "A clean shaven man, slight of build, you say, Mr. Bates?"

"Aye, my lord," Bates agreed.

He turned to Kevin. "Have we anyone on board fitting that description?"

"Nay, m'lord. All the workers are burly lads with facial hair."

He stroked his mustache. "Who the devil can this villain be?" He frowned at Kevin, swallowing hard to control his anger. His very breath burned in his throat as he fought the frustration rising to choke him. "And if you swear you never left your post unattended, how did this scoundrel get in the office to sign receipts without you noticing?"

"Oh, he didn't conduct business in this office, my lord," Bates offered.

Braiton stared at the man and countered icily. "Where then, Mr. Bates, was the deal made?"

"On the pier, my lord. I was informed I needn't bother coming to the warehouse. A surplus of wine was handy in a wagon on the dock, and the receipts in his pocket."

Braiton banged a fist on the desk. "I've never

conducted business from a wagon on the pier, like a peddler. 'Tis most definite this lad wasn't one of my workers."

"It's obvious you've been set up by someone who wishes to see you ruined," Morgan said.

"But who would want to do such a thing, m'lord," Kevin said. "You have no competitors in Ireland."

He shook his head vehemently. "This hooligan doesn't want to compete with me, Kevin, he wants me closed down."

"And before your demise the scoundrel fattens his own pockets with profits from the difference between your prices and the one's he's invented," Morgan summed up.

"Aye," he agreed. "'Tis safer for him that way, and after my business folds, there's a better chance at building his own company with the readies he's cheated my customers out of."

"Then he simply gathers all of your former customers together and offers them your original prices," Kevin concluded.

He nodded in agreement. "That seems the way of it, Kevin."

Kevin stroked the thick red beard framing his jaw. "There's just one thing that doesn't make sense to me. Why was Lord Wade the only client the rogue schemed?"

"He is the most influential client I have. Angering him would result in him taking his business elsewhere. Other clients would soon follow," he explained.

"But if no one has been let in here and your man swears he didn't leave his command, how in blue blazes did this imposter get his hands on the wine he sold Mr. Bates and the receipts?" Morgan said.

"That, my lord, is a question I have yet to find the answer to myself. But I will," Braiton vowed, arching a brow. "You can bet your life on it."

****

Raven's retching became a morning routine for her, and she was thankful Braiton left early each day. With his business problems taking up most of his time, he never noticed the daily bouts of nausea. Keeping it from Molly, however, was not as easy since she was the one who emptied the basin she used after her breakfast decided to come up.

"You need to tell Lord Shannon, m'lady, he's got a right to know," Molly scolded, while swabbing her neck and face with a cool, damp cloth.

"No, Molly, not now," she said between gasps. "He has too much on his mind. Telling him now would not be wise, trust me on this."

"Very well, m'lady, but you can't keep your condition a secret much longer. Already I've opened the seams on some of your dresses. And he does have a right to be told."

She closed her eyes. "Yes, Molly, I know…I know."

After Molly left the room, though she fought for rest, sleep would not come. Guilt tugged at her heart and nagged her thoughts. Was she really sparing Braiton the added concern or buying herself more time?

"Dear God," she whispered. "What should I do?"

****

Braiton spent his days walking the pier, asking ship owners and dock workers questions. No one knew of the clean shaven lad. Exasperation followed him on his search. Other clients were notified of the scheme. With their cooperation to deal only with him or Kevin, further ruination was no longer a threat. But not knowing the culprit's identity haunted him daily. He also realized the thief could not have acted alone, having inside help. Who among his workers betrayed him?

"Any luck, m'lord?" Patrick inquired as he climbed into the bian.

"Nay, Patrick. It looks like another lost afternoon."

"Somethin' will turn up, m'lord. The hooligan can't hide forever."

"'Tis not likely he'd stick around, Patrick."

"At least you've put a stop to his shenanigans before more damage is done."

"Aye, 'tis true, I have done that. But as things stand now, I'm still in a financial bind. Reimbursing Lord Wade took quite a bite out of my profits. I may not be able to voyage next year to America or the Orient. My customers will seek other importers for new and exotic goods if they can no longer purchase them from me. Business will dwindle and eventually die."

"At least you can take comfort in knowing the rogue cannot strike you again," Patrick said encouragingly.

He sighed. "Well, not in the way he's done this time. But if he's bent on closing me down, God knows what other ways he's got up his sleeve to try."

"What other ways could there be, m'lord?"

"I'm afraid to even contemplate, Patrick, and too tired to worry further at this point. All I want to do now is go home and see my wife."

"Aye, m'lord, that I understand. 'Tis me Anna who sets everythin' right for me durin' difficult times."

He sat back in his seat and thought of Raven the rest of the ride home. She also was preoccupied with something, deep in thought, subdued and looking tired. Perhaps she was taking on too many responsibilities with the new school, spreading her hospitality too thin?

Guilt nagged at him now for neglecting her. He was gone all day and late into the night in the hopes of exposing the scammers. Focusing only on his own troubles, he failed to consider her. She'd been devoted and caring to him, staying awake and waiting for him to come home, then comforting him until he fell asleep. Filled with remorse for his selfishness, he departed with haste from the bian when it came to a stop before the mansion, and took the stairs two at a time to her chamber. He knocked on the door, and upon her agreement for him to enter, he found her sitting cross-legged on a rug in front of the fire.

He smiled and plopped down beside her. "Old habits die hard, do they not, my lady?"

She frowned. "I do not understand."

He gestured around the room. "In case you haven't noticed, lass, this chamber is well stocked with chairs to sit upon. Yet you can always be found sitting on the floor."

"The chairs have no room for me to sit cross-legged," she said. "And sitting in such a fashion makes me feel more at home, less lonely."

He pushed aside a lock of hair from her forehead. "'Tis all my fault you're so lonely."

"Your fault," she gasped.

"Aye, lass. I have been selfish."

Her eyes widened. "You have been nothing but generous, my *shikaa*."

"Aye, with material possessions, but not with my time. I cannot remember when we last spent a day together, riding and enjoying each other's company."

She shrugged. "You have a lot on your mind. I understand it was important for you to be away."

"I've been a fool to not have realized sooner time with you is also important." He smiled. "So, will you forgive this fool and go riding with me?"

"Now?"

"Aye, lass right now."

Sparks of excitement lit her face. "I would like that very much."

He stood, extending a hand to her. "Excellent. I'll have Dooley get Grania and Dayden ready then, while you change into your riding habit." He walked to the door, and then hesitated. "By the way, lass, your horse's name, does it have a meaning to you?"

She smiled. "It was an endearment my father used often to refer to me and my sister, Sunny. Dayden, in Apache, means *little girl.*"

He stroked his mustache and mulled over the name in his thoughts. "Aye, you have named her well."

****

Raven rode with ease beside Braiton, the bite of Ireland's autumn stinging her eyes. She secured her hood and nestled her chin beneath the large collar of her cape to keep warm.

He gave his horse an affectionate pat as he rode. "Grania, I haven't given much time to you, either."

"Now it is my turn to ask you, does Grania have meaning?"

"Aye," he said, eyes twinkling. "The story of Grania O'Malley, a warrior queen of the Western islands about three hundred years ago, was my favorite history lesson."

She brought Dayden to a slow walk. "I have shared many of the folklore of my people. Will you share yours while we ride?"

He nodded, matching his horse to the other's pace. "'Twould be wise of me to start my tale with Owen O'Malley, Grania's father, who was a fearsome soul. 'Tis said he was a tall man with a thick beard curling about his jaw. Brown-eyed and wearing his dark hair about his broad shoulders, Owen's lungs bellowed, and he shook the ground when he walked. 'Twasn't hard to understand why folks called him, *Black Oak, King of the Western Sea.*"

A shiver ran down her spine. “He sounds frightening.”

“Aye, for sure, but in spite of his frightening presence, Owen O’Malley was a kind man. He could weave a good tale, and oddly enough, he loved his daughter, Grace.”

She frowned. “What is so odd about a father loving his daughter?”

“In those times a man didn’t take well to a girl child, and only after a son received his share of affection, did a daughter receive hers.”

“Then I am very pleased it was not that way for my family. My father doted on his daughters, and I enjoyed every minute he spent with me.” Thinking of her father made her heart yearn for home. “Please, go on with your story.”

“Grania bore a strong resemblance to Owen’s own beloved mother, black-eyed Maria from Spain, and I believe ’tis why he lavished his heart upon the lass. And he wasted no time taking her to sea with him. As soon as wee Grace was out of nappies, he stood her upon a crate before the ship’s wheel and urged her to steer the *Dorcas* while he stood behind her. He held his precious daughter steady with calloused hands, his eyes on the horizon.”

“From that time on did she sail the seas?”

He smiled, the dimple in his chin deepening. “Aye, lass, she did, in spite of her mother’s attempts to teach her womanly skills. She also ignored the proper way a lady should dress, and donned lad’s clothes; woolen breeches, linen shirt, and a short jacket, which she waterproofed with wax. Her long dark braid was tied up and covered with a cap.”

“My mother once did the same, dressed herself in boy’s breeches and shirt and stuffed her hair up into a hat.”

He frowned. “Why did she do this, lass?”

“To save my father, who had been captured by a

white lawman, by the name of Ryan Duffy, and taken to a military fort to be hanged."

Braiton's frowned deepened. "What was his crime?"

The injustice of the way her people were treated caused her next words to crack with emotion. "He was an Indian, not as heroic as Crazy Horse, but brave just the same."

"And who is Crazy Horse?"

"He was the Sioux leader in 1876 that joined with Sitting Bull to defeat General George Armstrong Custer and his army at a place called Little Big Horn. In the end, Crazy Horse was forced to surrender to the troops due to starvation and killed while trying to escape. But my people, because of the heroic way Crazy Horse defended the threatened people, have made him a symbol of leadership," she said.

They rode on, neither of them speaking for several moments, then she broke the silence. "I would like for you to finish telling me about Grania."

He nodded. "She cut off all her hair when she was but fourteen so she could sail with her father to Spain. She earned the name, *Granuaile,* which in Gaelic means *Grace of Gold.* Further voyages took her to Scotland and Portugal, and she learned from her father how to be a skilled swordsman, wielding a blade with a deadly force to reckon with. She could best any man who crossed swords with her. Owen even taught the lass how to fight."

"My father taught my mother the warrior's fight, as well as all of us children."

He chuckled. "Then I shall be careful not to anger you."

"Did Grania ever marry, have children of her own?"

"Aye, my lady, she married and was widowed thrice. After giving birth to her fifth child, a son, while on a voyage overrun by the Turks, Grania rose from her birthing bed to fight with her men, saving her vessel."

She gasped. "Did she quit the sailing after that?"

"Nay, my lady, the woman's calling was the sea, 'twas on a ship she felt at home. Wild, free, unencumbered by conventional means, Grania O'Malley reigned for forty years as a sea pirate and gunrunner. 'Twas how she made her living. A clan leader and captain, she's credited with commanding a fleet of galleys. At the height of her power, perhaps thirty men manned the oars and another fifty to one hundred warriors were armed for whatever new adventure lay ahead. She fought her foes, the English Saxons, who had a stronghold on her beloved Ireland, and became mother of the Irish Rebellion. For a year's time she was even imprisoned in a Limerick gaol, by the Earl of Desmond. Then she was sent to a prison in Dublin to be hanged, but finally freed after a nearly a second year passed by Lord Justice William Druary."

"Truly not a featherhead," she commented.

He chuckled again. "Nay, that she wasn't." His expression turned thoughtful. "Perhaps my admiration for such a brave lass, as Grania O'Malley, is what's made me irreverent toward women who have empty heads and shrinking spirits." He searched her face. "You would have fought well beside her, my lady."

She laughed sardonically. "I do not think I could lead one hundred warriors into battle."

"I have a strong inkling you'd try your damnedest," he said with confidence. "I would heed your judgment, fight under your command."

Her eyes widened. "You would put your life in my hands?"

"Aye, without hesitation." He arched a brow. "The only trouble I see encountering is keeping the other men at bay from wanting to taste your charms."

Her cheeks warmed. "I have a strong inkling you would try your damnedest."

He laughed. "Aye, that I would."

Again they rode in silence, her taking in the lush scenery. The leaves adorning the clusters of trees had turned red and gold. She sighed. "I enjoy all seasons, but I love most the colors of spring."

"Then come with me, and I'll show you a place still aglow with the colors you crave." He tugged on Grania's reins and turned off the path.

She followed him with anticipation to the shores of the Shannon River.

"This is the most beautiful and finest river of the west; large in width and rimmed with lush dense forests," he said as he led her to a small clearing where deep dark pink flowers grew.

"See, my lady," he said, pointing to the spray of blooms. "There lie your colors of spring."

He dismounted, helped her off Dayden, and together they made their way to the colony of flowers.

"They are beautiful, Braiton." She bent down on one knee and felt a petal. "What are they called and how did you know they bloomed here?"

"They are the fuchsia flower, and as a lad, I'd come here often." He looked out to sea. "After my mother died, 'twas the only place I found peace."

She remembered his ship was named after his mother. *The Sweet Maureen.*

"Tell me about your sweet Maureen."

He turned his gaze to meet hers. "Aye, she was sweet, my lady. And by no means was she a featherhead, though her illness left her frail and fragile." He made his way to a tree and leaned against the aging trunk. "She never ventured far from her bed, so I'd climb in beside her to keep her company. She'd read aloud to me for hours, entertaining us both." He smiled with his memories. "A witty woman, she was, and I admired her wisdom."

She came to stand beside him. "Were your father and mother close?"

He shrugged. "That's hard to say, since my father worked long hours. I suppose in their private time they had loving moments. I know he had an endearing name for her, called her his Lilly, because her flesh was so wane. Spidery veins peeked through her transparent skin, reminding me of little blue trails upon a map."

She rested a hand on his arm. "You miss her, Braiton?"

"Aye, that I do, lass." Again he gazed out across the river. "I remember well the day she died." He sighed. "I was no more than ten, just beginning manhood. I wanted to explore, hunt, and ride with friends. Climbing beneath the quilt with your mother and listening to her read was for younger lads. So, my visits to her bedchamber weren't as frequent." His tone wavered. "The day she died I ran from her deathbed and into my father's study. He kept there a rare and beautiful collection of porcelain pipes on a shelf behind his desk. I smashed the lot of them."

She gasped. "Why did you do such a thing?"

He turned to lock his gaze with hers. "I wanted him to hurt me, beat me, humiliated me, and punish me."

"But why, my *shikaa*?"

"Because I was guilty for not spending more time with my mother, and if he reddened my backside till it burned, justice would have been served."

"Did your father beat you?"

"Nay, he did nothing, left me to my torment." He

glanced around the clearing. "And so I'd come here and in the privacy of this quiet place, I'd cry, ashamed of myself for abandoning my mother."

"Oh, Braiton," she whispered, wrapping her arms around his waist and placing an ear to his heart. "You did not abandon your mother."

He stroked her hair. "What would you know about it, Raven?"

"I know if I had a son, I would be blessed for him to experience the excitement of growing up." She raised her eyes to meet his misty, green orbs. "I would not deny him his right to live life to the fullest. My love for him would trust his love for me. Never would I feel he stayed away to hurt me." She reached up and caressed the side of his face with the tip of a finger. "It is time you forgave yourself. Put the guilt to rest."

He brought her hand to his mouth and bestowed a kiss upon her fingers. "You are but one perfect flower, my lady; rare and beautiful, like the fuchsia that grows to bloom in autumn—a ray of hope amongst the dismal sorrows of life, sprouting strong and determined."

Her heart raced with his touch. "What do you think makes one flower so much more perfect than the others?"

Taking her by the hand, he led her to the patch of fuchsia, and looked down at the thriving blooms.

"'Tis the seed planted with love, from which one perfect flower grows."

She smiled, placing a hand to rest upon her stomach and spreading her fingers over her belly. "And love always finds a way."

He glanced over at her, returning a smile. "Aye, Raven, that it does."

Chapter Twenty-One

The bouts of nausea subsided and the fatigue ebbed. With renewed energy Raven was able to accomplish all she must each day. What she was not able to do, was tell Braiton he was going to be a father. She made numerous attempts, only to cower in the end. And Molly's constant badgering did not help her frame of mind.

She sighed and squared her shoulders. This would be the night. This had to be the night. Her growing belly would tell all soon, anyway. She found Braiton in his study, sitting in an overstuffed chair and puffing on a clay pipe. Clearing her throat, she opened her mouth to speak when her efforts were interrupted by a messenger delivering the news Shamus O'Neill was dead.

The elder man passed in his sleep two nights before. At his request a private service was held the next day in his memory, his wife and children the only attendants at the ceremony. He was buried in the family plot at the edge of the estate.

She had not known Lord O'Neill long, but treasured the time she did have with him during the week they spent at Glenview. She truly enjoyed reading aloud to him the sonnets he loved.

Braiton looked at the letter in his hand and sighed. "He was the last of my father's cronies. He mentored me, took me under his wing at a time I needed the most help."

"I am so sorry, my *shikaa*. He will be truly missed."

"Aye, he will." He looked up at her. "And Rory

will be paying us a visit within a few days. He wants to discuss his father's holdings and shares with my company."

He chuckled sardonically. "He's not wasting any time in assuming his place in the family affairs. Shamus is barely cold in his grave, and his son is ready to talk business." He ran a hand over his eyes. "The last thing I need right now is a visit from Rory. With the warehouse scandal not yet solved, I'm in no frame of mind to go through Shamus's accounts."

He stood and made his way to the window, looking out at the quiet night. "Was there something you wished to speak to me about, my lady?"

She bit her bottom lip. "No, not a thing."

****

The day Rory O'Neill arrived, Braiton was more out of sorts then he expected. And to top off his foul mood, Raven declined joining them for lunch. Not that he could blame her. The O'Neill siblings were anything but hospitable toward her. He had Molly take a tray up to her bedchamber and dined with Rory himself.

"Driving the poor lass mad, are you, Braiton," Rory teased from his seat across the table.

He took a sip of his coffee and steered the conversation away from his wife. "I find it disrespectful of you, deciding to conduct business so soon after your father's death."

Rory raised a brow. "Are you insinuating I'm not grieving, because I choose to carry on with what needs to be done?"

He placed his cup on the table. "'Tis not an insinuation, but a bold faced fact."

Rory sat back in his seat, a derisive grin curving his lips. "And you own the market on how to properly grieve?"

"I know what's appropriate," he snapped.

"And 'tis always important to look appropriate,

isn't that right?" Rory challenged.

"You miss my meaning entirely," he said, locking his eyes with the other man. "For God's sake, Rory, the man was your father."

"What would you have me do, sit around in mourning clothes like the women and sniffle into a handkerchief?" Rory shot back. "Nay, I think not. I have a business to run now, and there's not a better time than the present to get a feel for my new duties and responsibilities. My mother and sister are depending on me to make sure the household finances run as usual."

He sipped his coffee. "After I get matters squared away with you, I will return to Glenview and act accordingly."

Braiton felt disgust for the other man, right down to his toes. Standing, he straightened his waist coat. "Then let's be off. Your father's accounts will not take long to summarize. He was a man who thought ahead, was well organized. If you're as wise a business man as he, you should have no problem continuing to run Glenview's affairs."

Anna stepped into the room to clear the table. "Should I plan on Mr. O'Neill joining you for dinner, m'lord?"

"Aye, there's not much for us to do at the warehouse," he said.

"I will not be returning to Shannonbrook, Anna," Rory corrected. "So I'll ask you to bid Lady Shannon farewell for me. Please let her know how much I regret not being able to enjoy her company on this visit."

He frowned. "You would travel at night when there's not a need?"

"Aye," Rory said. "As a matter of fact, I prefer it. I like the dark peace of night waters."

He made his way to the foyer. "Then, let's be on our way."

****

Raven fell asleep in the overstuffed chair in Braiton's study, waiting for him to return. Anna said they would not be long, yet a glimpse at the mantle clock showed the hour to be way past six. Wiping the sleep from her eyes, she stood and made her way to the door. Kathleen Grady's voice sounded from the foyer, nervous and shaking as she conversed with Brian.

"What is it, Kathleen," she said, entering the large vestibule.

"Lady Raven," Kathleen began, her large green eyes filled with concern. "Forgive me for this visit at such a late hour, but I fear for our husbands."

She motioned for Kathleen to take a seat on the hallway davenport and sat beside her. "Why, Kathleen?"

"This afternoon Lord Shannon and another man came by the cottage for Kevin."

She nodded. "The other man was Rory O'Neill. Braiton had business with him at the warehouse, and I am sure he needed Kevin along."

"Aye, that's where Lord Shannon said they'd be, but he also said he'd be needin' Kevin for only an hour, and that was around one o'clock. He promised they'd both be home long before 'twas time to be eatin' the evenin' meal." Kathleen gestured to the grandfather clock. "But as you can see, 'tis way past six now."

Raven glanced over at Brian. "Has Lord Shannon sent a message home saying his plans were changed?"

"Nay, m'lady, if he had you would know."

She frowned. "Yes, well, sometimes his messages get waylaid, especially if he trusts Daniel Brodie with the delivery. The man has a good heart, but cannot pass a pub without stopping in." She took Kathleen by the arm. "Come, we will be more comfortable talking in the drawing room." She smiled. "I am sure my husband will be home soon. In the meantime, stay and wait with me." She turned again to Brian. "Please bring us a pot of tea, Brian. Mrs. Grady looks chilled to the bone."

"Aye, m'lady," Brian agreed and hurried off to the kitchen.

She wrapped an arm around Kathleen's shoulders. "Did you walk all the way from the village?"

"Nay, not all the way. I was able to catch a ride on a wagon with one of the tenants. It brought me as far as the gate," Kathleen said.

The path from the gate to the mansion's door was dark, winding, and lined by dense woods. She remembered her own attack while walking about her village at night and quivered inside. "That is a long, frightening walk, especially for a woman at this hour."

Kathleen nodded in agreement. "I had no other choice, m'lady."

After Brian brought them the tea and a plate of Anna's pumpkin cookies, Raven dismissed him. "I am sorry my husband has been keeping yours out so late, Kathleen. He has been very worried over business troubles. I am sure the men are just discussing those problems and lost track of time."

"I don't think that's happened, m'lady."

"How would you know different, Kathleen?"

Kathleen frowned. "From me cottage I can see the warehouse. Kevin works in the room at the rear of the buildin'. I can see the window o' his room from the porch. Around four o'clock, I emptied a dish pan o' soapy water out back of me house, and I saw the light in Kevin's office go out. I hurried back inside to finish dinner, knowin' 'twould not be long before he'd be arrivin' home. But he never *came* home."

She bit her bottom lip. "And you are sure that

was at four o'clock?"

"Aye, m'lady, I'm positive," Kathleen said. "I waited an hour more before walkin' over to the warehouse to see what was goin' on. I tried the door and 'twas locked. There was no sign o' anyone around."

"Perhaps they decided to take the discussion to the pub?"

"I thought of that, but Kevin has to pass our front walkway to get to the street the pub's on. Knowin' I thought he was comin' home for dinner, I'm positive he'd have stopped in to let me know the plans changed."

Kathleen's words disturbed her. "I can see now why you would be worried, but there has to be a good explanation."

"I only pray you're right, m'lady."

She sighed. "It would be wise for us not to get carried away with believing the worst." Her gaze landed on the book Shamus O'Neill gave her, lying on the table beside her chair. Reaching for the volume of sonnets, she opened it to the first page.

"While we wait I will read aloud to calm us."

Kathleen nodded in agreement and sat back in her chair.

She scanned the first page, her gaze resting on the inscription. Fear gripped her heart. "Lord, help them," she muttered, closing the book and glancing over at Kathleen.

The other woman's terror-filled eyes matched the panic spiraling down her spine.

"What's wrong, m'lady?"

She put the book aside and cleared her throat. "I know you mentioned you have hunted, but how skilled would you say you are with a gun?"

Kathleen's eyes widened. "I've gotten me share of game, why do you ask?"

Raven stood, her stomach knotting. "Come with

me to my husband's study."

Kathleen followed. "Tell me, please, m'lady, what's wrong?"

She did not answer Kathleen, but went to the large desk by the window and opened the drawer. She took two large pistols from the drawer and loaded them with trembling hands.

"Saints preserve us, m'lady," Kathleen moaned. "What's happenin'?"

"I believe now our husbands may be in grave danger." She handed a gun to Kathleen. "And we need to help them."

Kathleen gripped the gun with an experienced hand. "Shouldn't we go for the men tenants to help us?"

She shook her head. "There is not enough time to get word to all of them. By the time they all gather, set about a plan—"

"I agree," Kathleen interrupted. "But how can we, just two women, be o' any help?"

"I am sure we can conjure up as good a plan as any man." She made her way to the kitchen, thankful all the help were not around, and lit a lantern. Together, she and Kathleen ran to the stables. They were in luck. Dooley was gone for the day. And the fewer questions she had to answer, the better. She reached for the men's clothing hanging on a peg by the door.

"Here," she said, handing Kathleen a shirt and breeches. "Put these on." She began to undress from her own clothes. "It is safer for us to appear as two boys, then to go off riding in the night as two unescorted women."

"What about our hair?"

She glanced around the stable and spotted a cap and a wide brimmed hat hanging on another peg by a horse's stall. Taking them from the hook, she tossed Kathleen the cap.

"Take down your hair and braid it, then stuff it up into the cap and pull it down around your ears," she instructed, while doing the same. In no time, they looked like a pair of farm lads. She showed Kathleen how to secure the pistol in the drawstring of the breeches, and then looped a rope around Dayden's neck and led her from the stall. In one fluid motion she mounted the horse, sitting tall upon her back.

Kathleen gasped. "Aren't you goin' to saddle her?"

"There is not enough time," she said, extending a hand to Kathleen.

"But we will just fall off."

She sighed. "I have been riding this way for as long as I can remember."

Kathleen's lips thinned. "Then 'tis I who will fall off."

"Come, Kathleen." She extended her hand lower. "Just dig your knees into the horse's side and hang on to me."

Kathleen mounted and they raced out of the stable.

The chill of the night stung her face, her heart pounded, but she rode as swift as she dared with a novice on board. Poor Kathleen, her teeth chattered and arms shook as she hung on for dear life. Burying her face against Raven's back, the other woman recited the Lord's Prayer. She silently prayed along.

When they arrived at the warehouse it was dark, desolate, just as Kathleen described. She spotted the carriage and brought Dayden to a halt beside it.

"Patrick would never leave the carriage unattended."

"Then they're all still inside the warehouse?" Kathleen said, scrambling off the horse.

"But where?" Raven dismounted and tied

Dayden to the carriage. "I have only been here one time and not for very long."

"I take Kevin his lunch on me way to the schoolhouse. I know the lay out well," Kathleen offered. "With the doors locked, we can't enter through them, but I know o' another way." She took Raven by the hand and led her to the east side of the warehouse.

"Through there," she said, pointing to a large metal cylinder."

Raven frowned. "What is that?"

"'Tis a chute used for discardin' old crates and packin'. The trash is thrown down the tube and falls into the vat below, then burned." She neared the large silo. "If we could get on the barrel's rim and climb up the chute, we can get into the warehouse. We'd come out on the second floor, in the last room of the buildin'. That's where the items to be trashed and burned are stored."

In her youth Raven had climbed many trees. Looking the situation over carefully, she did not doubt for a minute she could do as Kathleen suggested. But could Kathleen?

It was as though the other woman read her mind. "I used to climb trees when I was just a wee lass, so I can do this. How about you?"

"Same here," she admitted. "You are looking at the village's champion tree climber."

Kathleen chuckled. "I didn't do too bad meself, except I tore me stockin's and stained me dress every time. And every time Papa thrashed me bottom with the switch." She sighed. "I couldn't sit for days."

Raven grabbed hold of the edge of the barrel, coated with soot and grime, and hoisted herself up on the rim. Kathleen did the same. By the time they crept their way to where they could reach the metal tube, they were both covered in ash.

Kathleen was the first to inch her way up the chute, hands and feet braced against the sides to keep from falling down the tube and into the dirty barrel. Her pistol scraped the metal cylinder with each move.

"Kathleen," she said, her voice echoing throughout the tube. She cringed and lowered her tone. "Can you reach your gun and move it onto your hip?"

"I fear I'll hit the trigger, since I can't even see me own hands in front of me face," Kathleen whispered.

"Then can you feel for the drawstring around your waist and tighten it?"

"I'll need both hands to do that, and without securin' meself, I'll slide. Then we'll both end up at the bottom o' that grimy vat."

She blindly reached for Kathleen's foot. Upon finding the right one she braced it with the palm of her hand. "Try to pull the drawstring now."

The tunnel was alive with Kathleen's erratic breathing, but within moments the other woman announced with a sigh of relief, "'Tis done."

They made their way to the top of the chute and climbed out. A sliver of moonlight from a tiny window shed a bit of light into the room, revealing boxes and wood piled high against the walls.

Kathleen pointed to the right. "The way out is beyond those crates."

Raven groped her way through the debris, hitting a knee and a chin, stifling the cries of pain. A creature scampered past her foot and she cringed. "I dare not ask what that could be."

"'Tis probably a rat, m'lady," Kathleen whispered. "They're all over the place."

They came to a door; beyond it voices could be heard. "Do you hear that, Kathleen?"

"Aye, m'lady, 'tis comin' from the middle storage

room, which would explain why no light can be seen from the outside. That room has no windows."

"How can we get there from here?"

"Through this door and to the left," Kathleen instructed.

The voices grew louder as they snuck through the opening and crouched behind a pile of wood. From their position two men could be seen, their backs to them. One was tall and broad shouldered. The other was small and slight of build. Braiton and Kevin were tied to their chairs, arms behind their backs. The smaller man held a gun on Braiton, the larger man pointed his weapon at Kevin.

Kathleen gasped and reached for Raven's hand. "Who are these men?"

"They must be the two scoundrels swindling my husband." She took a deep breath and focused on the lighting of the room. Only one lantern was lit and it did not shed past where the men stood. It would be possible to sneak up from behind and still remain hidden in the shadows.

"Kathleen, make your way to the area behind the bigger man. The darkness is in your favor and you will not be seen. When you hear me hoot like an owl, shoot him in the foot, then hide behind the wood pile there."

"What about you, m'lady?"

"I have a plan of my own, so do not be concerned for me. Just listen for the hoot, then shoot and hide."

"Hoot, shoot, and hide," Kathleen whispered, giving Raven's hand a squeeze before she slipped away.

****

Mouth parched, shoulders throbbing, Braiton secretly worked the ropes binding his hands. Besides experiencing physical and mental stress, his heart was raw with emotion. He was unable to psychologically wrap his mind around the situation at hand and hurt deep with betrayal.

"Why are you doing this, Rory?"

"'Tis how it has to be, old friend. My father's will states all his holdings with your company be governed by you. But in the event your company folds, the holdings are mine."

"Correction, dear brother, the holdings would be divided equally, that was the deal." Joleena moved closer, her topaz eyes filled with hate. "If you were only a wee bit smarter, Braiton, and married me instead of that little half-breed, all this could have been avoided."

He smiled sardonically at the thought of Joleena O'Neill in Raven's place. "You're far from the woman she is."

"And you're in no position to anger me further." Joleena brought the gun's muzzle to rest against his chest. "I hold all the cards now. Since 'tis no longer possible to see you as my husband, I'm afraid I must see you dead."

He gritted his teeth, trying again to free his hands from the ropes that bound him. "You're mad, both of you. Do you really believe you'll get away with murder this time?"

Rory chuckled. "Ah, I see you've been talking to mother." He shrugged. "Except this time suspicion will be placed on the small built lad." He smiled and glanced over at his sister.

He glared at Joleena, seething with a mixture of hate and disgust. "Then 'twas you dressed in men's clothes, as you are now, who swindled Lord Wade."

Joleena's wicked laughter filled the storage room, rising to the high rafters. "Aye, 'twas me. A clever plan, don't you think? After I sold Wade's assistant the goods, I climbed aboard our vessel. That's where I stayed while Rory visited you. Not a soul was aware I was even along."

"I was able to get the receipts easily enough,"

Rory confessed. He smiled at Kevin. "Your trusted foreman trusted me as well to be in your office."

"So sorry, m'lord," Kevin said.

"You had no way of knowing, Kevin," he said, working further at the rope. He had to get himself free. He wouldn't die at the hands of these degenerates.

"Oh, he wasn't the only one of your men who helped," Rory snickered. "'Twas your man, Brodie, who brought the wagon full of goods to the dock. I led him to believe they were my father's purchases. After I offered him a few shillings for his help, he was off to the pub."

"So you see, Braiton darling, 'twill be impossible for anyone to piece together what happened, let alone blame Rory or I of the crime."

His heart hammered in his ears. Would his captors really get away with murder? Certainly such fools couldn't have thought of everything? He was sure if he thought hard enough he would find a loop hole, something he could use against them. But what? How effective would his threats be, tied to a chair. Again, he worked at the rope and prayed for an answer, which came to him from the shadows in the form of an owl's hoot.

A shot rang out.

Rory wailed in pain and dropped his gun. He fell to the floor, holding his foot. Blood poured from between his fingers. He rocked back and forth.

Braiton's gaze swept the darkness for the gunman. When none could be seen, he directed his attention to Joleena, who by now was concerned for her brother's welfare. While looking over at Rory, she lowered the hand holding the gun. Braiton took this opportunity to kick upward, knocking the weapon out of her grasp.

Rory regained a measure of his senses by this time and reached for the gun he dropped, aiming the barrel at Kevin's head. Another shot rang out, hitting Rory in the wrist. The gun flew from his hand and landed at Kevin's feet. Kevin kicked the gun to the other side of the room, where it was lost in the shadows.

Joleena's eyes rounded with confusion as a young lad stepped from the shadows. In one fluid motion, the stranger had Joleena on her stomach, pressing the barrel of the pistol between her shoulder blades. "Do not move one muscle, or I will shoot."

Braiton frowned. The lad's voice was that of a woman's…one he knew well.

"Raven?" he questioned. "Is it you, lass?"

"In the flesh, my *shikaa*."

His heart dropped to his toes, fearing now for his wife's safety. Though she appeared to have subdued Joleena quite successfully, there was still the threat of Rory coming to his sister's aid. Injured, as he was, would Raven be able to match strength with him. Braiton struggled against the ropes again, fighting for composure. Bad enough he and Kevin found themselves in such a situation, but not his Raven. *Nay, Rory will not take her life, too.*

Raven's voice broke through his inner panic as she called over her shoulder. "Kathleen, hurry and untie your husband and Lord Shannon."

From a pile of wood, out stepped Kathleen Grady.

She knew enough not to come alone, but now would he see both women harmed?

Kathleen didn't hesitant for a moment. She ran to her husband and freed him before Rory was able to make a move to help Joleena. While Kevin bound Rory's bloody wrists with the rope that once secured his, Kathleen ran to Braiton and released him from his binds.

He held his rope out to Raven, who was now

keeping Joleena pinned to the floor with both her knees planted squarely on her captive's back. "Care to do the honors, my lady?"

"With pleasure," she said, handing him the pistol.

"Run and get the constable, Kathleen," Kevin said.

Kathleen nodded and hurried out the door to get the authorities.

"Nay," screamed Joleena. "I cannot spend one day in prison."

"You haven't a choice in the matter, lass," Braiton said, his lungs breathing much easier now that both Rory and Joleena were restrained. "And 'twill be much more than a day for both of you. I've an affidavit signed by Evangeline O'Neill stating her suspicions you and Rory were the cause of her son and daughter-in-law's death."

"Then you have spoken to Lady O'Neill?" Raven said.

"Aye, lass, the morning before we left Glenview." He smiled, pride swelling his heart for having such a clever and resourceful wife. "As you asked me to do."

"Please don't send me to prison, Braiton," Joleena pleaded, tears streaming from terror filled eyes.

"Ah, but think of the adventure of it all, lass. After the vermin nestle deep within those amber curls, they'll be sheared to the scalp. Perhaps you could weave with them a nice basket. And think of the new clothes you'll be given. Can't say they'll be anything warm or fashionable, but then again the guards will be glad to heat your flesh with their own."

"Nay, nay, I can't go to prison, Braiton," she screeched.

"You should've thought of that before, Joleena," he snapped, a hatred he never knew existed hardening every fiber of his being. "But then again, you didn't think you'd get caught, did you now?"

"Have you no mercy?" she sobbed.

His tone was as cold as his heart at that moment. "Nay, lass, not for you."

Joleena turned her head and glared at Raven. "You...you little bitch, how could you have figured all this out?"

"The inscription on the first page of the sonnet book Lord O'Neill gave me was written in the same hand as the signature on the receipts. It read: To my loving father, Shamus O'Neill. The fancy way the letter "*I*" is dotted, in a swirl, like a dancing snake, got my attention. And it was signed: Your loving daughter, Joleena."

Rory groaned from his place on the floor. "I'd say she's definitely not the twit you mistook her for, little sister."

Nay, never a twit. Pride again coursed through his veins for his wife and the action she took to save him...although he'd clearly have a talk with her when he got her home about taking such a risk.

After the constables arrived and took Rory and Joleena away, he was able to fully size up the mode of dress Raven and Kathleen were garbed in. "It must be the fashion for all you lassies to dress like lads."

Raven flashed him a playful smile. "Maybe I should tell Tilly of the new idea."

He ran a finger down her smudged cheek. "How is it you're covered in soot?"

"The doors were locked, so Kathleen and I climbed up the trash chute. How else do you think we got in?"

He chuckled. "My lady, I was so stunned to see you leap from those crates, how you got here was the furthest thought from my mind." He smiled down at her. "'Tis most definite, Grania O'Malley would've had you fighting by her side."

"I was not the only one who came to your rescue." She smiled over at Kathleen. "If it were not for Kathleen's visit warning me something was wrong and her knowing how to get into the warehouse..." her voice trailed off.

Kathleen, visibly shaken, wrapped her arms around herself. "I cannot bear to think what might have been, had we not come."

Kevin pulled her close. "You and Lady Shannon are the two bravest lassies I know, and your husband's are extremely grateful."

"My sentiments, exactly," Braiton chimed in, his admiration and respect for his wife mounting in volumes. Even dressed as she was and covered in soot, she still posed a delectable sight.

"Now, lass," Kevin said, taking his wife by the hand. "I'm starvin'. Let's go home and eat."

Kathleen looked back at Raven. "Thank you, m'lady, for listenin' to me."

Raven smiled. "It is I who thanks you, Kathleen."

He took an audible breath. "I'd say home is where we should head as well, my lady."

Raven looked around the storage room, frowning. "Where is Patrick?"

"At Shannonbrook with his wife, where he belongs," he said.

"But I have not seen him all day."

"Ah, well, 'tis probably because he went fishing, since I gave him the time off. 'Tis his most favorite thing to do, outside of eating Anna's cooking."

Her frown deepened. "Then who drove the carriage here?"

"Rory talked me into driving it myself. We'd taken the carriage out alone many times when we were lads. He said 'twould be like old times." He sighed. "He wanted Kevin to join us, so 'twould look as though he was really going through his father's accounts. He even made a point to let Anna know he regretted not staying for dinner. He said he'd be sailing for Bunratty after we were through with business." He sighed again, his friend's betrayal wounding him deep. "But once we were all gathered here, he held a gun on me while I wrote a message to be delivered home, saying I would be in town until nine o'clock."

"Your death would have looked as though it happened long after he left," she said.

He nodded. "Except for the fact I gave the note to Brodie. " He chuckled. "For once I'm glad the lad is so unreliable. 'Twas then Joleena arrived, dressed as she was and tied Kevin and I to the chairs.

"The authorities would be looking to question a man of slight build, summing up the swindler came to finish the job," she said.

"Aye, Rory thought he covered every corner." He shook his head, the scale of the crime evident. "Such a scheme didn't hatch overnight. The two of them planned this for a long time."

"But they could not have gone completely through with it if Lord O'Neill did not die." Her eyes widened. "Good heavens, Braiton, you do not think they had anything to do with his death, too?"

His heart sickened to think of his mentor as a victim of Rory and Joleena's greed. "I don't know, Raven. Anything's possible with those two. I guess the investigators will have their hands full with this case. And if there's anyway I can assist them, I shall. Rory and Joleena O'Neill will not see the dawn of a free day until they're very old...perhaps not at all."

She placed a hand on his arm. "I am so sorry, my *shikaa* you have been betrayed by those you believed were friends."

As always, she picked up on his inner feelings. The woman was a rare gem indeed. He searched her face. "I'm just thankful they didn't count on the fact I have such a resourceful wife."

She looked down at her soot-stained clothes. "Right now I am a messy wife."

He picked up her hand and kissed it. "I'd say you're dirtier than Brawn was when we brought him home. I think 'tis in order I prescribe for you what I did for him, a bath."

She giggled. "I can just hear Anna now."

Chapter Twenty-Two

It was 1864 when Raven's mother, Amanda Gregory, better known as Golden Lady, married Proud Eagle and brought the Thanksgiving celebration to the Apache village. Now, twenty-eight years later Raven did the same for the folks at Shannonbrook in Ireland. After describing the holiday to the servants, they did the best they could to comply. Several turkeys were roasted on outdoor pits and under her guidance the trimmings were prepared.

All of the household staff, the stable help, the ground keepers, warehouse workers, and tenants were invited to dine and give thanks with her and Braiton. And there was much to be thankful for. Her husband's business was once again thriving, the tenants all reaped a plentiful harvest, and the children were able to go to school.

They all gathered in the great room of the mansion, where several long tables were set up with food. Everyone helped themselves to the meal, and then took their plates to various areas of the estate to eat. There was laughing and singing at every turn, all enjoying her country's feast. She knew her mother would have been proud of the way she shared Thanksgiving with the Irish, and wished her parents and siblings were along for the fun.

Her husband smiled as she poured a cup of tea for Molly. "Lass, I admire the warmth and spirit that springs forth from you. You are like a burst of sunshine."

She glanced around with satisfaction at all those

savoring the food that took days to prepare. "I believe the Irish like Thanksgiving."

He chuckled. "Aye, but 'tis you they love."

The month of December sped by and soon Shannonbrook was aglow with holiday cheer. A large tree was erected in the great room, decorated with glass balls and china figurines. She never saw anything quite as grand. Gifts were delivered daily from Braiton's clients, business acquaintances, and friends. Soon the space beneath the tree was filled to capacity. As thrilling as it was to receive packages wrapped with brightly colored paper, ribbons, and bows, there was only one delivery she waited for. Each day that passed, she worried it would not arrive.

Two days before Christmas she was in the kitchen making cookies with Anna, when Brian announced a delivery for her. Running through the mansion, her clothes coated with flour, she found the large package waiting for her in the study. Her gift to Braiton was finally here, now she prayed he would be pleased with it.

On Christmas Eve, Braiton escorted her to midnight mass at the big cathedral in the village. She wore a cranberry colored velvet gown and matching cape, trimmed with white fur. Candles glowed, illuminating the stained glass windows and the choir raised their voices, heralding the hymns like a host of angels. Riding back to Shannonbrook, she sat quiet in the bian, lost in deep thought. With a heavy heart she missed the family and friends who usually shared this occasion with her.

Braiton reached for her hand. "You're so quiet this evening, my lady. Is anything wrong?"

She sighed. "I was just picturing my mother making my father a Christmas meal, then sitting around the fire pit telling stories and singing songs."

"I'm sorry they cannot be here with you."

"I am too, my *shikaa*." She squeezed his hand. "But they have each other, and I can only imagine how Sunny is reacting to Christmas in England. If Aunt Kaylena celebrates it as grand as we do at Shannonbrook, I am sure my sister is crazy with excitement."

He smiled. "What of your brother?"

She cocked her head sideways with thoughtful musings of Gabriel. "He will be calm on the outside, but filled with excitement on the inside." She narrowed her eyes. "He must always play the steadfast warrior, you know."

He laughed, the dimple in his chin deepening. "Well, we men have to keep up a uniformed front."

Still holding his hand, she brought it to rest on her lap. "Are you not excited to open all the gifts beneath the tree?"

"I like giving much better than receiving, my lady."

"Yes, well, that is what the Bible teaches, and it is the right thing to do, of course. But I must admit, in truth, I like receiving a lot better."

He laughed again. "And the truth shall set you free."

Brian had mugs of eggnog waiting for them when they arrived at Shannonbrook. Braiton handed her a package from beneath the tree, his green eyes sparkling. "I was going to wait till morning to give this to you, but since you like receiving," he teased, "perhaps you should open it now."

Her spirits were renewed as she tore away the fancy wrappings and raised the box's lid. Inside was a leather violin carrying case, her initials engraved on a gold plate by the latch. She sprang the catch with trembling fingers and caressed the deep blue velvet lining.

"This is magnificient," she marveled, running a hand over the rich, soft, leather. "It will be a lot easier carrying the violin to the schoolhouse now."

"Then you like it, my lady?"

She stood and placed the case aside. Cautiously she hugged him, keeping just enough distance from him, so he would not feel the baby bulge rounding her belly. "I love it."

He stroked her hair. "I'm so happy you're pleased."

She raised her gaze to his. "You have done more than please me, Braiton." Standing on tiptoe, she placed a kiss upon his lips, then whispered against his mouth. "*Ashoge*, thank you from the bottom of my *biijii*, heart."

The nearness of her, the warmth of her body against his, made the blood rush through his veins. He yearned to pull her closer and plant the most passionate kiss upon her full, soft lips. But his secret torment held him in control. Instead, he returned her affection with a tiny peck upon her forehead.

"I have something for you as well," she beamed.

He smiled at the child-like excitement in her eyes. "Do you now?"

"It is in my chamber," she said, taking him by the hand and leading him upstairs. "It was the only place I could think to hide it, where I was sure you would not snoop."

He pretended to be shocked. "Me, snoop? Never."

She giggled. "Anna told me all about the way you crept around the mansion looking for presents. I was not taking any chances."

He gave a playful scowl. "Anna has a wagging tongue, besides I was only a lad at the time."

She brought him over to a large object covered with a blanket. "It was too big to wrap with colored paper."

"May I unveil it?"

"Yes, my *shikaa*."

He was not prepared for what he saw. Before

him, framed in gold, was a portrait of Raven standing with moccasin-clad feet, one foot upon a large rock. A hand was upon her hip, the other holding a spear. Her chin was lifted in a proud pose, hair falling to her waist. She was clothed in a traditional Apache dress, which hung only to her knees. In the background a river flowed, the water as blue as her eyes.

The painting took his breath away. “Raven, where did you pose for this?”

“On the reservation, just days before I left for England.”

He ran his fingers over the canvas. “Who is the artist?”

“My sister, Sunny. She painted this from a sketch she drew of me.”

“She paints extraordinary,” he marveled, taking in each detail of her face.

“Yes, she is quite good, absolutely loves to draw. Sometimes she would be so engrossed in her artwork, she would forget to eat. She begged anyone going into town for a tablet of paper and lead sticks. Before we left America, she sketched most of the people in the tribe; left them something to remember her by.”

“How did you commission her to do this for you?”

“In her letters to me she wrote how Aunt Kaylena enrolled her in art lessons and her discovery of painting with oils. In a return letter, I asked if she would paint with the oils the sketch she did of me on the reservation, as a Christmas gift to you.”

He was mesmerized by the painting. “Is it exactly like the sketch?”

“My hair is different. In the sketch I am wearing the nah-leen, as a maiden in my tribe would do. Only the married women wear their hair down.”

“Aye, I remember you explaining that to me,” he

said.

"Well, I figured, since I was now married and you enjoy my hair free, the change would please you more."

"Aye, lass, it does." He dragged his gaze from the painting to search her face. "I can't think of anything as wonderful as this glimpse of you in your native dress, the proud spirit of your people portrayed on your face." He smiled. "You and Sunny are a talented pair. One sister plays the violin, the other paints."

"Then you like your gift?"

"Aye, I do, my lady."

"I thought it might look nice hanging over the library mantle."

"Nay, 'twill be hung over the mantle in the drawing room, where everyone who enters Shannonbrook will be able to admire it."

Her cheeks turned crimson. "Are you sure you want that?"

"Aye, lass, I'm quite sure." He caressed the side of her face with the tip of a finger. "I want everyone to know how proud I am of my Indian princess."

She smiled. "Merry Christmas, Braiton."

"To you as well, Raven," he said, lifting her chin with the tip of his finger, and bestowing upon her lips the kiss he'd been denying himself all evening.

Chapter Twenty-Three

Several times she wanted to tell Braiton she carried his child, but it was not the sort of news to be shared without the time to talk further, especially in this situation. With the aftermath of the holidays and his preparations for a business voyage to France, a convenient time never surfaced. Before she knew it he was gone for six very long weeks. Each day she missed him more and more. Her tiny waist continuing to swell. It would not be long before everyone knew her secret.

In five months time I will give birth, and my husband has yet to know he is going to be a father. She rubbed her belly with loving strokes. *As soon as he returns, I will most definitely have to tell him.*

But his return fell just a week before St. Patrick's Day, a time the Irish celebrated with exuberance. Her time was consumed with writing out and sending invitations to those prominent people in Limerick and the surrounding Clare County, as well as a visit and verbal invite to those tenants on the estate who could not read. She made sure no one was excluded from the gala. Since all the festivities would take place outdoors, she prayed for good weather.

The day of the St. Patrick's celebration, Braiton couldn't help but think what an interesting day it would be with such a mix of social classes. His wife was exquisite in a bright yellow and cream, brocaded gown and matching hooded cape, walking by his side. With her arm looped over his, she smiled and greeted the guests. She especially cared for and enjoyed the tenants, complimenting the women on how stunning they looked in their best dress and embracing the children. He listened to the sweetness of her laughter and watched the soft curve of her mouth as she spoke. She was genuine, considerate, and became a friend to them all.

He always prided himself at being a landlord who paid his workers fair wages and charged tenants reasonable rent, but Raven encouraged him to extend himself beyond what was expected. She made sure he had peppermint sticks on hand to give out to the children and jugs of water or ale brought out to the workers. She'd sing and play the violin in the garden, with a group of children gathered around her. When she wasn't tending school, she helped the women bake bread. She was never idle and always pleasant to everyone.

He studied her now, today she simply glowed. The twinkle in her eyes, her beaming smile, and the brilliance of her yellow ensemble, reminded him of a ray of sunshine. The thick ebony curls framing her face, shone; each lock entwined with ribbons to match her gown. Her beauty surpassed every woman there, and his heart swelled with love for her.

Gazing around at the other men, he found them watching her throughout the day. Their eyes gleamed with a mixture of admiration and lust. There'd not be a one among them who would deny her their affection, should she be willing. Just the thought of another man touching her, and her yielding to their caresses, made his insides clench. If he dwelled on such a thought for too long, he knew it would drive him insane.

They strolled toward the river, her arm draped around his, a sapphire gaze searching his face, a smile curving full, luscious lips. "Is it the festivities that have brightened your eyes or the anticipation of spring?"

"Neither, there is another reason for what you see. And I think this would be the perfect time to tell you."

His smile deepened. Knowing her as he did, the reason could be almost anything. Raven had a knack for keeping him surprised. "I'm almost afraid to ask what that reason might be, lass?"

She took an audible breath. "I pray you will be as happy as I am about it, Braiton."

"I'm sure whatever makes you as happy as you seem, will do the same for me."

"I am...actually, I should say, we are going to have a—" Screams from the children playing on the bank interrupted her.

Raven turned from Braition in time to see a child's head sinking below the surface of the water. Without hesitation, she ripped off her cape and ran to the child's aid. Picking up the hem of her skirt, she hurried into the water and swam after the drowning victim.

Paralyzed by the Shannon River's frigid waters, her heart pounded as she dove deep. The weight of her garments encumbered her attempts to reach the child. She fought the odds with all her strength. Reaching out, she grabbed the child by the hair and pulled his face to the surface. With an arm wrapped around his neck, she fought in desperation to keep them afloat. The shocking cold water slapped painfully against her ribs. Her legs grew numb. Out of breath and losing her grip on the child, she struggled to shore.

Just when she thought she could go no farther, someone took the child from her. Then a pair of strong arms plucked her from the watery chill and held her close. She looked up into her husband's eyes and opened her mouth to speak, reassure him she was all right. But the words did not come. His voice calling her name was the last thing she heard before everything in her world darkened.

Braiton ran to the mansion with Raven in his arms. “Someone find Terrance Murphy,” he shouted. He burst through the doubled doors and past Molly.

“Saints preserve us,” she screeched.

He took the stairs two at a time to Raven’s chamber. “Get towels, blankets, put more wood on the fire,” he demanded over his shoulder.

“Oh, sweet Mother of God,” Molly sobbed, following close behind.

“Stop your blubbering, woman and do as I’ve asked,” he snapped. With trembling fingers he ripped apart the bodice of her dress, stripping Raven of her clothes. He had to remove the wet garments from her flesh to keep her from fever. Molly returned with all he requested and wrapped her in a blanket as he dried his wife’s hair with the towels.

He rubbed Raven’s hands. “Come on, lass, open your eyes,” he whispered, fearful he was losing her. “Don’t do this to me, Raven. Don’t be leaving me, now lass. Not like this…not like this.”

Terrance Murphy burst into the room and pushed Braiton aside. “How is her breathin’?”

He moved to the foot of the bed, fear gripping his heart. “Shallow.”

“Have you noticed any bleedin’?” Terrance listened to her heart with the instrument he pulled from his black bag.”

He frowned. “Nay, why would she bleed?”

“In her condition, suddenly bein’ emerged in freezin’ water could shock the babe she’s carryin’. She’s miscarried once. I dare not take a chance she’ll do the same again.”

He was numb all over, the blood draining from his head. He grabbed the bedpost to keep from collapsing. “A baby?”

“Aye, m’lord, a baby.” Terrance glanced his way and frowned. “For God’s sake, get a hold of yourself.

You act like you're hearing the news for the first time."

Molly came beside him and took him by the arm. "Come away, m'lord," she said, leading him out of the room and to his own chamber. "Let's let the good Doctor Murphy take care of your wife."

He made his way to a chair and sat, stunned. "She's having a baby?"

Molly put more wood on the fire. "Best you get yourself out o' those wet clothes, before you catch your death as well, m'lord."

"You knew, Molly?"

She knelt to remove his boots. "Aye, m'lord."

He swallowed the lump in his throat rising to choke him. "How far into the pregnancy is she?"

"She's about four months along, m'lord."

His voice trembled. "Why didn't you tell me?"

Molly stood. "She didn't want to cause you further worries, m'lord. At the time she learned o' the news, you were goin' through so much at the warehouse. M'lady felt you had enough upon your shoulders." She shifted her gaze to the floor. "I promised her I wouldn't tell you."

He inhaled a calming breath. "I understand your loyalty to her, Molly, but not your discretion. Something of this magnitude should have reached my ears, way before this."

"'Twas not me place, m'lord."

"Leave me be, Molly," he snapped. Again he'd been betrayed—now by his own staff.

She wrung her hands in front of her. "Please don't be angry with me, m'lord."

He stood, making his way to the veranda doors. "Just go!" he bellowed, not able to stomach looking any longer upon the woman's face. "Terrance might need your help in tending my wife."

"Aye, m'lord," was Molly's meek reply before she left the room.

He looked out onto the lawn below. People were still milling about, enjoying the rest of the St. Patrick's Day celebration.

She's four months along.

He ran a hand through his hair and did the math, his calculations bringing him to the time they were at Glenview. Closing his eyes he saw her laying beneath him, submitting to his touch, his kisses, his… 'Twas not a delicious dream he'd been having, but a flashback of what he'd done. He made love to her the night he drank too much whiskey with Lord Wade, and given her a child. He groaned and opened his eyes, remembering the morning after. His head pounded, his stomach queasy, but he made sure to ask her if he'd compromised her in any way. She denied he did. Why had she lied?

He moved to sit on the bed, his thoughts swirling. Then everything became crystal clear. He knew exactly why she lied. She feared she wouldn't be able to leave Ireland when the time came. An annulment would be out of the question if the marriage had been consummated. Strange enough, he was filled with disappointment. Some small part of his heart wanted her to stay, remain his wife. Bowing his head with sorrow, he realized how impossible that would be. She couldn't stay in Ireland, and 'twas to his advantage she felt the same.

****

Raven was sitting up in bed, sipping tea when Braiton came to her later that evening. He knocked on her door, and she bid him to enter, scooting over a bit so he could sit at the edge of the bed.

"I just wanted to see how you were doing, lass." His large green eyes scanned the length of her. "Nothing hurts?"

She forced a smile. "All is well."

"I'm glad, I'm glad," he said.

She searched his face. “We need to talk, Braiton.”

He chuckled sardonically. “That, my lady, is an understatement.”

She sighed. “I am so sorry, my *shikaa*.”

“’Tis I who is sorry, my lady, for losing my control and putting you in this position,” he said, gesturing to her belly.

“I would have told you sooner, but I feared—”

“I know what you feared, lass,” he interjected. “But there is no need. Our agreement still stands as ’tis. The marriage cannot be dissolved by annulment, but can by divorce.” He stood. “And since this whole mess is my fault, I will take full responsibility for it all. No shame will be placed upon your good name.” He walked to the door. “I’ll leave you now to your rest.”

Alone again in her room, tears filled her eyes and streamed down her cheeks. The pounding of her heart echoed in her ears, and she was overwhelmed with an acute sense of loss. She felt a wretchedness of mind she had never known before. The despair gripping her heart physically engulfed her with pain.

Placing her hands over her belly, she wrapped her unborn child in a cocoon of anguish. *He really wants us gone.*

She choked on a sob and whispered, “And here I was hoping he would ask us to stay.”

Chapter Twenty-Four

Ireland in the spring was a welcomed sight to behold. The garden was green, lush, and alive. Raven stood admiring the new blooms when Braiton came up beside her. "I have been thinking, after the baby arrives, 'twould be necessary for you to have help."

"I have Molly and Anna," she said, then smiled. "And you."

His eyes widened. "Me? I know nothing about babies."

She gave him an affectionate pat on the arm. "Then, like my father did, you will learn." He sat down on a garden bench, looking like the air was taken from his lungs. She giggled. "It is not all that bad, my *shikaa*."

He frowned. "I'm just trying to be practical here, Raven. Anna and Molly have their own duties. Besides, neither of them is getting any younger."

"Oh, Braiton, never let them hear you say that."

He arched a brow. "Aye, that's the truth." He cleared his throat. "As for myself, though I'm not against learning, I'm at the warehouse most afternoons, and sometimes for the better part of the day. You'll need someone you can rely on for those times, at least."

Her brow creased in contemplation. "I know of no one trustworthy to care for our child."

He cast a triumphant smile. "Ah, but I do."

"Who?"

He stood and took her by the hand. "Come and see."

He led her to the drawing room, where a young woman waited. Thin framed and a crop of auburn curls piled atop of her head; she stood admiring Raven's portrait.

"'Tis a beautiful likeness, don't you think?" Braiton asked the woman.

"Aye, 'tis at that," she replied, turning to face them.

Raven gasped. "Sinead." Running to embrace the other women, she held her close for a moment, then set her at arm's length. "Let me look at you."

Sinead cast a shy glance to the floor. "I'm just the same as I've always been, m'lady."

She took Sinead by the hand. "I am so happy to see you."

Sinead met her gaze. "And I you, m'lady."

"What do you say, Raven?" Braiton said. "Do you trust the lass with the care of our child?"

She turned to smile his way. "I trust her fully."

"'Tis settled then," he said, with a satisfied nod of his head. "Now, I'll leave you two alone to discuss the position," he added, making his way to the door.

She motioned for Sinead to take a seat. "Lady O'Neill no longer has a use for your services?"

"Nay, m'lady. With Miss Joleena gone, Tessie is all she needs."

She rubbed her large belly with a gentle hand. "Well, you are needed here, if you wish to stay."

Sinead's face brightened. "Aye, m'lady, 'twould be so grand if I could."

She stood and took Sinead's hand. "Come, let me show you the nursery and the adjoining room that will be yours."

"'Twill be such a joy helpin' you with the wee one." Sinead took an audible breath. "I can't tell you how happy I was when Lord Shannon sent for me." She gave Raven's hand a squeeze. "I promise to love and care for your babe with all o' me heart."

She smiled. "I cannot ask for anything more, Sinead."

****

Spring turned to summer. A tranquil breeze blew, bursts of sunlight beamed in the pale blue sky, birds sang, flowers swelled to their lustrous beauty, and so did Raven's belly. She sat naked on a chair in her chamber, her rounded stomach resting on her thighs, while being prepared for bed. She sighed as Molly washed her back with a cool cloth. "The flowers are not the only things in full bloom."

"And like the flowers, you're just as beautiful, m'lady," Molly said, moving to bathe her bulging belly. "'Twon't be long now till you hold the wee one in your arms."

"I cannot wait for that time, Molly." Along with her time nearing to give birth, so was the time to leave Ireland. In spite of her agreement with Braiton, she remained hopeful once he saw his child, held the babe in his arms; he would ask her to stay. He was, after all, attentive to her needs, made sure she ate properly, got enough rest. He even insisted Terrance check her once a week, relieved each time to learn all was well and the baby was thriving.

She stood and raised her arms for Molly to slip the summer nightgown she chose over her head. The light, linen material was cool against her hot flesh. It fell gracefully over her belly and danced around her ankles.

"Aye, m'lady, you're as beautiful as any flower."

She smiled at her reflection in the mirror and caressed her abdomen. "Not just any flower, Molly, one perfect flower."

Molly placed a hand over hers. "Aye, m'lady, 'tis as perfect as it gets."

****

Braiton sat at the edge of his bed with his aching, throbbing head in his hands. Though he was exhausted, he couldn't sleep. Terrance assured him all was well with his wife and child, yet still he worried. Many women died during child birth. How could he live on, if he caused her death? Each day her eyes held the glow of a nurturing and loving mother. How would she live on if the child were still born?

Lately his hands shook, eyes blurred, and his appetite dwindled. Terrance laughed when he explained his symptoms, saying they were typical of an expectant father. But he knew different, saw the same happen to his mother. Before long she couldn't do the simplest of things for herself. She had to be fed, washed, and her bloomers changed like a wee one. All dignity stripped from her, and yet her mind was as clear and sharp as ever.

He rose from the bed and paced his chamber floor. He couldn't bear the thought of Raven seeing him in that condition. Knowing her heart to be a kind and good one, she'd insist on caring for him. How could he watch her struggle to stay hopeful while wiping and washing his body? The humiliating thought of her tending to his personal needs heated his face. He walked over to the open veranda doors, inhaling the night air. Again he would know no rest. Like a festering sore anguish gathered to torment his spirit. He knew, after the baby was born, she and the child would have to leave.

****

No matter how many times Molly or Sinead cooled Raven's flesh, it still sweltered. Stuck now to the sheets, sleep would not come. She threw her legs off the bed and struggled to sit. When she gained her balance, she stood and made her way to the open veranda doors. A small breeze played with the moist curls framing her face. Taking a deep breath, she struggled to remain calm. Lately she became agitated easily, breaking out in tears over the smallest thing. As she gazed out into the darkness the child she carried beneath her heart, stirred. She smiled to herself, remembering earlier in the day taking Braiton's hand and placing it over her belly.

He felt the baby move and a slow grin spread across his face. A second time the kick was more intense, and she winced. His face changed, eyes filled with concern. "Are you in pain, my lady?"

She laughed and reassured him, more then a dozen times after, it did not hurt. "It is a strange and wonderful sensation to experience," she explained. "To imagine, within my body there is another body growing, is so miraculous."

"Aye, miraculous indeed," he agreed.

My dear Braiton, do you really feel that way…will you change your mind about our agreement and let us stay?

****

Raven rested upon the garden chaise, not able to do much else. She resembled a stuffed turkey. Sighing, she raised her eyes to the heavens and declared aloud to herself, "Ah, what I would give to go riding."

"You're hardly in a condition to do that, my lady."

She turned to find Braiton in the doorframe. "Well, a girl can dream."

He arched a brow. "Aye, that she can." He came nearer. "But I have another idea that might please you." With that said, he was off. Within the hour, he returned and escorted her to the side entrance. A small wagon was parked there. She recognized it as the one Clancy used to bring vegetables to the village market. "I thought, instead of the large carriage, this would make you feel more as though you were riding," he explained.

She nodded in agreement. "Good thinking, my *shikaa*." The gray mare hitched to the farm cart stomped a foot, anxious to get going. "My sentiments exactly," she said, allowing Braiton to help her aboard.

He guided the small carriage down the long, winding path, over a small bridge, and to the river. The day was warm, but a breeze blew in from the water. The simple cotton frock she wore, void of undergarments, rustled against her swollen stomach. Within moments the gentle wind grew lusty and drops of water pelted her skin.

Braiton raised his gaze to the dark clouds blanketing the sky. "We're in for a storm, and by the fierce way 'tis coming, we'll never make it back to Shannonbrook." He frowned and glanced south. "There's a hunter's cottage down that path, 'twould be wise for us to take cover there till it passes."

She hung onto the carriage's rim as they jostled down the unpaved road. With each jolt, her stomach bounced, and she winced. Then it happened. A gush of water broke from her loins and soaked her feet.

She gasped. "Braiton, hurry and get me to the cottage."

He turned to look her way, and seeing the puddle on the carriage floor, his face paled. "Saints preserve us, lass. I should have never taken you from the comforts of home"

A sharp pain pierced her middle and she groaned, holding her abdomen. "The baby's coming."

"Nay, lass, not now...not here," he choked out hoarsely.

By the time they reached the hunter's cottage, the rain soaked them through and through. He carried her inside and placed her on the tiny cot, leaving her only long enough to tie the horse beneath a wooden port built alongside the small house.

He helped her off with her wet clothing and covered her with a quilt. "I'm going to make a run for

Terrance."

She reached for his hand. "No, Braiton, do not leave me here alone."

He frowned. "I can be back within the hour, my lady."

She glanced out a window at the angry storm. "In this weather you cannot promise the roads will remain passable." Pain ripped through her, and she gasped. "I do not believe there is time for you to get help."

He swallowed hard. "But I know nothing of such things, Raven."

She bit back another pain. "I have helped birth many babies, and I will tell you what to do."

He combed the fingers of his other hand through his hair. "Raven, I cannot..."

Tears sprang to her eyes. "You have to, Braiton," she interrupted. "Please, I need your help."

"Aye, my lady, that you do." He sighed. "Tell me then, what must be done."

"You will need blankets, string, a basin to fill with water, and a knife."

He nodded, leaving her only long enough to fetch the things she requested. Luckily, all the items needed were available, though the hunting knife had to be cleaned with whiskey he found in a cupboard. He placed everything on a table beside the cot.

"What now, Raven?"

Another pain consumed her, slicing through her like a warrior's spear. Never did she experience anything so unbearable. She threw her head back, and a long, high-pitched sob escaped her throat.

Braiton fell to his knees beside the cot, her agony mirrored in his eyes. "Mother of God, lass, what can I be doing for you?"

"There is nothing you can do," she gulped.

"If Terrance or Molly were here..."

"They could do no more for me then you are

doing," she cut him short. Another pain washed through her body, and she reached for his hand. He winced with the bone crushing grip, but did not pull away.

The storm raged on, pelts of rain hit the windows and roof. For what was an eternity, she labored, rested, then labored, again, until she cried out. "Is everything ready?"

"Aye lass," he said, gesturing to the things set out on the table.

"Then help me to stand."

His eyes widened. "Nay, Raven."

She gasped. "It is easier when standing. This is the way the women of my tribe give birth.

"But the child will fall head first onto the floor."

"You will get down on your knees behind me and catch the baby," she said. "Now, please help me to stand." With gentle hands he lifted her.

Bracing herself using the mantle, she spread her legs and crouched. Intense pain tore through her, pressure increasing, and she pushed. His trembling hands, outstretched between her thighs, were soon covered with her blood.

"The babe comes now," she cried out.

"Aye, I see the head." His words filled with awe.

The last pain gripped her harder, longer. With great effort she pushed one last time, till the baby fell from her womb.

"I hav...him...him, Raven. 'Tis a boy. We have a son," he rambled on excited.

"Tie the cord with the string and cut it from me," she instructed. "Then tend to the baby."

He turned his attention to the crying child, wrapping him in a blanket and placing him at the foot of the cot. She tended to what came after the birth, and then crawled upon the tiny bed.

"You have to wash him with the water. The tribe's midwife warms the water in her mouth before spraying it all over the baby."

He chuckled. "Won't just washing him with a cloth do, my lady? I'm making quite a mess as 'tis."

She smiled. "It will do fine. You have done fine, Braiton. *Ashoge*, thank you." After he washed and wrapped the baby in a clean blanket, he handed her their son. She brought the infant to her breast. Braiton sat at the edge of the cot and watched their son take his first bit of nourishment. She looked down at the infant and stroked his soft cheek with the tip of a finger.

"What shall we call him?"

He reached out and touched the baby's hand. "The Gaelic word meaning brave is Casey."

She smiled. "Mothers wish for their sons to be kind and good, fathers want them to be brave." She raised her gaze from the babe to his. "Is that not true?"

He ran his hands over weary eyes. "Aye, our son will need to be very brave." He sighed, a cloud of sadness passing over his face. "And 'twould be nice to have his middle name be Broderick, after my father," he added. "Does that stand well with you, my lady?"

She tried out the name. "Casey Broderick Shannon." She nodded. "I like it, a good strong name for a good strong boy." She reached over to caress Braiton's face. "You look tired, my lord."

He turned his mouth into her hand, bestowing a kiss upon her palm. "'Twas you who did all the work."

She glanced again at her son, feeding at her breast. "Casey Broderick Shannon had both his parents working today. Each of us did our part in giving him life." Looking back at Braiton, she found him curled in a ball, deep in sleep. She rested her head back upon the pillow and smiled, "That, is a very good idea, my *shikaa*."

Chapter Twenty-Five

Braiton truly believed Ireland welcomed autumn much better than his wife did. She was adamant about not wanting the cold months ahead to come. However, his son relished the passing time, growing bigger and stronger with each day. As proud parents often did, they marveled over the babe's little accomplishments. Though he did his best to distance himself from his wife and child, preparing them all for the time when they'd part, one ear always heard what went on with them both.

On his thirtieth birthday he requested no fuss be made and spent the day in his study, staring out the window. Today marked the beginning of the time he dreaded. At thirty, his mother began her battle with the illness that took her life. And she wasn't the only victim. At precisely the same age his grandfather, and his mother before him, all succumbed to the same fate. Mother, son...mother, son, was the pattern; and he was next.

****

Raven worked for weeks on Braiton's surprise, and though he asked for no acknowledgment of the day, she wanted him to have a gift from her. He was so good to her, taking care of all her needs and those of their son's; she could not let his birthday pass without some recognition. She rapped on the study door and waited for the deep, rich voice to grant permission to enter. She found him standing by the window and made her way beside him.

"I wanted you to have this," she said, handing him a brightly wrapped package.

He hesitated before taking it. "'Twasn't necessary to bother, Raven."

"It was not a bother, my *shikaa*." He tore the paper, pulling from the scraps a buckskin pouch. "It is for your compass." She reached for the small bag and turned it over. "On the back I have made a strap, so you can fasten it onto your belt. In this way you will always have the compass handy."

He chuckled. "Is this a polite way of telling me I need to keep track of my direction?"

She smiled. "It is not a bad thing for all of us to do."

He took the time to examine the pouch. "The craftsmanship is exquisite, the design so intricate." His gaze rose to meet hers. "I had no idea you were so talented with leather."

"On the reservation I was always making something out of animal hide." She glanced down at his boots. "My next gift will be moccasins. Once you put them on your feet, you will never want to wear anything else."

"Extremely comfortable, are they?"

She met his gaze. "More then you could ever imagine."

He sighed. "Do you know what I was doing last year on my birthday, Raven?"

She shook her head. "Do tell."

He smiled fondly. "I was rescuing a young woman from the clutches of a rogue in Silver City."

She gasped. "That day was your birthday?"

"Aye lass, and up till that point it was pretty uneventful."

"Leave it to me to be the event of someone's day."

"You have been the event of every day since, my lady." He made his way to his desk and sat down. "I don't remember you saying when your birthday was."

She moved to stand in front of the writing table. "That is because I did not. Anyway, it has already long come and gone, my lord."

He arched a brow. "And you gave me no chance to honor it?"

She smiled down at him. "Ah, but you did, in a most generous way."

He frowned. "Am I losing my memory along with my direction?"

She giggled. "I turned twenty on the day you brought me to Tilly's for all those beautiful clothes." She cocked her head sideways. "Then there was Brawn, he was another unexpected present."

"Oh, aye, good ole' Brawn." He sat back in his seat. "Why didn't you let me know?"

She shrugged. "You had done enough already. And I have intruded long enough on your request to be alone." She made her way to the door.

"Raven," he called after her. She turned to look his way. "Thank you for such a wonderful gift. I'll cherish it always."

She smiled. "I am glad, my shikaa. Happy birthday," she said, taking a moment to search his face before she left the room. Lines of worry creased his brow; his emerald eyes showed tortured dullness. Both concerned and disturbed for his well-being, she added, "And I wish you many more healthy ones to come, Braiton."

He took an audible breath. "My wish is for the same, my lady."

Braiton waited for her to shut the door behind her before he looked over the pouch again. She must have spent hours on the stitching. It was perfect. He rested his head back upon the chair, smiling to himself. His wife was the most loving and giving person he knew. With just a glance of those deep blue eyes she could undo him completely, send his senses reeling. She'd become such a part of his life, and unless he did something fast, she'd also become a part of his pain. The wee one was nearing his tenth week, and Raven's strength had fully returned.

Both mother and child were healthy enough to travel. It was time he kept his part of the agreement they made aboard *The Sweet Maureen*. He gave her his word he'd send her to England within a year's time, to be with her family, and that time was arriving soon. He stood, made his way to the stable, saddled Grania, and rode to the village. Today, he would keep his promise.

****

Braiton left word that upon his return he would have a surprise for Raven. She was as excited as a child on Christmas morning and asked Molly for the hundredth time, if she had any idea what the surprise was.

"Nay, m'lady," Molly replied, as she did the many times before. Lacing the bodice of a light blue, satin gown, she added again, "He only said what I've been tellin' you, and then requested you wear one o' your favorite dresses."

"I cannot imagine what he could have for me, Molly," she said, bending to smooth the full skirt.

Molly chuckled. "And you won't be findin' out any too soon either, if you don't stop fidgetin' and let me be done with the lacin'."

When she entered the dining room, she was taken back. She was not the only one garbed in elegant attire. The table was draped with a lace clothe and set with the good china and silverware. Two tall white candles were lit; crystal goblets filled with wine, and in the center sat a vase filled with a fuchsia bouquet. She gasped and brought a hand to her throat.

"Braiton, this is all so beautiful."

"As are you, Raven," he said, escorting her to the

chair placed beside his. After taking his own seat, he handed her a goblet and raised the other in a toast.

"To a year well spent."

She smiled and clicked her glass against his. The sweet taste of the wine glided down her throat. A delicious meal of roasted chicken bathed in a creamy sauce, boiled potatoes smothered in cheese, and fresh green beans were on the menu. It was followed by coffee and lemon cake, served to them in the drawing room. Braiton sat in the overstuffed chair by the fire, puffing on his clay pipe. For this evening, she remained sitting in a chair, her dress too elegant and the skirt to full to sit cross-legged on the floor.

"Such a beautiful dinner was a wonderful surprise. *Ashoge*, my *shikaa*."

"I have another, Raven." Braiton pulled from his jacket pocket a white envelope. He stared at it a moment before handing it to her. "In there you'll find an agreement kept."

Her fingers fumbled with the seal. Once opened, she pulled out three slips of paper. She frowned and looked over at him, her mind spinning with bewilderment. "I do not understand."

"There you have three passages to England, lass, aboard the luxury ship, *The Donahue*. The agreement we made is now fulfilled by us both."

She held the tickets against her heart and swallowed hard, then stood and made her way to the window, looking out onto the front lawn.

"Ah, yes, our agreement."

"You, Sinead, and Casey leave the day after tomorrow. Come the spring, I will bring Brawn and Dayden by cargo ship, if I am able." He cleared his throat. "If the situation should be otherwise, Captain Kirby will make the voyage without me."

"But Casey was not part of the agreement, Braiton."

"Aye, 'tis true, Raven, and I'll take full responsibility for my lack of control." He stood and made his way beside her. "You will be given adequate compensation for your trouble."

She turned to face him, anger swelling her heart. "Compensated for my trouble?" she repeated. "Casey is not trouble; he is my son, our son. Not some business deal you can settle with money."

He reached for her hand. "I didn't mean for it to sound like that."

She pulled away. "Then how did you mean it to sound?"

He combed his fingers through his hair. "I just meant you and Casey will never want for anything. All your financial needs, and much more will be met."

She bit her bottom lip. "I do not want your money."

"'Tis Casey's right to have it," he said.

"It is also his right to have a father," she snapped.

Braiton turned away from her and walked to the fireplace. Gripping the mantle, he stared into the fire. "He will have a mother, an aunt and an uncle to love him." He took a deep breath to still his racing pulse. "'Tis best he never knows me."

"Why…why is it best, Braiton?"

His heart pounded in his ears. "'Tis what you want as well, lass."

She neared him. "That is not true."

He spun around to face her, his voice rough with anxiety. "Then why did you lie to me?"

She blinked baffled. "I have never lied to you."

"Ah, but you have, Raven. Twice to be exact. The first time was in Glenview, the morning after we consummated Casey. I asked if anything happened between us, and you denied it did."

Her tone was velvet, yet cold and exact. "I

believe you asked if you did anything to compromise me."

"Aye, and you denied it," he snapped.

"But I did not." She inhaled sharply and held her breath for a second. When she finally spoke, she weighed each word. "You far from compromised me, Braiton. I willingly accepted your touch. Willingly received your kisses, and kissed you in return. The words we shared, the tenderness, the way you looked at me, when you…" the words caught in her throat.

Again she took a breath, her eyes filling with tears. "It was the most beautiful and thrilling moment of my life, and I never want to forget it. You want to know why, Braiton?" She didn't wait for his answer. "Because I have fallen—"

"Nay, don't," he interrupted. "Don't say it," he said, turning away from her, unable to bear the sorrow etched upon her beautiful face. "Please, say no more." He glanced at her portrait above the mantle and everything in him cried out to stop what was happening between them. To take her in his arms and hold her close; admit he never wanted her to leave him. But he couldn't be so selfish. She was better off away from him and with her family.

Her voice broke with emotion. "Is it what you really want, for us to leave and never return?"

"Aye," he lied, swallowing hard the strangling grief choking the life from him. "'Twas our agreement."

"Yes—yes it was," she said, her tone resigned. "Then I should give you back your mother's ring."

"Nay, I wish for you to keep it. 'Twill never be placed upon another woman's finger, and you can save it for when Casey…if Casey…" he couldn't finish the sentence, his emotions rising to suffocate him. But his thoughts shouted his fear. *If Casey lives long enough to wed.*

He heard her walk to the door, and he clenched

his fists to his side. Then she halted her departure.

"You said I lied to you twice. When was the second time?"

He shook his head. "It matters not now, Raven."

"It does to me. Tell me of the second time," she demanded.

"When you kept your pregnancy from me, fearing I would not let you go."

"Is that why you think I said nothing?"

He could only nod.

"I kept silent because I did not want you to be forced to let me stay. I have known right along you could never grow to love me because of what happened on the reservation."

He glanced back at her. Tears streamed down her face, falling to her collar and staining the satin material of her dress. "Raven, that's not—"

"I am a tainted woman, already touched by another," she interrupted. "Spoiled goods; nothing any man of your means would desire...unless he was filled with whiskey and half out of his mind. Am I not right, Bration?"

His heart broke for what she believed, and if he could tell her the truth, he would. But he remained silent and again turned to gaze at the flames. For her sake, 'twas better she hate him. He forced a stern tone.

"Then I would say there's nothing further for us to talk about, lass."

The silence was deafening. Finally she said, "Then I will say goodnight."

He closed his eyes, hating what he'd done to her. "Nay, 'tis farewell I'll be saying to you now, lass. I leave in the morning for business in Killarney and won't return for several days." His flesh went cold, in spite of his nearness to the fire.

"I see," she said. "Then I will take this last time to thank you for all you have done for me, and to ask you make sure the school continues for the children."

Her words, *last time*, hit him like a brick between the eyes. "I give you my word it will." His stomach twisted within him. Even now she cared for others. "God's speed on your journey, I wish you happiness with your family and in your life, Raven."

"I wish the same for you, Braiton," she replied softly, then ran from the room.

He waited for her footsteps to vanish up the stairs before he made his way to the study. Trembling, he poured himself a glass of whiskey. Numb all over, he sipped his drink and walked to the window, staring out at the night. He'd accomplished what he'd set out to do. Raven wouldn't be around to watch him waste away to nothing. She'd have a chance at a normal, happy life. He prayed the same for his son.

He ran his fingers through his hair; disgusted with himself for the way he treated her at the end. She deserved so much better. Never would he forget the hurt on her face, the tears in her eyes, the way her voice trembled. Nor what she said to him. It took courage to admit the things she did; especially believing he didn't feel the same. Only a woman who cared with a pure heart could open herself to confess such emotion. Only a woman with the stamina of Grania O'Malley, which his Raven was.

Except, after this night, she wouldn't be *his* Raven anymore. He squeezed his eyes shut. He'd never see his son again either. The lad would never run through the mansion, open gifts on Christmas morn, or climb a tree at Shannonbrook. The whole of the place will be so empty now with them gone. He would die alone. A thought worse than death itself. Tears welled in his eyes and cascaded down his face. He leaned against the window casement, shame, sorrow, and guilt piercing his heart and he wept.

****

Braiton didn't sleep a wink all night, envisioning the agony on her face. Forever it would be etched in his brain to haunt him. Maybe 'twas what he deserved.

At sunrise, he made his way to the kitchen and filled a satchel with provisions. Anna, also up early, stepped from the pantry. "Is there anythin' I can be helpin' you with, m'lord?"

"Nay, Anna, I have everything I need."

Anna sighed, coming to stand beside him. "Why are you sendin' her and the wee one away?"

He continued to fill his pack. "You know perfectly well, why."

"A man should try his best to never be separated from the woman he loves."

He met her gaze. "Not even if 'twere to spare her the grief of watching him die?"

Her eyes never wavered. "Nay, m'lord, not even then."

""Tis a bit of a selfish way of thinking, isn't it Anna?"

"Nay, 'tis you who is selfish, m'lord, for robbin' her o' a choice. She has a right to know the truth. She deserves that much."

"We don't always get what we deserve, Anna." He arched a brow. "Did my mother deserve to die as she did? So young and without dignity."

"'Twas a sin the way Maureen suffered, but her demise was not in anyone's power to change. You can change what's happenin' now. Lady Raven has a right to choose her own decision, not one you've made for her."

He frowned. "She's a warmhearted lass who pities a starving dog. Hell and damnation, Anna. You know very well what decision she'll make?"

"But 'tis hers to make, m'lord."

"Nay, Anna, I'll not do that to her. I'm sparing her the grief."

Anna folded her arms across her chest. "Is it grief you're sparin' her or your own pride."

His face warmed. "I grant you, woman, I'd rather not have her seeing me weak and dependent, but 'tis her sorrow for me I will not place upon her." He stormed out of the kitchen and to the stables, saddling and mounting Grania. He rode to the hunter's cottage, where he'd really stay till she left. He'd lied about business in Killarney. He'd lied to her all along.

He stood in the door and looked about the room. His gaze rested on the cot where she lay writhing in pain to give their son life. At the table in the corner, they ate a meal of jarred jam and stale crackers he found in a cupboard. They talked about their childhood, telling stories about the friends they made and the things they did. By dusk, Brawn led Patrick and Dooley to the cottage. Raven and the baby rode comfortably in the bian back to Shannonbrook.

She brought him encouragement, hope, and love. *Aye, much love.* In all she did, giving life to his son, helping others, there was love. And if his reasoning wasn't purely out of concern for her, then he'd done her a very big injustice. He'd done an injustice to them all.

Remorse's tang coated the back of his tongue; he ran outside, fell to his knees, and retched beneath a tree.

Chapter Twenty-Six

Anna stood numb in front of the basin, washing each dish. “We cannot allow her to leave, Patty,” she said through her tears. “She and the wee one belong here. We cannot lose another one.” She turned to face her husband, his eyes also brimming with tears. “You know what must be done.”

“Anna, me love, you gave your word.” He took both of her wet hands in his. “’Twas a deathbed vow, to be exact. There’s nothin’ more sacred then keepin’ such a promise.”

She bit her bottom lip. “I can no longer keep silent, Patty. Especially when ’twill destroy so many people’s lives.” She pulled her hands free from his grasp and wiped them on her apron. “I must tell m’lady the truth.”

****

Raven glanced around the bedchamber she had grown to consider hers. To leave Shannonbrook would pierce her heart like a poison arrow. As the memories of the day she arrived flooded her thoughts, she swallowed hard the lump growing in her throat. Now the trunks were all packed with the beautiful clothes he bought for her and everything was ready to go. She spotted the ship tickets lying on the dressing table and reached for them, pressing them to her heart. Soon, she would be far away from the man she loved. Weak with grief, she collapsed to the floor and sobbed.

It was Anna who came beside her, pulling her to her feet and gathering her into a warm embrace, cradling her like a baby.

"There, there, lass," she comforted, rocking with her back and forth.

"Oh, Anna, he wants me gone," she choked out through her tears.

Anna stroked her hair. "Nay, he doesn't want you gone, love. He believes he has to let you go."

She pulled back to look into the elder woman's sad eyes. "Is it because of our agreement?"

"Nay, lass, 'tis because he doesn't want you to watch him die."

She gasped, the thought tore at her insides. "Braiton is dying? Tell me this cannot be true."

"Come, lass," Anna said, leading her over to the bed.

She sat at the edge and wiped the tears with the backs of her hands. "I do not understand, Anna. What is he dying from?"

Anna sighed. "Lady Maureen died of a terrible disease, one that took her father and her grandmother. All o' them began to experience symptoms not long after they turned thirty. Braiton fears he inherited the family curse."

"And he just turned thirty," she said, realizing now why her husband did not want to celebrate his birthday. Suddenly, she understood the reason he looked so tortured and sullen the day she presented him with the compass pouch.

Anna nodded.

A cold knot formed in her stomach. "Oh, Anna, he cannot be dying, he just cannot," she moaned.

Anna reached for her hands. "Calm yourself, lass."

"Is there nothing Terrance can do for him?"

"He isn't dying, m'lady."

She blinked, baffled. "But you just said his mother…and the rest of the family all—"

"Lady Maureen 'tisn't his mother," Anna interjected with a whisper.

She frowned. “Now, I really do not understand.”

Anna arched a brow. “Aye, well, ’tis a wee bit complicated.”

“Then who *is* his mother?” There was a long, brittle silence.

“Me daughter, Aubrey,” Anna finally confessed.

Her eyes widened. “Your daughter?”

Anna sighed again. “Aye, she was me only little girl, me sweet Aubrey Rose. ’Twas the stars in her father’s eyes, she was. When she and Broderick were just wee ones, I took care o’ them together. They grew close, like siblin’s, so I thought. Then by the time they turned fourteen, things changed. They saw each other in a different light, and one day Broderick’s mother, Lady Cora, caught the two o’ them smoochin’ behind the stables. Within a week Broderick was gone, sent away to school in Dublin.”

“What happened to Aubrey?”

“She moped around like a sick pup, hadn’t much o’ an appetite and didn’t laugh anymore.” Anna’s eyes filled with tears. “The whole thing to watch was heart breakin’. Seven long years passed, and durin’ that time, me Aubrey turned down many a marriage proposal. I knew she was waitin’ for Broderick to return, hopin’ when he did he’d declare his love and wed her.”

“But instead he returned with a new love,” she surmised.

“Aye, m’lady, ’tis the truth of it. His father, Nolan Shannon died and Lady Cora, beside herself with grief, sent for Broderick. Upon his arrival he brought with him his intended.”

“He was engaged to wed Maureen?”

“Aye, he was, and me Aubrey’s heart was broken. She grieved so, the day o’ Broderick’s nuptials, even tried to take her own life by jumpin’ into the Shannon River. If ’tweren’t for Clancey, the grounds keeper, comin’ upon her when he did, she would've succeeded." Anna wiped her tears with the hem of her apron.

"Lady Maureen was never a hardy sort, always pale and fragile. She was prone to faintin' spells and most o' what she ate sickened her stomach. About six months into the marriage she became with child, but lost it three months later. The next year she had two miscarriages. The last left her bed bound for months after, 'twasn't able to do much o' anythin'. Broderick grew restless. Watchin' Aubrey work about Shannonbrook, all healthy and vibrant, gave him ideas no married man has the right o' havin'."

She smiled. "Aubrey was a beautiful lass, turned many heads with her flowin' red hair and large, green eyes—"

"Just like Braiton's," she interjected.

"Aye, the same," Anna agreed. "Broderick's heart desired her, and bein' she was still in love with him, it didn't take much for them to get themselves into a compromisin' situation. Not long after, Aubrey discovered she was with child."

"Where is Aubrey now, Anna?"

Anna lowered her gaze to the hands she held clasped in her lap. "She died givin' birth to Braiton, m'lady."

She covered Anna's hands with her own. "I am so sorry, Anna."

Anna raised her gaze. "I am, too, m'lady."

"What happened then?"

"Lady Maureen was a smart women, knew what was goin' on. I think she turned a blind eye because she couldn't be the wife Broderick needed. When Aubrey died, I went to her with wee Braiton, laid him beside her. Knowin' she would never sire an heir to Shannonbrook, she took the babe and raised him like her own." She tipped her head sideways. "I believe 'twas then she won back Broderick's heart and respect. He watched her with Braiton. The love she shelled out upon the wee lad was heart warmin'. For a tad, Shannonbrook ran smooth and all the people residing here. Then when Braiton was four, Lady Cora, her mind growin' idle, set her bedchamber on fire. She perished in the blaze, leavin' half o' the old mansion uninhabitable.

"Broderick ordered the new mansion built and within a year's time the family was able to move. But 'twasn't long after Maureen's disease took hold of her, tormentin' her for the next six years. By the time she was thirty-six, she was gone. On her deathbed she made me vow never to reveal to Braiton she was not his mother."

"And what became of Broderick?"

"After Lady Maureen died, Broderick was into his cups more than out. Didn't go along on his business voyages anymore, sent Molly and her husband Chauncey, who was captain at that time, on without him. The poor man drank himself into an early grave."

"And so you and Patrick, Braiton's grandparents, stayed on for his sake?"

"Aye, m'lady, that we did. He was such a young lad, just turned twenty and had so much responsibility to bear. 'Twas me Patrick who helped him run the place in those early days, like a granddad would. Later, Broderick's old time friend, Shamus O'Neill lent a hand. Bein' a business man himself, he mentored Braiton, taught him how to handle the shippin' business."

"I am sorry, you and Patrick have had to keep your relationship to Braiton quiet all these years. I remember the times I enjoyed with my own grandmother, White Dove. My heart goes out to Braiton as well, for not knowing the same pleasure. But now he is a man, do you not believe he deserves the truth?"

"If 'twere made known, he'd be shunned by

society, called a bastard, lose his title, and would not have inherited Maureen's fortune. Though Broderick's business flourished, 'twas Maureen's money that got it started."

She frowned. "So all the hell my husband's been through, thinking he is her blood child and would die as she died, was all for the sake of money?"

Anna nodded. "'Tis the way with those o' means, m'lady. And there was Maureen's brother's son, five years older than Braiton, still alive. M'lord would have lost everythin' to him."

"Where does Maureen's nephew live, Anna?"

"When he did live, m'lady, 'twas in Dublin, where Maureen's family is from. But recently he died. Molly's son, Michael, has a congregation in Dublin and knew of the man. He sent us word o' his death just before Braiton sailed for America. When m'lord returned with a wife, I believed he made peace with his notion o' dyin'."

"And you saw no reason to tell him Maureen was not his mother," she concluded.

"Aye, m'lady...until now."

She took an audible breath. "And all this time I believed I was too damaged for him to—" the words stuck in her throat. "You see, Anna, on the reservation I was taken against my will."

"Aye, m'lady, me sister told me, and o' the miscarriage aboard ship. There's not much we keep from each other, but be rest assured. Your secret will go no farther than me and Molly's ears. We only wag our tongues between one another." She leaned closer and whispered. "Not even me Patrick knows, and Dr. Murphy never talks about what ails those he treats."

"Then Molly must have also told you about the Sea Patrol and why Braiton really married me."

Anna nodded. "Perhaps 'twas the reason in the beginnin', but I've seen how he looks at you, how his face brightens when you walk into the room. M'lord has nothin' but the highest regard for you." She smiled and added. "We all do, m'lady."

The highest regard, but not love. "Then if what you say is true, Anna, and he is not ashamed of my past, why does he still want me gone?"

"'Twas not you he's ashamed o', never was, m'lady. 'Tis more how he believes he'll succumb to the illness. He wanted to spare you seein' him in the condition he saw his mother." Again, she smiled. "A man who cares deeply for a woman cannot bear to see her in pain."

"Then I am not so sure he would even believe you, Anna. He will think you are just trying to change his mind about sending me and Casey to England."

Anna's face brightened. "But I have proof, m'lady. Lady Maureen left a diary, and in it she tells o' the night Braiton was born. After her death, I went lookin' for the journal, thought it best I put it aside for Braiton to one day read. But before I could take it, Broderick locked it away in a trunk, which is stored still at the old Shannonbrook ruins. All these years I've not been able to find the key."

"Anna, I think I know where the key is," she said, rising from the bed and making her way to the large armoire.

Anna stood and followed her. "How is that possible, m'lady?"

She opened the double entry and pushed aside the mirror hanging on the back of the right door, revealing a secret compartment. She stuck her hand inside and pulled out a key for Anna to see.

"Could this be the one you are looking for?"

Anna examined the key. "Aye, m'lady, I'm sure 'tis the one." She frowned "But how did you come by this secret place?"

"One day, not long after I arrived at Shannonbrook, I was admiring the flowers etched along the mirror. As I traced their imprint with the tip of my finger, the mirror moved. Upon a further look, I discovered the compartment and the key. But not wanting to be caught snooping, I replaced it and kept the secret to myself." She smiled and took the key from the elder woman. "Now tell me, Anna, exactly where can I find the trunk?"

****

Ireland's crisp autumn air stung Braiton's face as he pushed Grania hard. Never would he run her this way for fear he'd make her lame, but this morning he needed to be at the pier before *The Donahue* sailed. He thought of Anna's words all night and decided he couldn't let Raven leave, not without her knowing the truth. She deserved that much from him. Now, he prayed he wouldn't be too late to intercept her departure and beg for her forgiveness. All he wanted was to take his family home.

He dismounted and ran to the edge of the dock, spotting what he knew to be *The Donahue* already out to sea. He was too late. Raven and his son were gone.

He rode back to Shannonbrook enveloped in a shroud of sadness. Upon entering the clearing, the ruins of the old mansion loomed ahead. It was a constant reminder of days better left forgotten. *If I only could forget, wipe the slate clean and start over.*

He would love her like no man ever loved a woman. She was his rapture, the sun shining on a cold day warming his heart and everything she surrounded. He knew the emptiness; the loneliness he felt before she came into his life would be double hard to bear now. He'd tasted her love, basked in its rays, and he'd never be the same again.

He slowed Grania and studied the old building. His heart swelled with anger for the legacy he'd been left. He was weary of the grip it had on him, controlling his every move. Digging his heels into his mount, he rode to the groundskeeper's cottage.

Clancey sat on a stump, enjoying an apple when he rode up. The other man stood. "What can I be doin' for you this mornin', m'lord?"

Braiton pointed to the ruins. "Clancey, my man, I'm sick to death of that eyesore blocking my view of the river. I want it leveled. Gather Kelly, Shelby, and some of the other men and have a go at it."

Clancey took a bite of his apple. "The only way we can get her down, is to burn the rest o' her, m'lord."

"Then do it, Clancey. Burn it all to the ground!"

****

The stairs squeaked, as did the family of rats dwelling in a corner. Torn, faded tapestries, at one time priceless, hung on the wall. Raven held the lantern high, stepping with care over loose slabs of stone and other debris littering the floor. She made her way to the last bedchamber on the left, where Anna said she would find Maureen's trunk.

The chamber door hung from its hinge, and when she pushed it aside, it fell with a bang. Dust blew everywhere. She coughed and glanced around the cold, dark room. A winged back chair lay broken to one side of the fireplace along with an old wash basin. Faded, gold drapes hung frayed and stained from the veranda doors. A rug was rolled up to one side, thick with cob webs. In a far corner, hidden partially by a broken full length mirror, she spied the trunk.

Making her way through the mess, she knelt in front of the coffer and placed the lantern on the floor beside her. Her fingers trembled as she turned the key in the lock and opened the lid. More dust flew, this time in her face. She rubbed the grime from her eyes, then reached for the lantern, holding it high over the trunk. With her other hand, she pushed aside the mildewed gowns and flowered hats, searching for the diary. At the bottom of the trunk she found the leather bound journal and pulled it free from its hiding place. She sat back and held it to her heart. Between its pages was the key to unlock Braiton's prison.

Setting the lantern down, she brought the book to its light and took care in turning each fragile page. Maureen's handwriting, delicate and weak like the women herself, stared back at her. When she came upon the pages she sought, she herself experienced the anguish and torment, the sorrow and despair Maureen was living. Tears blurred the words and fell from her eyes to stain the already yellowed pages.

Maureen's beautifully sculpted words expressed how much she loved her husband, longed to nurture his seed. She envied Aubrey's vibrancy and beauty. Her illness kept her a prisoner in her room, and she dreamed—yearned to ride the hills beside Broderick, to dance in his arms at society balls, and be able to make love to him. With each page she turned, pity swelled in her heart for Maureen. She read farther, falling deep into the previous Lady Shannon's growing ache. It was the same pain consuming her own heart when she readied herself to leave Shannonbrook.

"You could not be the wife you wanted to be in your own marriage, Maureen. But please help me be the wife I choose to be in mine," she whispered to herself.

****

Braiton took refuge in his study. Brian set a lunch tray on the table beside him and poured a cup of coffee. He glanced at the flames dancing in the fireplace. "'Tis way too quiet here without her, Brian."

"Without whom, m'lord?"

"Without my lady," he mused.

"But Lady Shannon is still here, m'lord."

He stood. "The devil you say, man. She didn't leave?"

"Nay, m'lord, she decided against it."

He stunned Brian by wrapping his arms around the other man's slender frame and twirling him about.

"'Tis grand news you bring me, Brian. And grateful, I am, she's a spirited lass who pays not a wee bit of attention to anything I say, or my foolish behavior." He set Brian down. "Is she in her chamber?"

Brian adjusted his jacket. "The last time I saw her, m'lord, she was makin' her way to the nursery. No doubt to feed the wee one."

"Aye, 'tis my son's lunch time as well." He smiled. "Then I shall catch up to her there," he said and raced out the door. Bounding up the stairs, a surge of joy coursed through every fiber of his being.

By some miracle, he was given the second chance he prayed for earlier. At that moment, all he knew was he needed her, wanted her, and loved her. To live without her, for whatever time there was left, would be unbearable. 'Twas time she knew the truth, not only about his illness, but of his love for her as well. And he did love her, more then any man could love a women.

"Raven," he called out, opening the nursery door.

He found Sinead drying the baby. "She's not here, m'lord."

He came to stand beside the changing table, looking down with pride upon his son's face. Naked, the lad kicked and smiled up at him. He stroked the babe's face. "Through with your afternoon bath, lad?"

Sinead giggled. "'Tis one o' many, m'lord. He doesn't stay clean for very long, especially here," she said, indicating the infant's tiny bottom and washing the area with a wet cloth.

He chuckled and his son smiled again. "Do you know if my wife is in her chamber, lass?"

"Nay, she's not there. I believe she went downstairs, m'lord. You might try askin' Anna. The two o' them have been together most o' the mornin'."

He nodded and kissed his son on the forehead before he hurried to the kitchen. He found Anna chopping mutton for the evening meal.

"Would you know where my lady is, Anna?"

Anna bit her bottom lip. "Aye, m'lord, and I can explain."

He frowned. "Explain about what, Anna?"

"'Twas all me doin', m'lord, so if you're to be angry with anyone, then let it be me."

"What on earth are you going on about, women? If you know where I can find my wife, then just tell me."

Before Anna could say another word, Patrick burst into the kitchen from the back entrance. "M'lord, the old mansion is on fire."

He nodded. "I know, Patrick. 'Twas I who ordered it done." He turned his attention back to Anna. "Now, dear woman, would you tell me where to find Raven."

Anna's eyes welled with tears. "Sweet Mother of God, this is all me fault."

Patrick put his arm around his wife's shoulders. "What's your fault, me darlin'?"

"Sendin' Lady Shannon over to the old mansion," she said.

****

Raven would have sat the entire day reading Maureen Shannon's deepest thoughts, if it were not for the smell of smoke. It stung her eyes and caught in her throat. She tucked the diary beneath her arm and reached for the lantern, making her way to the hall. By the time she reached the end, it was completely consumed by smoke. She raised the lantern high, searching with watery, burning eyes for the stairway.

Upon finding the landing, she glanced over the rail. The stairs were engulfed in flames and the floor below a raging inferno. Fear gripped her heart. There was no way for her to get down…no way out.

She was trapped!

Chapter Twenty-Seven

"Raven? Raven, can you hear me?" Braiton's frantic call fueled the panic looming in Raven's chest.

The smoke, limiting her air, restricted a reply. She cleared her throat and forced the words to come.

"Here, Braiton…I am up here."

He stood at the end of the foyer, shielding his eyes from the intense heat as he glanced up the stairs. "Lass, you're standing too close to the edge of the landing."

"There is no way for me to get down." The heat was unbearable and she coughed, choking out hoarsely, "Leave before it is too late for you."

"Nay, lass, I will not leave you here."

A beam plummeted to the floor, crashing down beside him. Still, he stood steadfast in the midst of the bellowing fire.

"*Ugashe*, go," she screamed. "Get out of here, now!"

"Nay, not without you, lass."

She fell to her knees, cradling the diary to her chest. The book and all that was in it would burn with her. She could not let him send Casey away. She coughed, smoke filling her lungs. "Please promise me you will take care of our son, Braiton."

"Damn it, Raven, stand up!" he shouted.

The energy drained from her. "It is no use. *Hidisho*, it is finished. Just *ugashe*, save yourself."

"Nay, lass, get to your feet!" he bellowed.

She could not move, the pain in her chest smothered her.

"Stand, damn it! Stand, Raven!" he demanded.

"My chest, the pain…I cannot…I cannot breathe," she gasped.

"Think of your warrior training, lass. Conquer the pain through thought. Can you do that, Raven? Do you remember?"

She did remember and nodded.

"Then do it, my lady," he urged. "I know you can. You must."

His encouragement became her strength to stand.

"That's the way lass. Now get to the last room on the left. There is a set of double doors there, and beyond it a wee bit of a veranda still stands. Go, Raven, get out on the balcony, and I'll get you down."

She walked, legs trembling, the length of the hall and again entered Maureen's chamber. Stumbling to the exit, she tried the knob.

Locked, the doors are locked!

She scanned the room, now filling with smoke, and spotted a broken fireplace brick. Grasping the block and shielding her eyes with Maureen's diary, she broke the door's pane. She used a broken chair leg to smash away at the remaining glass. Never did she think she would come to bless the cumbersome garments she wore, until now. If it were not for all the padding the petticoat and gown afforded, her flesh would have been torn by the jagged shards of glass still protruding from the frame. Squeezing through the opening, she stood rigid against the outer wall, fearing one false move would send her crashing to the ground. She glanced down, it was a long drop.

She licked her dry lips and prayed. Whatever Braiton planned, he better do it fast. Smoke billowed through the veranda doors, and she knew the flames now reached the second floor.

Braiton ran to the shed a few feet from the

burning mansion.

Patrick joined him there. "What can I do to help, m'lord?"

"I need a long rope, Patrick. A very long one. And leather gloves. Do you think those things would be in this shed?" he said, trying the door.

"Aye, m'lord, they would for sure, but God only knows where the key might be. Perhaps Clancey..."

"You could tire the sun with your talking, man," he interrupted. "I haven't the time to hunt for Clancey or the damned key." He lunged forward with a booted foot and kicked in the door. Fragments of wood flew into the air.

Upon entering the shed, he tossed aside anything in his path, till he found a pair of gloves and a rope. Slipping the gloves onto his hands, he ran with the rope thrown over his shoulders to the large oak tree he climbed as a lad. It weathered well, standing tall and strong. The grab holds he used as a child to assist him to the top, hopefully would again. He prayed he'd remember where all the old crevices were.

With his heart in his throat, he climbed the tree and braced his legs around the highest limb, which brought him just above the veranda where Raven stood trapped. He physically ached with the immense fear for her life. Every nerve in his body tingled and he fought the pain, moving ahead to save her. 'Twas what he knew he had to do because he could never bear it if anything happened to her. She had become each and every breath he took.

Raven's eyes were squeezed shut, and her back hugged the outer wall.

"Raven," he called to her. She opened her eyes and glanced down. "Nay, don't look at the ground, lass. I'm above you, in the tree."

She raised her gaze to meet his. "Braiton, thank God you are here."

"I'm going to lower down to you the end of a rope. I want you to tie it around your waist," he instructed.

"I will not be able to reach it from here, and I am too afraid to move," she said, standing stiff against the wall. "Inhaling the smoke has made me dizzy."

He could see his mother's bedchamber now engulfed in flames. 'Twouldn't be but a few moments till they reached her. Choking with fright, he swallowed the panic rising in his throat and forced his voice to remain calm. Setting Raven into a worse panic then she already was wouldn't help the situation a bit.

"Sit down then, and scoot yourself closer to the edge."

She gave him a taut nod, tucked a book she held beneath her arm, and slid to a sitting position. He lowered the rope and watched her tie it with trembling hands around her waist.

"Do you have the knot secured, Raven?" *Hurry love, every moment counts.*

She tested the rope. "Yes, it is strong."

"Now listen carefully, lass. I want you to dangle your legs off the side of the veranda, then ease yourself away from the ledge. If you don't go off the side gently, I'll lose my grip and you'll slam into the tree's trunk."

Raven made the mistake of glancing down. Nearer to the edge, the distance down looked even longer. Brawn barked, ran, barked, and ran, back and forth. Molly and Anna cried into their handkerchiefs and Sinead stood holding Casey. Brian, Patrick, Clancey, and Dooley were positioned at the base of the tree. All eyes were frozen on her, their horror stricken faces mirroring her own fear.

She lifted her gaze to focus on her husband, sitting above her in the tree. "I cannot do this Braiton."

"Aye, you can, Raven. You must," he snapped with anxiety. "Then I can lower you to the ground."

"I am afraid the two of us will crash below."

"My lady, I will not let that happen." Hoping to somehow shock her into compliance, he hardened his tone. "Saints preserve us, lass, we're running out of time."

She took a quick look over her shoulder, the flames danced through the broken doors.

"Please, Raven," he pleaded. "You can do this, lass, I know you can."

Panic soaked through to her bones. She took Maureen's diary from beneath her arm and threw it to the ground. At least he would know the truth. Then she released her grip on the rope and covered her hands over her eyes.

"Nay, don't you do that! Don't you dare give up! 'Tis not your right to do to our son. He needs his mother, and I…I need my wife."

She opened her eyes, raising them to meet his. Tears streaked down his soot-stained face.

His voice broke with emotion. "Nothing makes sense without you, lass. In the eyes of God and all that's holy, I declare these words for all to hear. I love you, Raven Amelia Shannon. I love you with all my heart! You are *shi'aad*, my wife. Do you hear me? And you will not leave me to live in this life alone."

His words echoed through her soul and swelled her heart with happiness. A new determination was born deep inside of her, giving her the courage to ease off the veranda's ledge, whereby his strong arms lowered her safely to the ground.

Chapter Twenty-Eight

After such a chaotic day, the quiet evening was a welcome relief. Raven sat in the rocking chair, nursing Casey, with Brawn at her feet. Braiton walked into the room and knelt down in front of her, his green eyes watching with admiration their son's tiny mouth drawing nourishment from her breast.

He reached over and placed a finger in the babe's hand, and smiled with pride when the child curled his tiny fingers around his.

"He's a strong one at that."

She nodded in agreement. "Like his father."

He watched in silence as she finished the babe's feeding, then took the child from her and held him close to his heart. He kissed the top of the infant's soft head before placing him in the cradle. Then he covered his son and stroked his tiny cheek with a thumb. She was overwhelmed by his tenderness, contentment swelling her heart.

He turned to her and extended a hand. "Come," he whispered. "I have something to show you."

He led her to his bedchamber, shutting and locking the door behind them. She spotted her wardrobe, dressing table, and in the corner of the room her writing table—a vase filled with a bouquet of fuschia on top. She frowned. "Why are my things in here?"

He moved to embrace her. "A wife belongs with her husband."

There were no shadows across her heart tonight, and she exhaled with contentment. "Thank you, *shikaa* for saving my life."

"'Twas you who saved mine, twice now, I might add," he said.

She searched his face. "You have read the diary, then?"

He nodded. "The part that mattered, the rest is not my business. 'Tis meant to be only Maureen's."

She brought her hands up to cup each side of his face. "You may not have grown beneath her heart, but you grew in it. Maureen loved you very much and for all her intentions and purposes, she was really your mother."

He traced the curve of her mouth with the tip of a finger. "Aye, that she was, my lady. And that she'll always be."

His gentle touch ignited a fire within her. "The past does not matter anymore, Braiton."

He smiled. "I decided the same last night, 'tis why I rode this morning to Shannon Harbour to stop you from leaving. But *The Donahue* had already sailed." He pulled her close. "I don't have the words to explain the miserable state I was in. When I returned to Shannonbrook, I ordered Clancey to rid me of the old mansion, the eyesore that 'twas. I wanted a clean slate, was sick of the memories haunting my life. Then I came into the study and sat before the fire. 'Twas then I'd decided to sail to England and bring you home."

She moved her hands to the nape of his neck, playing with the curls there. "Home, such a wonderful word."

His smile broadened, the cleft in his chin deepening. "Aye, 'tis at that, my lady. And when I learned from Brian you did not leave our home, I went searching for you. 'Twas then I discovered you were at the old mansion." His gaze melted into hers. "I nearly went insane, knowing I ordered the place burnt to the ground." He captured a lock of her hair and brought it to his lips, inhaling her scent. "I don't know what I would have done if I lost you, Raven."

"Did you mean what you said about loving me with all your heart?" she whispered.

He lowered his face to hers. "Every word of it, my love. And right now I am drowning in the depth of your eyes, hoping never to surface again."

She arched a brow. "Not even for one breath of air?"

"You will be every breath I take, Raven. I cannot—will not live without you or my son."

His warm lips consumed hers, his tongue probing the soft corners of her mouth. Filled with desire, she explored around his, running her tongue over his teeth and biting his lower lip.

He moaned and slipped the straps of her nightgown off her shoulders. The garment cascaded to the floor, gathering around her ankles. His eyes roamed the length of her, slow and easy, feasting on her nakedness. A mischievous grin curved one side of his mouth.

"I have dreamt of this moment from the first time I set eyes on you in Silver City. I couldn't get you out of my head then, and I don't plan on ever having to in the future." He gathered her into his muscular embrace and carried her over to the bed. The heart wrenching tenderness of his gaze heated her flesh.

"You are mine, to love and cherish forever." Green orbs twinkled. "I have locked the door and instructed the servants we're not to be disturbed."

She smiled. "You are wise, my *shikaa*."

He took his time undressing. The prolonged anticipation, almost unbearable, filled her whole being with wanting him. Not once did she cast her gaze away, but instead drank in his every move, every ounce of his flesh.

He lay beside her, his warm, naked body pressed against hers. There was a tingling in the pit of her stomach. Her heart jolted, and her pulse pounded as his searing kisses traveled down her neck, to her breast. His lips covered the peak, his tongue circling and playing, stoking a growing fire within her. The pink button hardened with his attention.

He raised his eyes to meet hers. "Raven, *m'annachd*, my best beloved, you're all mine."

"And what of you, *my* best beloved," she whispered.

He smiled. "I, too, am *yovrs onli*, yours only."

She wrapped her arms around his shoulders, stroking the muscles there as he slid his hand down her thigh and entered her with a finger. Arching her back and spreading her legs, she thrilled to the delicious spasms he invoked, growing hot and moist. She closed her eyes. His touch sent waves of excitement through her, and her passion piqued.

"I'm not intoxicated by the fire water this time, Raven, just by love." And Braiton would savor every moment of her writhing body. Her pleasure heightened his, the passion melting his resolve.

She opened her eyes, wetting her full lips with a swipe of her tongue. "*Wo'ina*, I love you, Braiton. I always have."

"And I you, Raven," he whispered, moving above her. Hard and throbbing, he brushed against her thigh. She bent her knees and raised herself to receive him. His fullness penetrated her warmth, and he groaned with pleasure. Each thrust into her, not only fueled his excitement, but hers as well. The double connection, the duel passion soared his desire. He was free to love her, to take his yearning to great heights, and there would no longer be an aftermath of guilt or fear…only rapture.

Her outcry of gratification sent him wild, and he trembled within her. A quiver surged through his veins, his ecstasy mounting. He exploded, shattering within her. As an exclamation of delight escaped his throat, he filled her, his climax making them as one.

Spent and exhausted, every muscle in his body relaxed, he rolled onto his back and pulled her close.

"Will you marry me, Raven?"

"I am already married to you, my *shikaa*."

"Nay, I mean in the eyes of God, saying our vows at a church with flowers and music and you dressed in a beautiful gown."

"I always wanted to wear the gown my grandmother and mother wore. Perhaps I can have Sunny send it to me."

"I'd be so pleased to see you in it, my love. Then after we'll have a dinner here at Shannonbrook, invite everyone to share in our day. We can combine the whole thing with your twenty-first birthday."

She snuggled against him. "It all sounds so grand, Braiton, but all I truly need is to know you love me."

"And I do, lass, but my heart is so happy, I want to declare it to the world," he said, caressing her back. Even touching her soft flesh reeled his senses.

She giggled. "Like you did this afternoon while perching upon the tree limb?"

He chuckled. "Aye, my love, just as I did then, only this time I want all of Limerick to hear."

"Perhaps Molly's son, Michael the priest, can leave Dublin and his congregation for a few days to perform the ceremony. I think it would be nice for him to be present, join in on the festivities. He is, after all, your cousin."

Learning of all the family he now had was still so astounding. "Aye, he is at that. And this poses another thing to be done."

"What would that be, my *shikaa*?"

"I'll have to build a new mansion, one much bigger this time."

"You do not think this one is big enough?"

He kissed her temple. "Nay, at best, not for very

long."

She nestled her face beneath his chin. "You plan on making our family larger?"

"Aye, lass, that I do. And with discovering Anna, Patrick and Molly are family, 'twould be only right to accommodate them as such. I thought I'd give them the whole of this mansion, let them be served and pampered for a change."

"Well, I know you would have a hard time separating Anna from her kitchen."

He chuckled. "Aye, 'tis true."

"And I have learned Dooley is smitten with Sinead, so soon they will need more room as well. Did you know she refused to leave for England, too?"

He clicked his tongue. "What are Dooley and I to do with you willful women?"

She pulled back to look at him and cast a mischievous smile. "Love the bloomers off of us, I would say."

"Aye, 'tis a wise solution you have there, my lady," he agreed. "Tomorrow we'll draw up the plans together, and when we return from visiting your family in England, the construction can begin."

She kissed his throat. "Thank you, Braiton."

****

Content to listen to his steady breathing beside her, Raven prayed nothing would ever drive them apart. Finally her marriage was like her parent's, something she always yearned one day to have. She rose from the bed and slipped on her nightgown, stopping to smell the bouquet of fuschia before tiptoeing to the nursery.

Brawn lay beside the cradle, guarding his new little charge. She bent down and scratched him behind the ears. "You are a good dog, my friend," she whispered, as she peered down at her son. He slept in peace, a little hand tucked beneath a chubby cheek. She walked to the window and gazed out.

Faint clouds of smoke still rose from the ruins, curling in the early morning sky.

Braiton came up behind her, wrapping his robe-clad arms around her waist. "The past is gone forever, my love," he whispered in her ear. "It floats away with the smoke."

She turned in his embrace to face him. "And it shall never return."

"Nay, never," he agreed.

She glanced over at the cradle, where their son slept in the corner of the room. A warm glow flowed through her, and she glorified in the moment. Wrapped in a silken cocoon of euphoria, she returned her gaze to look deep into the shifting emerald lights of Braiton's eyes. "It is the seed planted with love, from which one perfect flower grows."

"Aye, my lady," he said, pulling her close. "And love always finds a way."

She smiled. "That it does."

A word about the author...

A former Assistant Editor for *Independence Today* newspaper and an RWA member, Roberta C. M. DeCaprio's back list consists of two previous paranormal romances published by Wings Press, entitled *Coma Coast* and *The Vanity*, as well as a mainstream paranormal published by Write Words Inc., entitled *Family Secrets*. It also includes an historical and a fantasy published by The Wild Rose Press, entitled *A RIVER OF ORANGE* and *THE GOLDEN LADY* (the first book in the **Between the Rifle and the Spear** Series).

To read excerpts from these books, log on to: www.robertadecaprio.com.

www.ingramcontent.com/pod-product-compliance
Lightning Source LLC
Chambersburg PA
CBHW070202260626
47160CB00002B/422